# A Time of Torment

# A TIME
# OF TORMENT

A Charlie Parker Thriller

## John Connolly

**EMILY BESTLER BOOKS**
—
**ATRIA**
New York   London   Toronto   Sydney   New Delhi

**ATRIA** BOOKS

An Imprint of Simon & Schuster, Inc.
1230 Avenue of the Americas
New York, NY 10020

First Emily Bestler Books/Atria Books hardcover edition August 2016

**EMILY BESTLER BOOKS / ATRIA** BOOKS and colophons are trademarks of Simon & Schuster, Inc.

For information about special discounts for bulk purchases, please contact Simon & Schuster Special Sales at 1-866-506-1949 or business@simonandschuster.com.

The Simon & Schuster Speakers Bureau can bring authors to your live event. For more information or to book an event contact the Simon & Schuster Speakers Bureau at 1-866-248-3049 or visit our website at www.simonspeakers.com.

Manufactured in the United States of America

10   9   8   7   6   5   4   3   2   1

Library of Congress Cataloging-in-Publication Data

Names: Connolly, John, 1968– author.
Title: A time of torment : a Charlie Parker thriller / John Connolly.
Description: First Emily Bestler Books/Atria Books hardcover edition. | New
    York : Emily Bestler Books/Atria Books, 2016. | Series: Charlie Parker ; 14
Identifiers: LCCN 2016011399 (print) | LCCN 2016017541 (ebook)
Subjects: LCSH: Parker, Charlie "Bird" (Fictitious character)—Fiction. |
    Private investigators—Fiction. | Assassins—Fiction. | Cults—Fiction. |
    BISAC: FICTION / Mystery & Detective / General. | FICTION / Thrillers. |
    FICTION / Literary. | GSAFD: Mystery fiction. | Suspense fiction.
Classification: LCC PR6053.O48645 T56 2016 (print) | LCC PR6053.O48645
    (ebook) | DDC 823/.914—dc23
LC record available at https://lccn.loc.gov/2016011399

ISBN 978-1-5011-1832-6
ISBN 978-1-5011-1835-7 (ebook)

*For David Torrans and Claudia Edelmann*
*of No Alibis bookstore, Belfast*

# 1

Like a dog, he hunts in dreams.

—Alfred, Lord Tennyson (1809–1820), "Locksley Hall"

# Chapter

# I

They're circling now, then falling, descending in a slow gyre, dropping so gently that their approach can barely be discerned. They are hawks in the form of men, and the one who leads them is a being doubly transformed: lost and found, human and bird; youngest of them, yet strangely old. He has endured, and in this endurance he has been forged anew. He has seen a world beyond this one. He has glimpsed the face of a new god.

He is at peace with himself, and so he will wage war.

Faster they come, the spiral narrowing, the three almost as one, their coats mantling in the chill fall air; and not a whisper of their approach, not a passing shadow nor a sparrow startled, only the stillness of a world waiting to be shattered, and the perfect balance of a life, perhaps, to be saved and a life, perhaps, to be ended.

The clouds part, pierced by a shaft of light that catches them in flight, as though they have attracted, however briefly, the attention of a deity long slumbering but now awake, roused by martial clamor and the raising of armies in the name of the Captain, the One Who Waits Behind the Glass, the God of Wasps.

And the old deity will set His child against them, and the hawks will follow.

———

**IT WAS A LONG** time since the Gray Man had considered the possibility of being caught, for the Gray Man did not truly exist. He had no physical form. He dwelt alongside another, sharing the same skin, and only at the final breath might there have been a glimpse of the essence of his true nature, although even then he preferred to remain unseen, concealed by darkness. He was not above causing pain, although this was as much a matter of whim as any particular tastes that he might have possessed. A death was only the beginning, which was why he had survived undetected for so long. He could make a kill last for years. Physical pain was finite, for ultimately the body would surrender the soul, but emotional agony was capable of infinite variations, and the subtlest of modifications might release from the wound a new torrent of distress.

In the persona that he presented to the world, the Gray Man was a reverse chameleon. His name was Roger Ormsby, and he was small, colorful, and greatly liked. He was in his early sixties, with an impish humor. His hair and beard were white, but neatly trimmed. He proudly carried before him his little potbelly, like a happily expectant mother demonstrating the pleasure she takes in her burden. He favored red suspenders and vests of unusual design. He wore tweed in winter and linen in summer, preferring creams and tans but offsetting them with tastefully bright ties and handkerchiefs. He could play the piano, and waltz and two-step with ease, but inside Ormsby was a foul thing animating him as a puppeteer works a marionette, and only an expert might have detected the sterility of his renditions of beloved classics as his fingers moved across the keys, or the joyless precision of every move he made on a dance floor.

Ormsby did not discuss politics or religion. He took only frivolous subjects seriously, and as a consequence was much valued as a dinner guest. He was a happy widower, faithful to the memory of his departed wife to the extent that he would do no more than flirt with the less lonely widows of Champaign, Illinois, but not so in love with the ghost of his departed spouse as to allow the loss of her to cloud his spirit or the spirits of others. He was always in demand as a companion for theater, movies, and the occasional light opera, and the absence of a sexual component to his relationships meant that he moved in and out of social situations with ease. He was a Friend of the Library, a member of the Audubon Society, a regular fixture at lectures on local history, and a generous—but not overgenerous—donor to good causes. True, there were some who disliked him, for no man can be loved by all, but in general such naysayers were regarded by the majority as willfully ornery, unable to accept that someone might simply be a force for contentment in the world.

And so Roger Ormsby bobbed through life in his vibrant plumage, advertising his presence, hiding nothing, but when he closed his front door behind him the artificial light in his eyes was suffocated, and the face of the Gray Man was pendent like a dead moon in the blackness of his pupils.

This is what Roger Ormsby did—or, if you wish, what the Gray Man did, for they were two aspects of the same entity, like a coat and its lining. He typically targeted his victims carefully, spending months in preparation. He had been known to engage in crimes of opportunity, but they were riskier now than they once were, because cameras were everywhere. In addition, it was difficult to gauge just what one might be appropriating in such a situation, for Ormsby required a very particular set of social circumstances from his victims. They couldn't be loners, isolated from their families and friends. He did not desire discards. The more beloved they were, the better. He wanted offspring who were cherished. He wanted teenagers from happy homes. He wanted good mothers of children beyond the age of infancy. He wanted emotional engagement.

He wanted many lives that he could slowly and painstakingly destroy over a period of years, even decades.

Ormsby made people disappear, then watched as those who loved them were left to wonder at their fate. He understood the half-life of hope: it is not despair that destroys us, but its opposite. Hope is the winding, despair the unwinding. Despair brings with it the possibility of an ending. Taken to the extreme, its logical conclusion is death. But hope sustains. It can be exploited.

Ormsby's actions had caused some to take their own lives, but he considered this a failure, both on his own part and theirs. The ones he killed were merely the first victims, and also the least interesting to him. He liked to watch those who remained as they tried to cope with what had been visited upon them. He knew that they would wake each morning and briefly forget what they had lost: a mother, a son, a daughter. (Ormsby avoided taking adult men. He was stronger than he looked, but not so much that he believed he could tackle a grown man, especially not as he grew older.) Then, seconds after waking, they would remember again, and this was where the pleasure lay for Ormsby.

He was not above goading, reminding, but that was a dangerous business. He had sent items to relatives in the mail—a necklace, a watch, a child's shoe—to enjoy the commotion that followed. He had forced children that he had taken to write letters to their mothers and fathers, informing them that they were in good health and being looked after. (Adults, too, might be persuaded to write similar missives, but only under threat of physical harm.) He might wait years before sending such notes, depending on the age of the child and the reaction of the parents. He dropped the letters in mailboxes far from home, often when he was on vacation, and always ensured that he was not overlooked by cameras.

The Internet made it easier for him to monitor the progress of his real victims, but Ormsby was wary of leaving an electronic trail. He concealed his searches amid random examinations of newspapers and magazines, often in public libraries or the kind of cybercafes frequented by immigrants. He did not attend public gatherings for the disappeared, or church services at which the congregation prayed for their safe return, because he believed the authorities monitored such events. It was usually enough for Ormsby to know that the suffering he had inflicted continued unabated. If nothing else, the Gray Man had a vivid imagination. This was how Ormsby could survive for so long without killing: as the years went by, so too his store of victims increased. He could dip in and out of destroyed lives. He was an emotional vampire.

Now, as he drove home, he thought that this metaphor had a pleasing precision under the circumstances. He recalled a scene from Bram Stoker's *Dracula*, in which the Count returns to his castle and throws to his three vampire brides an infant contained in a sack. At that moment, the trunk of Ormsby's car also contained a child in a sack. Her name was Charlotte Littleton. She was nine years old, and represented one of his rare crimes of opportunity: a child playing with a ball as the afternoon sunlight died, an open gate, the ball drifting into an empty street of big houses set back from the road . . .

Good fortune: God—if He existed—finding His attention briefly distracted.

And inside, the Gray Man danced.

# II

Ormsby's wife had died suddenly when she was in her early forties and her husband was in his midthirties. It was a blessing, of a kind. By then, Ormsby, the Gray Man, had already begun playing his long game, and was concerned that his wife, who was not a stupid woman, and even actively curious, might begin to take an interest in his activities. Sometimes he wondered if, had her heart not simply failed unexpectedly while she was testing the firmness of avocados at a sidewalk market—such a curious detail, and one that had led him to avoid avocados ever since—he might have been forced to get rid of her. He wasn't even certain why he had married her to begin with. He suspected he had craved some form of stability, given his own family background of divorce and acrimony, and a mother whose maternal instincts extended no further than occasionally taking it upon herself to heat some mac and cheese instead of delegating the task to her only son. Ormsby's relationship with his late wife had been affectionate, if almost entirely passionless, a situation that had not troubled either of them unduly.

But perhaps also, even then, he was already creating a framework for his life, and an identity for himself, that would arouse the least amount of suspicion: Roger Ormsby, contentedly if unexceptionally married, with a job selling painting and decorating supplies that required him to spend time on the road, staying in dull motels, mostly eating alone, but always watching, always listening.

He heard a thumping from the trunk of his car and turned up the volume on the radio: a news program on NPR, which was just the kind of show to which a man like Roger Ormsby might have been expected to listen. He used to smoke a pipe too, puffing contentedly on it as he drove, but then he'd learned about throat and tongue cancer, and decided that Roger Ormsby would be sensible enough to let this particular pleasure go. He missed the pipe, though. It had given him something to do with his hands.

He'd have to kill the girl quickly, of course. The unplanned ones were always difficult. He might not have taken her had winter not recently crept into the air, giving him an excuse to light the furnace in his big, old house. He'd spend the night questioning her, find out as much as he could about her family, then put an end to her: a single blow to the head, knocking her out cold, then strangulation. He didn't want her to suffer.

After that, the game could begin.

He fantasized about the months and years to come.

And the shadows that were following him, the arc of the hunters, went entirely unnoticed.

———

IN A CURIOUS WAY, Ormsby had been inspired to pursue his particular appetites by base conflicts in lands that he had never visited, and in which he had little interest on a political or social level. He had found himself fascinated by the actions of the military dictatorships in Argentina and Chile, which routinely "disappeared" those with whom they differed, leaving the families to mourn phantoms, nearly certain that their loved ones were dead but unable to let go of them until they could identify their remains and lay them in the ground, although the chances of this were remote when the military's favorite methods of dispatch included dropping the bound bodies of living captives into the sea from aircraft, or, in the case of the Chileans, using railway ties to ensure that the corpses didn't float to the surface.

And then there were the Irish terrorists who dragged widowed mothers from their homes and tortured them in secret before shooting them in the head and burying their bodies on some desolate stretch of beach. When the deed was done, they returned with clear consciences to their own families and communities, there to pass the desolate, orphaned children on the street, continuing to do so for decades after in a strange dance of murderers and victims, each party knowing the identity of the other but never confronting the truth of what had been done, and so the dance went on. Ormsby, who was depraved beyond comprehension, thought that he might have enjoyed fighting for freedom if he could have passed some of his time so pleasantly: the misery for those left behind lay in not knowing, in uncertainty. It was sadism refined to its purest essence.

Ormsby's house appeared before him. He turned into the driveway and activated the garage door. The garage connected directly to the house through the utility room, which in turn had another door leading to the basement. It meant that he was able to move his victims easily, and without being noticed. He pulled into the garage, killed the engine, and hit the button on his key fob a second time, causing the door to begin its descent. He was already out of his car, and poised to open the trunk, when he saw that the door had frozen.

Ormsby stared at it. He tried the button again. Nothing happened. The door didn't even jerk slightly, as might have been expected if the mechanism had somehow become fouled. He took a flashlight from the shelf and checked the door's workings, but could see nothing wrong. The street beyond appeared empty, but the door was not even a quarter of the way down, and while the light was fading, it was not yet dark enough to guarantee he wouldn't be seen by one of his neighbors if he tried to move the child.

Regardless of this, he couldn't just leave the door unsecured. The garage was connected to his house alarm, and the button on the fob automatically deactivated it. His home was now vulnerable, and it wasn't as if he could call someone to take a look at the door, not with a child tied in a sack in the trunk of his car. The girl was kicking again: he could hear her, and the lid of the trunk shook with the impact.

He tried the button one more time and, miraculously, the door began to descend. He held his breath until it stopped again an inch or two from the floor. It wasn't perfect, but from outside it would appear closed. He'd worry about it again in the morning, once the girl was dead.

Ormsby turned on the garage's interior light. Only now did he open the trunk of the car. The child in the sack was wriggling, and screaming against the material. He'd managed to get cable ties around her hands by working fast, but not her legs. They remained free, and the best he'd been able to do was cinch the drawstring of the sack around her shins and tie it off. He'd been forced to hit her once to stun her, but he hadn't enjoyed it, and had no desire to do it again.

Ormsby spoke.

"If you continue making noise, you'll force me to hurt you," he said, "and I don't want to hurt you. Keep quiet and listen to me."

The child stopped moving. He could see the sacking inflating and deflating where it was closest to her mouth. She was sobbing.

"I'm going to help you out of the car. If you struggle, you risk falling, and the floor here is hard. Also, if you try to lash out at me, you'll make me strike you, and I hate striking children. Nod if you understand."

There was a pause, and then he saw the girl nod.

"Good. Now I'm going to help you out of the trunk."

He leaned in carefully, still wary of her, and he was right to be. As soon as she sensed him drawing close, she tried to swing at him with her legs, hoping to catch him on the head with her knees or her feet. Objectively, he had to admire her spirit, but he couldn't risk incurring a broken nose, or even a bruise to his face. Any injury might be enough to raise suspicions, even in the case of harmless Roger Ormsby.

He stepped back.

"I warned you," he said. "Now you're going to make me do something I didn't want to do."

The girl began wailing and writhing. Ormsby was just drawing back his hand to give her a sharp slap on the head when the doorbell rang.

Ormsby listened. He wasn't expecting anyone. He could try to ignore the bell, and hope that whoever it was went away. On the other hand, if one of his neighbors had seen him pull into the garage they'd know he was home, and if he didn't answer they might begin to worry. The last thing he needed was for the police to be called.

And what if it was the police? Suppose he had been seen? The street had appeared to be empty and unwatched, but one could never be sure . . .

The bell rang a second time. Ormsby struck the girl once to subdue her before he closed the trunk again. He moved through the house, turning on a lamp as he entered the hallway. He saw a shape through the glass fan of the door: a tall figure.

Ormsby paused when he was still five feet away.

"Who is it?" he called, but received no reply.

Ormsby shuffled his feet and tried again.

"Who's there? What do you want?"

Finally, the voice spoke. It sounded to Ormsby like that of a black man.

"Delivery for Mr. Cole."

Ormsby relaxed.

"You have the wrong house," he said. "Cole lives in fourteen thirty-seven, across the street. This is fourteen thirty-six."

"You sure? Says fourteen thirty-six on the slip."

"Well, your slip's wrong."

"Shit," said the man, and Ormsby saw his shape ripple as he took in the street. "Don't look like anybody's home over there. Maybe you could sign for it, save me a wasted trip."

Ormsby experienced a creeping sense of unease.

"I don't think so," he said. "I don't open my door to strangers after dark."

"It's not dark yet."

"Even so."

"Shit," said the man again. "Okay, you have a good evening."

He went away. Only when Ormsby heard his footsteps moving down the path did he slip into the living room and ensure that he had departed. The caller was wearing a jacket, and didn't look like any delivery man Ormsby had ever seen, but as he paused at the sidewalk, Ormsby saw that he was holding a box. The man hung a right, and was lost behind the tall hedge. Ormsby waited, but he did not reappear.

Ormsby returned to the garage and opened the trunk of his car.

The sack lay limp and flat on the rubber matting.

The girl was gone.

# III

Let us leave Roger Ormsby for now, staring into the empty trunk of his clean, well-maintained car, in his big, anonymous house with its many unused rooms, the whole surrounded by a pretty garden with beds that flower throughout the year, for Ormsby prided himself on his plants, and they flourished thanks to his care and attention, the addition of copious amounts of old coffee grounds . . .

And human ash.

———

IT WAS ONE MONTH earlier, and the town of Rehoboth Beach, Delaware, had witnessed the final exodus of its summer tourists. The boardwalk concessions had closed, along with those bars, restaurants, and stores that relied exclusively on the season for their income. Here and there rainbow flags still flew, for Rehoboth was as gay-friendly as such towns came, and anyway, the pink dollar was only pink in a certain light. Once it arrived at the bank, it was as green as any other.

In the bathroom of a house at the edge of the town limits, the lawyer Eldritch was shaving, working at his sparse whiskers with an old straight razor. His was the only room with a mirror, and even then it was barely large enough to enable him to see his own face. Beyond the bathroom was his bedroom, and downstairs was his home office, where he continued the work of reassembling the records he had lost in the explosive fire that had destroyed his original business premises in Lynn, Massachusetts, some years earlier. Eldritch had almost entirely recovered from the physical injuries he received in the blast, but he remained frailer than before. His right hand shook slightly as he cut swaths through the shaving foam.

Beside him was a window that gave a partial view of the sea through some trees. A man stood smoking on the lawn, his back to the house. This was Eldritch's son, although the old lawyer had long conceded that he was his son in name only. At the moment of his birth, something had colonized his being: a wandering spirit, an angel, a demon. Call it what you would, but it was not human.

The doctors were surprised that the child had lived: his umbilical cord had become wrapped around his neck during delivery, asphyxiating him. The boy had, in fact, been born dead, and only the swift actions of the attending staff had resuscitated him. Eldritch and his late wife—who lived barely long enough to see her boy begin to walk—had feared brain damage or some other disability, but their son appeared to be entirely healthy, if unusually quiet. Eldritch could only remember him crying, really bawling, a handful of times, and he had slept for seven hours a night throughout his infancy. Other fathers told him he was blessed. Mothers, too.

But he was not blessed: his son *had* died, and just as his soul left his body another force had taken its place, one that had only gradually revealed itself to Eldritch as the years passed. Even now, after many decades, it remained something of an enigma to him. As it grew and matured, so too did it alter Eldritch's own nature, so that a once ordinary attorney with the usual slate of minor civil and criminal work became an examiner of the consciences of men, an assembler of evidence of base acts, and he presented his records to this being, who decided if action should be taken. The man now smoking on the lawn was an instrument of justice, although of whose justice Eldritch was uncertain.

Eldritch had been raised Lutheran, but his faith quickly became a half-remembered matter irregularly indulged, like the expensive coat that he only wore to church for his biannual attendances at Easter and Christmas. Then, as the creature that hid itself in the guise of his dead son became manifest, the reality of a world beyond this one concretized for Eldritch, but it was not a realm that bore any resemblance to the paradise of which the preachers spoke. From the little that Eldritch could glean, the being responsible for the creation of the universe had been silent for millennia. For all anyone knew, He might even be dead. (Perhaps, Eldritch's son had suggested, spurred into an astonishing blasphemy by a rare indulgence in hard liquor, He had killed Himself in despair at what He had created.) God, to give the entity a name, might have been unheard and unseen, but other creatures were waiting, and listening, and it was best not to draw their attention through loose talk.

Kushiel: when Eldritch had asked his son for his true name, that was the one he gave, but he did so with a crooked smile, as though this, too, were part of some great cosmic joke to which Eldritch was not privy.

Kushiel: Hell's jailer.

But to those he hunted, he was the Collector.

Eldritch finished shaving and washed away the remains of the foam. Just as his son stank of nicotine from the cigarettes that had stained his fingers a deep ocher, so, too, could Eldritch smell his own mortality. His body odor had changed, and no matter how clean he kept himself, or how much cedarwood aftershave he used, he could still detect it. It was the stink of his physical form in decline. It was the reek of the mud in the bottom of the pond of existence, and flies buzzed around it. He wondered how much time he had left. Not long. He felt it in his bones.

He carefully turned the mirror so that its reflective surface faced the wall. The Collector—let Eldritch think of his son as others did—was strict about this. He had a distrust of mirrors. He had once described them as "reflecting eyes." Eldritch had thought it a superstition, until an incident involving a dead child killer named John Grady. The Collector had retrieved a mirror from Grady's former home, and, just before he removed it from Eldritch's presence, he had turned it toward the lawyer. Eldritch had seen his own features and, behind them, those of another: the terrified face of John Grady, who, in death, had somehow sequestered himself in a reflected version of his house, wandering through it with the ghosts of dead children, believing himself to be immune from justice, until the Collector proved him wrong.

But Eldritch knew that the Collector had seen other faces looking back at him from polished surfaces, and one face in particular, for behind the surface of mirrors moved the Buried God, the God of Wasps, the one whom even the Collector feared. If God slept, the Buried God did not. The Buried God watched, and waited to be found.

Eldritch entered his bedroom and put on a clean shirt. He was going to see a movie, and later he would have a quiet dinner in one of the local bars that remained open. He was rereading Montaigne's *Essays*. He found a kind of consolation in them.

He went downstairs and called from the open back door to say that he was leaving. He received only a slight wave of the hand in reply, but the Collector did not turn around. Even six months before, it would not have been possible for Eldritch to leave the house in this way, because the Collector would not have permitted it. They were being hunted by the detective named Charlie Parker and the men who stood with him, all of them seeking revenge for the death of one of their friends at the Collector's hands. But a truce of kinds had been declared, and they were safer now, although Eldritch knew that the Collector remained wary of Parker.

*Sometimes*, Eldritch thought, *I think he fears Parker almost as much as he fears the Buried God.*

Eldritch got in his car and drove onto the road, turning right for Rehoboth. He didn't even know what movie he'd go see. They all started at the same time, more or less. And they were all the same, more or less. It would be enough just to sit in the darkness and forget, for a while.

———

THE COLLECTOR TOOK ANOTHER drag on his cigarette, and listened to the sound of his father's car fading away. There was a new moon in the sky. He tracked the progress of a dying insect, its flight erratic, until it finally fell by the feet of the man who was holding a gun on him.

"I knew you'd come," he said, as Charlie Parker emerged from the shadows.

The Collector had not seen Parker in more than a year, and was astonished by the changes in him. It was not simply the physical alterations wrought by his suffering, although his injuries, and his ongoing recuperation from them, had left him thinner than before, and his hair was speckled with white where the shotgun pellets had torn paths through his scalp. No, this was a man transformed within as well as without, and the unease that the Collector had always experienced in Parker's presence, a glowing ember of concern, suddenly exploded into flame. Parker had died three times in the hours following the shooting, and each time he had returned, like some biblical prophecy made real. Now he was no longer as he once was: he burned with conviction. The Collector could see it in his eyes, and feel it as surely as a static charge.

The Collector had never been in as much danger as he was at this moment.

"Are your confederates with you?" he asked.

He stared past the detective, expecting to witness the arrival of Angel and Louis, the men who walked with Parker, but the woods remained undisturbed.

"I'm alone."

"How did you find me?"

"I sniffed you out."

The Collector's right arm twitched once in response, for he understood that the detective's reply contained a truth both literal and metaphorical. Somehow he had tracked him down, and not through Internet searches or the words of informants. No, Parker had hunted him by following unseen trails. The Collector would never be able to hide from this man again, assuming he was permitted to survive this encounter.

"They gave me their word," said the Collector. He had struck a bargain with Angel and Louis, although perhaps he had been naïve to expect it to be honored. "If I helped them find the ones who attacked you, then you would leave my father and me in peace."

"Had I been in a position to advise them, I'd have told them to kill you along with those who hurt me."

Something remained unspoken.

"But?" asked the Collector.

"It would have been a mistake."

"And why is that?"

"Because I may have a use for you."

The Collector managed to laugh.

"You, use *me*?" he said. "And what makes you think I would even countenance such an arrangement?"

Parker's expression did not alter, and neither did the gun waver in his hand.

"Because you're a dog, and all dogs need a master. I'm about to bring you to heel."

The cigarette in the Collector's hand had burned down almost to his fingers. He let it drop, and carefully moved his right foot to crush the butt.

"What did you see," he asked, "during your time between worlds?"

"I saw a lake," the detective replied. "I spoke with my dead child, and the ghost of my wife whispered to me."

"And what did she say?"

A flicker of the eyes, caught by the Collector.

"That's none of your business. It's enough for you to know that this world is altering, and your purpose will change along with it. And I'm tired of looking over my shoulder, tired of wondering if your blade is about to flash in the darkness."

"I have no intention of killing you. I don't believe I ever had."

"Nevertheless, I don't care much for you walking in my footsteps, or those of my friends. I've found you once, and I can find you again. You'll come when I call, and you'll do as I say."

"Or?"

But the word held no real defiance. It was the response of one who has already surrendered, and is simply seeking to salvage some dignity from the terms.

"I'll feed your father to the FBI as an accomplice to murder, and then I'll help them to track you down. You're a mystery to them, but they suspect your existence. I'll confirm it. But it'll be me who puts an end to you, and whatever you are, or whatever lives inside you, will wander in darkness. You won't return. I guarantee it."

"You don't have that kind of power."

"Don't I?"

The Collector swallowed.

"And if I agree?"

"You can go about your work. I don't have the time or inclination to chain you up in a yard just to feed you scraps, but you'll come when I summon you."

The Collector watched the scudding of clouds. He felt a tightness at his neck, as of a restored collar tightening.

"May I have another cigarette?"

"Go ahead."

He moved his left hand very slowly to the pocket of his coat and retrieved the pack and his matches. He put a cigarette between his lips and lit it. He inhaled deeply, but it both smelled and tasted wrong. He removed the cigarette and looked at it in disappointment.

"All this," he said, "because of a brush with death?"

"No," said the detective. "All this because a god has awoken."

He reached into one of his own pockets, withdrew a cell phone, and tossed it to the Collector.

"When it rings, you answer. When I call, you come."

He lowered his gun. He had no more need of it that night. He turned his back on the Collector and returned to the shadows.

# V

Although he did not yet know it, Roger Ormsby's current dilemma was a direct consequence of that confrontation at Rehoboth Beach, and of others less recent. Not that the revelation, when it came, would be of any comfort to him.

Quite the contrary, in fact.

For the moment, all he could do was pick up the empty sack from the trunk of his car, as though expecting some shrunken version of the child to be revealed beneath it. He then checked under the car, and found the space there unoccupied. The gap between the frozen garage door and the floor was too small to have permitted the girl to escape through it, and there were no hiding places in the garage itself, which meant she had to be somewhere in the house. In her situation, he would have made straight for the front door, so he must have passed her as he was returning after the conversation with the delivery man, probably as she was hiding in the kitchen, or in the interconnected living and dining rooms.

Ormsby grabbed a pistol from under his tool rack and hurried from the garage. He half expected to hear the sound of breaking glass: the front door was locked and the windows secured, so the only way the child could get out would be by shattering a pane. He glanced into the kitchen, but it was empty. He didn't even bother checking the stairs, or consider the possibility that she might be in one of the upstairs rooms: it would make no sense for her to go up.

Ormsby paused at the door to the living room. The drapes were drawn, and it was dark inside. He didn't want to risk having the child run at him. There was any number of heavy objects in the room—cut-glass vases, lamps, bronzes. Even a glancing blow from one of them might be enough to lay him flat on the ground, and once he was down he would be vulnerable to further attack.

"Missy, are you in there?" he called.

He received no reply, but he thought he could hear a small snuffling sound.

"Look, I'm sorry I hurt you, but I did warn you, and I'm a man who keeps his word. I don't want to cause you any more pain, honest I don't."

He tried to come up with some excuse for what was happening that might be acceptable and understandable to a child.

"I need some money, that's all," he said. "I'm going to send a message to your mom and dad, they'll pay me what I want, and then I'll let you go. They love you, right? If they love you, they'll pay up, and pretty soon this will all be over. In the meantime, you can watch TV, and eat whatever you like. I've got a full larder, and all kinds of movies. There's even a computer you can play games on. How about that? So you show yourself, then we can get you comfortable and set about returning you to your family. What do you say? We got a deal?"

Something cold touched the side of his neck. He didn't have to see it to know it was a gun.

"No," said a male voice, and Ormsby recognized it from the exchange at the front door only minutes earlier. "I don't think that deal will be acceptable at all."

Ormsby considered trying to bring his pistol into play, but it was in his right hand and the man was slightly to his left. Ormsby would be dead before he could use it. Still, he didn't panic. The Gray Man wasn't the kind to do so.

"Are you police?" he asked.

"What do you think?"

"If you're police, then you've entered my home illegally."

"You a lawyer?"

"No, but I know the law."

"Watch a lot of TV, huh?"

"I read."

"Good for you."

"Don't patronize me."

The barrel of the gun nudged Ormsby gently.

"Frankly, Mr. Ormsby, I can do whatever I please, and you'll do whatever I tell you, beginning with dropping that gun in your hand."

Ormsby did as he was told.

"You're no cop," he said.

"Took you long enough to figure that out."

"So what do you want?"

"You, Mr. Ormsby. We want you."

*We?*

A light went on in the living room, and the muzzle guided Ormsby inside. He saw the girl sitting in an armchair, wrapped in the big wool blanket that Ormsby sometimes used to keep out the cold. There was some bruising to her face, but she didn't look frightened. Ormsby wondered why she wasn't scared, until he saw the man standing behind her.

He was unshaven, and of indeterminate age, so that he might have been anywhere between forty and sixty. He wore a green combat jacket that was old and battered enough to have seen service in Vietnam. Ormsby's first thought was that he looked like a homeless person, and therefore his house was in the process of being burgled. It led him to believe, however briefly, that he might yet be able to talk his way out of this. He had some valuables, and a little hard cash. Depending on how unscrupulous these men were, they could be reasoned with. If their tastes ran in a particular direction, he might even be in a position to offer them the girl herself. It didn't matter much to Ormsby how she died, just *that* she died. He could deal with the men later, just as soon as he managed to get his hands on another weapon. He had plenty stored around the house, just in case.

Then Ormsby saw that the man's left hand was hanging over the top of the armchair, and the girl was holding on to it with her right, so that their linked arms hung across her body like a protective shield. She appeared to be deriving strength and consolation from his presence. She trusted him. He was watching Ormsby with the dead gaze of a farmer about to behead a snake that has threatened one of his herd. If he was a burglar, then he wasn't the kind to hurt a child. Ormsby felt some of his hope ebb. All was not yet lost, but he'd have to be clever. It did not even cross his mind that they might have come for the girl herself. He had been so careful for so long that he found it almost impossible to conceive of being caught; or, if such an eventuality ever troubled him, it always involved men in uniform, and detectives with badges, and these were neither.

"Sit down," said the voice from behind, and Ormsby took a second armchair, which now allowed him to see the one with the gun. He was tall, black, and bald, with the faintest of gray goatees. Unlike the other, he appeared faintly amused: if the smaller man would have beheaded Ormsby with a single blow, granted the opportunity, this one gave the impression that he might first prefer to toy with his prey.

Even as Ormsby watched them, assessing the odds, the Gray Man was trying to figure out how they had got in. It wasn't too hard, once he set his mind to it. The jamming of the garage door had been no malfunction: these men had somehow overridden his own control, and because the door remained up the alarm system had been disabled. When the black man rang the doorbell as a distraction, the other must have raised the door, entered the garage and taken the girl, then continued into the house, keeping her quiet when Ormsby returned to his car, before admitting his colleague.

But then Ormsby heard the front door closing, and footsteps approaching from the hall. The figure that appeared in the doorway was of average height, with a build that was just on the heavier side of slight. He moved slowly, and took in his surroundings as though faintly appalled by all that he was seeing. And although Ormsby had listened to him drawing nearer, and seen with his own eyes how he stepped into the open doorway, still it was as though this man had descended upon him, alighting in his home like a bird of prey landing by wounded quarry. He paused on the threshold of the living room, enshadowed, taking in Ormsby, then the girl. Ormsby saw his head tilt, and once again he was reminded of the movements of a hawk. He remembered what he had been told many years before.

*If you're lucky, and careful, you'll die in your own bed, and no one will ever learn of what you've done. But if the odds change—and the odds always change, it's just a question of how much—then the hunters may find you, and if that happens you will tell them nothing about us.*

*Because there are worse things than being caught.*

The stranger stepped into the room, the light catching the white markings in his hair before losing itself in the cold fire of his eyes.

And deep inside Roger Ormsby, the Gray Man whispered the hunter's name, and tried to find a hiding place in the disused hollows of his heart.

# VI

B ack, back through the years, to a younger Ormsby, and the first warning that a hunter might someday come . . .

————

ORMSBY WOULDN'T HAVE CALLED it blackmail, exactly. Oh, the threat was there, and it was made explicit to him by the woman who had arrived at his door shortly after he'd killed a boy named Joseph Slocum, who'd made the mistake of running off to sulk in a culvert near his home after an argument with his mother. The smell of his burning still lingered in the basement, and a new game was about to begin.

Ormsby had been surprised by how much the woman knew about him: she didn't have all the names, just two, but her information was enough to damn him, especially since it included photographs of him snatching the boy. They looked like they'd been taken through darkened glass, and Ormsby vaguely recollected a van parked nearby when he'd taken Slocum.

But the woman didn't want to give what she had to the police. Instead, she offered Ormsby a deal: her silence in return for a favor, should it be asked of him, and he had acquiesced because, really, what choice did he have? Five years went by, and Ormsby had begun to believe that the debt might never be called in when the woman contacted him again. This time, she gave him the name of a child—a girl—and the time and place at which she would be most vulnerable. The woman would even arrange for the girl's mother to be otherwise occupied—a fire in a trash can, nothing serious—to give Ormsby the time he needed.

Ormsby did as he was asked. He didn't even need to know the reason the child had to disappear, because he could guess it. He wasn't a fool. The parents of a missing child have no time for any concerns other than their own, and, handled correctly, such a disappearance guaranteed a lifetime of distraction. This particular girl's parents—campaigners, proselytizers, do-gooders—just needed to be turned aside from their mission. So Ormsby took the girl and began a fresh game, and the woman never contacted him again, except to give him that warning about luck and care, and the importance of remaining silent.

And now the test was about to begin.

———

PARKER WALKED PAST ORMSBY without giving him another glance, and approached the girl. He saw her grip tighten instinctively on Angel's hand. Parker went down on one knee before her, like a man paying homage to the image of a saint.

"You're Charlotte, right?" he asked.

She nodded.

"But your family calls you Charlie."

Another nod.

"That's my name, too."

She looked dubious, but Angel squeezed her hand and said, "It's true."

"So, may I call you Charlie, as one to another?"

She looked to Angel, and he nodded.

"Yes," she said.

"Thank you. In a few minutes, Charlie, we're going to contact your parents, and the police, and we'll tell them to come get you. But first, we need to talk with this man here—his name is Ormsby, although you don't need to worry about that—because we don't think you're the first child he's taken, and out there are other mommies and daddies who've lost sons and daughters to him. We can't bring their children back, but we can give their moms and dads a little peace by letting them know the truth.

"But I understand what you've been through, and it may be that you don't want to wait. So if you ask it, we'll make the call to your parents right now, and hope that the police can get what they need from Mr. Ormsby back at the station. My guess, though, is that Mr. Ormsby will tell them nothing. You see, we got to him just a little too late, otherwise we'd have stopped him from taking you. But unless someone saw what happened, then it's possible that he might be able to lie his way out of this. People like him are very good at lying. If that happens, then he'll get away not only with what he did to you, but what he did to all those other children.

"So it's your choice, Charlie. Can we have the time that we need?"

She thought long and hard, so long that, for a moment, Parker believed she might refuse, and he would have kept his word to her if she had. But instead she said, "Yes, you can talk to him."

Parker thanked her, then rose. He reached into his pocket, and handed her a cell phone.

"Angel will take you into the kitchen to wait while Louis and I stay here with Mr. Ormsby, if that's okay. Do you know your mom's number, or your dad's?"

"I know both."

"Then pick one, and put it into that phone. If you get frightened, or worried, or feel that we're taking too long, you just press the green button. Nobody will try to stop you, and no one will be angry. We're just grateful for the chance you've given us."

Charlie looked past him to where Ormsby sat, and the purity of her hatred for him shone from her face.

"I'll wait until you tell me to call," she said.

Angel continued to hold her hand as she climbed from her seat, and accompanied her to the kitchen, leaving Ormsby alone with Parker and Louis. Once she was safely out of the room, Parker placed an upright chair directly opposite Ormsby.

"Do you know who I am?" Parker asked.

"An intruder in my home," said Ormsby. "A pedophile who broke in here with his deviant friends after I rescued that little girl from them."

"My name is Parker."

"I don't care."

"How many others have you taken?"

"I don't know what you're talking about."

"Elizabeth Keynes."

Of all the possibilities, it had to be that one: the favor, the debt.

"Never heard of her."

"You're lying. The cries of dying children echo in this house."

"I don't even understand what language you're speaking. It's just noise to me."

"Aren't you afraid of what we might do to you?"

"You mean kill me?" Ormsby laughed. "You won't do that."

"Why not?"

"Because if you kill me, you lose. You get nothing."

"We could torture you."

Ormsby stared hard at the man who sat across from him.

"No, you won't do that, either. It's not in you." Ormsby inclined a chin toward Louis. "Maybe it's in your friend here, but I don't believe you'd let him do the kind of harm that you wouldn't be willing to inflict yourself."

"So you *do* know who I am?"

"Like I told your friend, I read a lot. I've seen your picture. I know what you are."

"What do you think will happen if we hand you over to the police?"

"I'll tell my story of how I found the girl wandering, and brought her home. Maybe they'll believe me, maybe they won't, but a good lawyer will sow enough doubt to get me off. The law will probably go poking into my past, trying to tie me to whatever you or someone else says I may have done, but they'll find nothing. I'll move on, and those kids you keep speaking about will remain missing, and their parents still won't know whether to mourn them or continue praying for their return. I'm not a young man. Death will come for me soon, and the earth will swallow up every secret I've ever kept."

"And what if I don't hand you over to the police?"

"You mean you just walk away from here with the girl? Yes, I suppose you could do that, but you'll get nothing in return. This is a seller's market, Mr. Parker, and I'm not selling to you, not for any price."

Parker got to his feet. Ormsby couldn't help flinching, but the detective simply walked away from him and stood by the picture window at the rear of the house. The drapes were drawn. He opened them.

"Mr. Ormsby," he said, without turning around. "Would you come here, please?"

"You heard him," said Louis. "Get up."

Ormsby rose from the chair and joined Parker at the window. He saw a man standing on the back lawn, smoking a cigarette, but that wasn't what drew Ormsby's immediate attention, or caused him to sway on his feet. It was a woman, as close to the glass on the outside of the house as Ormsby was to the pane inside. She wore a tattered red dress, soiled with blood and dirt. Her skull was entirely hairless, and the sockets of her eyes were empty. Her skin was gray, and wrinkled around the mouth like the surface of an apple long past its best. She opened her lips, and Ormsby saw the exposed roots of her teeth where her gums had receded. She reached out her left hand and the glass squeaked as she drew her fingers down the pane, leaving behind flakes of tissue like the residue of dead moths.

Behind her, more figures appeared, male and female, crowding around the man who smoked his cigarette and regarded Ormsby calmly and coldly.

"I won't give you to the police," said Parker. "I'll give you to the ones that you're seeing."

Ormsby stepped back from the glass, from the dreadful longing of the woman beyond it. Somehow, he found his tongue.

"What are they?"

"They're hollow, and without mercy, and that's all you need to know, for now. When they take you, you'll discover the rest."

"And the one with them?"

"Summary justice: the instrument that will send you to join them."

Ormsby felt as though he had wandered into a dream trap.

"It's not possible."

"You can tell him that yourself. I'm sure he'll be fascinated to listen to your theory."

And it seemed that the one on the lawn heard him, for from the folds of his coat he produced a knife that shone in the moonlight.

"You'll just let him kill me?"

"If I have to, but that's only where your troubles will begin. There is no oblivion. The punishment goes on, and in time you'll find yourself on the other side of a glass, staring at someone just like you."

Even in this moment of abject fear, and confronted with the reality of his own damnation, Ormsby tried to bargain.

"Why should I give you what you want, if this is what waits for me?"

"Because now you know. Now you have time."

"For what?"

"For repentance. To make amends. But the moment I hand you over to the one with the blade, that chance will be gone."

Ormsby retreated from the window, and sat back down in his chair. He was the Gray Man, and the Gray Man was him, and both sides feared what waited beyond the glass.

"I agree," he said, for what choice did he have?

"You'll confess all to the police?"

"Yes."

"If you renege, he'll come for you," Parker warned.

"I won't renege."

"I believe you." Parker gave his attention to Louis. "Call Ross. Tell him we have another one."

Parker turned back to the window of Ormsby's house. The Collector appeared to be alone in the garden, still smoking his cigarette. Parker shook his head, and the Collector threw the cigarette on the ground in disgust before stalking off into the dusk.

# 2

Oh! how many torments lie in the small circle of a wedding-ring!

Colley Cibber (1671–1757), *The Double Gallant*

# VII

The one who stood in the late fall sunshine, disoriented by his first moments of freedom, was already damaged when he entered Maine State Prison, and the years inside had not served to repair the fractures to his mind and soul. Instead they had added physical injury and emotional turmoil to his list of burdens, and a desire simply to fade away.

Nobody was waiting to greet him as he stood outside the prison gates. His lawyer had offered to send someone to collect him, but there had been confusion about the time of his release—an error with the paperwork, it seemed—and he was now among those rarest of prisoners, the ones who found themselves released early through bureaucratic incompetence, if only, in his case, by a few hours.

He was many things: a convicted felon, a former husband, a disgraced hero.

An innocent man? Perhaps, but then so many made the same claim . . .

With luck, though, nobody would even remember his name. It would make whatever was to come a little easier. In the meantime, he would find the man named Charlie Parker and tell him his tale. Among his possessions was a newspaper article concerning the apprehension of Roger Ormsby, a man who had thrived on torment. Parker had found him, and would understand that others like him existed.

A prison van pulled up, and he got in. It would take him to the Rockland Ferry Terminal, and from there he could hop a Concord Coach Lines bus to Portland. They'd given him $50 and a bus ticket upon release, and he had another $240 that he'd earned in the workshops. He didn't speak to the officers in the van, and they did not speak to him. He had been a model prisoner, but it didn't matter. They knew the crime of which he had been convicted, and they distrusted and disliked him for it.

He regarded the falling of leaves as they drove, like all the dead days descending.

———

FROM THE PARKING LOT, three men in a clean Chevy pickup watched him go. They and their kind had taken almost everything from the prisoner. He had just one thing left, and soon they would take that, too.

They pulled out of the lot and passed the van on the road, not even glancing in its direction, before driving on to Rockland, where they parked by the terminal off Main Street, and there they waited.

The van pulled up and disgorged its passenger. He walked to a pay phone and made a call, then bought himself coffee and a cookie while he waited for the bus to arrive. When it came, he got on board, and they shadowed him all the way to Portland. One of them went inside the terminal to watch for his arrival, and the ex-prisoner was greeted by a very large man in a very large suit that was still too small for him, who took his bag and escorted him to a black Mercedes sedan.

The tracker returned to the Chevy.

"The lawyer," he said.

"He looks like a clown," came the reply from the man in the backseat. He had red hair and a feral aspect, like a creature frozen in the process of transformation from human to animal.

"If he is, he's a clever one."

Only the driver remained silent. He had not seen the fallen hero since the trial, and was surprised by how much he loathed him, and by his desire for him to suffer more than he already had.

Together the lawyer and the ex-con drove to a mixed-income property on Congress Street, not far from Longfellow Square, which was roughly divided between private tenants and those supported by the Portland Housing Authority. They went inside, and the lawyer was alone when he emerged twenty minutes later.

"He's fallen far," said the feral man.

"He's still falling," said the tracker. "He just doesn't know it."

Only now did the driver speak.

"Oh, I think he does."

They drove off. They knew where to find him, and could take him anytime. They would wait a little longer—a couple of days, but no more than that—just in case the opportunity presented itself to inflict fresh miseries upon him, or life chose to do it for them.

When they finally came for him, he might even be grateful.

# VIII

S AC Edgar Ross of the Federal Bureau of Investigation's New York field office arrived at Blue Smoke on East Twenty-seventh Street shortly after seven that same evening. He had been running behind schedule all day, and was surprised that he was only half an hour late stepping through the door of the restaurant. He spotted Conrad Holt sitting at the packed bar, half-interested in the playoff game showing on the big TV screen, and moved through the postwork crowd to join him.

"Thanks for keeping a seat for me," said Ross.

The deputy director gestured with his Bloody Mary at the masses thronging the bar.

"What did you expect me to do, put my purse on it? I might just be able to order you a drink, now that you've got here at last."

"Bad day."

"Can you remember when you last had a good one?"

"Not really. Gin and tonic. Hendrick's, if they have it."

Holt called the order, and the bartender asked if he wanted it with cucumber. Ross declined. He thought the gin tasted just vegetal enough as it was.

"They were going to give away our table," said Holt.

"Did you tell them who you were?"

"I thought charm might work better."

The Hendrick's arrived. Holt settled up as Ross took his first sip, and a hostess appeared with menus and led them to a table at the back. Despite the noise at the bar, and the earlier threat of being bounced, they found themselves by a window with no neighbors for the time being.

"I don't even know why I still look at the menu here," said Holt. "I always have the same thing."

"Which is?"

"Fried chicken. Steak tips for an appetizer, if they're on. Mostly the chicken is enough."

Ross didn't care much for fried chicken. He was a red meat man, regardless of his physician's admonitions to the contrary. Not that Dr. Mahajan would have signed off on fried chicken without wincing either, but it wasn't as if Ross was about to Snapchat him a picture of whatever ended up on his plate. The waiter came to take their order. Ross settled for the brisket, with fries on the side. Dr. Mahajan would just have to up the dosage on his cholesterol medication. Holt, meanwhile, ordered the fried chicken, with a side of collard greens.

"I saw the Ormsby memo," said Holt, once the waiter had disappeared.

"He refused counsel," said Ross. "He had his rights read to him. It's clean."

"Clean once the details of how Parker and his friends got to him were airbrushed from it."

"Clean is relative, but we're being careful."

"So you say."

Holt finished his Bloody Mary, then called for a glass of wine. Ross stuck with his gin. In retrospect, he should have asked the bartender to make it a large one, and easy on the tonic. He'd managed to keep the arrangement with Parker under the radar for months, but he knew it couldn't last. Ormsby's crimes were too serious and vile for the details of his apprehension to pass unexamined at Federal Plaza, and Holt was nobody's fool. It was still not yet common knowledge that Parker was on a federal retainer, with a degree of protection that also covered his friends, both of whom were criminals and one of whom was a professional killer, albeit semiretired, or so Ross hoped. He needed Holt—to whom he answered, technically at least—to support what was, by any standards, an unorthodox and risky piece of business.

"How did you redirect the money to pay Parker?" asked Holt.

"Fax paper and typewriter ribbons. I like to think of sections of the stationery budget as a discretionary fund."

"Do we even still use typewriter ribbons?"

"If anyone asks, I'll tell them we type up sensitive documents."

"And faxes?"

"The War on Terror takes many forms."

Holt nodded. "God bless unwinnable conflicts."

His wine arrived, but he didn't touch it.

"How long did you think your deal with Parker would go unnoticed?"

"Not as long as it did."

"There's a part of me that wishes I still didn't know. Why did he consent to it?"

"He didn't. The approach came from him. He offered."

"Again, why?"

"I think," said Ross, as Holt took a tentative sip of his wine, "that he intends to be more proactive in his investigations."

Holt almost choked on his chardonnay.

"*More* proactive?" he said. "Jesus, he's practically shitting dead bodies as it is. And you've signed us on to his crusade?"

"I thought it might allow us to direct his energies when the situation required it."

"Seriously? You think you can control him?"

"He's a tethered goat. On a long chain, admittedly, but tethered nonetheless."

Holt looked doubtful.

"Does he need the money that badly?"

"He finds it useful. To be honest, I'm still not sure why he signed up."

"And the two lunatics with him?"

"The cash covers their bar tabs, if nothing else. And the one called Angel sends me letters." Ross couldn't bring himself to look Holt in the eye as he spoke. That goddamned Angel.

"What kind of letters?"

"He's convinced that federal agents receive keys to restricted restrooms. He wants one for himself."

There was a pause that spoke volumes, then:

"Restrooms."

"Yes. Special ones, in Amtrak stations and airports. Museums, too."

"Jesus."

Holt, hopeful that no more sudden shocks were about to come his way, risked a second attempt at his wine, successful this time.

"Am I the only one who hears a ticking sound?" he asked.

"With respect, you're asking a lot of questions for someone who'd prefer not to know."

"Why do you think I'm asking them here, and not back at Federal Plaza?"

"Parker is part of what's to come," said Ross. "The closer we keep him, the better equipped we'll be to react when it happens."

"You know, I'm the only deputy director who doesn't believe that you're insane. And sometimes even I'm not entirely convinced."

"I'm touched by your faith in me."

"Are you monitoring him?"

"He uses a cell phone for work, and we have ears on that, but I'm sure he knows. He has others, but he changes them regularly. We're on his e-mail as well, but he's smart, and doesn't commit anything of value to electronic communications."

"And you're sure he has the list?"

Parker had negotiated his deal with Ross by passing him part of a list of names retrieved from the wreckage of an airplane in Maine's Great North Woods. The list, Ross believed, contained the identities of those who were in league with various elements, all of them united by one aim: to find the Buried God, release it from its captivity, and just maybe bring about Armageddon, all of which Ross had most assuredly *not* put in any official memos.

"What we've received so far checks out. He's promised more. I also believe that he used the list to track down Ormsby."

"Parker's playing us."

"Perhaps."

"To what end?"

"I think he's looking for something."

"What?"

"A pattern."

"And what will this pattern reveal?"

"A name. A controlling influence."

Holt wore the expression of a man who believed that he might accidentally have ingested a wasp, and would find out for sure only when it started to sting him.

"And if he screws up?" he said. "Or dies? We'll lose everything. That list, wherever it is, will be gone forever."

"If that were to happen, then I believe the rest of the list would find its way to us. My understanding is that Parker has made arrangements."

Their food arrived. Ross thought that Holt's fried chicken looked very good, even to someone like himself who generally eschewed it.

"Do you like him?" asked Holt.

It was a strange question. Ross wasn't sure that he had an answer. He did think that he understood something of Parker's essence, even if the man entire remained an enigma to him. Ross had been educated by Jesuits, and had, for a time, considered entering the order until sanity prevailed, even if he suspected that he had simply exchanged the possibility of one ambitious, secretive institution for the reality of another. The Jesuits practiced "discernment," which required listening and waiting in order to establish what course of action God might wish in a given situation. Parker, too, was a man who listened and waited, but for what voice Ross could not say. Also, the actions of Jesuits, unlike those of Parker, did not typically run to guns and violence, or end with entire communities being put to the torch.

"I think he's a good man," he replied, eventually.

"God preserve us from good men," said Holt. "Do you trust him?"

"Yes," said Ross, without hesitation.

"Funny," said Holt. "I never took you for the trusting type."

He cut into his chicken.

"What about the other two?"

"We only ever had suspicions, but no real proof."

"You could have found proof, if you'd tried hard enough."

"Maybe I didn't want to."

"That's what worries me. How's the brisket?"

"Moist."

"You still should have ordered the chicken."

"I think you're right."

"If this falls apart," Holt said, "you'll burn. You know that, don't you?"

"If this falls apart," Ross replied, "we'll all burn."

Chapter

# IX

F ar to the north, amid the anonymous furnishings of his apartment, the newly freed man lay awake, unable to sleep away from
the noise of the prison, and wondered again how his life had
come to such an end.

He was a Disgraced Hero, a Fallen Idol. He'd once had a wife, but
no children. That absence of children was fortunate, he supposed: he
couldn't begin to imagine the grief they would have endured once their
father's alleged offenses became known. Even moving to another state
wouldn't have saved them: the Internet could make prey of anyone. As
for his wife, well, they hadn't been getting along so well before everything went wrong, but he still remained shocked and hurt at how
quickly she had abandoned him.

He'd told her he was innocent—had told the same thing to anyone
who would listen, from the police who first interrogated him, to the
jury that had subsequently convicted him and the judge who sentenced
him, and even to those fellow prisoners who were willing to associate
with him, or with whom he could safely associate in turn, which wasn't
many. He'd told his lawyer, too. The lawyer said that it didn't matter, but
it did. It mattered to the Hero before he was toppled from his pedestal.

Only his mother and father had continued to believe in him—they,
and a handful of friends, but his parents were almost entirely alone in

visiting him regularly. His mother had died first, and then his father just six months later. He'd applied for compassionate release to attend their funerals and been turned down on both occasions, even though a sympathetic corrections officer had offered to transport him from the jail to the graveside and back after the death of his father. Incensed, the Hero had even gone so far as to apply to the U.S. District Court for a temporary release order, only to have the state object on the grounds that the nature of his crimes made him an ongoing danger to the community, and he was also considered a flight risk due to his intelligence and the belief that he might have some funds hidden away, according to his ex-wife. So his mother and father had gone into the ground without their only child to mourn them, and nobody came to visit him after they were gone.

His parents had left him some money, for which he was grateful as he'd been wiped out by the divorce, despite anything his ex-wife might have claimed to the contrary, although she managed to get her hands on some of his inheritance, too. The bequest might have been enough to enable him to resettle in another state, were it not for his status as a registered sex offender and the requirement to engage with probation and counseling services in Maine on that basis. He'd been given a list of his conditions of probation, which included, on top of the standard requirements—refrain from using drugs and avoid excessive alcohol intake, find a job, pay the court-determined probation and Department of Corrections supervision fees—an injunction against contact with anyone under the age of eighteen, and any use of a computer with an Internet connection. The latter stipulation meant that he had to get the private detective's number the old-fashioned way, through a phone call. He'd bought a TracFone, and his lawyer had registered it for him online.

He was barely out of prison, but already he recognized the difficulty of adjusting to the outside world: it was either too loud or too quiet, too cognizant of his presence or too unaware, too random or too regimented. There were aspects of it that he no longer understood, and

others that appeared to have vanished entirely while he was incarcerated. He had eaten dinner in a bar earlier that evening, but at first he
had been unable to pick up the silverware. It was the first time in five
years that he had been presented with utensils that were not plastic, and
he was afraid to use them. He wondered if the reason so many former
inmates reoffended was simply that they wanted to be back in a world
they understood.

He dialed the number and waited. It went straight to voice mail.

For a moment, he struggled to find his voice. He thought about
hanging up, and remaining silent, but he believed that he did not have
long left. If he was right, they would come for him soon, because all
that was left to take was his life.

But they had not broken him completely. Despite everything, he had
endured, and now he would tell his story.

"Mr. Parker," he said. "My name is Jerome Burnel . . ."

Chapter

So how did it come to pass? How did Jerome Burnel, the Disgraced Hero, lose everything? It began when Jerome Burnel was no kind of hero at all, when this tale was not even his.

Almost six years earlier, this was the stumble that led to the fall.

———

CORRIE HAD BEEN SIZING up the guy for the last hour. She was good at what she did, or thought she was: after all, she'd had enough practice by now.

He was neatly dressed: shirt, jacket, and trousers, not jeans. His shoes were clean and well shined. He wasn't wearing a wedding ring, which was a problem. She'd found that the ones who wore a ring were more likely to be amenable to the kind of pressure under which they would ultimately be placed, simply because they had more to lose. He was on his third drink, though, which was a plus, and she'd seen the way he looked at some of the girls who were passing. He was in the market, even if he didn't know it yet.

She didn't care much for the bar itself. To begin with, the music was terrible—the kind of faux-country seemingly beloved of city boys slumming it in Portland—and even though the bar was new, it already smelled of stale, spilled beer that hadn't been properly cleaned up, and of half-eaten peanuts crushed into the floor. On the other hand, because it was a recent arrival to the strip of noisy bars down at the Old Port, and the bouncers weren't familiar to her, or she to them, it represented virgin territory. She and the others had almost worn out their welcome in Portland. To stay much longer would be to risk inviting attention.

She drifted over, swaying in time to the music because it made her appear drunker than she was. She was drinking bourbon, but heavy on the ice and soda. Good bartenders tended to assume that girls who drank like her were trying to be careful and responded accordingly, but the dunce in this place had already offered her one on the house, which she'd declined. He'd pretended to act all hurt in response, but then the pretense had become reality, and when she'd tried to order a second drink he'd ignored her. She didn't make a fuss. She didn't want to give him more cause than necessary to remember her.

Corrie slipped onto the stool to the right of the mark.

"Hi," she said.

He turned to look at her. His eyes were slightly different colors: one bright blue, the other closer to green. It could have made him appear odd, but instead she found it hugely attractive, helped by the fact that he was slim but not too thin, and dark-haired without any gray that she could see. Up close, she could tell that he was older than she'd first assumed: early thirties.

"I saw you looking at me," he replied.

"I didn't think you'd noticed."

"Hard not to, when a pretty girl is giving you the eye."

"You didn't let on."

"I figured you'd come over, in your own time."

He said all this without smiling. The words sounded flirty, but his manner was neutral. He wasn't arrogant, she thought. He was simply commenting, as he might have done on a change in the weather.

"Well, I'm here now."

"Yes, you are."

"Buy you a drink?"

"Aren't I supposed to ask *you* that?"

"I don't know. It's the twenty-first century."

"So it is. Still, I figure that's how this thing is supposed to go."

Corrie tried not to bristle. Did he figure her for a hooker?

"What kind of thing?" she asked, trying to keep the edge from her voice.

He moved his gaze away from her for the first time. "Just a conversation between a man and a girl in a bar: man buys the girl a drink, they get to talking. I've seen it done before."

Again, she experienced a peculiar sense of disconnection, of this individual as a kind of observer of his own life. Perhaps she'd made a mistake in choosing him. For this thing of theirs to work, she needed lust, and a loss of inhibition. This one seemed too much in control of himself.

But then he let his right hand drop to his thigh, brushing her leg as he did so, and she gently rubbed herself against it. After a moment, she felt his hand slide onto her jeans. No, she hadn't made an error after all.

"What's your name?" she asked.

"Henry." Which it wasn't.

"Like the king."

"Which one?"

"Any of them."

"Yes, just like one of the kings."

"I'm Lise," she said, although he hadn't asked, and it wasn't her name either.

"Hello, Lise."

"Hello, Henry."

"What can I get you?"

"Bourbon and Coke," she said. "Easy on the ice."

"And the soda?"

She sipped through her straw, draining the watery residue at the end of the glass she had so carefully nursed until now.

"Easy on that, too."

———

THE VOLUME OF THE music rose. Dancing wasn't permitted, but somehow they found themselves standing close to each other, and she thought she could feel the hardness of him against her. He wasn't from around here, he told her, but she could have guessed that by the way he held himself apart from his surroundings. When she pressed him, he gave her only "south of here," which wasn't much. Given that they were just below Canada, most places were south. She was used to evasiveness, though, particularly from the married ones. Henry said he wasn't married, but a lot of them told her that. The ones who were honest often qualified their status with unflattering descriptions of their wives, or admitted just to being unhappy. A handful were genuinely sad and lonely, trapped in relationships because of kids, jobs, mortgages, or simply because they didn't believe that anyone else would have them. She was always sorry for those ones, afterward.

As for Henry, she couldn't detect a mark on his ring finger, the little telltale band of white that spoke of a symbol set aside. She'd have spotted it easily in his case, because he had outdoor hands. He was here on business, he said. What kind? Stock acquisition. Corrie didn't know what that meant, and Henry wasn't interested in telling her. Corrie was smart enough to suppose that everyone, on some level, was engaged in stock acquisition. Only the job titles varied.

"I like you, Henry," she said. "I prefer slightly older men."

"And why is that?"

"They know what they want. And they're kinder than young men."

And she meant it.

"Kinder, how? Like with money?"

"Sometimes," she said, then added the lie: "But this isn't about money."

"No?"

His tone caused her to frown. Although this was all a game, and one he was destined to lose, it annoyed her that after the couple of hours they had spent talking, he was still capable of making such an implication.

"I'm not a hooker," she said.

"I never said you were." He didn't sound defensive, or even amused. There was only that weird neutrality again. "But money always comes into it, in one form or another, even if it's only for dinner and a movie. Kindness takes many forms. I know that you didn't mean it just as dollars and cents, but it's part of it. Folks who are tight with money tend to be tight in other ways too, or that's been my experience. But the opposite isn't always true either, now that I think of it. I've met plenty of men who threw money around and were still motherfuckers."

It was the first time he'd uttered a cuss word since they'd met. It didn't bother her. She kind of liked it. What he said also made sense to her. She started to realize that, under other circumstances, she might almost have enjoyed making the fantasy a reality, and being with a man like this, if only for a little while. She shrugged the thought away, and found that the action was as much physical as mental, for her body actually moved in a kind of shiver. Henry's mouth twisted.

"What was that?" he asked.

"Someone walking over my grave," she replied.

"That'll come, someday," he said. "No point in rushing it. You want another drink?"

"No, I've drunk enough, or enough here. But I'm having a good time with you. Do you have somewhere we can go?"

"Don't you?"

"I have a roommate."

"Male or female?"

She decided not to lie about it, although the way Henry was staring at her so intently, she felt like she had little choice.

"Male."

"Boyfriend?"

"Sometimes."

"But not serious."

Oh, you have no idea, she thought, but settled for repeating herself. "Sometimes."

"Just not tonight."

"No."

He called for the check, and paid in cash from a fold of bills. He kept it concealed from Corrie so that she couldn't catch the denominations, but it looked thick.

"Which hotel are you staying at?" she asked, as they walked from the bar. She tried to take his arm, but he kept his distance from her: not much, just enough.

"I'm not at a hotel," he said. "I'm in a private house."

That was unusual, but not sufficiently so to cause her to reconsider. Apartments were one thing—the buildings could be hard to gain access to, and access was a major factor in this business—but a house wasn't such a concern. Houses were more vulnerable than apartments, and definitely easier than hotels, as long as the alarm system was turned off. With hotels there was always the question of cameras and, in the better ones, hotel security. Motels were ideal, especially the big chain ones: they were so used to pizza deliveries and prostitutes that their staff barely batted an eye at passing strangers because everyone was a stranger to them, didn't matter how many cupcakes or cookies they offered you at check-in.

"Did your company find it for you?"

"I suppose it did, in a way."

―――――

HIS CAR WAS PARKED on Middle Street. It was a Toyota compact, and not at all what she was expecting. It was kind of a chick car, in her opinion, if the gods of feminism could forgive her the generalization.

"Rental?" she asked, as she got in. It was pretty clean, but didn't smell like a rental.

"Yeah," he said. "Some small outfit the company uses. It was all they had."

"Huh."

She tried to remember how much he'd had to drink. At first it had seemed like a lot, but now that she was in the car she recalled plenty of ice melting, and fresh shots of Jack being ordered before the last was finished, after which he'd pour the new into the old. He'd sipped throughout the evening, and she suspected that she might have imbibed a lot more than he had. But she'd been careful, even if she had been forced to dump almost an entire measure on the one occasion that he'd gone to the bathroom.

"Where's the house?" she asked, as he pulled out.

"York," he replied.

"That's a ways from Portland. They couldn't have found you somewhere closer to the city?"

"I have to drive a lot," said Henry, "so one place is as far away as another. And I like some quiet. I've never been much for towns and cities."

Corrie pulled down the visor, revealing one of those illuminated mirrors with a little pull-back plastic shield. She checked her makeup and her teeth, then adjusted her angle so she could see the road behind her. A couple of cars were following Henry's. One of them would be theirs.

She was about to flip the visor back in place when she spotted a stain on the mirror. She leaned in closer to check, although she already knew what it was: a small smear of lipstick. She didn't comment on it, but it confirmed her growing suspicion that Henry was lying to her about the car, and maybe about the house and the company as well. She was used to lies—the whole success of the venture depended on them, because lies made men vulnerable—but she was disappointed in him. Not afraid, just disappointed.

Still, it made her feel better about what was to come.

The house looked like a family home: two floors, an attic window, and a two-car garage. It even had a pool, although it was currently protected by a plastic cover that had come loose at one corner and now flapped in the night breeze. The property was private, set back from a tributary road with a row of maturing trees in place of a fence. A light burned in one of the upstairs rooms, and another in the room that faced out onto the pool, leaking through the drapes to cut a fiery line across the grass.

Henry parked beside a large gray van bearing muddied New Hampshire plates, and something about the sight of it gave Corrie the shivers. It made no logical sense—it was just a van—but Corrie had been engaged in these minor acts of predation for long enough to be able to tell when a situation felt wrong, and she now realized that she'd made a dreadful mistake in targeting Henry.

She rubbed her face, then covered her mouth.

"You okay?" asked Henry.

"I'm really sorry, but I don't feel well."

"Come inside. I'll get you a glass of water."

Corrie shook her head.

"No, I have to go. I'd be grateful if you could take me back to town, or I can just call a cab to come pick me up."

She took her cell phone from her purse. She kept a couple of cab companies in various cities on her list of contacts, along with a handful of individual drivers who were particularly trustworthy or simply knew how to turn a blind eye, but they were mostly for show. The emergency number was listed as "CN" for "Come Now."

Henry's left hand closed over hers, and his right plucked the cell phone from her grasp.

"What are you doing?" she asked. "Give me back my phone."

"We're going to have a drink and a talk," said Henry, "just like we agreed. I don't know what you're getting all excited about."

"I told you: I don't feel so good."

Henry returned the phone to her.

"Go ahead," he said. "Call a cab. I'm done driving for the night."

Corrie was surprised, but she had no intention of calling a taxi, and never had. The others would be close, and she wanted them to know that they had to move fast. They could go ahead with it if they wished, but she didn't intend to spend any longer alone with Henry than was necessary, and she sure as hell wasn't about to step into that house with him, no matter what he said. Her right thumb hovered over the CN listing.

The front door opened, revealing the silhouette of a man. She couldn't see his face, but he was tall—much taller than Henry. His frame was stooped, as of one who had spent too many years connecting painfully with a world created by and for those who were shorter than him, and now warily anticipated contact. She couldn't be certain, but he seemed to be wearing a shower cap.

"Who's that?" she said.

"I forgot to mention that I have a roommate too," said Henry. "You ought to meet him."

That was it for Corrie. She was about to hit the call button when a hammer blow from Henry's right fist impacted on the bridge of her nose, breaking it instantly.

The second punch knocked her out cold.

# Chapter

# XII

His name was Todd Peltz, but he hated it, and preferred to be known as TP. Sometimes he thought TP sounded like a kid's name, and at others that it made him sound like a rapper. He wasn't too happy about either possibility, but the third option—that he might remain Todd fucking Peltz—was the worst of all.

He was about to turn twenty-five, and had known the inside of a couple of county jails for minor assault stuff, and one dumb DUI, but that was all in the past. TP had a temper—would never have denied it—but he'd worked hard at learning to control it, and he'd curbed his alcohol consumption, recognizing that one fed the other. It was his curse to be just slightly too intelligent to settle for honest, menial work, or at least not for any length of time, yet not disciplined enough to be able to commit himself to long-term self-improvement. He was the kind of man who liked to boast that he had never hit a woman, and never would, as though this were a claim worthy of note, and one that somehow separated him from the masses. TP looked hard—six feet tall and rangy, with the long-muscled limbs of a climber or a middle-distance runner—but there was also a kind of gentleness to him. He loved Corrie Wyatt, and she loved him in return, enough to lure luckless men into situations where they would be vulnerable to TP's particular brand of pressure. His eyes were soft, but when threats or acts of violence became necessary they assumed a glassy emptiness, as though the better part of TP chose to absent itself at those moments and turn its gaze elsewhere.

Sitting beside TP in the passenger seat of their junk-cluttered Dodge was Barry Brown, the BB to Todd Peltz's TP, had Brown consented to such a diminution of his given name, which he most assuredly would not. Brown was of similar height to his friend, but broader and flesh-ier. He was smarter than TP, even though he assumed the subservi-ent role, but that was Brown's nature: he was a natural manipulator, and he found it easier to operate from behind the scenes than on the stage. When they studied *Othello* in high school, he was the only kid in his class who empathized immediately and intimately with Iago. In another age, and with better opportunities, Brown might have made a fine, ambitious courtier, a Cromwell or a Walsingham. He didn't want to be the titular godfather after watching the first two Coppola movies: he wanted to be a cleverer Tom Hayden, the *consigliere*, the fixer. He wore spectacles instead of contact lenses because he liked the way they made him look, and had trained himself to speak only when necessary. It had turned out to be a useful skill. He discovered that silence made a lot of people uneasy, and they would often say something to break it, thus revealing themselves in the process.

It had been Brown's idea to use Corrie as the worm on the hook, although he had been careful not to suggest it to TP in those terms, instead working slowly to insinuate the notion into TP's head so that his friend believed the plan to be entirely his own. Corrie had been a harder sell, but TP wasn't above a little manipulation himself, and had convinced her that she would never be in any real danger. Brown got on well enough with Corrie, but he knew that she would have preferred if it were just her and TP making their own way in the world. Brown thought that Corrie would have been perfectly content to work in a coffee shop or a bar, and support her boyfriend while he played com-puter games, or tinkered with cars, and came up with big schemes for getting rich that would never reach fruition because he didn't have the energy or drive to pursue them. Eventually, Brown knew, she would have grown frustrated and left him, maybe with a child in her arms that she'd then have to raise alone. In a way, Brown thought, he was keeping them together by instilling a degree of ambition in TP that would otherwise have been absent.

So far, their scheme had gone entirely to plan. The first man targeted was a married fifty-something conventioneer in Boston. It had been almost too easy: a couple of drinks, some flirtation, a little chat about how he reminded Corrie of her favorite uncle, one on whom she'd always secretly had a crush, then back to his hotel room. When the knock came on the door—which Corrie made sure she answered, permitting the two masked men to enter—the mark was already down to his boxers, with a hard-on from which he could have hung a flag. Corrie was in a similar state of undress, and stayed that way while BB showed the conventioneer the gun, and explained how it was going to go down. They photographed his driver's license, which he kept in his wallet alongside pictures of his wife, kids, and first grandchild. They noted his address before, at gunpoint, taking pictures of him in a series of suitably compromising positions with Corrie. Finally, they got him to reveal the PINs for his debit and credit cards, after which Corrie got dressed and withdrew cash to the daily limit on each card, then went and had a cup of coffee until just after midnight, so she could take a second run at them. When she returned, they gave the conventioneer back his wallet, debit card, and one of his credit cards, and told him not to report the second card missing until a further twenty-four hours had elapsed. They assured him that his bank would cover any losses, and it wasn't like they could do too much damage anyway with a $5,000 credit limit. If they encountered any problems using the card, then his wife would find out just what he'd been doing on his free night in Beantown. No violence had proved necessary, which was just the way they liked it, and they'd netted a total of $3,000, and a number of laptop computers bought on the second card, which they'd sold for twenty-five cents on the dollar.

Afterward, Corrie ditched her cheap wig, and they pulled the scam twice more in Boston and its environs before heading slowly north: Portsmouth, Concord, and now Portland. Brown hadn't wanted to net that night's sucker, though. He felt that it was time to give the operation a rest and lie low for a while. They had enough cash to get them comfortably through the winter, and he was convinced the last mark—a salesman in Portsmouth, who'd required a tap on the head to curb his indignation—might take the risk of not remaining silent about what had happened. It was TP who had argued for one last effort, and Corrie had agreed, just because it was TP who was asking.

But Brown and Corrie had recently spoken together at length for the first time in weeks—maybe even the first time ever—without TP present, and it was clear to Brown that Corrie was growing increasingly uneasy about their business enterprise. Brown wasn't surprised. She was the one taking the major risk. True, he and TP were always on her heels, and they made sure to let only the minimum amount of time go by between Corrie and the mark entering the hotel, and their knock sounding on the door. But suppose they were stopped by security, or their car broke down, or they just screwed up, none of which was beyond the bounds of possibility? Then, my friends, Corrie would most assuredly be on her own, and the big "r" word—"rape"—was never far from her mind.

Corrie and TP were staying in one room of a motel out by The Maine Mall, and Brown was across the hall. It meant that he couldn't hear them screwing, which was a relief on a lot of levels. He'd been forced to listen to them when they'd all shared a small one-bedroom apartment down in Quincy, Brown already struggling with sleep thanks to the sadistic springs on the sleeper couch without TP's grunts and Corrie's cheerleading as a soundtrack. When they'd first been on the road, and watching their cash, he'd taken the second bed in the motel rooms, or sometimes just slept on the floor, and TP would gesture to the door when he wanted some quality time with Corrie, leaving Brown to wander until they were done, or smoke and read a book while sitting on a plastic chair, maybe catch a movie if there was a theater nearby. Brown hated having to do that. It made him feel about nine years old, and an inch tall.

Brown was in love with Corrie. It had taken him a while to realize this, and attempt unsuccessfully to come to terms with it. He was self-aware enough to speculate whether one of the reasons he'd suggested using her as bait was to punish her for sleeping with TP and not him, but now that they were deep in the whole mess, Brown was starting to regret ever involving her. He could see the strain it placed on her. She was more jittery than before, and he knew that she was having trouble sleeping. He'd tried pointing all this out to TP, but TP was enjoying the money, and, as he pointed out to Brown, it wasn't like they were whoring Corrie out.

Except they were. That was the truth of it, but TP either wouldn't or couldn't recognize it. Just because he and Brown intervened before the main show had to commence didn't make it any less demeaning and dangerous for Corrie. And so, after talking with her that evening, Brown was determined to find another way for them to make a little easy money. He knew some guys up in Bangor, and he and TP now had enough ready cash to be able to buy a decent quantity of blow. Screw weed: the economy looked like it was improving some, and to Brown that meant the demand for coke would increase. You just had to hang out in the right bars, and make the right connections with the Friday-night asshole set, the young men in suits who started drinking straight out of the office, and were already whooping it up by 8:00 p.m. Brown had started laying the groundwork with TP as they waited for Corrie and the mark to emerge, and he thought that he'd made headway.

Then Brown saw the guy with Corrie, and alarm bells began ringing in his head.

"Hey," he said to TP.

"What is it?"

"I don't like what I'm feeling here."

"Not again. Come on, I told you: I'll think about the coke thing, and we already agreed that this would be the last one for a while."

"Seriously, man: that dude is wrong."

"Everybody's wrong to you."

"He's not drunk."

"He looks drunk to me."

It was true that the mark was walking a little unsteadily, but Brown wasn't convinced. He'd caught a glimpse of the guy's eyes as he passed their car, and they'd resembled pools of polluted mud. And the way he'd looked at Corrie, like one of those slaughterhouse workers who enjoy torturing the pigs before they die . . .

"I say we call it off," said Brown.

"You've got to be kidding. They're at his car."

"We drive up, we call out to Corrie, and we offer her a ride," said Brown. It was something they'd come up with at the start. Corrie always wore a scarf. If they saw her take it from her neck and put it in her bag, it was a sign that something was wrong, and she wanted to bail. So far she'd done that only once, with a company executive who'd whispered in her ear about what he was going to do to her once he got her back to his hotel room, and it wasn't anything that Corrie wanted done to her, not even by TP.

Scarf into bag; TP and Brown rolling up alongside, shouting out "Hey, Linda!"—the name she was using that night, because she never used the same one twice—"What you doing? Want to hang with us?"; Corrie apologizing to the executive, because she had to go with her friends; the executive objecting; TP getting out of the car, the executive still mouthing off; TP just about keeping his temper in check, knowing that it could be bad news if they attracted the attention of a passing cop; Corrie getting in their car; driving away; Corrie telling them what the guy said to her; TP insisting on going back and giving the executive a beating he wouldn't forget, and only the best combined efforts of Corrie and Brown convincing him that it would land them all in jail.

"She hasn't taken off her scarf," said TP.

He was right. She hadn't.

"It doesn't have to be her call," said Brown.

"If she's okay with him, so am I."

"TP—"

"I said no."

TP hadn't raised his voice—he rarely did—but Brown knew the tone. The discussion was over.

Now here they were, watching the house in front of which the car was parked, the trees masking it from the road so they couldn't even see what was going on.

*A house*, thought Brown. *Not a hotel, but a house. We've never tried it in a house before.*

He told himself that it might be simpler than a hotel because there would be no security.

*But what about an alarm? And what if the guy isn't alone in there?*

TP took the gun from under his seat and tucked it into the waistband of his pants. Brown didn't own a gun. He didn't much care for them. But he was glad, just this once, that TP had no such qualms.

Then TP said something that he'd never before said to Brown.

"You were right," he said. "We should have called it off."

# XIII

TP and Barry Brown entered the yard of the house, Brown leading, skirting the car and van in the drive, moving quickly to the back of the property where they had the best chance of gaining access without being spotted. They hadn't even discussed the possibility of a simple knock on the door, not since TP had recognized that Brown might have been right about the mark, which meant that Corrie had become the mark instead. Now, in unison, each pulled down his ski mask, obscuring his features. Brown hoped that TP didn't find cause to use the gun. They were in enough trouble as it was.

Brown heard a slapping sound as they reached the backyard, which caused him to tighten his grip on the bat he was carrying. He'd made the bat himself, wood turning being one of those skills that he just had, and from which he thought he might someday be able to make a living, or supplement a regular income. Brown's view was that a gun did only two things well—it threatened, and it fired—while a baseball bat had a multitude of uses, and, unlike a gun, was capable of inflicting harm in subtle increments.

TP paused beside him. There was a stirring in the yard, but TP's eyesight wasn't great at the best of times—although, thanks to the miracle of self-diagnosis, his condition was not yet serious enough to merit glasses or lenses. It was left to Brown to pick out the tarpaulin over the pool before them. One corner of it had come loose, and the sound of its flapping had gradually risen in tempo and volume as the wind increased. Brown figured that the tarp must have become detached recently, because the noise was loud and annoying, the kind that came between a person and sleep. It would even have been persistent and distracting enough to draw the attention of neighbors had the house not been comparatively isolated and sheltered.

He risked a glance around the corner, and saw that, as at the front of the house, the drapes had been drawn across the windows. Glass patio doors led to a deck, and farther along was a wood door with a small glass window, possibly leading to a kitchen or utility room. Brown could see no sign of illumination within, and the rear windows on the second floor were also dark.

To his right, that damned tarp kept flapping. It was possible that it might draw someone from inside, which would be good, especially if both the patio and secondary door were secured. He glanced at the area of the pool revealed by the tarp and saw that it still had water in it. Brown didn't know much about pools. His family had never owned one, nor had the kinds of families with whom they'd associated. He assumed that pools had to be drained for winter, but perhaps the people here hadn't managed to get around to it yet, or were holding out for one last warm weekend. Good luck with that in Maine.

Sections of the backyard were lit by solar-powered lamps, one of which stood not far from the exposed corner of the pool. It cast a little light on the water, and Brown thought he caught a glimpse of something lying at the bottom of the shallow end. It was strangely regular in form, and he experienced the immediate sense that, whatever it was, it had no business being there.

He drew closer to the pool. Behind him, he heard TP whisper.

"Hey, where are you going?"

Brown was exposing himself to anyone who might happen to glance out a window, but he didn't care. Curiosity had snagged him with its hook, and now it was drawing him in. What *was* that?

He stood at the edge of the pool and looked down. A television set, one of those big, expensive flat-screen models, lay on the tiles. Lengths of rope or cable crisscrossed it, binding it tightly to what was beneath, anchored by the TV to the bottom of the pool.

Brown was looking into the eyes of a dead boy.

# XIV

orrie returned to consciousness to find herself lying facedown on a couch in an unfamiliar room. Her hands had been pulled behind her back and secured with what felt like metal cuffs. She could feel them biting into her wrists. Her legs wouldn't move, and she saw that they were held together with wire. She had been gagged with a length of cloth.

She tried to control her panic. TP was on his way, and Barry with him. They had to be close. Any moment now she would hear the ringing of the doorbell, or the breaking of glass, and then Henry the Asshole would wish that he'd never made his way to Portland. She hoped Barry would break his legs, and maybe his arms, too, just before TP killed him and his creepy friend.

She heard movement behind her, and Henry appeared to her left. He was holding a pistol in his hand. Of the other man, there was no sign.

Henry put the muzzle to Corrie's left eye. She just had time to close it before she felt it pressing hard against the eyelid. The click of the hammer locking caused a little part of her to come loose inside.

"Not a sound," said Henry. "Not a movement."

———

THE BOY IN THE pool had dark hair. He was probably not yet a teenager, to judge by his size, although the distortion caused by the water made it difficult to tell. *He hasn't been down there very long*, Brown thought. For the most part he looked undamaged, apart from the way his mouth bulged. Brown couldn't be sure, but it appeared that a ball had been jammed into it. The ball was red. It protruded from between his upper and lower jaws like a half-eaten apple.

Brown gazed down at the boy, and the boy gazed back. The gentle lapping of the water in the pool caused his hair to move. One of his hands was visible, but Brown couldn't see the other. He wondered if the boy had somehow managed to get his left hand free, and tried to push against the big TV as he drowned. That assumed, of course, that he'd been alive when he went in the water. If he was, did whoever was responsible for throwing him in the pool stay to watch him die?

Brown felt the weight of the bat in his hand, and the grain of the wood against his skin. It brought him back, and with that he thought of Corrie. She was in the house with whoever had killed this boy.

Now Brown was really glad that TP had his gun with him.

He turned to speak to TP, who was staring at him from the back wall of the house. Brown pointed at the pool, but TP just shook his head. He didn't want to see whatever was down there, because it didn't matter. Only Corrie mattered now.

TP moved to the patio doors.

———

UPSTAIRS, ON THE SECOND floor, Henry's companion left the bedroom he'd been cleaning and stepped into the hallway. His name was Gideon, although it would be many years before that fact became known. For now, like his companion, he was sailing under a false flag. He was, as Corrie had quickly surmised, both excessively tall and excessively thin, like a stick insect given human form. His eyes were very small, and partly obscured by heavy lids, making him virtually blind in the upper visual fields on the lateral gaze. The hair on his head was a uniform half-inch in length, and already gray, even though Gideon was only in his thirties. He also suffered from asthma, gout, a peptic ulcer, and undiagnosed pancreatic cancer. He was a creature of the shadows and the depths.

Gideon had slept on a bed while they were in the house, but he always remained fully clothed, and the plastic garbage bag in his left hand now contained the pillowcase and the cover from the comforter, as well as the used towels from the bathroom. Earlier he'd poured bleach down the drains in the bath and the sink, although both he and Henry had been careful to use a drain stopper to catch any stray hairs. They had also worn double-layered plastic gloves and shower caps during their entire time in the house. While Henry was away, Gideon had vacuumed and cleaned, doing his best to ensure that they left as few traces of their presence as possible.

He passed by a second bedroom to his right. A dead woman was tied to the bed. Gideon had used her, but he'd been careful to wear a rubber. He'd cleaned her, too, after he killed her. Gideon was also responsible for killing the boy at the bottom of the pool. He had lost his temper when the boy attacked him. He had no idea why he chose to toss him into the pool with the TV to weigh him down, except that Gideon didn't like TV and didn't like the boy either. Henry had been absent from the house when Gideon murdered the boy, but he hadn't said anything when he came back, although he'd been surprised to find the boy in the pool. The tarp had held until the wind picked up. Gideon thought that he'd better retie it, even though they were about to leave.

The woman had been too old to keep. She was the boy's mother, but he must have been born when she was already in her forties, because her driver's license said that she was fifty-four. Her husband was five years older. Henry had killed him. He'd shot him in the chest, and he was now lying in the basement, where it was cool. It had been Gideon's decision to keep the woman alive for a while. Henry didn't have the same obstacles to intimacy as Gideon. Women liked Henry. They most assuredly did not like Gideon, so he took his pleasures where he could.

This trip—or "range," in their parlance—had produced a good haul: some designer clothes; jewelry; cash; a collection of coins and stamps; a couple of expensive phones; a handful of transportable electronic items, including some tablets; even a collection of old books that Henry thought might be worth something. Most of it was in the van, with the more valuable items hidden in a pair of compartments under the driver and front passenger seats. It was a shame that the woman had been so old, but Henry had made up for that. The girl downstairs would do just fine, although Gideon wouldn't be given a chance to spend time with her, except maybe right at the end. He was glad that he'd used the other woman while he could.

Past the bedroom in which the dead woman lay was a hallway window overlooking the backyard. Gideon paused there to take in, for a last time, the view of the lawn and the flower beds, of the pool—and the figure of the man who was staring into it.

Gideon dropped the bag and scuttled down the stairs.

———

TP TESTED THE PATIO door, expecting to find it locked, but it moved under the pressure of his left hand. He listened, heard no sounds of movement inside, and slowly began to open the door wider. He looked over his right shoulder to see Brown coming to join him, and even in the moonlight his face displayed his shock at what he had seen in the pool. A body, TP figured. What else could it be? But it wasn't Corrie's. There wouldn't have been time for that. And all that mattered right now was Corrie.

He turned back toward the drapes, lifting them with his left hand, the other holding the gun. He saw Corrie lying on a couch. He saw—

———

BROWN HEARD A SOUND like a paper bag bursting, and TP toppled backward and fell to the ground on his back. Another bag burst, and Brown was punched hard in the gut, pirouetting with the force of the blow and landing on the tarp covering the pool. It bowed under his weight, but held. Water flowed over him, but it wasn't deep, and he could keep his face above it. Still, he was hurting now. The water was cold, but not cold enough to cancel out the heat of the pain in his belly.

A man appeared by the pool, watching him. He was tall but hunched, his legs too long for his body, his fingers too long for his hands. His eyes were barely there at all. One arm hung free, and the other was holding on to TP's left hand. The man had dragged TP from where he had fallen to the edge of the pool. TP's face was turned toward the water, and Brown could see, just below his right eye, the entry wound from the bullet that had killed his friend.

The man smiled, and Brown saw that his teeth were so perfect they could only be dentures, an impression confirmed when he ejected them into his right hand and dropped them in a pocket of the old army jacket he was wearing. But his hand was not empty when it reemerged from his pocket, and was instead holding one of those plastic boxes in which folks kept their mouth guards. He allowed TP's arm to fall, freeing up two hands, and used them to place a new set of dentures in his mouth. Once they were in position, he displayed them to Brown. Each consisted of a pair of long blades set into the acrylic base at slight angles, leaving a gap in the middle of each row. The man reached down, lifted TP's right hand, bit off the top half of TP's index finger, and chewed for a time before spitting the resulting mess into the pool close to Brown's head, the blades of the dentures now stained red.

Brown felt himself dying. He just prayed that it would come before this creature went to work on him.

A second man appeared, the one responsible for bringing them here, the one who had taken Corrie. Beside the other, he appeared unutterably normal. Brown tried to speak. He wanted to ask the man from the bar to prevent Corrie from being bitten, but death was stealing away all his words as a preparation for the great silence to come.

"Time to go," he heard the man from the bar say.

The other one kicked at TP's body, and it landed on the tarp by Brown's feet, yet somehow the cover still held, although Brown felt himself beginning to slide. The man from the bar produced a knife and cut at the ropes holding the tarp in place—one, then another—until they came away, and TP and Barry Brown drifted slowly down to join the dead boy.

# XV

Years later, and a life away, Jerome Burnel, the Disgraced Hero, withdrew money in cash from his bank account. His hand trembled as he filled in the slip. He used his passport for identification, since his driver's license was no longer valid. He watched the teller take the passport away and show it to a supervisor, and some kind of consultation followed before the teller made a photocopy of the relevant page and returned the passport to him. Burnel thought that her expression was different when she came back, that it bore a trace of distaste, but perhaps he was just projecting. After all, he wasn't exactly infamous, and he'd been behind bars long enough to allow most people to have forgotten about him. But the teller was in her fifties, and who knew what kind of memory she had, or what notes had been appended to his banking record. His name was unusual, and so was his history. She didn't look up at him when she told him to have a good day, and the security guard at the door appeared to give him a more hostile examination than before as he left.

The private detective had called back while Burnel was sitting on a bench in Deering Oaks Park. He'd bought himself a sandwich and coffee at the Public Market House at Monument Square and carried them over to a bench, where he ate most of the sandwich once he was certain that no children were nearby. He fed the remainder of his meal to the pigeons. The detective didn't have an office, which Burnel considered slightly unusual. Then again, this was a mobile age in which entire companies were run from a laptop and a table in a coffee shop. The detective had agreed to meet with Burnel later that afternoon in a booth at the Great Lost Bear on Forest Avenue, a bar that Burnel had frequented before he was married but less so after, as his wife hadn't much cared for beer—hadn't much cared for Burnel either, as it turned out, even before everything went to shit for him.

Burnel had spent the morning in the Portland offices of the Maine Department of Corrections on Washington Avenue, his first contact with the probation service since he'd been released. His probation officer, Chris Attwood, was a specialist in sex offenders, but he'd treated Burnel courteously, and Burnel couldn't help but warm to him. Attwood had explained each step of the process to Burnel. It began with a Level of Services Inventory, which was basically a risk-assessment report on Burnel, accompanied by what was known as a Static-99, a further profiling tool used solely for sex offenders. The Static-99 was a lifetime score, and would remain with Burnel to the grave; since it was based on static factors—his age at arrest, his history, the severity of his crimes—it could never improve, and Burnel's best hope, according to Attwood, was that it might remain stable, which would eventually result in an easing of the conditions of his probation.

Attwood told Burnel that he'd been placed on the maximum end of the offender scale, even though he'd never even touched a child, and— as he didn't bother telling Attwood, because what good would it do?— he was innocent. The maximum rating meant that Burnel would have to endure a home check every month; bimonthly face-to-face meetings with Attwood, usually at Washington Avenue; collateral contacts with employers, when Burnel eventually found work; and weekly group counseling sessions, which Attwood told him had been found to be effective with sex offenders. If he completed counseling, and a significant period of time passed without violations, the probation service would back off as much as it could. He was also required to register as a sex offender, and would remain on the registry for ten years. For all this, he would pay $25 every month as a contribution toward the cost of his probation.

Then, to his surprise, Burnel was given a polygraph examination. Apparently it was standard, and he'd receive one every year while on probation, but Burnel still didn't care for it. He answered all the questions honestly, although the intermingling of general questions—his name, his mother's name—with others relating to his alleged crimes threw him a little, and he found those that dealt with his life before his arrest more disturbing because they reminded him of all that he had lost. He had another interview with Attwood after the poly, during which Burnel thought that the probation officer was marginally less friendly than before, but that might just have been tiredness.

Finally, he was allowed to leave. Attwood told him to take some time before he went looking for a job. He advised him to get comfortable with the outside world again, to take walks, to find his feet in the city. Burnel had nodded and said that he would try. He had no intention of looking for work. He believed that he would be dead soon, so what was the point?

He finished feeding the birds, and then walked back toward the Old Port. The daylight was too bright, and he had too much space in which to move. He paid to see the only R-rated movie showing at the Nickelodeon, just so that he could sit in the dark and be reasonably sure that no kids would be present. Only four other people were in attendance, and they were all safely a couple of decades older than he was. The movie was a comedy, but Burnel didn't laugh much. He barely noticed the images on the screen, if the truth were to be told. He just sat at the back of the theater and wept.

# XVI

C hris Attwood sat at a table across from Philip Gurley, the repre-
sentative of RPL, one of the companies responsible for polygraph
testing for the Department of Corrections. Before them were the
results of Burnel's examination.

"Do you think he's lying?" Attwood asked.

Gurley glanced at the results again.

"As you and I both know," said Gurley, "there are men and women who
ace the poly even though they've got butchers' hands. Those ones just
look through you when you ask the questions. Burnel wasn't like that."

"Meaning?"

"That maybe he's convinced himself that he didn't commit the
crimes of which he's accused."

"Which doesn't mean that he's innocent of them."

"Not at all, but as I said: the kind who can cut themselves off from
reality like that are pretty unusual, and they give off their own stink."

"And you didn't smell it off Burnel?"

"No, I did not."

"So, was he telling the truth?"

"Possibly."

Attwood picked up the polygraph results, placed them in a folder,
and closed it.

"You want me to run him through again?" asked Gurley.

"I don't know."

"It doesn't make a difference if he's innocent or not, does it?"

"Only to him," said Attwood. "He's in the system now. We'll do our best for him."

Gurley stood.

"It was quite something, what he did, wasn't it?"

"What was?"

"That business at the gas station. The shooting."

"Yeah, it was something, all right."

"He doesn't look like the type."

"No," said Attwood, "they rarely do."

# XVII

It was shortly after four thirty in the afternoon, and raining heavily, when Charlie Parker arrived at the Great Lost Bear. He hadn't set foot in the bar in many months, not since before he was shot. The Bear hadn't changed. It was still dimly lit and comforting, the kitchen beginning to bustle in preparation for the evening rush, although on a wet Wednesday the term "rush" was likely to be a relative one.

Dave Evans, the owner, was standing at the host's station, regarding a piece of paper over the top of his glasses in a manner that suggested it contained something insulting to his mother. He didn't look up, not even when Parker's shadow fell upon him.

"I thought you were dead," said Dave.

"I was."

Dave flicked his attention from the document to the detective, and studied him in the bar's distinctive light.

"You look okay for it. We have regular customers who look worse than you. *I* look worse than you."

He put down the paper and shook Parker's hand. Dave had come to visit Parker a couple of times when he was recovering in the hospital, but hadn't seen him since. He'd read about him, though. The business up in Boreas had made the national papers, not just the locals. Dave had been under the impression that all the old Nazis were dead, and any that weren't were probably close to being measured for a coffin, but trust Parker to unearth ones who could still bite. Next thing, he'd be discovering Martians in Millinocket.

Parker was different now. For starters, he was thinner, with a few more lines on his face, and his hair was speckled with new white. He also seemed quieter, more distant, although Dave figured that being shot and left for dead, not to mention dying and being brought back a few times, would do that to a person.

But it was his gaze that was most altered. If it was true what they said about the eyes being the windows to the soul, then Parker's soul burned with a new fire. His eyes held a calm conviction that Dave had not seen in them before. This was a fundamentally changed man, one who had come back strengthened, not weakened, by what he had endured, but who was also both less and more than he once had been.

For the first time that he could recall, Dave was frightened of Charlie Parker.

"Is my office still free?" asked Parker. He had a favorite booth that he liked to occupy at the Bear.

"It'll always be free for you," said Dave. "There's a place behind the bar, too, if the mood strikes."

He didn't know how Parker was doing for money, and he didn't want to appear to be dispensing charity. He wanted to help, if he could, and if it was needed. The offer was sincerely meant, but Dave couldn't deny the sense of relief he felt at Parker's reply.

"You know, I think I may be okay. But thank you."

"Well, if you change your mind, just say something."

"I will. A man should be coming in to ask for me. His name's Burnel. Will you send him over when he arrives?"

"Sure. You want some coffee?"

"Coffee would be good."

"It's on its way. Just the two of you?"

"No, four. Angel and Louis will be joining me."

"Right."

Dave tried to form his features into a pleased expression at the news, but they didn't want to cooperate. Even after all these years, he had not yet grown comfortable with having those two men in his bar. He had heard how some of the city and state detectives who drank in the Bear talked about Angel and Louis when the bar was quiet. "Tame killers" was one of the more polite descriptions. Most of them didn't even bother with the adjective.

Angel and Louis had come into the Bear on a number of occasions while Parker was in the hospital, and during his subsequent recuperation, which had made Dave more nervous than when they used to arrive accompanied by the detective himself. Worse, once or twice they had been with the Fulci brothers, and every time the Fulci brothers entered his bar, Dave endured a disturbing mental image of his beloved establishment being disassembled around him, and the bricks used as ammunition against the forces of reason.

Parker watched the struggle play out on his face.

"You do know that Angel and Louis like you, right?"

"How can you tell?" asked Dave. Angel he could almost understand. He smiled occasionally, even if it was the kind of smile that could easily conceal its opposite. But Louis—he didn't smile much at all, and when he did it was like the final expression that a mouse saw on the face of a cat before the claws came down on its neck.

"They have a way of making their negative feelings known," said Parker.

"But not positive ones," said Dave.

"No," Parker admitted, "not so much."

He went to the last booth at the left of the bar, and sat facing out. He had already researched Jerome Burnel, and knew the details of his case. The name had seemed familiar as soon as he played the message, and a few minutes on the Internet had filled in any gaps. Parker's little Moleskine notebook now contained a list of details and names, including those of the prosecuting and defense attorneys at Burnel's trial.

Burnel had served five years for his crimes. The case had received a considerable degree of coverage because of Burnel's history, with most of the newspaper reports taking a similar line: the word "hero" recurred, but always in association with terms such as "tarnished," "shamed," and "disgraced." The media had built up Burnel, and in its rush to atone for doing so it tore him apart as he fell.

The initial investigation into Burnel had commenced after an anonymous tip-off was received by the U.S. Post Office on Forest Avenue in Portland. The Fourth Amendment protected first-class letters and parcels against search and seizure without a warrant, and an anonymous tip-off didn't offer probable cause to obtain one, but no such protection applied to other classes of mail, and one of the packages on its way to Burnel had been sent via Media Mail. It was opened, and found to contain one hundred sexually explicit images of children, whereupon a warrant was obtained for a search of Burnel's property, which unearthed further material and resulted in his arrest and successful prosecution.

Ordinarily, Parker wouldn't have bothered with a case like Burnel's, but he found it interesting that Burnel had declined to plead guilty in return for a possible reduction in his sentence, even in the face of all the evidence against him. Time served for child sex offenses was hard time: any halfway decent lawyer would have made that clear to a client, and Burnel's lawyer was one of the best. Burnel was a first-time offender, and his past actions might have caused a judge to look more favorably on him, especially if the prosecutor was prepared to play ball. Weighted against Burnel, though, was the amount and nature of the pornography involved: thousands of explicit and often violent images, many of them stored on his computer, and some involving very young children. Since part of that material had been sent to him through the U.S. Mail, federal jurisdiction applied in the case. But in an unusual move, the U.S. Attorney's Office for the District of Maine ceded authority to the state, mainly because it could not be conclusively established that Burnel had sent material across state lines, or ordered it to be sent to him. Similarly, explicit images found on a series of USB drives in Burnel's garage could not be linked conclusively to interstate activity. Still, Parker was certain that, in declining jurisdiction, the U.S. attorney would have wanted some guarantees that Burnel would receive an adequate sentence, equivalent to at least the minimum of five years required for possession offenses under federal law. In the end, he'd been sentenced to eight years, reduced to five after an appeal, and a fine of $50,000. Now he was out, and seeking to hire Parker.

And Parker would have declined, had it not been for two things. The first was what Burnel had done before all this had come to pass, the act of heroism that had briefly made him famous. The second was a small detail that Burnel's attorney had been smart enough to raise at his trial, even if it hadn't yielded much in the way of results. No images of child pornography had been found on Burnel's laptop, which he routinely took with him when he was out on the road. Instead, the only images discovered were on his desktop computer at home, which was not even password protected. Parker didn't know a lot about Burnel, but what little he had discovered didn't lead him to suspect that the man was a fool, and only a fool would store explicit, illegal material on an unsecured home computer when he could easily have kept it on his private laptop.

Angel and Louis arrived while he was still mulling over the problem. They had taken a long-term lease on an apartment in the East End of Portland, overlooking the water, and seemed content to move regularly between the city and their New York base. It was good news for Portland's better restaurants, once they'd grown used to Angel's distinctive taste in attire and concluded that he wasn't about to steal any of the silverware.

Parker hadn't seen them since the arrest of Roger Ormsby. Tracking Ormsby had been a time-consuming business, and required calling in some additional manpower. The money funneled to Parker from Ross enabled him to pay reasonably generously for such services. Angel and Louis had tried to decline compensation, but this was a new order that Parker was building, and it also helped that it was the feds' money, and not his, that was going into their pockets.

"He here yet?" asked Louis, for Parker had told them about Burnel's call.

"He said five," said Parker, "and it's only ten to."

"I still don't understand why you're even agreeing to spend time with him," said Angel. As a child, Angel had been hurt by men with similar tastes to Burnel's, and his rage at them had never ebbed.

"Curiosity," said Parker.

"I don't like it."

"I know."

Parker didn't tell Angel that he shouldn't have come. Angel had wanted to be there, and it wasn't for Parker to prevent him, even if that had been his wish. Some part of Angel desired to look upon Burnel, as though he could see in his face the ghosts of others like him, now long departed from this world, and feed them to his flames.

And Parker wanted Angel to look at Burnel, and to be present as he told his story.

Because Angel would know if Burnel was telling the truth.

# XVIII

B urnel arrived one minute early, and Parker guessed that he might have been waiting somewhere nearby, or even just making circuits of the block to pass the time. He recognized Burnel from the pictures he'd found while researching him, although the man had suffered the premature aging of the prisoner, and carried the weight of years of bad food and restricted movement.

There were those who claimed to be able to spot an ex-con by his carriage and appearance, but most of them were liars, and the remainder just unreliable. Had Parker not known about Burnel, he might simply have taken him for a middle-aged man of average height and build, with only a hint of nervousness about his reaction to being in the enclosed space of the Bear. He kept his head low, but his eyes flicked from face to face, just as they would have in the state prison, checking out which inmates to avoid, which ones were neutral, which friendly— and there would not have been many of the latter, not for a man like him. Parker had no illusions about what Burnel would have gone through: beatings, bodily fluids in his food, and worse. Much worse.

"Is that him?" asked Angel.

"Yes," said Parker.

Beside him, he felt Angel tense. Would Angel have been one of Burnel's tormentors, had they found themselves imprisoned behind the same walls? Parker liked to think that he would not, but who could say? It was only at moments like this that something of the rage kept tamped down by Angel found a spark and began to smolder. Louis gave only a single glance at Burnel, and revealed no clue to the direction of his thoughts.

Parker stood and raised his hand in greeting. Burnel spotted him and came over. He kept his distance from the handful of men seated at the bar, following a curve instead of a straight line to reach the booth.

"Mr. Parker?" he said.

Parker nodded and put out his hand. Burnel's handshake was tentative initially, but firmed up in response to Parker's grip.

"Thank you for agreeing to meet with me," said Burnel.

"It's no trouble."

Parker introduced Angel and Louis as his "associates." Louis lifted a finger in greeting, while Angel allowed Burnel a flexing of the muscles around his mouth, like a man in the doctor's office trying to decide if what he was feeling was pain or merely discomfort.

"I was under the impression you worked alone," said Burnel.

"That impression is occasionally useful. Please, have a seat."

Louis rose and slipped into the next booth, taking his glass of red wine with him. Since Parker had occupied the last booth, it meant that their conversation would not be overheard. Angel and Parker were drinking coffee, and the latter asked Burnel if they could offer him the same, or if he'd prefer something stronger.

"I haven't had a drink since I got out," said Burnel.

"Really?" said Parker.

"I thought it would be the first thing I'd want—well, one of the first," Burnel continued. He spoke hesitantly, as though uncertain that he still possessed all the words he might need to express his thoughts. "But when it came down to it, it wasn't."

"What was?"

"I don't know," said Burnel. He appeared genuinely confused.

"It's a shock, isn't it?" said Parker.

"Being free?"

"Yes."

"I suppose it is. I had all these plans, all these ways in which I'd spend my first days once I got out of there, but none of them came to pass. I drank some good coffee. Mostly, I just like walking. I like to feed the pigeons, too, although someone told me that it's not allowed. I don't know if that's true. I hope it isn't. I'd like to get a dog, but—"

He stopped, and smiled apologetically.

"You don't need to hear this," he said. "It's not important. And I'm not free, not truly, because they put all kinds of conditions on my release. For now, I can't leave the state, and I have to talk to therapists and probation officers. When I stop to sit down, I need to make sure there are no children nearby. I'm not permitted to access the Internet. My name is on the sex offender registry, and that's bad enough, but then I picked up yesterday's paper in a coffee shop, and there was an article about my release, with an old picture of me alongside it. I've changed, but not so much that someone wouldn't be able to identify me on the basis of a photograph. Already, people are looking at me differently, or I think they are. I can't tell if they've figured out who I am, or if I'm just imagining it."

"It'll get easier," said Parker.

"No, it won't," said Burnel, "but it's not going to trouble me for long."

"Why is that?"

"Because I'll be dead."

Burnel examined the fingers of his right hand. The nails were unbitten, but the cuticles were ragged and torn where he'd picked at them. He began doing it again while Parker and Angel watched, working obsessively at the area around the fingernail on his right index finger, tearing off a strip of skin to expose a small triangle of pink flesh.

"Are you talking about taking your life?" asked Parker.

"No." Burnel didn't look up. "I'm talking about someone else taking it from me."

"Have you been threatened?"

"No."

"Are you afraid of the consequences of your name appearing on the registry, or that picture in the newspaper?"

"No." Burnel relented. "A little. I'm careful about walking the streets after dark, and I always check my surroundings when I approach or leave my apartment building. But that would just be a beating, if it came, and I've taken beatings. I didn't care much for them, and I don't want any more, but that's not how I'll go, not at the boots of some thug who believes he's doing the community a service by kicking out my lights."

"Then what do you mean, Mr. Burnel?"

Burnel ceased damaging his skin. He had drawn blood, and that seemed to content him. He wiped away the rising red bubble with his left thumb, and stared at Parker.

"I didn't do what they claimed I did," he said. "I didn't gather child pornography. I didn't order it. I didn't look at it. It wasn't mine. All I did was stop for coffee in the wrong gas station at the wrong time, and that's why I'm going to die. It's why all of this has happened. Had I just kept driving, then I wouldn't be here talking to you now. I might still have a future."

He smiled.

"You know, I think I will have a beer, if it's okay with you."

"What kind?" asked Parker.

"Just beer. Any beer. It'll all taste good."

Parker called for an ale from the Maine Beer Company. He figured he might as well keep the money local. When it arrived, Burnel took one long mouthful to start, but sipped the rest. By the time he finished telling his story, there was still a little left at the bottom of the glass, and Parker's coffee had long gone cold. The light in the bar had changed, and the noise level had increased, but none of the four men really noticed, not until the end. By then Louis had joined the group, for Burnel spoke softly, and there was little danger of anyone eavesdropping on them.

A man driving on a dark fall evening, a gas station appearing in the distance: to stop, or to go on. On such decisions were lives saved, lives ended, and lives destroyed . . .

Jerome Burnel was just five days past his fortieth birthday on the night that changed his life. He worked as a manager for a chain of jewelry stores that kept their connections as low-key as possible, preferring to present themselves as independent family operations while enjoying the better terms that bulk-buying brought. In practice, they were owned by a man named Owen Larraby down in Boston, whose good fortune it had been to marry a very beautiful Jewish woman named Ahuva Baer. Ahuva had familial connections to New York's diamond district, which was how Larraby had met her in the first place, when he was starting out in the trade under Rabinow & Saft over in Queens, one of the few goyim to graduate from their dusty university of gemology.

Rabinow & Saft was now long gone, as was Ahuva Baer, who had died far too young at fifty-three. Owen Larraby was still alive and kicking at seventy-nine, although he had never remarried after his wife's death, and showed no more interest in women than politeness dictated. This was entirely understandable to anyone who had ever met his wife, including Jerome Burnel's father, Andreas, who had, for many years, been Larraby's agent in the Northeast, and Jerome himself, who had taken over his father's role when back problems prevented the old man from putting in the required miles on the road. But Andreas con-

tinued to exert a considerable degree of influence over his former territory through Jerome, who only occasionally chafed at his father's daily
calls, Andreas Burnel clearly being of the belief that cell phones had
been invented for no better purpose than to ensure his son didn't screw
up nearly half a century of careful networking.

But the trade was changing. While households were spending more
than ever on jewelry and watches, people wanted more for less, which
was the same everywhere, from books to beans. Sometimes Jerome
would watch the hucksters on the home shopping channels and wonder
at the foolishness of those who had not yet realized that, when it came
to jewelry, what seemed like a bargain never really was. In the jewelry
trade, or the part of it inhabited by men like Owen Larraby and the
Burnels, you got what you paid for, and nothing cheap was ever worth
its price. That was one of the lessons Andreas Burnel had drummed
into his son. The other was an understanding of desire: theirs was an
industry driven not by the items themselves, but by those who wished
to possess them. That was why the hucksters could make so much
money selling tat to rubes: the desire to own what glowed and sparkled
was ingrained in everyone, and if you couldn't afford the best, you'd
take whatever imitation of it you could afford, and ignore the voice of
doubt that whispered of madness.

Traditionally, that desire was at its height during two periods of
people's lives: from their mid-twenties to mid-thirties, when thoughts
turned to marriage; and from fifty-five to sixty-four, when older folk
reached the peak of their earning power, and figured there was no harm
in treating themselves and their spouses to a few luxuries before the
time came to start worrying about hospitals and who'd get the Rolex
in the will. The trade had primarily positioned itself with those two
groups in mind.

But since the retirement of Jerome's father, the largest increases in
jewelry spending had occurred among the youngest consumers—the
under twenty-fives—and the oldest, who were over seventy. The young

had more money than before, and the old were living longer. The only thing that hadn't changed was what most of them spent their money on, and that was diamonds. Loose or mounted, it didn't matter: the cash gravitated toward diamonds, either from revenue generated in direct sales or through ancillary services like maintenance, polishing, and repairs.

What this meant was that, more than ever before, Jerome Burnel needed to have diamonds available for his stores, and sometimes at short notice, which, in real terms, translated as "right now." On that particular evening, the one that changed everything, he was carrying $120,000 worth of them in a specially designed pocket in his jacket. He also carried a briefcase, but it was a decoy, and contained only rhinestones and cubic zirconia packed in clear sleeves for show. In the event of a robbery—which, so far, had never arisen, praise Jesus and all the saints—he would simply hand over the case without objection, and hope that the thieves were smart enough not to compound theft with murder.

Only recently had Burnel started carrying a weapon, after a couple of guys he knew had been targeted and robbed, one so violently that he now had a plate in his head and could only talk out of the left side of his mouth. The pistol made Burnel feel more ill at ease than any quantity of diamonds secreted about his person. He hated the weight and shape of it. He was always uncomfortable carrying it in the holster on his belt, even though the little Ruger weighed less than a pound and could pretty much fit in the palm of his hand. He had practiced drawing it from its leather holster in front of the bathroom mirror, but it made him feel slightly ridiculous, as though he were playing at being a gunfighter. At first, the gun had fit too snugly in the holster, which he'd chosen because the dealer said that leather was better for concealed carry. Unfortunately, a concealed weapon wouldn't be much use to him if he couldn't get it out of the holster, but Owen Larraby, who knew about guns, told him to wet the holster, put the gun in a ziplock bag, and place the bagged gun in the holster overnight. That had helped some, but Burnel had still been forced to buy some Mitch Rosen Leather Lightning in order to loosen the sheath enough for an easy draw.

All of which assumed that, if the worst happened, Burnel would have time to arm himself, and then be able to shoot any prospective thief, neither of which seemed very likely to him. He just couldn't see himself killing another man, not even to save a pouch of diamonds. He'd paid a couple of visits to the local range to gain the minimum proficiency required for his permit, but he'd felt uncomfortable with some of the company he was keeping. He wasn't a gun nut, and there were men— and two women—beside him on the first visit with enough weapons to take on the Islamic State. Later, when he returned with the Ruger, he told the guy in charge why he'd bought the revolver, and the guy had shuffled him off to the edge of the range, and brought the silhouette target right up close.

"Just get used to firing at the shape of a man," was the advice Burnel received. "Aim for the torso. Nothing fancy."

Burnel had fired and reloaded, fired and reloaded, until his ears rang, the grip of the gun was slick with sweat, and the center of the man-shaped target was torn apart. He hadn't removed the gun from its holster since, not even to clean it. It sat on his belt and dug into his belly. He hadn't told his wife about it. He couldn't have said why, except that he had an inkling of how Norah would respond to the sight of him with a gun on his belt. There would be laughter: maybe not the mocking kind, for he had long ago learned to identify her varying tones of disapproval and strained amusement at her husband's ways, but simply a spontaneous reaction to the improbability of what she was seeing. He was, he had come to realize, a disappointment to his wife in so many ways, just as she was a disappointment to him.

That was one reason why, when the gas station appeared before him, he decided to pull in for a coffee. He was less than an hour from Portland, and home, and didn't even particularly need a coffee or a rest stop, but increasingly he was happier alone than he was in his own house, and was spending more time on the road than ever before. He'd even begun hunting for new accounts as far north as Presque Isle and Fort Kent, just to give him an excuse to spend an extra night or two in a motel, and was branching out into one-off pieces by local crafters in an effort to expand his range, which offered him further opportunities to travel. Norah didn't seem to mind. They both knew that the time was approaching when they'd have to discuss a separation, and divorce. Maybe things might have been different if they'd had a child, but perhaps not. They were just wrong for each other, and kids would merely have made an unpleasant situation sadder and more complicated.

He wondered if Norah was having an affair. He didn't think so, but he was surprised at how little he was troubled by the possibility. As for himself, he wasn't the kind, not that any women were currently throwing themselves at him, demanding that he take them in interesting ways. If—or when—he and Norah divorced, he'd try again, but until then he'd just do without significant female comfort, whether physical or emotional. He didn't believe he could handle the stress of his troubled home life and a second, secret existence as an adulterer. He'd give himself a heart attack.

The gas station was a comparative rarity, which was why he'd chosen it for his respite: a mom-and-pop operation, with none of the brash, impersonal neon of the big providers. The building itself was painted red and white, so that it looked more like a small coastal diner than anything else. A mural of two dogs had been added to the wall at the far right, and beneath it was a water bowl and a second container filled with dog treats. Inside, the registers were to the left, and to the right was a seating area with pine tables and stools, and a ledge that looked out over the forecourt. Burnel had stopped there for gas on a few occasions, but never stayed any longer than was necessary to fill up and pay. He recalled that a sign beside the coffeepot identified all muffins and pastries as homemade, and they sat on wooden shelves, resting on the paper on which they'd been baked instead of sweating inside plastic wrap.

Burnel parked at the side of the gas station. The dampness in the air hit him as soon as he stepped from the car, and by the time he was inside the first drops had begun to patter on the ground. The interior was warm, and smelled of fresh coffee with a faint underpinning of gasoline. Music was playing: some light jazz that wouldn't frighten the horses. From behind the counter, a man in his early seventies and a girl in her twenties who resembled him so much that she could only have been his daughter were engaged in conversation with an elderly woman who was leaning against the empty newspaper stand, holding a cigarette pack in one hand and an unlit cigarette in the other, which she was using to emphasize a particular point and guide the argument, like a conductor wielding a baton before an orchestra. The older woman was wearing mismatched house slippers and a raccoon-fur stole that looked like the contributing raccoons had departed this life many decades earlier, but put up a good fight before they went. All three greeted Burnel as he entered, then returned to their discussion, which centered on the price of heating oil, always an issue in Maine as winter loomed.

The older woman's name was Kezia, judging by how often the man behind the counter was being forced to say "Now look, Kezia" and "Don't go all wrathy on me, Kezia" in response to her diatribe. Kezia, in turn, referred to him as Bryce, and seemed to be appealing to his daughter as a voice of reason, as in "Paige, you tell your father, Bryce, here . . ." as though the older man were suffering from some form of selective deafness, or had forgotten his station in life. It was all pretty good-natured, though, and both of the old-timers struck Burnel as serious wigs.

The coffee was hot and smelled of vanilla. He filled a paper cup and selected a muffin from the shelf. It didn't have the cold, unpleasantly moist texture of a pastry that had been defrosted for consumption. He'd become expert in such matters during his years on the road. He went to the counter, paid for his food, and took a seat at the window. He had brought his satchel with him—the briefcase, complete with its worthless stones, remained in the car—but he left his laptop untouched, even though he still had some work to do. It would give him an excuse to avoid Norah when he got home. She always left him alone when he was working. If nothing else, she knew the value of a dollar, and Burnel brought many more of them into the house than she did. Norah owned 51 percent of a vintage clothing store in South Portland, and was also the manager. Burnel was far from being a fashionisto, but even he could tell that most of what his wife sold had been tasteless crap back in the seventies, eighties, and nineties, and was tasteless crap now, which was why so much of it stayed on the racks gathering dust. Norah's partner, Judie, had a better eye, and it was she who found the premium items capable of supporting the kind of markups that kept the store in business.

So, instead of checking e-mail and collating orders, Burnel removed a copy of *The Count of Monte Cristo* from his bag and picked up where he'd left off earlier in the day. The book was a monster, and he only ever got to read it when he was traveling, or when Norah was out. If she saw him with a book in his hand, she took it as a sign that he was free to be disturbed. Norah didn't read. She didn't watch TV either, except for fashion and makeover shows. Mostly she just smoked and talked to her friends on her cell phone, or stared into space, imagining other existences that fate had so far denied her.

Burnel heard two vehicles pull into the gas station's lot. He glanced up in time to see the lights of a gray van die, a dark sedan beside it, followed by the appearance of two men who walked slowly toward the building in which he sat, seemingly untroubled by the rain. Initially, Burnel thought that some distortion of the glass, combined with the patterns of the rain, had conspired to alter the appearance of the taller of the two, but as they entered he saw that the new arrival was unnaturally thin, his fingers twisted by what was probably early onset arthritis. His heavy eyelids might have suggested someone trapped between sleeping and waking were it not for the spiderlike gleam of his dark eyes. When they flicked toward Burnel, he felt as though small, sharp legs were crawling across the skin of his face, and he could not help but try to brush them away.

The gray van looked familiar to Burnel, but he couldn't quite place it. He thought that he'd seen it earlier that evening. It wasn't distinctive, exactly, just memorable for the wrong reasons, like a bad party or a poor meal.

The shorter of the two men went directly to the counter and asked for a pack of cigarettes. While he did so, the taller man turned to the door and twisted the lock, securing the door.

"Hey," said Kezia. "Chupta?"—the five words of the question flowing neatly into one.

When she received no reply, she shouted to Bryce, "Hey, Bryce! This fella's gone and locked the door."

The tall man turned and punched her hard in the face. The blow sent Kezia to her knees, and left her attacker shaking his gnarly hand in pain. By then, his companion had pulled a gun and was pointing it at Bryce and his daughter.

"No alarms," he said. "No screams. Kill the lights outside. Dim the ones in here."

He kept the gun on Bryce as he moved to a set of switches on the wall beside the registers. Meanwhile, his partner advanced on Burnel and pulled him from his stool, sending him sprawling to the floor. The lights outside were extinguished, and seconds later only a handful at the back of the store remained lit.

"The registers are near empty," said Bryce. "My daughter went to the bank this afternoon."

"Shut up," said the gunman. "Get to the back, down by the sodas."

He gestured with the gun, and Bryce and Paige started to move. Burnel noticed that Paige hadn't said a word since the men entered. She had gone gray at the first sight of the gun. Some atavistic sense had told her that this could not, would not, end well. Later, with the blood still fresh on her, she would tell the police that she had watched the expression on the gunman's face as he looked at her, and in his eyes she had seen an image of herself despoiled and then gutted like a fish.

"You!" The gunman looked toward Burnel. "Help the old woman up."

Burnel, who had stayed down, stood slowly. Monitored by the tall man, he went over to where Kezia lay slumped amid fallen packs of bubble gum. He noticed that she was still holding on to her cigarette, although it had snapped when she fell. She was bleeding from the mouth, but conscious, and the look on her face was profoundly hostile as she glared at the man who had hit her.

"Fucker," she said, as Burnel assisted her in standing up, and the tall man responded by displaying his very white, very even teeth. They clicked as the two rows met, then clicked again, and again, and Burnel knew that, in his mind, this scarecrow was already biting down on flesh.

"Hush, now," said Burnel, and she was smart enough to heed him and stay quiet until they both reached the back of the store. Paige and Bryce were already seated against the wall by the side of the coolers. To their left was a closed door protected by a combination lock.

"Is anybody back there?" the gunman asked Bryce.

"No, it's just us."

"If you're lying—"

"I'm not. Please, take what you want, but don't hurt anyone"—he looked over at Kezia, whom Burnel was easing into a comfortable position—"any more than you already have."

"Are you telling me what to do?" The gunman's tone was very even, but Bryce was too smart to be lulled by it.

"No, I'm asking. Begging, if you like."

The gunman nodded.

"That's better. Cell phones out and on the floor. Now."

Kezia's had fallen from her pocket as she fell, and the tall man added it to the rest. Bryce's was on his belt, Paige's in the back pocket of her jeans. Both tossed them at the gunman's feet, but Burnel had already beaten them to it with his own. He, too, had a holder on his belt for his phone. It was on the opposite side from his gun, and he very much did not want to give these men a reason to search him, because not only might they find the revolver, but also the gems in their pouch. In fact, he was surprised that the men hadn't bothered searching their captives to begin with, but perhaps they believed themselves to be better judges of character than they were.

"What's the combination for the door lock?" the gunman asked Bryce.

"Five-zero-zero-five-six."

"What's in there?"

"Storage. An employee restroom. The office."

"The recording system for your security cameras?"

A pause.

"Yes."

"A gun?"

"No."

"You sure?"

"Yes."

The gunman exchanged a look with the monstrous other. Burnel saw that his right hand was not as gnarled as his left. It now reached beneath his overlong jacket, and Burnel heard the sound of metal on leather. When the hand reappeared, it was holding a short machete.

"Jesus," said Kezia, and Paige began whimpering.

"Please," said Bryce again. "Please . . ."

"My bro—" the gunman began, then paused. "My *friend* here," he corrected himself, "is going to keep an eye on you all while I take a look behind that door. He doesn't care much for firearms. He's better with a blade. Don't make him prove it."

He pointed his gun at Paige.

"You, missy. Up you get. You're going to open that door for me, and show me around."

Paige didn't move. She knew what was going to happen behind the door.

"No," she whispered.

The gunman squatted before her, and pushed the muzzle of the gun against her mouth so hard that the sight split her lip.

"I think you misheard me," he said.

He snagged the sight under her teeth, and used it to draw her to her feet. As he did so, he looked from her to Burnel.

"And you," he said. "I like your jacket."

Which was when the Sagadahoc County sheriff's deputy pulled up outside.

**XX**

**B**ack at the Bear, Burnel took a sip of beer.

"Have you ever been in that position?" he asked Parker. "You know, at the mercy of someone without mercy?"

He smiled at his own formulation, and Parker was given a brief glimpse of the man Burnel once was—and, somewhere deep inside, might still be: clever, but not overly so; confident and educated, but not arrogant. But the kind of man to store child pornography in both physical and electronic form, and not secure it?

That remained to be seen.

"We all have," said Parker, which was when Louis joined them. "Well," Parker added, regarding Louis, and reconsidering his own answer in light of his presence, "most of us."

"And you survived," said Burnel. He looked from Parker to Angel and Louis then back again.

"The fact that you have an audience suggests we did," said Angel. His tone gave no indication that his attitude toward Burnel had softened in the course of his tale.

"And the other party involved?"

"It's happened on more than one occasion," said Parker.

"The *parties* involved, then."

There was silence for a time, until Louis answered the question.

"They didn't come out of it so good."

"But," said Parker to Burnel, "we have that in common, don't we?"

"Yes," Burnel replied, "I think we do."

And he returned to his story.

Chapter

# XXI

S agadahoc County is the smallest county in the state of Maine, with a lot of inhabitants of Scots-Irish Presbyterian heritage, of which Deputy Ralph Erskine was one. He was named after a prominent eighteenth-century Presbyterian churchman, a statue of whom stood in the center of the town of Dunfermline in Scotland. Deputy Erskine intended to have his photograph taken alongside his namesake just as soon as he had enough money on which to retire, and thus enable him to make a pilgrimage to his ancestral homeland.

Erskine felt that he'd gotten off easy when it came to his nomenclature: his older brother, Ebenezer Erskine, was also named after a Scottish cleric, who had been, in turn, the older brother of the original Ralph Erskine. All of this had come about because Deputy Erskine's late father, a man of impressive miserabilism, had been a teaching elder in the Presbytery of Northern New England. Upon his death, it was revealed that, in addition to leaving various small sums to his family in his will, and larger sums to his beloved church, he had also set aside a figure of $500 for a "modest celebration of his life," as long as it was spent on nothing stronger than tea and lemonade. Just to be sure that everyone got the message, his will had included the relevant portion of the constitution of the Reformed Presbyterian Church of North America, which advised that "it is altogether wise and proper that Christians refrain from the use, sale and manufacture of alcoholic beverages." It had given Deputy Erskine no small amount of pleasure to redirect some of that $500 toward the purchase of a bottle of fifteen-year-old Balvenie, which he and Ebenezer had shared by their father's graveside.

Deputy Erskine was one week short of his fifty-third birthday when he pulled up outside the Dunstan family gas station. He had a wife, four children, and a grandchild. He also had a liking for the pastries cooked by Bryce Dunstan's wife, Dot. Since he was prediabetic, this was a weakness that his own wife regularly warned might kill him someday.

On this particular evening, Erskine had not intended to indulge himself with a crafty muffin, as he'd just eaten a Firehouse sub back in Topsham, but the absence of lights at the gas station had drawn his attention. Bryce sometimes closed up early if the mood struck him, but early for him was nine, and that was still more than an hour away. Erskine pulled up outside, walked to the door, and tested it. Most of the lights were out, apart from a couple at the rear, and he caught signs of movement. He rapped on the glass and called Bryce's name, but received no reply.

"Hey, all okay in there?" he asked.

Bryce appeared at the back of the store and waved to him.

"Fine," he shouted. "Just closing up."

But he did not approach the door.

Ralph Erskine was slightly overweight and, when under stress, was inclined to stammer. He'd never aspired to be sheriff, or even chief deputy. Neither did he want to be a lieutenant, a sergeant, or a corporal. Promotion might have meant more money, but it would also have involved administration, and additional paperwork, and meetings, and Erskine hated meetings more than he hated hemorrhoids.

None of this meant that Erskine was not smart. He just liked being a patrol cop, and he was good at it. It was as though he'd been bred for it in the womb. Now he felt instinctively that something was wrong at Dunstan's, and only the requirement to establish some certainty about it prevented him from returning to his car and calling for backup.

Erskine kept his voice as casual as he could.

"Come on, Bryce. I'm cold and damp, and I need a cup of coffee. Do the Christian thing here."

The old man's face was hard to see from where Erskine stood, but he was pretty damned sure that Bryce was listening to someone standing to his left. He could glimpse it in the slight inclination of Bryce's head. Erskine turned his body and let his hand slip to his holster, where he gently undid the strap securing his weapon.

"I just threw out the pot," said Bryce, finally.

"Then you can darn well make another one. You can afford it, prices you charge."

Bryce started walking toward the door, but he moved like an actor playing a role, a performer with an unwanted audience. Erskine watched him come, but his eyes were also taking in the spaces around Bryce. The angle of the shelves obscured his view, but he didn't want to make his surveillance too obvious. Dot might be back there, or Bryce's daughter, Paige, and if Erskine was right, then they weren't alone.

Bryce reached the door but didn't unlock it.

"I'm real tired, Ed," he said. "And I don't feel so good. If it's okay with you, I'd like to just finish up and head home."

Ed. Not Ralph: Ed. Ralph Erskine and Bryce Dunstan had known each other for decades. This wasn't a mistake.

Erskine held his gaze. "Sure," he said. "I understand. Is Dot around to help you?"

"No, but Paige is here."

"Nobody else?"

Bryce licked his lips. "We had a couple of folks in here earlier—" he began, which is when the man who called himself Henry appeared from behind the register and shot Ralph Erskine through the glass. The first bullet took Erskine high on the left shoulder, but he managed to draw his weapon before the second bullet hit him in the chest.

Bryce Dunstan cowered, and covered his head with his right hand, as though that could ward off any bullet that might come his way. Ralph Erskine lay on the ground outside, spangled by broken glass, the life bubbling redly from him. A final gush came from his mouth, and then Erskine grew still.

From behind his splayed hand, Bryce risked a peer. The gun was now pointing directly at his face.

"You stupid old bastard," said the gunman.

And Bryce closed his eyes, squeezing them tighter as he heard the first shot, only opening them to discover why, against all expectations, he was not dead.

———

BURNEL WAS WATCHING THE tall man, who had been forced to crouch down to avoid the possibility of being glimpsed by the deputy at the door. It increased his resemblance to a great pale insect, his head bobbing as he tried to hear what was being said by the deputy and Bryce, and keep them in view through the gaps in the shelving. His right hand held the short machete against Paige's throat, while his left was buried in her hair. Burnel saw that the tall man's face was contorted with pain. He kept shifting position, and Burnel understood that he was profoundly physically as well as morally corrupt. The older woman, Kezia, had lapsed into shock and semiconsciousness. She mumbled to herself—not loudly, but just loud enough to concern the tall man, whose little eyes now latched on to her before moving to Burnel.

"Shut her up," he said.

It was the first time the tall man had spoken, and he slurred his words, so they came out as "Shuzurup."

Kezia was to Burnel's right. He wasn't sure what to do. He supposed that he could cover her mouth, but that might make things worse.

What if she came out of her daze and panicked, or started kicking and screaming? Burnel didn't know how far sound might carry from where they were. What if the cop heard her? But then, he thought, how much worse could the situation get? He didn't believe they were going to make it out of there alive. Men like these were beyond his experience and understanding, but they smelled of blood and the panicked excretions of their victims.

"Take it easy," he said to Kezia. He turned to her, twisting his body, leaning over to embrace her with his left arm, and then he heard the first shot. The tall man extended his upper body and raised his head, the better to see what was happening, the blade slipping marginally from Paige's throat, although he kept his grip on her hair, dragging her with him as he tried to discover who had fired. He was still looking away when Burnel, his right hand concealed by his body, reached under his coat and slipped the Ruger from its holster.

The sound of a second shot being fired reached them from the door. Burnel moved away from Kezia, pushing his jacket aside with his left hand, lifting his right. The tall man didn't even glance in Burnel's direction until the gun was already out and pointing at him, but by then the last sands in his hourglass were falling. Burnel thought of the targets at the range, removing the tall man's features and humanity from the equation, reducing him to a two-dimensional image hanging in space.

He had been aiming for the upper body, but the gun bucked in his hand, or maybe it was just the way that Burnel was trembling. Whatever the reason, the bullet hit the tall man beneath the chin, and punched its way through his tongue and upper palate before blowing a path through his brain and exiting from the crown of his head.

The tall man was still falling as Burnel got to his feet. His ears were ringing from the shot. Paige was screaming, and Kezia was muttering louder, but the sounds seemed to Burnel to be coming from a great distance away. He walked as though he were being compelled to move. He could feel a pressure at the small of his back, like a hand pushing him on. He stepped into the aisle and saw the door with its shattered glass, and a figure lying on the ground outside. He saw Bryce crouching to the right of the broken pane, and the gunman to his left, his body partially in the aisle but already turning in Burnel's direction. Burnel brought his left hand up to support the Ruger under the grip, and noticed that the weapon was no longer shaking.

He heard a shot from the front of the store, and a plastic soda bottle close to his head exploded, spraying him with liquid. Burnel didn't try to hide. He didn't look for cover. It was too late for that now. He and the gunman at the door were linked by unseen bonds. Burnel advanced, firing as he did so, but he didn't trust his aim at this distance. He needed to close the gap.

He saw the gunman flinch and change position. Behind him, Bryce, who had dropped to the ground as the shooting began, was inching toward the body outside the door. Burnel guessed that he was trying to get to the deputy's gun through the shattered pane. That was good. If Burnel died, then maybe Bryce would shoot the bastard who had killed him.

Two shots came close together. Burnel felt a tug on his jacket, and glass broke somewhere nearby. He fired again, and the gunman jerked like someone who has just received a powerful electric shock. His gun hand dropped to his side, and Burnel pulled the trigger once more, keeping his weapon as level as he could, surprised at how relaxed he felt, even with the adrenaline that he knew must be coursing through his system. The gunman jerked a second time, then turned and stumbled through the glassless door, tripping over the hand of the dead man on the ground, even as Bryce raised the deputy's weapon but did not fire, seeing something in the gunman's face as he looked back that told him his race was run, that any threat he had once posed was now negated, and Bryce should not trouble himself by inflicting any further damage on him and carrying this debased creature's death on his conscience.

The gunman was bent over as he staggered toward the van. He fired his weapon, but its muzzle was pointing at the ground. Bryce watched Jerome Burnel step out into the rain, his own gun still held steadily before him, his eyes unblinking as he followed implacably after his wounded quarry and shot him twice more, tracking him with the barrel as he collapsed on the oil-stained forecourt, then standing astride him and pulling the trigger over and over as the hammer clicked on the empty chambers.

Except Bryce Dunstan didn't mention that part to the police later, just as he claimed that the killer had tried to raise his weapon and fire, forcing Burnel to shoot him in the back to finish him off. Not that the cops or the district attorney, or even the media, cared too much about delving into the minutiae of the victim's death: they had a murdered sheriff's deputy, and an ordinary man who had avenged his killing while acting to preserve his own life and the lives of others. They had a narrative, and a hero, and that was enough.

For a time.

# XXII

Later, Jerome Burnel recalled that, as he stood over the dead man in the parking lot of the gas station, he was overcome by a fit of shivering, followed by a light-headedness that quickly became active nausea. He threw up in the weeds at the edge of the lot, then sat down hard among them and gently placed his gun on the ground, as though it were a dormant entity that might yet somehow be wakened into another burst of murderous activity by any sudden movement. But as the rain fell, it struck him that the police would want the gun as evidence, and leaving it on the filthy concrete of the forecourt might tarnish it in some way. He thought about putting it back in its holster, but he didn't want to be armed when the police arrived. He checked his pockets, and discovered that he had nothing with which to protect the gun.

Jerome Burnel realized that he was sobbing.

Paige Dunstan walked across the forecourt and stood before him. She had her cell phone in her hand, and Burnel assumed that she had just called the police. Behind her, Bryce was placing a dish towel over the face of the dead sheriff's deputy. Burnel watched Paige come, but couldn't remember quite who she was, and found himself unable to connect her with what had just occurred. It was, he told the three men in the Great Lost Bear, like coming out of a movie and meeting one of the actresses from it on the street.

As for Paige, she noticed that the dead man had bled a lot. She was glad. She hoped that wherever the son of a bitch was, he was still feeling the pain of those bullets, and would continue to do so until Satan himself grew bored of that particular torture and found another, more inventive one to replace it. The thought of what might have befallen her if he had managed to get her into the storeroom made her want to get to a toilet fast.

She turned her attention from the dead to the living.

"I don't even know your name," she said to Burnel.

"Jerome."

"Thank you, Jerome," she said. "I'm Paige."

"I don't know what I did," said Burnel.

"What?"

"It wasn't me. I didn't fire the gun. I didn't kill those men. I watched someone else do it, and he looked just like me."

Paige reached out a hand to him.

"I think you should come inside," she said. "You'll catch your death out here."

*Like him*, Burnel thought, and his eyes alighted on the body lying only feet away. He heard himself giggle, and wondered if Paige had heard him, too. He hoped not. That would be bad. He covered his mouth with his right hand to hide the sound. *He caught his death. The man who looked like me threw it, and he caught it, right in the end zone.*

"Jerome, are you—?"

Lights were flashing to the north as the police approached. Meanwhile a car had pulled up by the pumps, and a woman and a man were asking if everyone was okay, but the woman was already filming the proceedings with her cell phone. Meet the Buttinskys, Snoop and Nosey.

The sight of them brought Burnel back, and he was almost grateful to them. If he'd started laughing aloud, he might never have stopped. Burnel didn't want to be on film. He didn't want pictures of him with puke on his shirt to appear on the news, but most of all he didn't want to be on the news, period. Common sense was rapidly returning now that he had taken a step back onto dry land from the old Insanity River. He was concerned that the dead men might have friends, the kind to take it very much amiss that a jewelry salesman named Jerome Burnel, forty, married (for now), a resident of Portland, Maine, had splattered the brains and skullcap of one of their buddies all over a milk cooler, and put four holes in the other, including two in the back to finish him off. He thought about going over there and snatching the phone, but suddenly police cars and uniforms filled his vision, and guns were being brandished and orders shouted. He lost sight of the woman with the phone, but he would become very familiar with the video she had shot, just as many other people would. And all the while, a little voice whispered:

*But what if they have friends?*
*What if they have family?*

———

BURNEL DIDN'T WANT TO be a hero, didn't believe himself to be one, but he became a hero anyway. He'd asked if his identity could be protected, but there was little hope of that, even before the woman from the car sold her video to the TV stations. He declined interviews, but still the journalists called him. He refused an accolade from the Portland Police Department at their annual awards breakfast, but it was later delivered to him by a young officer who shook his hand and thanked him for what he had done. People stopped him on the street and asked to have their picture taken with him. Customer orders soared, but he no longer felt comfortable making road trips while carrying any quantity of gems, just in case someone took it into his head to target him. As a consequence, he was forced to spend more time working from home, which meant more time in Norah's company, and only she remained unimpressed by what he had done.

Because she knew.

"Big shot," she would say, her words distorting the accompanying cloud of cigarette smoke. "Big man with a gun. Now you're so afraid you can't even leave the fucking house."

And she was right: he was afraid. He didn't like being known. He didn't want to have to carry the gun anymore, but he'd need it with him if he traveled, because everyone and his mother now knew that Jerome Burnel was in the jewelry business and—

*What if they have friends? What if they have family?*

The dead men's bodies went unclaimed, and they were eventually buried in the indigent section of Augusta's West View Cemetery. Their drivers' licenses, identifying them as Henry Forde and Tobin Simus, were high-quality fakes that wouldn't have got past most cops but would have sufficed for casual use. Their vehicles—a '98 Saturn and a 2000 Chevy Express Cargo van—were recent cash purchases from dealers in Virginia and New Hampshire, but title transfers had not yet been initiated.

The police returned Burnel's gun. There was no question of charges being filed against him, although one state police detective, a man named Gordon Walsh, was curious about the final shots fired, and made Burnel go through his story a couple of times before leaving, if not satisfied, then not dissatisfied enough to investigate further.

Gradually, once the public had moved on, and if only to get away from his wife, Burnel went back on the road.

But the events at Dunstan's Gas Station were only part of the story, and just one of the reasons Jerome Burnel became a hero. When the police opened the back of the van they found, amid a wide variety of stolen items, a girl named Corrie Wyatt. She had restraints around her arms and legs, and a ball gag in her mouth. A chain around her waist anchored her to a ring that had been welded to the inner body of the van, possibly for that precise purpose. Wyatt directed police to a house in Gorham, where they found the bodies of Mason Timard, his wife,

Doreen, and their son, Nathan, along with the remains of Todd Peltz and Barry Brown.

Later, Corrie Wyatt would be one of the few nonfamily visitors to Jerome Burnel at the state prison in Warren, along with Paige Dunstan. Dunstan stopped coming to visit Burnel less than a year into his sentence. She married and moved to Oregon following her father's death from heart disease and the sale of the gas station, although she continued to write to him until shortly before she disappeared.

"Disappeared?" said Parker.

"It was in the newspapers," said Burnel. "She was a librarian in Ashland. One day, she didn't come home from work. Her husband was questioned, but he was in San Francisco on business when she vanished, and I don't think he was ever really a suspect. If they ever found out what happened to her, then I didn't notice, and I was looking."

Corrie Wyatt's visits had simply ceased a year or so after Burnel's imprisonment. He received no explanation, for she had never written. One minute she was just there, and the next she wasn't.

# XXIII

Burnel still had a couple of mouthfuls of beer in his glass—enough to finish his story, if he needed some lubrication. Only a scattering of customers remained at the Bear. It had been a quiet evening.

"About two months after the shooting, I got a call from my wife telling me to come home, that the police were at the house and wanted to talk to me," said Burnel. "She didn't say why. I thought it had to be something to do with those two men. I thought that maybe they'd identified them at last, or what I was afraid of had finally come to pass, and their friends had found me."

Burnel grew distracted for a moment. He followed the progress of a young guy who was heading for the men's room, and immediately began picking at his skin. His lips moved, but no sound emerged. Parker could see Angel watching Burnel. He believed that Angel's expression might have softened, but he could not be certain.

"Mr. Burnel?" said Parker.

"Huh?"

Burnel stopped picking.

"I thought I recognized that man," he said. "Or he recognized me. But I was mistaken. Probably."

They waited for him to continue.

"Where was I?" he asked.

"The call from the police," said Parker.

"The call. Right. I was in Kennebunk, so it didn't take me long to drive back. On the way home, I kept thinking about what I'd do if it turned out that I'd been targeted for revenge because of the shootings. What if they were Russians, or Chechens? I'd heard those people were pretty mean, worse than the Italians. If that was the case, the police might have to hide me somewhere for my protection, and all I could think was that I didn't want to be stuck in some apartment with my wife for months or years on end. By then our marriage really was in its death throes, and I'd have been tempted just to let the Russians or Chechens have me, as long as they promised to shoot me and make it quick.

"But the police weren't there to protect me at all. They had all of this . . . *material*, these pictures and films of children. They showed it to me. They asked me if it was mine, and I told them it wasn't, but I could see that they didn't believe me. I saw some of the policemen who had talked to me after the shooting, who'd patted me on the back and called me a hero, and I could tell how disappointed and disgusted they were. I was arrested, brought to the Portland Police Department, questioned, then taken to the Cumberland County Jail. The next day, I appeared before the district court, and bail was set at forty thousand dollars, because the district attorney said that the nature of my business, and the ease of transportation of gemstones, made me a potential flight risk.

"But I didn't have that amount to hand. Norah's store had gone bust, and I wasn't bringing in the kind of money that I had before. Looking back, I think I might have been suffering from PTSD, and my father had been forced to take back a lot of the day-to-day running of the business. Between us, we managed to pay bail, and they let me go."

So Jerome Burnel's name was once again in the news, but for very different reasons than before. His house was daubed with red paint, and the tires on his car were repeatedly slashed. His wife moved out and filed for divorce. They agreed to price the house for a quick sale, and his share went toward paying his legal bills. He moved back in with his parents. He did not work. His father retired officially and permanently from the jewelry business, his reputation tarnished by the crimes that his son was alleged to have committed.

Eventually, Jerome Burnel went to prison.

"Do I need to tell you what happened to me in Warren?" he asked.

"Only if you want to," said Parker.

"You can figure it out for yourself, but the beatings were the least of it. Even in protective custody, I wasn't safe. For more than four of those five years, I lived in hell. For the last few months, it was just purgatory."

"What changed?" asked Angel.

"I was everybody's punch, if they could get to me, but I had a core of tormentors, and their ringleader was a man named Harpur Griffin. He was released five months before I was, although he left me something to remember him by. On the day after his release, five men took turns raping me. They told me it was Harpur's treat."

Burnel finished his beer.

"This is what I believe, Mr. Parker: everything that happened to me was a result of my actions at Dunstan's Gas Station. I was set up so that I would go to jail, and be punished for what I'd done. It's also likely that those same people found Paige Dunstan and Corrie Wyatt, and made them vanish from this earth. Pretty soon, the same thing will happen to me."

He dipped into an inside pocket of his jacket and produced a brown padded envelope. He slid it across the table toward Parker.

"Inside there is all the money I have left, minus a few dollars to keep me going until they come for me. When I'm gone, I'd like you to look into what happened, if not for me then for Paige and Corrie, and for the family killed by those two men, and those friends of Corrie's that were shot."

Parker didn't touch the envelope. At best, Burnel was a damaged man; at worst, a self-deluded one. He was looking for a reason for all

that had occurred. He wanted to believe that there was a logic and purpose to his suffering.

And Burnel, guessing his thoughts, said, "Why would I lie about
the child pornography, Mr. Parker? Why now? What purpose would
it serve? I've done my time. Those lost years can never be returned to
me. My reputation will never be restored. Were I to live long enough,
maybe I'd get some sympathy job that the state or my lawyer helped to
arrange for me, surrounded by others accused of the same crimes, all of
us clearing garbage and weeds from public lots, but that existence will
never be a reality. I did nothing wrong. All I did was stop for coffee at
the wrong gas station, and soon I'll pay for it with the last thing I have,
just like Paige Dunstan and Corrie Wyatt paid. And here's the rub, Mr.
Parker: I don't mind paying that price, because I've paid all the others. I
just don't want it to be for nothing."

Louis called for more wine, and he was the first to speak again after
it came.

"That's quite the story," he said.

"And you don't believe it," said Burnel.

"I've heard stranger."

It was Burnel's turn to look skeptical, but his doubt faded under Louis's implacable gaze.

"I need the men's room," said Burnel. He didn't particularly, but he
sensed that these three men might want some time alone to discuss
what they had heard. He went into a stall to pee, and kept the door
locked, because he could no longer stop his body from shaking when
he entered a restroom.

"Well?" said Parker, when Burnel was gone. He waited for Angel to
speak.

"I think he's telling the truth about the child pornography," said
Angel.

"Good," said Parker, "because so do I."

"But as for the bigger conspiracy theory," said Angel, "it's a stretch."

"If he's telling the truth about the pornography, then someone set him up."

"My money is on the wife," said Louis.

"Ex-wife now," said Parker. "But what did she gain? It doesn't sound like he would have objected to a divorce, even before the shooting."

"Maybe she just plain didn't like him," said Angel.

"That's a big can of not-like to want to see a man jailed and raped," said Louis.

"We only have his side of the story," said Angel. "He could have been the husband from hell."

"You think? Man doesn't even strike me as the husband from heck."

"And then there's the two missing women," said Parker.

"Coincidence?" asked Angel. "Plus, we don't know anything about this Corrie Wyatt. Just because she stopped visiting him doesn't mean she's been abducted or is dead."

"But it is a bunch of odd," said Louis. He raised his glass to Parker. "It's your call."

Burnel returned from the men's room. There was fresh blood on the cuticles of two of his fingers. One more thing about him was probably true, Parker knew: he would not live long. He was a hanging leaf, waiting to fall.

Burnel did not resume his seat, but stood before them.

"I've held one detail back," he said. "I thought you might find it too odd, or think that I'd made it up, but while I was in the men's room I thought about something this gentleman said." He gestured at Louis. "He told me that you'd heard stranger tales than mine, and from what I've read about you, Mr. Parker, that may well be true."

Parker could see the effort it took for Burnel to go on talking.

"Shortly before his release, Harpur Griffin raped me for the last time," he said. "Two of his friends were holding me down. Griffin had gotten hold of some Adderall, so he was worse than usual. Mostly he stuck with cursing me for being a pedophile, a deviant, or even simply a fag—whatever term of abuse he favored at any particular moment. But that morning he was in another place: he was twitching, hallucinating. And violent, just so violent."

Burnel stared at a spot somewhere on the table, not looking into the faces of the men to whom he was speaking.

"Griffin leaned over to whisper in my ear. He said—

"*This is for the Dead King.*

"Over and over, in time with his thrusts—

"*This is for the Dead King. This is for the Dead King.*"

*Dead King. Dead King.*

Dead King.

# 3

Take to my side
And we'll walk on
To where the frost of the Dead King
Weigh heavy on the vine.

Espers, "Dead King"

# XXIV

To everyone in Plassey County, it was known as "the Cut," after the cleft in the hill that towered above its northern extreme. The Cut wasn't a large area—maybe only ten square miles in total—but it was all private land, and those who lived within its boundaries kept themselves to themselves, or as much as was possible in the twenty-first century.

Plassey County lay east of Charleston, at the point where forested hills began to turn to arable land. Technically, in Appalachian terms, it was a cove, a valley between two ridges, but it was shallow rather than deep, with the gentle declination of the terrain barely noticeable as one moved farther into the Cut's territory. That was the other thing: the Cut was both the place itself and its inhabitants. They lived in the Cut, and were the Cut. It was in and of them, and they in turn were of it. Sometimes its people were referred to in the singular, but just as often in the plural: the Cut "is," the Cut "are." It was of no consequence. It was all the same, for it was all the Cut. This might have proved confusing for outsiders, but the people of Plassey County did their best not to refer to the Cut at all, and certainly not to strangers. It was better that way.

Now and again, the Cut came into the towns of Mortonsville, Turley, and Guyer's Crossing—the three principal settlements in Plassey County—to buy supplies, or very occasionally see a doctor, although they were largely self-sufficient, and had been for generations. They grew their own fruit and vegetables, and raised pigs, a few cattle, and a lot of chickens. There were apiaries, too, but they'd been having problems with them lately, like so many other beekeepers. Oswald Hosey knew this because he kept bees and one of the Cut—Oswald thought it might have been one of the younger Gantleys, but he couldn't be sure—had come by a year or so back to discuss the matter with him. Pesticides, that was Oswald's opinion about it, but the Gantley boy said they didn't hold with such things in the Cut, and Oswald had tried to explain to him that it was all very well him and his kind not holding with pesticides, but unless he could keep his bees tied to the hive with lengths of thread, they were going to come into contact with pesticides whether he liked it or not.

At that the Gantley boy had taken off his straw hat, wiped his brow with his sleeve, and looked out with disgust upon the houses and farms that formed the greater part of the community of Guyer's Crossing as though, if it were in his power, he would have swept them and all others like them from the face of the earth. Then he'd thanked Oswald for his time and driven away. That evening, five pots of fresh honey were left on Oswald's doorstep, and Oswald had to admit that it was probably very fine honey indeed, although he could only judge it by the smell, because he sure as hell wasn't going to eat any.

Those were the kinds of encounters that local people had with the Cut: unanticipated, generally polite but distant, and rarely repeated. And on every such occasion, those who were not of the Cut would return to their homes overcome by a terrible unease, and would sleep poorly that night, and be tense and short-tempered with their loved ones, even as they tried to hold them close and keep them within whatever protection was offered by walls and fences.

The people of the Cut were not like them. They belonged to an older dispensation.

Guyer's Crossing stood at the western edge of the Cut, Mortonsville to the east. The other nearest towns were Turley, the county seat, to the south, and tiny Deep Dell to the north. Looked at on a map, it might have appeared that the Cut was surrounded, a relic of old times trapped in the new, but to its neighbors it seemed that it was they who were at the mercy of the Cut. It squatted like a cancer in the heart of Plassey County, a permanent source of potential threat, and they would not be aware of the metastasis until the bodies began dropping.

In defense of the Cut and its population—should they have needed any to speak out on their behalf, which they did not—much of the mythology surrounding it came from centuries earlier, when the first inhabitants of the Cut, who had colonized the place before other settlers, and fought the Shawnee to a guarded truce in order to maintain their claim on the land, clashed with speculators and new European immigrants.

The Cut folk—a mix of Scandinavians, Scots, and various mongrels—had been distrusted from the start. Their relations with the Shawnee were regarded as too close to make them good white men, an impression heightened by the system of communal land ownership that they practiced, itself learned from the Shawnee, for whom the idea of an individual having exclusive use of a piece of land was regarded as entirely alien. In 1774, the Cut had also declined to participate in what was known as Cresap's War, when a land speculator named Michael Cresap led a group of volunteers on a punitive mission against Shawnee villages in response to native attacks against new settlements. The Cut shared the Shawnee view that the rapid growth of the settlements constituted a threat to their own way of life, and when family members of the peaceful Mingo chief known as Logan were slaughtered by Cresap's forces, it was said that the Cut gave shelter to the rest. In return, when Logan's warriors began killing settlers in retaliation, the Cut was spared.

But the whispers around the settlements suggested that it was not only the Shawnee who had murdered white men and women, and the Cut had used the conflict to remove the more troublesome of its neighbors and extend its sphere of influence. Two entire families were put to the knife, including women and children, with a savagery that had not been seen even in the predations of the Shawnee. The rumors became so persistent that they reached the ears of the Earl of Dunmore, the governor of Virginia, and when Dunmore rode out to deal with the Shawnee under the chief named Cornstalk, he did so with the intention of curbing the activities of the Cut as well.

Dunmore had planned a pincer movement on the Shawnee, dividing his force into two armies, one led by himself and attacking from the north, the other advancing from the south with the speculator Andrew Lewis at its head. Lewis was a particular thorn in the side of the Cut, and it was said to be at the Cut's instigation that the Shawnee ambushed Lewis by the meeting of the Kanawha and Ohio Rivers. The result was heavy losses on both sides, with the Shawnee being beaten into a retreat, and eventually forced to sign the Treaty of Camp Charlotte, in which they relinquished their claim on the land south of the Ohio River. This soured relations between the natives and the Cut, with the result that, during the Revolutionary War, when the natives sided with the British, the Cut and its people found themselves aiming guns at their former allies. It says much about them that they did not hesitate to pull their triggers.

By then, the nature of the settlers in the Cut had been established: they did not mix, they did not cooperate with the institutions of government beyond the minimum required, and their existence was one of interdependence and mutual support. As the decades went by, and the eighteenth century became the nineteenth, then the twentieth, it was inevitable that the Cut would find its insularity threatened, as well as have some engagement with the modern world forced upon it. Men of the Cut fought in the Civil War, and later in the two world wars. Some even went to Korea and Vietnam. But they always held themselves apart from their comrades, and shared little of their lives back home.

In the beginning, the Cut was based around a core of twelve families, each living within sight of at least one other dwelling. A series of fences and walls, supplemented by thorny hedgerows and ditches, formed what were, in effect, ringed fortifications around a central compound known as the Square. Outsiders were not welcome, and rarely progressed beyond the first or second ring before being spotted and turned back.

Of course, some who trespassed were more than simply curious. There were rumors that the Cut was a source of silver and gold, and those who lived in the settlement used this secret wealth to support their lifestyle, a tale that was never confirmed despite various efforts at unlawful exploration.

Then, in the mid-nineteenth century, there rose talk of devil worship and child sacrifice, much of it inspired by a revivalist preacher named Wilbur Torey, a student of Lyman Beecher, the cofounder of the American Temperance Society. Torey pitched his tent in Mortonsville, and attempted to gain access to the Cut in order to determine which form of religious belief, if any, was being practiced by the majority of its population, since then, as now, only a handful of the Cut worshipped alongside the county's established congregations. Torey was run off by members of the Lydell family, who occupied the easternmost area of the settlement. When Torey tried another point of entry, he was turned back at gunpoint, and warned that the next time he trespassed, he'd be shot. Humiliated, and perceiving the Cut as an evil to be remedied before the Second Coming of Jesus Christ, Torey began to preach against it, and to sow fear and discontent among those who lived on its borders.

On the night of January 23, 1855, Wilbur Torey vanished. A search warrant was obtained for the Cut, the first great intrusion into the preserve since the earliest skirmishes of the previous century. The families of the Cut were held at gunpoint over a period of days while sweeps were made of the area by men and dogs, but no trace of Torey was found, and eventually the search was abandoned. It was only a century later that a body discovered in woods near Grantsville, in Calhoun County, was identified as that of Wilbur Torey. All the fingers on his right hand were missing, and a heat-related fracture was evident in the temporal bone of the head, along with fragments of a sootlike ash in his mouth, and blackening to the interior of the skull. No other signs of damage by fire were found on the remains. It was concluded that Torey's mouth had been filled with some form of flammable material that had then been lit, causing the staining and fracturing of the skull.

The presence of ash in the mouth indicated that this had been done while Wilbur Torey was still alive.

The search of 1855 was the last time that the outside world, and the forces of the law in particular, had interfered in such a manner with the life of the Cut. The senior families determined that no cause would be given for any further such incursions, and great care was taken to avoid confrontations that might lead to local, state, or federal forces taking an interest in their activities. But the people of the Cut did not simply turn the other cheek: instead, they methodically set out to make clear to their neighbors that the Cut was to be left untroubled, and any clashes with it would end badly for the other parties involved. Pets would disappear from yards; beatings were delivered by masked individuals; cars, houses, even businesses were burned out; and, in the most extreme circumstances, a handful of others went the way of Wilbur Torey, vanishing, never to be heard from again.

And although it was never spoken aloud, it was understood that this was the work of the Cut.

As will sometimes happen when a potential source of harm cannot be eradicated, and instead a way must be found to coexist with it, the four main communities in Plassey County grew adept at stepping carefully around the Cut and, for the most part, simply ceased openly to acknowledge its existence. There were even some advantages to doing so, for the Cut, in order to ensure its seclusion and discourage the attentions of law enforcement, took it upon itself to deal with those whose criminality threatened to undermine the peace of Plassey County. No biker gangs made inroads, and no meth labs flourished: meth producers, even the low-level shakers and bakers, were quickly put out of business under threat of going into the ground, and a brief attempt by The Pagans to establish a foothold had ended with one of their leaders being drowned in a quarry, anchored to the bottom by his Harley. Even crimes against property were the lowest in the state. If one didn't look too hard, one might almost have been able to convince oneself that the Cut was a peculiar force for good, enforcing order in return for solitude.

But the people of Plassey County knew better.

———

OBERON MOVED THROUGH THE Cut's central plaza in the early-morning light. His last name was Olhouser, although it was so rarely used that he had almost ceased to connect it to himself. It was also probably not the name that his ancestors had brought to the New World, which was now lost to all: Olhouser—meaning "the dweller by the old house"—was derived from the Cut. It had originally referred to the foundations of a ruined cabin discovered by Oberon's forebears on this land, one that the natives claimed had been built centuries before by a man with pale skin who carried a longsword. What happened to him, they could not say. Tribal lore claimed that he had simply vanished one day, leaving his dwelling to fall into ruin.

But the Olhouser name remained apt, because Oberon was the guardian of the blockhouse.

He was a huge man, just over six-six in his bare feet, with long gray hair that hung past his shoulders. He was almost sixty, but his hair had been that color since his late twenties, premature graying being a trait on his father's side. He was heavily bearded, and wore jeans and work boots, with a blue padded vest over his shirt to keep out the morning cold. His hands were scarred, and the left was missing the upper halves of the little and ring fingers, lost to carelessness with a buzz saw as a boy. His eyes were bright green and gave him an otherworldly aspect, which was why his father had endowed him with the name of a fairy king. But it was the way of the Cut to give notable names to its children, and the community was filled with those whose nomenclature paid homage to gods and rulers from the ancient world, and figures from the Bible.

To Oberon's left lay his home, sheltered by a glade of firs. The house was a two-story construction of wood and stone, and dated back to the early nineteenth century in this form, although his ancestors had occupied dwellings on that plot since the start of the eighteenth century. His wife, Sherah, was still sleeping when he left, as was his daughter.

Directly across the Square stood the home of Cassander Hobb, Oberon's lieutenant. Cassander was outside now, drinking coffee and smoking a cigarette. His sons were still in Maine. When they returned, Oberon would send them to range, hunting for vacant properties to strip of valuables, easy targets to terrorize and rob. Winter was coming, and the Cut would cease its ranging when the first snows started to fall. Until then, they would continue to find ways to supplement their wealth.

Cassander raised his cup in greeting, but did not make any move to join Oberon. Cassander knew where he was going, and what he would do once he got there. It was better to leave him in peace, Cassander thought. Oberon would share whatever conclusions he had come to in his own time.

But it was also true that a distance had grown between the two men in recent months. Cassander was younger than Oberon by a decade and even resembled the older man, although Cassander's hair was shorter and darker, and his eyes were brown, not green. He had two sons while Oberon had none, and Sherah showed no signs of producing a male heir. That in itself was not enough to force Oberon to step aside in favor of Cassander, but there was also the matter of Oberon's caution to consider. He was less prepared to take risks than before, and it was costing the Cut money. Cassander believed that Oberon was frightened by the modern world, and fear was like a crack in stone, a weakness in the edifice destined to grow more dangerous with the passing of time. Only in the matter of Jerome Burnel had he exhibited signs of his old self, and that was because of the personal nature of the hurt inflicted by Burnel on Oberon's line. But it was not enough for a leader to act solely in his own interests: he had to consider the needs of the whole.

And then there was Sherah . . .

All of this in the raising of a cup, and an exchange of nods on a crisp fall morning.

From the south of the Square ran one of the main routes through the Cut, passing by six more houses on its way to the county road, the first point of contact with the outside world. Similar roads ran to the east and west, forking after a mile in each direction to send a pair of narrower avenues north, the two joining just short of the Cut's northern border. From these main arteries emerged smaller trails and lanes, some big enough to take a vehicle, most barely large enough to accommodate a man. The principal ways in and out of the Cut were electronically monitored, so that any vehicle that passed a signal without deactivating the system immediately drew a response from the nearest family. Smaller trails used more primitive methods of surveillance and deterrence, including wires attached to bells, heavy-duty snares, and, in places, steel animal traps. It had been many years since the last breach of the Cut, but Oberon had not permitted the relaxation of its guard.

To the north of the Square, half a mile into the oldest forest of the Cut, stood an extraordinary structure: a squat, two-story blockhouse that had once been part of the original fortifications, when the main families had lived largely within the confines of the Square and its environs, surrounded by a palisade of sharpened logs. Those barriers were mostly gone, although parts remained visible in the forest and around the Square; Cassander used one such section as a tomato wall, just like his father and grandfather had before him. The blockhouse still stood, but nature had been permitted to have its way with it, to a degree, and for more than a century a great oak tree—now dying—had grown up and through it. But instead of allowing the blockhouse to fall into ruin, the people of the Cut had repaired and moved boards and roof slats where necessary, enabling the blockhouse and the tree to become a kind of single entity, a blend of the natural and the man-made. A door stood in its southern face, and a series of small glass windows, covered by bars, admitted light on every side.

To the left of the blockhouse was a former stable. Inside, Oberon had two bitches that were about to whelp, so he went to check on them first. All was well, or appeared to be so: his wife was better with the bitches than he was, but they all shared responsibility for them, the same as they did with the cattle, pigs, and chickens, the fruit trees and the vegetable gardens.

Oberon secured the door after him and took the path over to the blockhouse. He felt his breath shorten and his heart begin to race as it always did at such moments. Even after all these years, his sense of awe had not lessened in any way.

The key to the blockhouse was the only one attached to the piece of bone that served as the fob. The bone had been carefully carved into the semblance of a crown. It looked like it might have come from some animal, although one long dead, but Oberon knew it was actually part of the thigh bone of a woman named Corrine Dotrice, who died back in 1952 after years of good service to the Cut, although she might not have described it in those terms herself.

Oberon paused before unlocking the door. The trees were losing their foliage, and through the gaps he could see the sunlight gleaming on the catenary wires above the Square, designed to prevent a helicopter from landing on the only central area of the Cut accessible from the air. The wires had been in place since 1993, when the Cut watched with interest, and alarm, as the FBI laid siege to the Branch Davidian compound in Waco, Texas. The wire ran to three layers and, seen from below, resembled an intricate spiderweb. It was a deterrent not only to choppers but also to any attempt at rappelling into the Square.

Oberon was wary of the FBI, and the Bureau of Alcohol, Tobacco,

Firearms and Explosives, despite the best efforts of the NRA to defang it. The Cut sourced its weapons carefully—and largely legally—and kept them well maintained to avoid unnecessary additional purchases. Its people held no more firearms than required, although ammunition was plentiful. The two words that Oberon always kept in mind were "probable cause": the Cut gave the forces of law and order no reason to come poking around. Its needs were few. It did not even range as it once had, and its criminal activities were relatively low-key, and limited to supplying its basic needs. Some of its children had even left to go to college, or seek jobs in cities and towns far from West Virginia. But it was understood that, once they departed the Cut, their relationship with it could not be the same. When they returned for Christmas, Thanksgiving, or, inevitably, funerals, their freedom of movement was restricted, and certain parts of the Cut were off-limits to them, including anywhere north of the Square. No one broke the rules, for fear of causing difficulties for those family members still remaining.

But the Cut was changing. Four of its houses now stood empty, and two of those were well on their way to becoming derelict. The Cut educated its own children, and educated them well, but it could not entirely shelter them from the attractions of the world beyond its borders. It could not, and would not, prevent from leaving those who wished to go, and so its population was gradually decreasing. Still, two children had been born in the past twelve months, and those to couples bearing the names of two of the original Cut families, the Haywards and the Molines. Another marriage was scheduled to take place before Christmas. There was hope for the Cut yet.

But Oberon could not shake off a mounting sense of unease. It had been growing in recent weeks, and he was not entirely sure why. A shadow was forming. He glimpsed it out of the corner of his eye, like a tumor encroaching upon his vision. Soon it would touch them.

And so he had come to the blockhouse, there to commune with the Dead King.

# XXV

P arker offered Burnel a ride back to his apartment, but he declined and ordered a cab instead, which arrived within minutes. The three men watched him leave, the envelope of cash hidden beneath his jacket. Parker had decided not to take the money, not yet, although he told Burnel that this did not mean he was refusing to look into his case. He just wanted to make some calls before committing, a condition that Burnel accepted. He informed Parker that he would leave the money with his lawyer because he didn't want to keep cash at his accommodation for any longer than was necessary.

"'Dead King,'" said Louis, once Burnel had gone. "You think this Harpur Griffin gave himself a nickname in prison?"

"If he did, it would have come up again," said Parker. Before leaving, Burnel had confirmed that Griffin used the name only on that one occasion.

"So who's the Dead King?"

"Maybe I'll have to find Harpur Griffin and ask him."

"When you do, can we come too?" said Angel. "He sounds like just the kind of offender who might benefit from a conversation about his attitude."

"And some therapy," added Louis. "Mostly physical."

"And definitely not state-approved," said Angel.

"You're assuming I'm going to take Burnel on as a client," said Parker. "You've already started ticking the boxes. I can see you doing it."

Parker called for the check.

"I have some work of my own ɔ first. Then we'll see."

————

PARKER DROVE BACK TO his house in Scarborough. Like him, it still bore scars both physical and psychic from the attack that had almost ended his life. Despite the best efforts of the Fulci brothers, he could see the differences in paint texture where the holes in the walls left by bullets and shotgun pellets had been filled in. His office door had been replaced, but the newness of it reminded him of what he had lost. He no longer turned his back to the night when entering the house through the kitchen door at the rear, and had trained himself to use his left hand to turn the key in the lock so that his right could be near his gun. And even after almost a year, he had not yet recovered his previous comfort with the nightly creaks and settling of the old structure.

He'd been thinking about putting it on the market. He loved the marshes, and the smell of the sea, but increasingly the city of Portland had come to seem more appealing. It would mean less driving, for a start. Sitting in an upright position for any length of time continued to cause him discomfort: it was why he liked the booths in the Great Lost Bear, because they allowed him to stretch out. If he found a place in the heart of Portland, he would be able to walk to restaurants, bars, coffee shops, and even the movies at the Nickelodeon. He hadn't discussed a possible move with anyone, but it nagged at him. He had no reason to be rattling around alone in such a big space, and he was acutely aware of his own vulnerability. No one could have survived what he had with an undamaged sense of security.

Yet, curiously, he was not afraid. The reminders of what had happened irritated him more than anything, as did the precautions he felt he had to take to prevent any recurrence. Fear was not an issue: he knew that his dead child watched over him from the shadows, although he had received no visitations from her in weeks. He sometimes thought that he sensed her presence, usually when it was dark, and always when he was outside. She liked the marshes and the woods. She was a creature of the natural world. She was the movement among the leaves when there was no wind, and the footprints in damp grass where no one had walked. She guarded him, both for herself and, Parker believed, for her half sister, Sam.

Sam was not what he had believed her to be. She was his daughter, and more than that: she was a being in the process of becoming, but what might ultimately emerge from that metamorphosis could not be foretold. If Sam knew, then she declined to say.

But Parker suspected that she did know. He had seen it in her eyes. *They're listening, Daddy.* Until the time came, she had to remain concealed. *They're always listening.* No one could know how extraordinary she was because—*They'll hear us*—that knowledge would place them all at risk.

*They'll hear us, and they'll come.*

———

HE OPENED HIS NEW laptop, the one that had been sourced for him by Louis. In this Internet age, nothing was safe, and little could be done online without someone looking over your shoulder. The new machine, though, was about as secure as any could be, and the risk of snooping was minimal, especially with the Tor Browser. The information contained on it was also secured by so many firewalls and security procedures that Parker himself had to make an effort to remember them all, just in case he sent his own data into the void with an incorrect keystroke.

The computer contained all the information collated so far about the list of names retrieved from the wreckage of the plane in the Great North Woods. More details had been added to the profile of each person on that list—husbands, wives, children, jobs, businesses, bank accounts, cars owned, homes bought, stocks acquired, friends, enemies, acquaintances—and all these details were being cross-checked with those of others in an effort to establish points of connection and possible patterns.

The handful of people who knew of Special Agent Ross and his work were convinced that Parker was engaged in some private mission to hunt down the most dangerous men and women on the list, but they were wrong. Oh, occasionally one—like Roger Ormsby—might rise to the surface and become worth hooking and pulling in, but Parker was content to feed most of these individuals to Ross without even involving himself in their apprehension. The FBI and the police were better placed to deal with them than he was, even with the help of Angel and Louis.

No, Parker was convinced that concealed somewhere on the list—or beyond it—was the identity of one person. The list was the early work of a group of men and women who called themselves the Backers: self-interested, amoral, and engaged in the hunt for a buried deity. They called it the God of Wasps, or the One Who Waits Behind the Glass. They called it Abaddon, and the Old Serpent. It was the light that fell, the sun eclipsed: *"And I saw a star fallen from heaven to the earth. To him was given the key to the bottomless pit."*

The Backers were looking for that pit, and they were led by a principal, one who stood above them all. Parker believed that the names on the list, and the data on their lives that he was amassing with the help of Angel, Louis, and a handful of others, functioned as circles, or spheres of existence. Some of those circles overlapped, creating a complex series of Venn diagrams, and somewhere in those shaded sectors, either as a name or as a perceptible, repeated absence, lay the identity of that principal. Parker could spend a lifetime hunting the servants, or he could find the master and destroy him.

He worked long into the night, seated by his kitchen window, guarded by a dead child who kept her vigil from a pitch pine bog.

———

AND TO THE WEST, in a converted Vermont stable house, another child sat on the edge of her bed, staring out her window but seeing nothing of what lay beyond it. Instead, through the eyes of her lost half sister, Sam watched her father's face lit by the glow of a screen, and listened to the whisperings of a waking god.

Chapter

# XXVI

The day after his conversation with Charlie Parker, Burnel went to meet his parole officer for the second time at the Department of Corrections on Washington Avenue. It seemed that he was required to take another polygraph test, and a change in schedule meant that his first group therapy session had been brought forward to early that evening. It wouldn't be worth returning to his apartment, so he'd find somewhere nearby to grab a coffee and read for a while. He had bought a bunch of used science fiction and fantasy novels cheaply at the Green Hand Bookshop on Congress, not far from his apartment, and was currently immersed in Alfred Bester's tale of telepathy, *The Demolished Man.* He had never read such escapist works until he went to prison, preferring nonfiction and the kind of literature that advertised the good taste of the reader, but nothing better teaches a man the value of escapism than life behind bars.

He could have taken a bus—the damage inflicted on him in prison had left him in constant pain—but he chose to walk. He was growing a little more comfortable with the absence of walls surrounding him, and took pleasure in the freedom simply to be able to stroll down a street. Also, walking meant that he was less likely to attract the attention of the police, as he was very aware of the Portland PD patrol cars that cruised the city, especially along Congress and down by the Old Port. Sitting on a bench or at a bus stop for too long or, God forbid, taking time out over at Congress Square Park, was the equivalent of waving a magnet at iron filings. It was very likely that they would just have passed him by, because he didn't really stand out: it was he who felt his own sense of difference, and feared its transmission to others.

And always he was conscious of children: of keeping his distance from them, of not looking at them, for fear that even accidental contact with a school group by the Children's Museum, or a mistimed glance while walking near Portland High School on Cumberland Avenue, might be enough to alert the police.

His lawyer had called him that morning. A company in South Portland that sold the kind of trashy costume jewelry on which he used to look down had a vacancy in its purchasing department, and the lawyer had called in a favor. Burnel could start on Monday, if he chose. Surprising himself, Burnel had accepted the offer. Only later did he realize that he was making plans for some kind of future. It was a consequence of his meeting with the private detective and his two colleagues the previous evening, and the fact that they hadn't rejected his story outright, or his fears. By sharing what he believed, he had drawn them to him. Perhaps they could protect him. He might even be exonerated. More than anything, he wanted his good name back. He did not want to die with this stigma upon him.

He remained troubled by the sighting of what he believed to be a familiar face at the Bear. He couldn't quite place the man who had gone into the restroom while he was speaking with Parker, and he'd been gone when Burnel went to take a leak, but his features had reminded him of someone he once knew. He couldn't swear to it, but there had been a hint to them of the man who had used the name of Henry Forde. Burnel thought that he should have mentioned it to Parker, but he was afraid it might have been taken as a manifestation of paranoia to believe that he saw resemblances in the faces of strangers to a man he had killed.

Eastern Cemetery was coming up on Burnel's right, and the sight of its headstones threatened to turn his fairy tale of a future to so much ash. He fought against despair, because there might yet be hope for him. He saw three possible realities. The first was that he was right about everything, and his life had been ruined as a punishment for killing the two unknown men at Dunstan's Gas Station, a punishment that would conclude with his death. The second was that he was wrong to be fearful, and his years in prison had simply driven him insane. He would not be the first to break in that way, and he would not be the last. In time, and with help, he might recover his reason.

And the third? The third was that those who had chosen to torment him had forgotten about him, or believed he had suffered enough. He had lost his reputation and whatever was left of his marriage. He had lost his home and years of his life. His nerves were shot, and the damage to his insides from repeated physical and sexual assaults had left him a ruin. If they wanted to snuff out his existence as well, then they could do so, for all it was worth.

But even as he thought this, he understood that he did not want to die. He had never considered himself to be a strong man, or a survivor, but he had come through five terrible years of incarceration, endured times when he had considered taking his life, yet he was still breathing, and still fighting. He would take the job and get a better place to live. He would continue to feed the birds at Deering Oaks Park and on Eastern Promenade. He might even get himself a dog for company. He had always wanted a dog, but Norah was allergic to them, or claimed to be. Never mind: she was gone now, and a mutt from the pound would more than adequately fill the space that she had once occupied. This life, or what was left of it, was better than no life at all.

But suppose they were watching him, these unseen men, these servants of the Dead King? What if they judged that his continued suffering was better than bringing it to a violent end? If he tried not to look too happy (hardly difficult, under the circumstances); if he kept his head down; if he held himself like a man even more damaged than he was: would that be enough for them?

He arrived at the black railings of Eastern Cemetery, and paused to look at the little wooden shed with its granite abutment, the only standing structure in the graveyard. It bore a sign with the cemetery's name and the date of its establishment: 1668. The Victorian building was known as the Dead House, because it sheltered the door to the city's belowground receiving tomb. It was an entrance to the underworld, Portland's own little gateway to Hades. Burnel had read that special tours were being offered to enable people to explore the tomb, but he had no desire to take one. The ranks of the dead would eventually welcome everyone, and he didn't see the need for a preview of coming attractions.

Behind him, a van pulled up to the curb, hiding Burnel from the view of those passing opposite. The side doors opened and men emerged from inside. Burnel became aware of them at the same moment that he felt a sharp pain in the side of his neck, and the cemetery before him began to blur. His legs gave way, but he did not fall. Strong arms gripped him, bearing him away, and because his last thoughts had been of the underworld, Burnel had a sensation of floating. He was on a boat crossing dark water: Acheron, the river of pain, or Lethe, the river of forgetfulness. The current would take him into the Dead House, and beneath it he would meet at last the Dead King, this god against whom he had sinned, and who would find an eternal place for him in the Fields of Punishment.

Within seconds the sidewalk was empty and the van was heading west. It turned down Washington Avenue and passed the squat red-brick building housing the office of Adult Community Corrections, where Chris Attwood was rereading the file on Jerome Burnel in preparation for their second meeting, and wondering if a man could at once be so brave and yet so depraved.

By then, Burnel had lost consciousness. His final thought before his world turned black was:

*At least I was not mad.*

# XXVII

Relations between Parker and Detective Gordon Walsh of the Maine State Police's Major Crimes Unit were frostier than they once had been. The events in Boreas earlier that year had forced Walsh to recognize the awkwardness of his position where Parker, Louis, and Angel were concerned: these were men who appeared comfortable with black, white, and every shade of gray in between, with Angel and Louis tending toward the darker tones. Walsh had tried to use Louis's knowledge in particular to gain some insight into what might be happening in Boreas, partly at the urging of SAC Ross—and there was a man equally comfortable in the shadows, Walsh thought, with an agenda to match. The result was that Walsh had found himself badly compromised, and in a potentially career-damaging way.

Oh, he wasn't so naïve as to think that you could lie down with dogs and not get fleas, but the bite, when it came, was not from Louis or Angel, but from Parker himself. It was Parker who had pointed out that Walsh had been consorting with known criminals, including one—Louis—who might well have put a bullet through a man's head not twenty-four hours earlier. Since then, Walsh had given a wide berth to Parker and his charmingly dangerous (even dangerously charming) acolytes, so he wasn't overly happy to emerge from his office at the MSP's barracks in Gray to find Parker's midlife-crisis Mustang parked in the lot, and the man himself taking the cool lunchtime air, seemingly without a care in the world. Worse, he was leaning against Walsh's ride, so it would be hard to get out of the lot without running him down, not that Walsh was entirely above considering that possibility under the current circumstances.

"Hey," said Parker, just like that, as though he hadn't effectively blackmailed Walsh into silence earlier that year. Not that they'd ever exactly been close friends, but Jesus, you know . . .

"Get away from my car," said Walsh.

"This is your car?"

"You know it's my car. Step away from the vehicle. Step away from the lot. In fact, just head east and keep walking until you fall into the fucking sea."

He skirted Parker and unlocked the driver's door, but the damned private detective remained seated on the hood. Walsh got behind the wheel and started the engine. He even went so far as to give it a little gas, just in case Parker might take fright and flee, although that would have been more of a surprise than finding him there in the first place. Walsh saw a couple of officers peering over curiously. He felt as though he were having some kind of lovers' quarrel, a comparison that caused him to grit his teeth so hard that he thought he felt one of them shift in his gums.

Walsh took his foot off the gas. Parker walked to his door, and Walsh rolled down the window without looking at him.

"I'll buy you lunch," said Parker.

Walsh continued staring ahead. He thought about putting his forehead on the steering wheel and resting it there for a little while, maybe close his eyes and hope that a blackness took him, but he was afraid it might look like he was weeping.

"Cole Farms," said Parker. "Beef liver and onions. With extra bacon. I'll even spring for the Indian pudding to finish."

Walsh's shoulders sank.

"Give me the money in advance. I don't trust you to pay. I don't trust you, period."

Parker handed over two twenties.

"I may want a soda," said Walsh. "And I'm a good tipper."

Parker added another ten. Walsh dropped the cash in his cup holder.

"I'll see you there," he said. "If you die along the way, I won't miss you."

He pulled out of his parking space. By the time he got to the main road, Parker was already behind him.

*At least Ross will be pleased*, Walsh thought. Then:

*Fuck Ross.*

————

COLE FARMS HAD BEEN around for more than sixty years. It stood on Lewiston Road, close by the entrance to the Spring Meadows Golf & Country Club. The two men took a four-top, and Parker ordered a turkey sandwich while Walsh went for the promised liver and onions, with bacon and enough sides to cause the table to slope.

"You got some nerve," said Walsh, once the waitress had taken their order.

"You're still sore about Boreas."

"That's an understatement."

Parker recalled a body on a beach, bleeding into the sand. He remembered stepping over it and feeling nothing.

"I told you back then: I have no blood on my hands."

"What about on your conscience?"

"None there either, or not because of Boreas."

"That's what concerns me."

Parker brushed his fingers across the table, testing the smoothness of it, finding nothing, not even a crumb.

"There's a price to be paid for everything, Gordon," he said. It was the first time Walsh could ever remember Parker calling him by his first name. "Nothing comes free."

"I don't know what that means."

"Yes, you do. Something terrible came to an end in Boreas. I paid the price in pain. You paid it in silence."

"There are laws. I'm required to enforce them."

"Law and justice are not the same."

"I think you got away with organizing a killing. I'm reluctant to be associated with a man who could do that."

"And Ross?"

"Apparently Ross doesn't share my reservations. He told me you were on the payroll, although I understand that 'sucking from the federal tit' is the more accepted expression. You that squeezed for money?"

"It gives me flexibility. Some of my clients aren't in a position to pay much for my services."

"And then there's the price of bullets for you and your friends."

"We get a deal on those."

Walsh sat back, seemingly in disgust, but also just in time to make space for his food. There was a lot of it. Parker could see that Walsh was tempted to leave it untouched and walk away, but it smelled too good. He nibbled at an onion and was lost.

"Why are you here?" Walsh asked.

"Jerome Burnel."

Walsh looked at Parker over a French fry.

"I hear he just got out," he said.

"He came to see me."

"Why would he do that?"

"He claims he was framed."

"The kiddie porn? It wasn't my case."

"And the gas station shooting?"

"I was one of the team. Tom Stedler was lead."

"Stedler's long dead."

"Yeah. Went young. Didn't look after himself."

Walsh dipped a roll into a pile of liver and onion, making sure to get some bacon on there too.

"Thank God you learned from his mistakes," said Parker.

"I did. Never drink diet soda. At least sugar is natural."

"Burnel remembered you."

"Did he? Should I be flattered?"

"He gave the impression that you might have doubted some details about the shooting of the second man, the one who called himself Henry Forde."

Walsh shrugged. "The Dunstans corroborated Burnel's version of events. At the time, there was no appetite for tugging at threads. Forde had killed a sheriff's deputy, and he and Simus had slaughtered at least five other people. There was also the girl, Corrie Wyatt. It wouldn't have ended well for her."

"At least five others?"

"They'd cleaned the Timard house of valuables, but there were other items in the van that didn't belong to them. It took a while, but a watch found in the vehicle was traced back to a jewelry store in Rhode Island. The watch belonged to a sixty-eight-year-old man named Arthur Dines. Dines lived alone in a house just outside Westerly. The house is still there. Dines isn't."

"Where did he go?"

"My guess is into the sea, put there by Forde and his freakish half brother, and weighted down enough to keep him there."

"Wait a minute: Forde and Simus were related?"

"Twenty-five percent shared DNA, although that didn't come out until after Burnel went to jail, and wouldn't have made any difference to him anyway. You know, the brother—Simus—wore dentures, and kept a set in his pocket modified with blades. What kind of man would do something like that?"

Parker took a bite of his sandwich. It was good.

"Back to Burnel and the shooting of Forde. What was hinky?"

"Oh, just angles more than anything else. Had Forde been turning to fire a shot, as Burnel claimed, then the bullets probably wouldn't have hit him square in the back like they did. It looked to me like Forde was running—or stumbling—away when he was killed. Privately, Stedler agreed, but hey, Burnel was a hero. And he was. I'm not taking that away from him. He saved everyone in that gas station, and he faced down Forde like a gunfighter. But he did finish him off. Maybe Burnel has a streak of something in him. Call it ruthlessness, if you like. He's just harder than he looks—or was, before he went into Warren."

"He still denies that the child porn was his."

"Yeah, that was curious. He didn't cop a plea, and there was pressure on him to do it. He kept maintaining his innocence."

"Maybe because he *was* innocent."

"Do you believe him?"

"Angel does."

"And Angel is some kind of expert on sex offenders?"

"Yeah, he kind of is."

Walsh took in this information, and was silent for a while.

"If he's innocent, who set him up?" asked Walsh.

"It could have been his now ex-wife. They weren't close, to put it mildly."

"Nah," said Walsh. "There's not being close, and then there's hating, and a wife would have to hate her husband the way I hate taxes to set him up on child porn charges."

"Well, if Burnel isn't lying, then someone took the trouble to frame him. He thinks it was done because of the Dunstan killings."

"Revenge? If that was the case, then why not just shoot him?"

"Because it would be over too soon?"

"Then torture him first, and kill him later."

A woman and child who were about to sit at the table across from them reconsidered their decision and moved away. Walsh noted their departure.

"You see the effect you have on people?" he said.

"You're still here."

"You're paying for my time."

"That's bribery."

"Not if you don't get anything in return. You going to take Burnel's dime?"

"I think so."

"It won't bring you any joy."

"You'd be surprised. What about Forde and Simus?"

"No leads. They were specters."

"Fingerprints?"

"We got a partial match on Simus from a burglary in Roanoke, Virginia, in 2002. Lot of valuables taken, but the occupants were on vacation at the time. Lucky for them, because they had a nineteen-year-old daughter. Still have, thanks to a time-share in Kissimmee."

"Burnel says that both Corrie Wyatt and Paige Dunstan are missing."

Walsh picked some bacon from his teeth, scowled at it as though it had personally offended him, then ate it.

"Wyatt was a junkie."

"Before the killings?"

"No, after. Before them, she was just bait in a scam, rolling sad men for money. What happened at the Timard house broke her. She was drifting anyway, but the wind took her when her friends died."

"And Dunstan?"

"I haven't been following the case."

"But she's officially missing?"

"I'd have to check."

"Come on . . ."

"Look, last I heard she was still gone, but that doesn't mean there's a connection to what happened at her old man's gas station. Is that what Burnel is suggesting?"

"It is."

"You do know what paranoia is, right?"

"Yes."

"Well, remember that it's contagious. You should always wash your hands after contact with it."

Walsh finished his liver and onions in silence. Parker picked at his sandwich, but left most of it on the plate. He still had not fully regained his appetite. He sometimes doubted that he ever would. Walsh ordered the Indian pudding to go. He told Parker that he had somewhere he had to be. It might even have been true.

"Does Ross still pay you to report back on me?" asked Parker, as they headed for the door.

"He never paid me. I did it out of the goodness of my heart."

"And now?"

"I don't much care what happens to you one way or the other."

"But Ross does."

Walsh wouldn't meet Parker's eye.

"Yeah, he does."

"Make sure you spell all the names right for him," said Parker.

"I will," Walsh replied. "Remind me, though: do you spell 'prick' with a capital 'P'?"

———

PARKER RETURNED HOME. He did some paperwork, sent out some bills, then caught a movie alone at the Nick in Portland. He preferred the local theater to the big modern places out in Saco and Westbrook. He found the smell of it strangely comforting, although he had to stand up a couple of times and lean against a wall when his back started to hurt, but nobody minded, because he was in the last row and the theater was almost empty. Sometimes his skin felt too tight at the grafts, and at others he felt an ache where one of his kidneys used to be. While he stood, he reached instinctively for the small grip ball that he kept in his pocket, and kneaded it both to work his damaged left hand and to distract himself from the rest of his pain.

He thought of Jerome Burnel, and murderous, scavenging men.

# XXVIII

O dell Watson couldn't sleep. He was ten years old, and lived with his mother and grandmother outside Turley in a three-bedroom trailer that baked its occupants in summer and forced them to dress in layers in winter. Odell often had nightmares, but he had learned not to bother the women in his house with them. They both worked: his mother as a line cook, his grandmother as a cleaner, holding down three jobs between them, for his mother did a little cleaning on the side too, when her diner hours allowed it. She worked the breakfast shift at Shelby's Diner, so she woke at three thirty to be there by four thirty, so she could have all her prep done when the doors opened at five. Shelby's stood just on the other side of town, and Odell's mother sometimes walked to work if the weather was good, to save on gas.

It was Odell's grandmother who got him ready for school each morning and put him on the bus. Odell loved her, but she was an angry woman. She remembered her father being denied the right to vote because he couldn't say how many bubbles were in a bar of soap, or spell the word "burlesque," a term he had never heard before, and of which he did not know the meaning. When he returned two years later, he passed the literacy test, cast his vote, and immediately lost his bank credit and his job.

His grandmother was in Montgomery in 1965 when white men murdered a Michigan housewife named Viola Liuzzo, who had driven black activists from Selma to Montgomery Airport in the days when the emblem of Alabama's Democratic Party bore the words "White Supremacy." Her killers were later applauded at a Klan parade, but Odell's grandmother was among those on the courtroom steps nine months later when they were jailed for the killing. His grandmother married a man named Mason Coffee—"like the jar," as he always said—a veteran of the Korean War who served with the Deacons for Defense and Justice, black ex-soldiers who acted as armed escorts for civil rights workers in Alabama, Mississippi, and Louisiana.

Eventually, his grandmother and Mason moved back to Plassey County, West Virginia, with their only child, the girl who would become Odell's mother. Mason was now long dead, and Odell's father was gone. He lived in Baltimore, and sent money at Christmas and on Odell's birthday, if he remembered and had some cash to spare. It had been so long since Odell had seen him that he could no longer recall precisely what he looked like.

His grandmother would remind Odell that he was the man of the house now, and she told him the stories of Odell's great-grandfather and grandfather because times hadn't changed much for black folk, she warned, didn't matter what the law said. The law could be read whatever way the powerful wanted it to read. Odell only had to look out his window to see that, she said.

He only had to look at the Cut.

————

SOMETIMES HIS MOTHER OR grandmother was home when Odell got back from school, but usually the trailer was empty, which meant that Odell had already learned to take care of himself. Each weekday he let himself in, prepared a sandwich, drank some milk, did his homework, and watched TV or played with his Xbox until the women returned, often together if they'd been on the same cleaning job, both of them weary and smelling of disinfectant.

Odell worked hard at school, but he was an unusually subdued child, in part because of the life he led. He was loved at home, but it was a quiet environment, the two women spending much of their time sleeping when they were not working, leaving Odell to his own devices. When he got bored of TV or games, he read. He liked stories about spacemen, and superhero comic books. He was good at drawing, but he drew well only at home. He tried not to attract too much attention at school. Life was easier that way.

The nightmares had started coming back in recent weeks. They were always the same, in detail and in the unraveling: a girl in a torn dress, her boobies showing, running through the woods across from the trailer, drawing closer to the window from which Odell watched, and then being pulled down by the first of the dogs. After that came the men, and they called the dogs off and carried the girl away, all but the last of them, the one named Lucius. He had red hair, and kept looking back at the window from which Odell was watching through a gap in the drapes. In the nightmare, he approached the window, and Odell couldn't move. He wanted to go back to bed and pretend to be asleep, but his body wouldn't obey him and he remained frozen in place, even as he heard Lucius breathing outside his window, and saw the man's shadow moving against the far wall, his presence already invading Odell's little space.

The nightmare had returned maybe two dozen times in the years since, but five times in the last two weeks alone, and a few nights Odell woke from it because he'd peed his bed. On the first occasion, he'd been so frightened and ashamed that he'd roused the house, and his mother had cleaned him up and helped him to change his pajamas while his grandmother took the sheets from the bed and put newspaper down to dry the mattress. Both of them had been bad-tempered the next day because of their disturbed night.

The second time it happened, Odell's mother threatened to put him back in diapers, and his grandmother came home that evening with a plastic sheet that she put over the mattress, "just in case of accidents." It made Odell feel like a baby. He'd peed himself only once since then, and on that occasion he hid his pajamas under his bed, and cleaned and dried them himself when he got home from school. But the nightmare itself kept returning, and when it did he was unable to get back to sleep. He remained away from the window when he did wake, and instead reread old comic books with a flashlight under the sheets. He didn't want to use his bedside lamp. Odell's bedroom was little more than a converted storage room adjoining his mother's bedroom, but it was his space, and he loved it. He had to be careful, though, because the lamplight showed under his door. It also shone through the thin drapes, where it could be seen from the road, and Odell didn't want that to happen.

The nightmare was so persistent by now that Odell had almost forgotten it was real, all of it: the girl, the dogs, the man named Lucius—him most of all. Odell had watched it happen, except that first time—the real time—he'd managed to get back into bed before Lucius reached the window. Odell had heard his footsteps, though, and then his breathing. Odell stayed very still, and eventually Lucius went away, but Odell didn't move a muscle until he heard his mother wake hours later, just in case it was a trick and the man was still spying on him.

He could have told his mother and grandmother what he had seen. He should have, because it would have been the right thing to do, except the next day, when he was walking to the trailer from the school bus, a man had emerged from the woods next to where his mother parked her car, and the afternoon sun had caught the redness of his hair. Odell wanted to run and try to lock himself inside, but Lucius had been too fast for him, and was beside him before the message to move had even reached Odell's feet.

He knew Lucius's name because he'd heard his mother speak of him to her own mother, just as they sometimes whispered of others from the Cut: Oberon, Cassander. *But Lucius is the worst of them*, his mother would say. *The worst of any world*, his grandmother would counter.

Lucius said only one thing to Odell—"I know where your momma works. Don't make me take her for a ride."—before putting a finger to his lips, enjoining the boy to silence. Then he ruffled Odell's hair and vanished into the Cut.

Now Odell was sitting on the edge of his bed, trembling. His pajamas were wet again. He wanted to cry. That night's version of the nightmare had been a new one. This time the girl was in his room. Her boobies were very big, and as Odell stared at them little beads of milk bubbled from the nipples. The girl smelled bad. Her right thumb was missing, but the stump wasn't bleeding.

"Your momma's safe," she told Odell, and as she spoke a bug crawled through her hair. "They don't take colored folk."

That was when Odell woke, and it was all he could do not to start screaming for his momma, because he could still smell the girl in the room, just as he could smell his own pee. But he managed not to make a sound, and just sat, and shook, and wished that he'd never looked out the window that September night.

He heard a vehicle slowing down outside before grinding to a halt. Odell often heard vehicles coming and going at odd hours, because it was his family's misfortune to live within sight of one of the roads into the Cut, but they rarely stopped. A door opened. Odell didn't want to look, but a man's voice swore, and another said something in reply that Odell couldn't catch. The gap in the drapes was still visible. It drew Odell.

"No," he whispered. Why did it have to be here? Why couldn't they have stopped someplace else? The lady taken by the dogs was bad enough, but now this? Yet he was already on his feet. One step. Two. He pressed his eye to the opening.

The van was brown or black—he couldn't be sure—but he could see that the right front tire was flat. That was what the two men who stood beside it were talking about. A third joined them, and Odell recognized him from around town, although he did not know his name.

"We walk him," said the third man. "Benedict can change the tire, and follow on."

One of the others went to the side door of the van, opened it, and climbed inside. When he appeared again, he was leading a fourth man by a rope tied around his neck. This man had his hands tied behind his back, and a sack over his head. He had to be helped from the van so that he didn't stumble and fall. Once he was safely outside, the van door was closed behind him, and he was pulled toward the woods. The third man spoke to the one called Benedict, who was preparing to jack the van. When he was finished, he turned and glanced over at the Watson trailer.

*I shouldn't have done this*, thought Odell. *I shouldn't have looked.*

A hand closed over his mouth. He struggled against it until his mother's voice whispered to him.

"Hush," she said. "Hush."

She held Odell tight against her, and together they watched.

This time, unlike Lucius, the man did not approach the window. A voice called to him from the woods—"Need some help here!"—and he turned away, stepping around the front of the van and into the woods.

Odell started to cry against his mother's hand. She took it away from his mouth. His grandmother appeared at the door, a gown wrapped around her against the cold.

"I did it again, Momma," Odell whispered. "I wet myself. I'm sorry."

"Don't worry, honey," she replied. "It's not your fault. But don't say nothing about this, not to anyone, you hear me?"

He nodded. He understood. He didn't want Lucius or someone like him to take his mother for a ride. Outside, he heard Benedict remove the first of the wheel nuts.

"Come away, now," said his mother. "Come away and leave them to their business."

That night he slept in his mother's bed, wearing only clean underwear. They were both still awake—his grandmother, too, Odell guessed, because he couldn't hear her snoring—when the van eventually started up and drove away, disappearing into the forest.

Vanishing into the Cut.

Chapter

# XXIX

Sheriff Edward Henkel of the Plassey County Sheriff's Department pulled over to the side of the road and tried to control his breathing. He had almost hit a deer. He certainly would have, had he been traveling any faster, and the buck was big enough to have come through the windshield and killed him. It had appeared out of the mist so suddenly that he'd barely had a chance to register the animal before it was in front of him. He couldn't even remember hitting the brake; it was as though the car had been stopped for him by some outside agency, and his foot had ended up on the brake only as a matter of course.

Henkel's chest hurt. It had been paining him a lot lately, which was why he'd gone to see his physician in the first place. He'd been experiencing breathlessness as well, and a dizziness if he stood up too suddenly, along with nausea and lassitude, although he'd put it down to flu until the pain started. A quick Internet search revealed that, at forty-nine, Ed Henkel was experiencing all the warning signs of an impending heart attack. Like just about every man born since the time of Adam, he'd considered swallowing some medication and taking it easy for a few days because, first of all, there was no point in overreacting if it really was just the flu; and second, if he was having heart problems then his life could be about to change, and that was assuming he survived whatever was coming to begin with, because the biggest life change any man would ever experience was the ending of it.

Henkel was divorced, and his two teenage children now lived with his ex-wife and her second husband in Cleveland. Relations between them all were pretty good, even if Henkel didn't get to see his kids quite as often as he might have liked, and they were at the age when they didn't care much to be hauled off to Turley for two weekends a month just so their dad could feel like a real father once again. As a result, he'd agreed to monthly visits instead, simply to make the kids happy, and it had kind of worked: Dennis, his son, was now less hostile than he used to be when he came back to Turley, but Kim, the younger of the two, remained a monster. He was assured by other fathers with daughters of a similar age that this was not unusual among fifteen-year-old girls, and he should not take it personally. Even Irene, the woman who had bought the dry cleaners in Mortonsville, and with whom he had recently begun a tentative relationship, assured him it was just a phase and Kim would mellow in time, although this was before Irene was actually exposed to his daughter, an experience that caused her to modify her opinion somewhat, as well as consume the best part of a bottle of Merlot to help calm her nerves.

Henkel hadn't told Irene about the chest pains, or the sickness, just as he hadn't informed her of the visit to the doctor after he woke at 4:00 a.m. in agony and decided that, no, this wasn't like any flu he'd experienced before. He'd have to inform her about the subsequent angiogram, though, because they'd shaved away a section of hair at his groin in order to insert the dye tube into the blood vessel, and she'd be certain to notice any changes to his personal grooming in that area.

He wondered if death was now shadowing him.

———

THE MORTONSVILLE POLICE DEPARTMENT cruiser stood at the edge of a sparse patch of woodland that sloped down to a pond in which nothing swam or lived because of all the pollutants that had been dumped in it over the years. In summer it was a mass of insects, and gave off an acrid, chemical stink. It didn't smell a whole lot better in the fall, but at least the insects were fewer. On the other hand, the pond now appeared to have some competition in the stench stakes.

Chief Bentley himself had made the call to Henkel using his personal cell phone, so that the information didn't go out over the bands just yet. Bentley was a small, wiry man in his early sixties, and should have retired long ago, but he was tied to his town and his job. If he left the latter, then he'd probably have to leave the former, too, because he wouldn't be able to stand by and watch someone else rule the roost. Bentley was defined by his position in Mortonsville. Without it, he would feel himself to be nothing.

Now, as Henkel pulled in beside the Mortonsville car, he saw Bentley appear in a gap between the trees and wave his hat. Henkel picked up his own hat from the passenger seat, took a fresh pair of plastic gloves from the box on the floor, and trudged down to join him. The last of the season's flies buzzed around, and in the clear morning light he thought he could see a larger cloud of them deeper in the woods. He picked up the odor of decay as he drew closer, and was relieved when the first thing that Bentley did, even before they began to speak, was hand over a tube of mentholated ointment. Henkel smeared it over his top lip and around his nostrils. The smell was still there, but the menthol took the edge from it.

Henkel slipped on his gloves, and Bentley did the same with the pair hanging from a pocket of his pants.

"Who found them?" asked Henkel, the first word he'd spoken since he arrived.

"Charlie Lutter's boy."

"Uh-huh."

Perry Lutter was simple. He had a part-time job at Shelby's Diner washing dishes and sweeping floors, and liked to draw pictures of zoo animals to give to folks. He was the Lutters' only child, born when they were in their forties. Both were nearly eighty now, and Henkel wasn't sure what would happen to their son when they were gone. He figured the boy would have to go into some kind of home, because he sure couldn't take care of himself.

"He told his mother," said Bentley, "and then his father called me. He asked if the boy's name could be kept out of it. I said I'd do my best."

The bodies lay partly uncovered in a pit at the heart of the copse. Bentley saw animal tracks in the dirt—fox, probably, although he wasn't any kind of expert. His first thought was that the hole should have been dug deeper, maybe with stones laid on top of the remains, except there weren't many stones nearby fit for purpose. It suggested a rushed job, or the work of someone who didn't much care if the remains were found.

The bodies were both male, and Henkel thought they'd been in the ground for possibly a week. Maybe it was the way they'd landed in the hole, but they lay side by side, one with his head on the chest of the other, an arm draped loosely around him in an embrace reminiscent of consolation. They'd both been shot in the head at close range, the caliber of the bullet big enough to leave massive exit wounds that had distorted their features even before rot started to have its way with them.

"You look for ID?" asked Henkel.

"I checked their pockets, but they're empty. I didn't want to go disturbing them more than was necessary."

Henkel squatted by the grave. He wished that he'd used more of the menthol. Judging by their clothing and general appearance, he thought the victims might be in their late twenties, or even a few years younger. One of them had a barbed-wire tattoo around his right wrist. That might help with formal identification, although already Henkel had some idea of who they might be, and suspected that Bentley did, too.

"Dustin Huff," said Henkel, pointing at the body with the tattoo, the one with its arm draped around the other.

"Which makes the other Robbie Killian," said Bentley.

"Would be my guess."

Killian and Huff were out of Columbus, Ohio originally, but with business interests in West Virginia. They'd begun by selling weed, and quickly progressed to OxyContin, meth, and whatever else the market could bear. They were ambitious, and word was they'd cut a deal back home with some Mexicans to sell and distribute heroin. Killian's family was wealthy, at least by the standards of this part of the world, and willing to indulge their son with money as long as he stayed out of their hair, a source of funds from which Huff and Killian had drawn to start their enterprise. Sensibly, they'd stayed away from Plassey County, or so it had seemed until a kid named Lucie Holmes overdosed at a party in Deep Dell a few weeks back and almost died. Although nobody could confirm it, the suspicion was that the heroin she'd injected had been supplied, directly or indirectly, by Killian and Huff. Plassey County was an untapped market, and emboldened by their connections, the two young men had decided to make it theirs.

Then they had disappeared, and Killian's folks, though hardly in line for any awards for good parenting, were sufficiently concerned about their son's well-being to kick up a fuss, and Huff's widowed mother had added her voice to that of her wealthier neighbors. Now here were their sons, rotting in a shallow grave.

"This is Cut work," said Henkel.

"We don't know that for sure."

"Not many others around here who'd put two boys in the ground like this."

"Maybe these boys crossed their Mexican friends over in Columbus," said Bentley.

Henkel knew what the older man was doing. He might have enjoyed being chief, but like every other lawman in the county, going back to a time when they wore gun belts and handlebar mustaches, the pleasure and satisfaction that he took in his job were inversely proportional to his degree of involvement with the Cut.

"If they crossed men back home, then they'd be buried in a hole in Ohio. There'd be no percentage in coming all the way over here to get rid of them."

Bentley used his hat to swat at the flies, as though they represented all that was now troubling him, right down to their persistence in refusing to be dismissed.

"The Cut's been quiet for a long time," he said.

"Or just careful."

"Comes back to how this might not be something to be laid at their doorstep," said Bentley, grabbing at another straw. "Habitually, when they put someone in the ground, that person has a way of staying there."

"Yeah, well, even Homer nods."

"I don't know what that means."

"Means everybody makes mistakes."

Bentley stared down at the bodies.

"You know what Russ Dugar would have done with them?"

Dugar was the sheriff in Plassey County before Henkel, and a legendary figure in local law enforcement. Dugar hated being behind a desk, and consequently was the last lawman in Plassey to be killed in the course of duty—shot and left to die by the side of the road after stopping a man named Owen Bick on suspicion of DUI, only to discover that Bick was drenched in blood, having just killed his wife, and was in no mood to explain the situation to anyone, least of all the sheriff's department. Dugar died in the dirt, and Bick drove off having at last grasped the necessity of changing his clothes and dumping the car. He managed to remain undetected for three days, but it was his misfortune not to be found by the police but by the Cut, or so the rumor went, which had an understanding with Dugar, and was unhappy to find it threatened by Bick's actions. Bick's body was found hanging upside down from a tree just across the county line, suspended by wire over the remains of the fire that had been lit beneath him, scorching his head and torso black.

"Yeah, I know what he would have done," said Henkel. Dugar would have taken a spade from the trunk of his car, covered his face with a handkerchief, and reburied these bodies properly, and not another word would have been said about the whole affair. In the world inhabited by Dugar and his kind, Killian and Huff were asking for trouble, and shouldn't have been surprised when it answered their summons. Dugar's position on the Cut had always been clear: he wouldn't interfere with it as long as no civilians got hurt, and it went about its business without drawing too much attention to itself.

Dugar, his successor reflected, was almost certainly burning in hell.

Henkel heard a vehicle pulling up on the road above. Bentley went to see who it was, and returned accompanied by Rob Channer, who was one of Henkel's deputies, and far from his favorite. Henkel had effectively been arm-twisted into hiring him, and although the younger man was smart and efficient, Henkel had never warmed to him, for Channer made no secret of his ambition to be Plassey County's youngest sheriff ever.

Channer didn't seem bothered by the smell of the bodies. If anything, Henkel might have said that it appeared to excite him, but perhaps he was allowing his antipathy to color his worldview.

"Man, somebody sent those boys to the Lord with a vengeance," said Channer. "Woo!"

"How'd you find us, Rob?" asked Henkel.

"I passed Charlie Lutter's place, and he was having some trouble with Perry. Dummy laid his pop on his ass right on the front lawn. I thought I'd have to taser him. Between me and Charlie we got him calmed down, and that's when Charlie told me what happened."

Henkel would have put Channer in the ground beside Killian and Huff if he'd dared to taser Perry Lutter, but he said nothing about it. He took a final look at the bodies before ordering Channer to get the tarp from the trunk of his car. There were clouds forming, and he didn't want rain to wash away any evidence.

"Nothing more we can do for them now," he said. "Time to call it in."

While the Lutter farm was under the jurisdiction of Mortonsville, the bodies had been discovered outside the town limits, but neither Henkel nor Bentley had the resources to undertake a murder investigation. This was a matter for the state police.

Bentley didn't move, and Henkel saw that Channer had paused upon hearing Henkel's words, and was looking back at them.

"Be a good idea if word got out that these bodies have been found," said Bentley, and Henkel knew just what he meant.

*Tell the Cut, and do it before the detectives get here.*

"Everyone will know soon enough," Henkel replied.

"Yeah, but—"

Henkel faced down Bentley.

"I can't stop you from making personal calls, or even driving away from here," he said, "but if there's a problem, and the state police or the feds come sniffing around, you'd better be able to explain every action you took from the time this grave was found. That goes for you too, Rob. Understand?"

After a pause, Channer nodded. Bentley shrugged.

"I didn't mean anything by it," he said.

*The hell you didn't*, thought Henkel.

"Go on, now, Rob. Get that tarp. I'll inform the state police"—he turned again to Bentley—"unless you'd prefer to do it."

"It's all yours," said Bentley, but he had the decency not to look Henkel in the eye.

"Yeah," said Henkel. "That's what I figured you'd say."

He followed Channer up the slope, leaving Bentley behind to blend in with the general stink of corruption.

Chapter

Parker was drinking coffee at the Speckled Ax on Congress while reading about plans for another big development down by the Old Port and wondering how long the Portland he loved would continue to exist.

He could just about remember a time when the Old Port catered mostly to drunken lobstermen and the kind of sailors who gave the shipping business a bad name. Back in the early seventies, when he and his parents would come to Maine to visit his grandfather during the summer, they had avoided the area around Commercial Street. It wasn't just rough: it was actively dangerous. But most of the places that had once given the city its original tough reputation were gone. Four decades earlier, the city had sourced a federal grant to improve the Old Port area, and paid men on welfare to lay paving stones and plant trees. A handful of developers began buying properties in bulk on Fore and Wharf streets, recognizing that, if the Old Port was to thrive, it needed restaurants and bars, and not the kind of bars where tourists might get their heads busted by fishermen. A certain amount of character was sacrificed along the way, but for a time a balance was achieved between the city as it was and the developers' transformative vision of what it might become.

But for Parker and those like him, the Old Port now had too many hotels, and most people of his acquaintance couldn't afford to eat in the new restaurants that were opening down there. Somewhere along the way, the city had decided to transform itself into a gourmets' paradise, with cuisine and prices to match, which was all fine as long as the economy didn't tank again. Those outlets sat slightly uneasily alongside the noisy tourist bars on Wharf Street, whose drunken revelers attracted an unavoidable police presence. Back in the day, order in the Old Port had been maintained by a single female police sergeant mounted on a horse notorious for its meanness, but the Portland PD had dispensed with mounted patrols back in the 1990s, and now policing the Old Port required cars and multiple uniforms.

Meanwhile, the city had finally managed to close Sangillo's Tavern on Hampshire Street, the last of the Old Port's true dive bars. The closure had been on the cards ever since a shooting outside Sangillo's had left a kid in his twenties paralyzed, but it was still a shame to see it go after fifty years. The Fulci brothers, who had once removed the tavern's door to use as a battering ram in the course of a fight, were inconsolable.

Parker drank his Americano and watched the bums go by on Congress. The street still maintained its eccentricity—Strange Maine continued to sell VHS tapes, cassettes, vinyl records, and games for consoles that no longer existed, and the Green Hand, Yes Books, and Longfellow flew the flag for the printed word, alongside galleries and smoke shops and even the Video Expo adult superstore—but the encroachment of upscale restaurants had already begun even this far west of the port, and it wasn't hard to see a time when the folks who lived in the public housing along the street would be shuffled off to the margins where they wouldn't offend tourist sensibilities.

His phone vibrated. He'd muted the ringtone so it wouldn't annoy the other customers around him. He had decided that when he became governor, or world ruler—whichever came first—he'd pass a law forcing people to make and take all cell phone calls outside bars and restaurants, on pain of having their phones confiscated, or fed to them. He looked at the screen and saw that it was Gordon Walsh calling. He was surprised. They'd parted on better terms than before, but that wasn't saying much.

Parker picked up his coffee and stepped outside.

"Good morning, Detective Walsh," he said.

He didn't receive a greeting in return.

"Jerome Burnel just went off the reservation," said Walsh. "He missed a mandatory meeting with his probation officer, and he hasn't been seen at his apartment since yesterday."

Parker closed his eyes.

"Damn," he said.

"He may be running," said Walsh. "He wouldn't be the first."

"I need to make some calls. Who's his probation officer?"

"A guy named Chris Attwood. Seems okay. He waited until this morning before sounding the alarm. Said he wanted to give Burnel a chance."

Would it have made any difference if Attwood had called it in sooner? Parker wondered. Probably not. He wasn't entirely ruling out the possibility that Burnel had decided to take his chances elsewhere. Even if he had been telling the truth at the Great Lost Bear, and he was marked, it didn't mean he had to sit tight and wait for them to come for him. Yet Burnel didn't seem as though he had the energy to flee. The simple act of telling his story to Parker had used him up, leaving him exhausted. He had barely been able to walk to his cab. Simply recounting his version of events, and telling a tale that might not be believed but needed to be shared regardless, had counted as an act of rebellion for him.

"Have they searched his apartment?"

A probation officer didn't require a warrant to search a probationer's place of residence, just as a warrant wasn't required to rearrest him if he was in violation of the terms of his probation.

"They went in an hour ago. He didn't leave a note, if that's what you're asking."

"Any signs of a struggle?"

"None. Still committed to taking him on as a client?"

"Maybe."

"Then I hope he paid you in advance."

"That's one of the calls I need to make. I'll get back to you."

"Not my case. I just thought you'd be interested."

"Thanks. I mean it."

"Look, you may hear from Attwood. I gave him a call and told him Burnel had been in touch with you. Your prospective client is now officially in breach of the conditions of his probation. Unless he has a good excuse, there's a cell waiting for him in the county jail."

Parker didn't care too much whether Attwood contacted him or not. He had nothing to hide, and would give Attwood whatever information Burnel had shared, or most of it. First, though, he would take a ride over to Burnel's lawyer and find out if Burnel had left the envelope of money with him as he'd promised. It wasn't that Parker wanted it, but someone who was hoping to hide from the law would need all the cash he could lay his hands on. If Burnel had deposited the envelope with his lawyer, then he hadn't run.

He'd been taken.

Jerome Burnel's lawyer was a man named Oleg Castin, otherwise known as Moxie Castin, who operated out of an office on Marginal Way. He was famous in Maine legal circles for his inability to function without a can of Maine's favorite carbonated beverage to hand. Back in the nineteenth century, Moxie had been marketed as a patent medicine to cure paralysis, softening of the brain, and impotence. The pitch was entirely true, if Castin was anything to go by, since he ran marathons, had a genius-level IQ, and was reputed to be a penile swordsman of the highest order. Not that anyone would have known this by looking at him, since Moxie was about five-six and at least sixty pounds overweight, with the face and manner of a squirrel that was about to settle into hibernation.

There was no secretary at the reception desk when Parker arrived, but he glimpsed Castin through the open office door, lying back in his chair. Castin was wearing a pink shirt and yellow suspenders, and his pinstriped legs were resting on the open bottom drawer of his desk. His hands were clasped across his belly, and the face on his watch was big enough to adorn a church steeple. He managed to keep one eye open while Parker entered and took a seat.

"You're disturbing my nap," said Castin.

"I hope these aren't someone's billable hours."

"I do all my best thinking when I'm at rest, which also allows me to expend huge amounts of energy elsewhere in short bursts."

Parker had an uncomfortable image of a tumescent Moxie in situ with one of his many female conquests, expending some of that energy. Sometimes he worried about the workings of his imagination.

"I really don't want to know," said Parker.

"You here about Jerome Burnel?"

"That's right."

"I advised him not to hire you, but he wouldn't listen. You'll need to sign for the money."

The lawyer didn't appear to be unduly troubled by his client's apparent disappearance, even by his own mellow standards.

"You didn't hear?" said Parker.

Castin opened his other eye and turned his head toward Parker. In a more demonstrative man, it would have been the equivalent of grabbing the private detective by the throat and shaking the relevant information out of him.

"Hear what?"

"He didn't make his probation session yesterday. As of today, he's in violation."

"Why the fuck does nobody tell me anything?"

"You could try answering your phone."

"I got stuff to do this afternoon," said Moxie. "I need to build up my reserves."

He let his feet drop and swiveled his chair so that he was facing Parker. He picked up the desk phone and called Attwood, confirmed what Parker had already told him, and hung up.

"Hell," said Castin.

He reached for the can of his namesake soda that stood on the desk, drained it empty, tossed it into a basket in the corner, and retrieved another from a small fridge below the window.

"You want one?"

"No, thanks. I just had coffee. You think he ran?"

"He wasn't the kind."

"I don't know him as well as you, but that was my impression as well. How much money can he lay hands on?"

"I can't tell you that."

"Come on, Moxie."

"You taking the case?"

"I wouldn't be here otherwise."

Castin unlocked the topmost desk drawer, withdrew the padded envelope that Burnel had dropped off the previous morning, and handed it to Parker, along with a receipt book.

"Sign there."

Parker signed.

"So," said Parker, "does Burnel have access to funds?"

"Not much," said Castin. "I've had power of attorney over his accounts since he was inside. Most of his money's gone. Aside from what's in that envelope, there's just a couple of grand left, at most."

"Can you check to see if he made a withdrawal either yesterday or today?"

Castin accessed the account online.

"It's still there."

"Who runs without money?" asked Parker.

"Nobody."

"You defended him. Did you think he did it?"

"The porn thing? I didn't ask. It was none of my business."

"But he denied it."

"Yes."

"And did you believe him?"

"He wouldn't cop a plea. That's unusual. We had some traction because of what he'd done—you know, the shooting thing. I tried to convince him that it might be in his best interests to take a deal, but he sat tight."

"So?"

"That doesn't mean he didn't do it. He'd seen enough movies to know that anything involving kids and sex was going to make him unpopular in Warren. He didn't want to do any time at all. I don't blame him. You could take the view that he gambled and lost."

"But if he was telling the truth?"

"In the end, the truth doesn't matter. What matters is what they can prove, and what I can prove or disprove in turn. If their proof is better than mine, then I lose, and my client loses. I lost, and so Burnel lost too."

"Even for a lawyer, you're kind of cynical."

"Bleakly realistic. Privately, just sitting here and talking, Burnel seemed shocked at what had been found in his house, and it wasn't just surprise at being caught. But if he didn't acquire those images, then a person or persons conspired to make it look like he did. It's not impossible, but the 'Burnel is guilty' story was an easier sell."

He took another gulp of soda.

"Look, I probably did believe he was innocent, okay? The firm had represented him in the past—small stuff, all civil. I liked him. Still do."

"And you remained in contact with him while he was in Warren?"

"That's right. I don't believe in abandoning clients. I help where I can. I arranged an apartment for him on release, and I managed to find him a job, too. He told me he was going to take it when last we spoke."

"Which was when?"

"Yesterday morning."

"Did he say anything about the meeting with Attwood?"

"Just that he would be heading to Washington Avenue later that afternoon. He didn't sound like he had too much of a problem with going. It was early days for him. The frustration hadn't set in yet."

Parker heard a door open behind him as Castin's secretary returned. She was in her late fifties, and looked like she'd have kicked Moxie in the nuts if he'd tried anything.

"What was his wife like?" asked Parker.

"Hard. She stood by him at the start, and was present in court, but they weren't close, and neither of them pretended that the marriage wasn't heading for the rocks. It wasn't a big surprise when she filed for divorce."

"Any idea where she is now?"

"She left town. I think she was from somewhere in Virginia, or could be West Virginia, and she went back down there. No, wait: Ohio. She's somewhere in Ohio. Sounds like a song title, doesn't it? They'd been married for eight years when Burnel was convicted, and the judge ordered standard general support, which is half the term of the marriage, so she got four years of alimony, along with some traditional support for relocation. All that ended a few months ago. I can access the payment records for you, and find out the location of her bank."

"It would be a help."

Castin tapped the can on his desk.

"Maybe he'll show up," he said. "Some of them panic after release. The transition is just too damn hard. They get drunk, they get high, head to Florida—whatever. I'll make some calls, see if I can limit the damage."

He drained the second can and sent it the way of the first, then picked up his spectacles and gestured at the envelope.

"He told me that he didn't want a contract drawn up. He said I was just to give you the money."

"I'll keep a record of my hours, and return what I don't earn."

"I have a feeling you'll earn it all," he said, and he wasn't trying to be smart. "I'd recommend signing a general agreement with this firm, though. You'll get the protection of privilege, not that you're the kind of man who wouldn't be open and helpful with law enforcement if asked."

He produced a document from a folder and made some amendments to it in pen before handing it to Parker, who glanced over it before signing.

"I'll put together a file of relevant material and e-mail it to you," said Castin. "Hard copies, too, if you want them."

"Print everything, if you don't mind. Call me when it's ready, and I'll come by and pick it up. Do you have a spare key to his apartment?"

Castin searched another drawer, found a bunch of keys, and removed one marked with blue tape.

"Try not to disturb the neighbors."

"You own the apartment?"

"I own the whole building."

For a moment, Parker thought he should have become a lawyer. He could have learned to live with the shame if it enabled him to own apartment blocks.

"One last thing," he said.

"Yes?"

"Did Burnel ever mention a man named Harpur Griffin?"

Castin's face creased in pain.

"He did. He said Griffin made life hard for him inside. I tried to help by making some calls, and I think things eased up for a while, but, you know . . ."

He began flicking through the Rolodex on his desk, already working on putting out the fires that threatened to burn his client's bridges entirely. His hands paused in their work.

"He didn't run," he said.

"No, I don't think he did."

Castin nodded.

"He didn't believe he was a hero. He said he just got scared and shot some guys."

"I can understand that."

"Yes," said Castin, "maybe you can."

Chapter

# XXXII

P arker drove over to Burnel's building, and found the superintendent who had admitted Attwood and another probation officer
to Burnel's apartment that morning. Apparently Burnel wasn't
the only probationer living in the block, and the super knew the procedure when the probation officers came calling, which was why he
hadn't even bothered informing the management company that looked
after the building on Castin's behalf.

It didn't take long for Parker to search the apartment, because it was
small and Burnel hadn't been out of prison long enough to accumulate many possessions. He called Castin from the bedroom to find out
if Burnel had a storage unit, and if he'd removed much from it since his
release. Castin confirmed that he had rented a unit for Burnel out by the
Maine Mall, and had driven him there the day after his release. Burnel
had removed only one suitcase filled with clothes, and not much else.
Parker asked him to check with the storage company that the unit had
not been visited since then, as he didn't think the company would tell
him if he asked, and he wasn't in the mood for arguing with a function-
ary. Castin said he'd get his secretary to do it, and a few minutes later she
called Parker back to tell him that the unit had not been accessed again.
Parker thanked her, and stared for a time into Burnel's small closet. It
contained just a single suitcase, and enough shoes and clothing to fill it.

*Bad*, he thought. *Very bad.*

He then called Chris Attwood, and explained that he was working for Moxie Castin, and had been engaged to establish the whereabouts of Jerome Burnel. If he found him, he said, he'd bring him back to Attwood, and it would be up to Castin to work something out on behalf of his client. In return, Parker asked Attwood if Burnel had seemed troubled during his initial dealings with his department. Attwood told him that he hadn't been given a chance to get to know Burnel well enough to make a judgment, but his initial impression was of a man who was more sad than angry. He then informed Parker about the results of the polygraph examination, and his decision to order another.

"Why?" asked Parker.

"To make sure I wasn't wrong about him."

"In what way?"

"I didn't think he was sociopathic, but the first polygraph was clean enough to make me suspect he might be."

"Unless he was just telling the truth."

"That possibility had also crossed my mind," said Attwood, "but we're still looking for him. Innocent or not, he's under my supervision. Unless he's being held under duress, or is lying in a hospital bed with memory loss, he's in breach of his conditions of probation."

"You were at his apartment earlier, right?"

"Yeah."

"Well, I'm there now. Burnel's clothes are still in his closet, along with his suitcase. If he has any money, it's only pocket change, and he has nowhere to go anyway."

"There's always someplace to go, even if it's only someplace else."

"You should go into the fortune cookie business."

"If you hear of an opening, let me know."

Attwood hung up, leaving Parker in the silence of Burnel's apartment. Three rooms, the largest of them smaller than Parker's bathroom, and all smelling faintly of dust, cleaning products, and lost hope. Parker wouldn't have blamed Burnel for running. He might have run himself, in the same situation, but he'd have planned far enough ahead to make sure that he packed a change of clothing.

The superintendent was waiting for him in the lobby.

"Are you going to be coming back?" he asked.

"No."

"Is Burnel?"

"Nobody's coming back," said Parker.

"Does Mr. Castin know?"

Parker took in the empty lobby, the battered tables, the mismatched chairs.

"Yes," he said, "Mr. Castin knows."

# XXXIII

Parker called Angel from outside the apartment building.

"Burnel's gone," he said.

"What are you going to do?"

"Look for him."

"Any idea where?"

"No, but I know who I'm going to ask first."

Angel was silent as he thought about the problem.

"Harpur Griffin?"

"You read my mind."

"Can we come too?"

"I'll let you know when I think I've found him. I did get the feeling that you wanted to meet him."

"I want to hurt him."

"Maybe," said Parker. "Once you get to know him better."

# XXXIV

The Porterhouse stood on a block in South Portland that couldn't have been further from gentrification if it was permanently on fire. Its exterior was entirely black, with some painted green shamrocks added to one wall in a nod to Irish authenticity, along with an attempt at a single sad leprechaun whose shillelagh had been replaced by a poor, if optimistic, impression of an erect penis. In reality the Porterhouse was Irish in the same way Caesars Palace in Vegas was Roman, although they had this much in common: both had staged a lot of fights.

The Porterhouse's reputation for violence was so well known that it was referred to locally as the Slaughterhouse. Nobody had actually died there, not yet, possibly because someone took the trouble to drag the wounded to the nearest patch of waste ground and let them expire off the premises. It was the kind of bar where everybody knew your name, as long as your name was "Motherfucker."

Parker summoned Angel and Louis to join him once he'd confirmed, through delicate questioning and a total outlay of fifty dollars in tongue-loosening money, that Harpur Griffin was at the bar. It had taken Parker twenty-four hours to track him down, which was too long for his liking, allowing for the size of the greater Portland area. Sometimes, though, people just didn't want to be found.

Those who gave their custom to the Porterhouse didn't care much for having their afternoon drinking disturbed for any reason. It was possible that Griffin might have been changed for the better by his time at Warren, and would welcome them with open arms, but everything Parker had learned about him suggested otherwise, not least the fact that he did his drinking in the Porterhouse.

"You been in this place much?" asked Angel, as they pulled up outside.

"Yeah, I come here all the time. I was thinking of asking them to host Sam's next birthday party."

"Really? First you might have to get them to scrub the cock from that leprechaun's fist. He looks like he has a hell of a grip for a little man."

"I ought to warn you," Parker told Louis. "They won't have seen anything like you before."

"You mean black, or gay?"

"No, just clean."

———

THE INTERIOR OF THE Porterhouse wasn't terrible. The windows could have been a little bigger, and the wood a little lighter, but it smelled no worse than most of the bars in town, and considerably better than some. The music was generic adult rock, but not so loud as to rattle a hangover, and a couple of the bottles outside the well indicated a familiarity with decent liquor, even if none appeared ever to have been opened. It was the clientele that brought the tone of the place down. If they weren't the dregs of humanity, they were at least on nodding terms with them on this particular Saturday afternoon.

The woman seated on the stool nearest the door wore a white sweatshirt bearing the Stars and Stripes, and the slogan "These Colors Don't Run," which might have been more affecting if the colors hadn't actually run, staining the sweatshirt a faint pink. Her hands were so weighed down with rings and bangles that it should have been a struggle for her to lift her glass to her mouth, but judging by the bleary eyes she turned on the new arrivals, she seemed to Parker to be managing just fine. Her hair was streaked red and blond, as though an ice cream had melted on her head, and she bore a tattoo of a black rose on the left side of her neck. She looked past Parker and Angel to take in Louis, who watched a succession of feelings play out on her face—curiosity, mild lust, confusion, and irritation—until ingrained racism won the day and she turned away with an expression that suggested the Porterhouse's already poor standard of clientele had just plummeted to new lows.

To the right of the door sat a pair of skinny twentysomething guys wearing oversize jeans, wife-beater shirts, and the kind of tribal arm tattoos that seemed to be obligatory for every knucklehead who didn't belong to a real tribe. They were drinking Pabst Blue Ribbon and keeping track of their progress by stacking the ring pulls. Unlike the woman, they barely glanced at the new arrivals. Parker reckoned that if the cops took them into the parking lot, then turned them upside down and shook them, pills would drop from their pockets like hailstones from a doper's dream sky.

Farther back, the bar drifted into semidarkness, although Parker could just about pick out in the murk a hand-lettered sign reading SMOKING AREA, taped to a steel door in the far wall. True to form, the bartender had tattoos as well. The first read "Know Thyself" and ran along his left forearm. The second, on the inside of his right arm, announced "I Will Fear No Evil." He was in his forties, and heavy without running too much to fat. His eyes suggested that he had seen just about every kind of misfortune that a place like the Porterhouse could attract, but wouldn't be surprised if he might be about to see some more.

"Help you?" he asked.

"We're looking for a man named Harpur Griffin. Someone said that he was here."

One of the tribesmen at the table by the door lifted his head, but didn't move. Louis, who wasn't watching him, continued not watching him, except more closely than before.

"Someone, huh?"

"Yeah, someone," said Parker. "It might have been his mother. She's worried about him. She thinks he's not eating his greens."

The bartender nodded.

"Sounds like a nice lady. You a cop?"

"Licensed investigator."

"These two?"

"Concerned private citizens."

"Identification?"

Parker handed it over. The bartender spent a long time looking at it, long enough to let one of the two tribesmen, the one who had not reacted to Griffin's name, pick up a pack of cigarettes from the table and start to drift toward the door at the rear. He stopped in surprise when Louis, who had so far largely kept his back to him, shifted marginally in his direction and asked, "Where are you going?"

The tribesman held up his cigarettes.

"Smoke, man."

"Sit the fuck down," said Louis.

The tribesman sat the fuck down. He exchanged a look with his pal, who shook his head. The bartender, who had taken all this in, returned Parker's ID.

"We done delaying?" asked Parker.

"Just being careful," said the bartender.

"Great. Is Griffin outside?"

"Yeah."

"Alone?"

"No, he has two guys with him."

"You know them?"

The bartender shook his head. "From away."

"And these two?" Parker jerked a thumb at the tribesmen.

"Just trying to do a good deed. They didn't mean no harm." The bartender extended his upper body across the bar, in the manner of a man about to share a great secret. "Listen, I don't want any trouble."

Parker leaned in as well.

"Seriously, have you seen where you work?" he said. "Somewhere back there, I bet there's a mop sitting in a bucket of bloody water. If you didn't want trouble, you should have found employment someplace safer, like Fallujah or Kabul. Now we're going outside to talk with Harpur Griffin. We'll take three sodas, just so you don't feel like we're freeloading."

Parker placed a ten on the bar, and the bartender poured them three plastic glasses of soda over ice. They carried their drinks to the smoking area. The main door to the Porterhouse opened behind them, but nobody looked back, so absorbed were they by the progress of Parker and his associates.

As soon as they were gone, one of the tribesmen took his cell phone from his pocket and started to dial. A shadow fell over him, which was immediately joined by a second. It was as though a pair of mountains had just dropped from space and landed in the Porterhouse. If the bartender had started to believe that his day couldn't possibly get any worse, he was about to be profoundly disillusioned.

The tribesman, whose name was Dale Pittsky, discovered the massive twin bulks of the Fulci brothers staring down at him. They'd had difficulty parking, a consequence of owning a truck that was like a building on wheels.

The Fulci brothers rarely blessed the Porterhouse with their business. They preferred to avoid blighted institutions on the grounds that they brought their own trouble with them, and so drinking somewhere like the Porterhouse was like taking sand to a desert. They were on new medication, according to Louis, but it didn't appear to be working any better than the old one, although Paulie Fulci claimed it made everything taste like Grape-Nuts.

Tony Fulci reached out and took Dale's phone from his hand. It was an old flip-top, and Tony stared at it curiously, the way a paleontologist might have examined a particularly obscure fossil.

"I didn't think they still made these," said Tony. He handed the phone to Paulie, who amused himself by flipping it open and closed with a thumb that was roughly the size and shape of the top of a hammer. His fun came to an end when the phone snapped, leaving the screen dangling by a wire. Paulie shook it, like a cat trying to understand why a dead mouse wouldn't play anymore.

"That was the guy's fuckin' phone, man," said Tony.

"Sorry," said Paulie. He handed the stricken instrument back to Dale.

"It doesn't matter," said Dale.

"You know," Tony told Dale, "they got these things called smart-phones now. You should ask for an upgrade."

"I'll do that."

"Who were you calling?" said Tony.

"Nobody," said Dale.

"Aw, you must have been trying to call somebody. Here, why don't you use mine?"

Tony handed Dale a phone the size of a cinder block, encased in rubber.

"You don't mind if we listen in, do you?" asked Tony. "I mean, you might be calling France, or—" He tried to think of another country right off the top of his head, and failed, so settled for "somewhere."

Dale didn't take the phone. He was seriously wishing he'd never left the house that day. Fuck Harpur Griffin. Dale barely knew him anyway, and no longer saw any percentage in making a call for help on Griffin's behalf.

"It's not urgent," said Dale.

"If you're sure," said Tony. The massive phone vanished into one of the pockets of his jacket, causing it to bulge like a tumor. "In that case, why don't you just sit and wait until our friends have concluded their business, and then we'll be on our way."

Tony gestured to the bartender.

"You got any board games?"

"No."

Tony shrugged and turned back to Dale.

"You know any songs?"

# XXXV

The three men were sitting behind the Porterhouse, smoking around a wire-spool table with sawed-off beer cans as ashtrays. Parker had a description of Harpur Griffin, supplemented by a couple of mug shots courtesy of Moxie Castin's contacts. Griffin was the kind of man who had probably skated by on looks and a certain superficial charm in his youth, but his stocks of both were dwindling and he had nothing with which to replace them. His features were fading into vacuity, and his charm had curdled to sleaze. Jail must have been hard for him at the start. What Griffin inflicted on Burnel had probably been visited on him earlier in his incarceration. He was not tall—five-five or five-six—and wore dark blue Levi's, tan cowboy boots, and a white shirt. His hair was long and blond, and he was laughing about something, displaying yellowed jail teeth. The tabletop was littered with bottles of Bud and a handful of shot glasses, although the glasses—and most of the bottles—seemed to be piling up at Griffin's side of the table.

He was seated so that he was facing away from the back door of the bar, which meant he was careless, drunk, or simply didn't believe he had any cause for concern. Then again, it might have been the men with Griffin who provided him with an enhanced sense of personal security. The one nearest the door wore black jeans and a black shirt buttoned to the neck, along with a gray fleece to keep out the gathering chill that didn't appear to be bothering Griffin. He had scuffed black work boots on his feet, and hands that had put in some heavy manual labor. His hair was brown running to gray, and his face was heavily lined around the eyes and mouth, and pitted with flecks of black, as though a gun had once gone off too close to him. He had picked at the label on his bottle, and made a pile of the shreds on the table.

The one who sat alongside him was like a fox in human form. His features were distorted so that his nose and mouth were strangely elongated, lending him his vulpine aspect, accentuated by red hair flecked with silver, and sideburns that extended neatly almost to the corners of his mouth. His eyes were a very dark brown, and the nails on his fingers had been trimmed to points. He seemed almost to snarl at the three men approaching him, baring his teeth to reveal the spaces between them, so that they resembled pale fence posts long stripped of their wire.

The Gunpowdered Man and the Fox: they were quite the pair.

As though to a prearranged signal, Parker, Angel, and Louis spread out, never taking their eyes from the two silent men, for they, and not Griffin, were unmistakably the threat. Griffin, realizing suddenly that he had lost the attention of his listeners, turned to face the newcomers, but did not rise. He was that smart, at least.

"Help you?" said Griffin.

"I hope so," said Parker. He gave Griffin his attention, knowing that Angel and Louis had the other two marked. "I was wondering if you'd heard from Jerome Burnel lately."

"I don't think I know that name," said Griffin.

"You were in Warren with him."

"I was in Warren with a lot of guys. Pardon me, but I don't think you've told us your name."

He put the emphasis on both "us" and "your," which gave Parker all he needed to know about him. Griffin would always rely on a pack for support. Alone, he'd run.

"My name is Charlie Parker. I'm a private investigator. I could give you a card, but I figure your friend there would probably just add it to his collection of torn paper."

The Gunpowdered Man's face had not moved a muscle. He hadn't even blinked much, as far as Parker could tell. Parker thought that he'd encountered human-shaped voids like this one before: they could skin a man alive without breaking a sweat or quickening their pulse.

"I don't believe I have to answer any questions from a private investigator," said Griffin.

"That's right, you don't. But here's how it goes: you don't talk to me, and I feed you to the police, and then you have to get all lawyered up if you decide not to answer their questions. It's easier just to deal with me."

"And your friends—are they private investigators too?"

"No, they're just private."

Griffin took a sip of beer to give himself time to think.

"Just private," he said. "I like that."

"Aren't you going to make the introductions?" asked Parker. "Shame to have us all out here, and nobody knowing anyone's name but yours and mine."

"My friends are private too," said Griffin.

"From away, is what I hear."

Louis shifted his weight, like a big cat vacillating between a stretch and a pounce.

"These are Southern boys," he said, "the low-down kind." Louis sniffed the air, then added: "I can smell it on them—all grease, and blood, and damned ignorance."

The Gunpowdered Man tensed, and the Fox raised the index finger of his right hand in warning to his colleague.

"Aw, you don't like that, huh?" Louis continued. "Don't care to be called on your roots. I've been dealing with peckerwoods like you all my life, men whose mommas shit them out after their daddies put their pole in the wrong fishing hole. See, I'm a Southern boy too, but not your kind, and it's nothing to do with the color of my skin. I just got more self-respect than to keep company with a jailhouse rapist."

This time, the Gunpowdered Man was halfway out of his chair when the Fox gripped his forearm, digging those nails into his partner's flesh. And all the time the Fox's eyes flicked from Louis to Angel and back again, as though uncertain from which of them the first attack might come, but unafraid of either.

"Least we know who's in charge," said Louis, and he leaned back against the wall, content to have stirred the pot to his liking.

Harpur Griffin was gnawing at his lower lip. He pointed a finger at Louis.

"You take that back, what you called me," he blustered, but Louis didn't even bother giving Griffin the oxygen of his attention. Instead he remained focused on the Fox, the hint of a smile on his lips, his head bobbing slightly to music that only he could hear, a private soundtrack to the possibility of violence. To Parker's right, Angel stood with his hands clasped before him and his jacket open, ready to go for the gun.

"I said—" Griffin began to say, until Parker interrupted.

"He heard you," said Parker. "He just doesn't care."

"He's all biggity with his buddies close by."

*Biggity.* Interesting.

"He's kind of biggity even without them."

"He called me a rapist."

As Griffin grew more annoyed, his Southern accent grew more pronounced. Parker was sorry that Louis hadn't goaded the others into speech so that they might reveal themselves too. Southern, Louis had guessed, but there was a lot of the South to go around.

"That's right," said Parker. "He called you a jailhouse rapist because you sexually assaulted Jerome Burnel in Warren—more than once, from what I hear."

"I told you: I don't know that name."

"You raped a man and didn't even have the good manners to ask him his name?" said Parker. "That's uncouth. Let's try again: Jerome Burnel."

"Get the fuck out of here. We're done."

"You know, he was released from prison not long ago," said Parker, as if Griffin had not even spoken. "Unfortunately, he seems to have gone missing. That troubles me because he's my client."

"You hiring on for pedophiles?" said Griffin. He pronounced it "pee-doe-fills."

"So you do know him."

"Maybe I heard the name."

"Have you seen him since he got out?"

"No. Unlike you, I don't consort with men of that stripe. I'd rather watch two dogs screwing."

He picked up his bottle of Bud, drained what was left, then shifted his grip to the neck and made a little feint at Parker. Parker didn't react, but Angel's hand inched closer to his gun, and the Fox glared at Griffin in the manner of one dumbstruck by such foolishness.

Griffin laughed. "I was only fucking with you," he said.

He threw the bottle at the bar's back wall and watched it shatter.

"You made Burnel's life a misery while he was in prison," said Parker.

"If he's the same man I'm thinking of, then he had no cause to complain," said Griffin. "He was a deviant. There was a line to make him pay for his ways."

"What about you?" said Parker. "Did you get ten years for robbing from the rich to give to the poor?"

"I didn't fuck no children."

"Neither did he."

"Might as well have."

"Doesn't answer my question."

"The hell with your question."

"You got ten years for aggravated assault on a pair of old women in the course of a home invasion. One of them died six months later."

"That wasn't on me. Old people die. It happens. And I am done answering your questions. Go talk to the cops. Send them here if the mood takes you. I won't be hard to find. I'll tell them what I told you: maybe I remember this Burnel, and maybe I gave him a lick or two, but that's all I know. I'm done with Warren. That's another life to me now."

Parker took in the three men. The Fox was now staring at the table, and the Gunpowdered Man had returned to tearing his beer label into even smaller strips.

"Well, thank you all for your time," said Parker.

He headed for the door, not quite giving them his back, even though Angel and Louis remained close. He paused with his fingers on the handle, the door now open, the bar ahead dim before him after the daylight.

"I did have one more question," he said. "Who is the Dead King?"

Ah, there it was. The Gunpowdered Man scattered his strips of paper to the breeze, and the Fox's eyes were not on Parker, or Angel and Louis, but on Griffin.

"I don't know what that is," said Griffin, but he was speaking to the Fox, and each word was a lie.

"I heard you were shouting the Dead King's name all over Warren," said Parker, "like he was the Lord and you were testifying, but maybe I was mistaken. In the meantime, though, I'll keep asking around, just in case." He nodded at Griffin's companions. "I hope you boys enjoy your stay in the city."

He stepped into the bar, Angel and Louis following behind, never taking their eyes from the men at the table.

"I'll see you again," said Louis to the feral man, who did not reply, and then was lost as the door closed upon the trio.

"I heard glass break," said the bartender.

"And you came running, right?" said Angel.

"I'm not that dumb. But nobody got hurt, did they?"

"Not yet."

They moved quickly to the exit, Angel and Louis making no effort to hide the fact that their hands were on their guns, staring back at the closed door, waiting for it to spring open, waiting for the men to come. The Fulci brothers were already ahead of them, and they confirmed that the street outside was clear. Only when both their vehicles were away safely, and the Porterhouse was fading into the distance, did Parker breathe more easily.

"What do you think?" he asked.

It was Louis who answered.

"I think," he said, "that maybe Harpur Griffin ain't long for this world."

They met back at the Great Lost Bear. The Fulcis parked in the lot across the street so they could watch the door, while Parker, Angel, and Louis took a booth at the back—the same booth, in fact, in which they'd recently listened to Jerome Burnel's tale. Parker and Louis drank wine, while Angel had a beer. All felt in need of a drink, because the presence of the two men at the Porterhouse had been profoundly unsettling to them. Parker experienced a sensation of weight and oppression, as though he had passed through a storm and his clothing was heavier than before, and the clouds above yet threatened to spill more rain.

"Three possibilities," he said. "One: assuming Burnel hasn't simply run, taking only the clothes on his back, then those men had nothing to do with his disappearance, and the fact that they were keeping company with Griffin was purely coincidental.

"Two: they took Burnel, but they didn't leave town, which means Burnel is still somewhere in Maine, or even Portland. Anyone else want to guess Three?"

"They're the rearguard," said Angel. "Someone else took Burnel, and they were left behind to make sure that nobody beyond the probation service cared much if he was gone."

"And then we showed up," said Louis.

"And baited them. You even found a way to insult their moms."

"I don't think I want to meet either of their moms. The redhead looked like one side of his family made a habit of having sex with animals."

"And then you threw Harpur Griffin to them," said Angel.

"Yeah, they didn't like that," said Louis. "Old Harpur didn't care much for it either, judging by the way the blood left his face. It means they now have a choice to make: they can cut and run, and leave Griffin here to clean up the mess; or, more likely, they put Griffin in a hole, then go back to wherever they came from."

"Unless Griffin's dumb, then right now he's pleading his case to be left alive," said Angel. "Maybe he'll offer to try and take care of us for them."

"He didn't look that good," said Louis.

"Few people do," said Parker. "If he can't keep his mouth shut, and he can't come after us, then what good is he to them?"

"No good at all," said Louis. "Which is why you put his blood in the water to begin with by talking about this Dead King. You think Griffin might break, and if he does he'll turn to us."

"It's what I'm hoping. You think it'll work?"

"No. Like I said in the car, I think they'll kill him."

Parker sipped his wine. He realized that he didn't really care either way what happened to Griffin, beyond his potential usefulness as a possible lead to the whereabouts of Jerome Burnel. But Griffin wouldn't have shared what he knew willingly—Parker had understood that the moment he'd set eyes on him—and needed to be forced into a situation where information was the only currency he had to spend, and all that might save him. Other than that, Griffin was a minor blight on the human race, a stain that would fade with his passing. The men with him, though, were harbingers of a greater evil, outriders for whoever it was that called himself the Dead King.

"Worst case," said Louis. "They kill Griffin, then take a run at us, too."

"They won't try to hit us," said Parker.

"You sound very certain of that."

"We don't know their names, or where they came from, and they didn't strike me as the kind of men who like to make a fuss. If they come after us, they're guaranteed to bring heat down. No, they'll deal with Griffin, for good or bad, and then they'll be out on the breeze."

Parker's cell phone rang. He checked the number before answering.

"Shakey," he said, putting the phone on speaker so the others could listen in.

Shakey was formerly one of the city's homeless. In a way, Shakey was the reason Parker had ended up pierced by bullets and shotgun pellets, and in possession of one kidney less than when he'd started life, after Parker had agreed to look into the death of one of Shakey's friends. Sometimes, Parker thought, saying no to certain cases might have been a good skill to learn.

But he owed Shakey, too: without Shakey, Parker wouldn't have died and come back transformed. Without Shakey, the truth about Parker's daughter might not have been revealed to him. Shakey had been the catalyst.

And Shakey himself acknowledged that Parker had paid a heavy price for intervening, although the detective had never once suggested that a debt was owed. He was paying it off in his own way by being available when, or if, Parker needed him, which was why he was currently in the doorway of a former used-car lot in South Portland, watching the Porterhouse.

"They're coming out," he said.

"All three?"

"Yes."

"How does Griffin look?"

Parker had supplied Shakey with a description.

"Het up. Smoking. He's speaking to the men with him—not arguing, exactly, but he's pretty animated. Looks like he's trying to convince them of something. Now he's getting into his car. They're watching him go. One of them is taking out a phone. He's making a call. He's— Shit!"

"What?"

"I think they've seen me. Sorry about this, but—"

The next thing Parker heard was Shakey screaming a string of obscenities into the phone, accusing an unnamed other of stiffing him for seven bucks, of screwing someone named Little Petty behind his back, and, unless Parker had misheard, of shitting on his dog. By the time Shakey was done, even Parker was entertaining serious doubts about his sanity, and considering getting a new number. Finally, the connection was cut, and Parker was left staring at his silent phone.

"Did he say someone shit on his dog?" asked Angel.

"I think so."

"Does he even have a dog?"

"If he does, it's not one you'd want to meet."

After a couple of minutes had passed, the phone rang again, and Shakey was back on the line.

"You okay?" asked Parker.

"Yeah. They're gone. They think I'm a fruit loop."

"They're not the only ones."

"Nobody wants to mess with a crazy person, not even other crazy people," said Shakey. "Griffin went his way alone, and the others stayed in their car for a while, then left. I got plate numbers for both."

He read them out, along with a description of the vehicles, and Parker made a note of the details.

"What do you want me to do now?"

"Go home, Shakey—and thanks. You've done good."

Parker told him he'd be in touch. He'd drop some cash off for him in the morning. Shakey would try to refuse it, because he always did, but Parker would make him take it in the end.

He didn't think that the two men who'd been with Griffin would make a decision on his fate immediately, but he couldn't be sure. Using his smartphone, he ran the plate on the car they'd been driving, and came up with a dealer's reference, which meant that the car had probably only recently been purchased, and the paperwork remained unprocessed. The information found an echo in his memory, but he was tired and couldn't recall the source, so he set it aside.

He was using Griffin, forcing him into a position where he might have to give up what he knew to save his life. And if Louis was right, he'd done more than that: he'd potentially condemned Griffin to death. It troubled him a little, but less than it might have, and certainly less than it should.

He was not the same man he once was. His grandfather used to say that there were angels whom devils would greet on the street. If that were true, thought Parker, then let the devils raise their hats to him.

It would just make them easier to identify and destroy.

Chapter

# XXXVII

Harpur Griffin tried to recall the first time he'd heard of Charlie Parker. Griffin didn't read the papers much, the occasional big-game coverage apart, or watch news bulletins on TV. He wasn't a complete moron, but he was intellectually lazy and incurious, as well as the eternally fixed center of his own universe. Every individual spends a lifetime trying to disprove Copernicus by placing him- or herself at the heart of existence, but a small core of diehards manages to turn it into an art. Harpur Griffin was just such a man, spurred on by a suspicion, although he could never have expressed it in so many words, that he was just an emptiness with a name.

Although he had no intention of ever doing so, he might have been surprised, had he sat down in a conciliatory atmosphere with Parker, to discover that the detective's diagnosis of his character flaws was pretty much on the money. High school had been the high point in Griffin's life, allowing him to disguise his dearth of character by trying on various identities, each of which ultimately sat uneasily on him, while keeping himself surrounded by others who were at least as insecure as he was, but who would grow into themselves in a way he never would.

Eventually, Griffin had settled on mindless bullying as the pursuit at which he excelled, supported by a coterie of younger men and women who were almost as vacuous as he was, and superficially blinded by this wanton young god in their midst. He'd had his share of girls, too—his, and a lot of other people's—but a little confused fragment of his being had always held itself apart at even the most intimate of moments, watching a version of himself in the throes of sexual performance while wondering why he wasn't enjoying it more.

Fags—that was how he thought of them: rarely queers, or homos, just fags—got a particularly hard time from Harpur Griffin. He hated fags the way the pastor at his local church said God hated them—and God, according to Pastor Ricky, *really* hated fags, despised them more than Muslims and abortionists and feminists, and that was saying something, because God had no truck with any of those other folk, no sir. Pastor Ricky would get so worked up about all the fags in their midst that his face would turn purple, and he'd have to wipe his mouth with a big white handkerchief where the spittle had accumulated. Pastor Ricky saw fags everywhere—he had a nose for them—which was probably how he'd found the one with whom he'd been arrested in a men's room not far from the Charleston Civic Center, performing what his assistant pastor subsequently described as an "unspeakable act," although the assistant pastor's view was that Pastor Ricky had been tempted into the performance of the act in question by Satan, who had been angered by Pastor Ricky's unstinting refusal to capitulate to the forces of liberalism. This, Harpur Griffin thought, was a pretty ambitious spin to put on the whole affair, but he admired the assistant pastor for throwing it out there nonetheless.

Later, over coffee in the adjoining hall, members of the congregation wondered how a man as staunch as Pastor Ricky could have been brought so low, both figuratively and, since he'd been discovered on his knees in a men's room, literally. Griffin had known, though, because he and Pastor Ricky had often hated fags together, in their way. You had to understand their degradation, Pastor Ricky used to tell him, and Griffin had been quite happy to try, just as long as he and the pastor were on the same page about loathing them and all their works.

Sometimes, in his more enlightened moments, relatively speaking,

Griffin suspected that he might be slightly confused about his own sexuality.

Griffin had grown up in Turley, the beating heart of Plassey County, which seemed as good a reason as any to find someplace else to live as soon as was practical. Slowly, and not entirely of his own will, he'd drifted north, and in the absence of anything approaching a skill set, fell into small-scale criminality until he eventually progressed to larger-scale forms of aberrant behavior to which he was conspicuously ill-suited, which was how he'd found himself serving time in Maine State Prison. The first half of his term had been hard, and the remainder of his sentence wasn't looking as though it would be a whole lot easier, when the Cut came calling.

Growing up in Plassey, Griffin knew all about the Cut. Because he wasn't bright, and had been trying to impress what he liked to think of as his "crew," he'd even gotten in the face of some of their boys when they'd crossed paths at Oakey's, which was when his troubles had really begun.

Oakey's was situated about midway between Turley and Mortonsville, and was popular with the post-teen crowd for its liberal attitude toward IDs, as long as the kids drank in the room out back and responded appropriately to "the Bell," a buzzer that sounded at any sign of a police presence, as all kinds of business were transacted at Oakey's, compared to which serving alcohol to minors counted as the barest infraction of the law. If the Bell sounded, all alcohol in the possession of minors was to be dumped in a plastic garbage can with holes in the bottom that stood over a drain in a corner, and beer and liquor was to be substituted with flat soda from a dispenser maintained expressly for that purpose.

Anyway, on the night in question Griffin was not breaking the law by alternating shots of Canadian Mist—he had always been classy, he thought, even back then—with Miller High Life, as he had turned twenty-one three months earlier, although everyone with him was conspicuously underage. (As Griffin got older, the crowd around him stayed the same age. Only the faces changed.) Griffin didn't know what the three boys from the Cut were doing at Oakey's. Had he been a little more sober, he might have realized that, whatever the reason for their presence, it probably meant bad news for someone, and he should probably not try to find out if there was any more to spare for him. But by the time one of the Cut boys brushed by him on the way to the men's room—or he brushed by the Cut boy; it was all kind of fuzzy—Griffin was pretty soaked, and high on the adulation of his younger acolytes.

But Griffin also knew more about the Cut than was wise, because not everyone in the Cut embraced seclusion to the same degree. Griffin might have slept with men, but it didn't mean he was above sleeping with women when the opportunity presented itself. It had only happened a couple of times with the woman from the Cut, but the act had served to dilute some of Griffin's caution. The Cut was no longer as mysterious and threatening to him now that he'd had one of its women.

So when the Cut boy's shoulder hit him, Griffin didn't back down. Words were exchanged, and Griffin was only a breath away from crowing about how he'd screwed a Cut woman when one thing led to another, culminating in Griffin throwing a punch that, ninety-nine times out of a hundred, would have missed entirely, or struck a glancing blow, but in this case connected perfectly with the Cut boy's jaw, dislocating it instantly and sending him stumbling backward through the door of the men's room, where he slipped and fractured his skull on the tiles.

The red mist cleared from Griffin's vision, and with it came the realization of the identity of the boy he'd just hit. Griffin hadn't recognized him at first, not with the baseball cap low on his head, and a new growth of sparse dark beard on his face. He was looking down on Marius, the younger son of Cassander Hobb. He had just struck a prince of the Cut.

Which was when the Bell sounded.

Griffin had never sobered up more quickly. Nobody in Plassey dared raise a voice to the Cut, never mind a hand. What he had done might just be enough to earn him a shallow grave. Marius's two buddies were in the main room of the bar, and the men's room was otherwise empty, so Griffin did the smart thing, or maybe the only thing, as far as he was concerned: he climbed out the bathroom window and ran to his car, where he waited for the cops to go into Oakey's before he started the engine and headed south. Unfortunately, he had only $40 left in his wallet, which wasn't exactly enough to start a new life elsewhere, so he headed back to the apartment he had been renting on the edge of town ever since his mother kicked him out on his ass. He was sharing it with a stoner named Cody, who kept his cash in a rolled-up sock in his bottom drawer. Griffin relieved Cody of $373, with the full intention of probably paying him back sometime, packed a bag, and returned to his car. He'd just managed to get it started again—it could be temperamental, code for a piece of shit—when a truck blocked his way out, and the men appeared.

Griffin recalled pleading with them as they pulled him from the car, and then something impacted on his face, and he didn't remember anything else until he woke up days later in the hospital. The doctor informed him that he was lucky: the pressure of bleeding on his brain had almost killed him. But Griffin knew that he was luckier still: he'd heard the tales, and knew that he could have been burned alive.

After that incident, he never touched Canadian Mist again.

Cassander came to visit him on the day he was due to be released from the hospital, his busted right leg in a cast along with his broken left arm, which made balancing a bitch, and no mistake. Cassander was one of the leaders of the Cut, although folks who claimed to know said the Cut didn't have leaders, not really, but they were full of shit. Griffin knew a leader when he saw one, even if the Cut woman hadn't told him about the hierarchy that ended with Cassander and Oberon. But Cassander hadn't been among those who'd beaten him up. They'd all been younger men.

Griffin tried not to show his fear, although inside he was wondering if Cassander had come to finish the job. He managed to wet his mouth enough to ask about the boy, and was told that he was recovering in a hospital in Charleston. Griffin replied that he was glad, and he was: if Marius had died, or been left a vegetable, then the Cut would have found a way to burn him after all. He wasn't surprised that the cops hadn't come calling, though. That wasn't the way the Cut did business.

Cassander didn't say much. He just stared at Griffin for a time, as though wondering how something so dumb hadn't been dealt with by natural selection long before it had entered the orbit of the Cut, before informing Griffin that he might want to consider finding somewhere else to live in the very near future. Griffin, who'd been thinking along the same lines even before he'd ended up in Oakey's that night, confirmed that he would oblige just as soon as he could walk without falling over—or even sooner, he added, noticing the cloud that passed across Cassander's features at the possibility that Griffin might be considering postponing his departure for any reason.

"That was my son you hurt back at Oakey's," said Cassander, "but I guess you already knew that," and Griffin felt his every muscle tighten painfully.

"If he'd died," Cassander continued, "then you'd have died, too. I wanted to have you killed, and so did my older boy. He wanted to do the job himself, matter of fact."

Griffin just about managed to keep from throwing up. Everyone in Plassey County was wary of Lucius Hobb. He wasn't just crazy: he was cruel into the bargain. If there was a species of animal in West Virginia that Lucius hadn't tortured to death at some point, then it was only because he hadn't yet managed to capture it.

"But," Cassander continued, "someone else pleaded your case in private, just to me."

He leaned in closer to Griffin.

"There are those among us who'd castrate and burn you if they knew you'd been with one of our women," he whispered. "You remember that."

Cassander patted Griffin's busted leg—harder than Griffin might have liked, to be honest—and informed him that he'd be watching Griffin's progress in life with interest. Griffin had assumed this was just a turn of phrase, but it turned out that Cassander had meant it. So it was that about halfway through his sentence at Warren—nine years, after appeal—a message was delivered to Griffin from the Cut: a debt was still owed for the injuries suffered by their boy, and he could work it off by doing them a favor.

He could make Jerome Burnel's life a living hell.

Which was what Griffin did, aided by a supply of contraband—narcotics, pharmaceuticals, nicotine—that found its way to him on a regular basis, and which he used to secure his position by paying off his own harassers and redirecting them toward Burnel. A price was put on everything, from sexual assault to spitting in Burnel's food, and Griffin paid it every time without dispute. Mostly, though, he was happy to do the job himself, assisted, when required, by two trusted cronies. As a result, Griffin's remaining years at Warren had passed more than tolerably. He'd even been able to indulge his penchant for homosexual rape without anyone raising an eyebrow.

Pastor Ricky, he thought, would have been proud.

Harpur Griffin's debt had finally been paid in full that week, when Burnel was lifted from the streets of Portland. It had all gone smoothly, and the Cut had even come up with a small cash bonus for Griffin's efforts, some of which he had been spending at the Porterhouse when Charlie Parker appeared.

This brought Griffin back to what he knew of the detective, which wasn't good, even allowing for the fact that, as already established, he didn't much care for conventional news outlets. He'd kept the worst of it from Lucius and Jabal, at the Porterhouse, but he didn't believe that Parker's reputation could remain hidden from them for long, not in this day and age. The Cut might not have believed in leaving a trail by the overuse of cell phones or computers, but some cursory inquiries would dredge up enough about Parker to make them concerned.

And Parker had waited until right at the end, just when Griffin thought that he'd stonewalled him to a standstill, before lobbing his grenade: the Dead King. Thing was, Griffin didn't even know what the Dead King might be. He'd only heard the name used after he left Plassey, when he briefly fell in with some guys in Huntington who'd had their own difficulties with the Cut. They were led by a man named Cort Leebone, who had been dumped from the Mongols motorcycle gang for—well, Griffin wasn't entirely sure why Leebone had been shown the door, but he was certain it fell under the general heading of an inability to get along well with others. Leebone was now of a mind to court the Bandidos, and ally his little gang with them as puppet members, for four others had followed him out of the Mongols, and he wanted something with which to demonstrate his bona fides.

The biker gangs had continued to circle the Cut, despite the death inflicted on an unfortunate Pagan some years earlier. Some of their members were the kind of men who hadn't the sense to simply skirt an obstacle in their path: they needed to knock it down. The Cut's refusal to let them even ride the roads in Plassey County was a source of discontent, but wiser heads had decided that a confrontation with the Cut simply wasn't worth the trouble, although this decision was open to revision should sufficient intelligence about it become available to support an assault.

That information was what Leebone hoped to present to the Bandidos as his calling card, but it was proving more difficult to obtain than he had anticipated. One of his number had already been shot and killed in a garage in Wheeling, having been sent to Plassey to recce the Cut in the guise of a weekend rider, and Leebone was of a mind to ascribe his murder to "those fucking hillbillies," as he called them. Having learned of his own difficulties with the Cut, Leebone had approached Griffin, but there was little that Griffin could offer him that he didn't already know, beyond what the woman had told him.

It was Leebone, during Griffin's third meeting with him, who had first mentioned the Dead King. Leebone and his affiliates had taken over a glorified drug den, in which Leebone was keeping company with a dirty-blond junkie called Makayla—which Griffin wasn't even sure was a proper name, but what did he know—who was so thin she looked like a needle with tattoos. Leebone said that "Dead King" was the name the Cut gave to their chieftain—not Oberon, not Cassander, but another, one who was never seen. He had it on good authority, he said, and then he'd laughed in a way that made Griffin want to throw up. Leebone had been drinking, and reeked of Chivas. The smell reminded Griffin of his last encounter with hard liquor, as if the pains in his arm, leg, and most of his upper body weren't enough, even with the plaster removed.

Still, Griffin had briefly considered throwing in his lot with Leebone and his people in the hope of achieving some small measure of revenge on the Cut for what had been done to him. He rapidly dispensed with this notion for two reasons. The first was that he didn't believe Leebone, even with the possible assistance of the Bandidos, was close to a match for the Cut, which meant that Leebone would very soon find out what it was like to be dead.

The second reason was that, about an hour after mentioning the Dead King, Leebone decided to introduce Griffin to the source of his information: an eighteen-year-old boy tied to a chair with wire, his face bloodied and three fingers missing from his right hand—missing, but not lost, as Leebone was keeping them safely wrapped in an oil-soaked rag. The kid, said Leebone, was a premed at the University of Charleston. More to the point, he came from the Cut. According to Leebone, he'd already helped them with the beginnings of a map of the area, although Leebone confessed that he wasn't convinced of the accuracy of all the routes, or the safety of them, which was why he anticipated removing some more of the boy's fingers before he was done, after which he intended to burn him alive in true Cut fashion.

It was then that Griffin decided Leebone was well and truly fucked.

Griffin's performance in the hour that followed was probably worthy of some kind of acting prize. He even managed to swallow a couple of mouthfuls of Chivas, just to be sociable, but all that was really on his mind was getting as far away as possible from Huntington, and Leebone, and that boy in the basement, because sure as night followed day the Cut would find them.

It was 4:00 a.m. by the time everyone else was drunk and stoned enough for Griffin to be able to sneak away. He got in his car and started driving, because he did some of his best thinking while driving. Shortly after 6:00 a.m., he paused for coffee and breakfast at an IHOP. This was back in the days before every fool had a cell phone, so he broke a five into quarters at the register and made the call from the phone by the men's room.

Preston Phelps, who was a bartender at Oakey's, didn't sound too pleased to be woken at sparrow's fart by a man who was persona non grata in the entirety of Plassey County and most of its environs, but he quieted down some when Griffin told him about the boy in the basement. Five minutes after he put the phone down, Preston Phelps was on his way to the Cut.

The killings at Huntington were put down to interbiker violence, although they were carried out silently and efficiently, which wasn't usually the way with motorcycle gangs. Only Cort Leebone was never found. It was said that he might have managed to escape the carnage, although his bike was still among those outside the house when the police came.

And on the day after the Huntington killings, the wind carried a smell of burning meat from the Cut.

———

GRIFFIN HAD BEEN HOPING that his assistance in the matter of Leebone and the kid in the basement might have wiped his slate clean, but in his heart he'd known better: they had long memories in the Cut, and harbored grudges. But Jabal, sitting out back of the Porterhouse, had led him to believe that the incident of the fractured skull had been forgotten, thanks to his work dealing with Burnel, and Griffin's debts were now fully paid as far as the Cut was concerned.

As for the other one, Lucius, he didn't speak much; he just simmered. Griffin had no idea what might be going through his head at any time, and anyway, he wasn't even sure that Lucius was entirely human. Griffin suspected that a glimpse into the workings of Lucius's mind would reveal only the bleak, base appetites of a rodent or a hunting mammal—a bat, maybe, or a mink, something capable of an all-consuming viciousness.

Still, there Griffin had been—sitting with a drink in his hand, enjoying the fact that he had some money in his pocket, and a pass from the Cut—when out of a clear fall sky had dropped Charlie Parker with his talk of the Dead King. Griffin had denied to Lucius having ever uttered the name of the Dead King, but Lucius hadn't believed him, not least because Griffin's face had revealed the truth as soon as Parker began talking. Lucius had given Griffin one night to think about how to make amends, which Griffin took to mean that Lucius might want Parker killed.

Unfortunately, Harpur Griffin wasn't a killer, or at least not the kind that might be able to go up against Parker and the men who operated with him. The colored in particular had given Griffin a serious set of the creeps, reminding him of the kind of black boys he used to bait down in Plassey when he had the numbers to back him up, but to whom he gave a wide, careful berth when he was alone.

The Cut folk were the killers, thought Griffin, so let them deal with Parker if they were so concerned about him. He went to his refrigerator, took the last beer from the rack, and used it to add fuel to his growing sense of righteous indignation. All this because one of those inbreeders wasn't keeping an eye on where he was going at Oakey's, and then hadn't been able to take a half-decent punch without breaking like a china vase. And what was it with Parker anyway, nosing around asking questions about some pedophile? To hell with him. To hell with them all.

*I could run*, Griffin thought. Some guys he'd met in Warren had

offered to hook him up with work if he needed it—well, work in the
sense of running pharmaceuticals from Canada, but that certainly beat
the job his probation officer had forced on him, which was glorified
yard cleaning, and hard grind to boost, rain or shine. He disregarded the
possibility of flight almost instantly, though, because he knew the Cut
would come after him, and they'd find him without any trouble at all.

Suddenly he put the bottle down, and wondered if he'd been looking at this whole business from the wrong angle. Until now, he'd been
regarding Parker as the problem, and himself, or the Cut, as the solution. But this man Parker wasn't just some PI who made chump
change from bail skips and errant husbands. He was a hunter, and a
killer. From the little Griffin knew of him, he was also protected: no
man got away with what he had done without someone higher up
signing off on it.

The Cut would never leave him in peace, Griffin knew. If he ran,
they'd kill him. If he failed to come through on Parker, they'd kill him.
And even if he did somehow manage to contrive a solution to their
problem, they'd almost certainly kill him as soon as it was all done, just
for having a big mouth. Whatever way he examined the situation, Griffin believed that he was heading for the grave.

So instead of feeding Parker to the Cut, maybe he should feed the
Cut to Parker. A man who was protected could find a way to protect
others. If he had federal contacts, then maybe he could get Griffin into
one of those safe houses—room, board, cable TV, a PlayStation—while
the feds descended on Plassey County with the full force of taxpayer
dollars.

Except what did Griffin have to sell? That was the problem. All he
could offer Parker was the approach made to him at Warren, and the
instruction to torture Jerome Burnel. He could throw in Cort Leebone
and his buddies as well, although for it to be worthwhile he'd have to
admit to his own involvement in turning the Cut on them. The rest
was just rumors, and even added together, it didn't sound like enough

to earn him much more than a cup of bad coffee from Parker or the police.

Unless he agreed to wear a wire.

All Griffin knew about wires was what he'd seen on TV cop shows and in movies, but he figured that the technology must have progressed far enough to allow him to wear a microphone resembling a button or a pin without the necessity of wrapping himself in duct tape. Conspiracy to commit murder had to be worth a lot, and that was what Lucius was suggesting, albeit not in so many words, or not yet. But, if necessary, Griffin could entice him into saying it aloud. He hadn't entirely exhausted his store of charm left over from early adulthood.

Griffin grabbed his laptop and went searching for Parker's details. The PI didn't have a website—who, in this day and age, didn't have a website to promote his business, Griffin mused, until the answer came to him: someone who didn't need one—but his details were available on the website of the Maine Licensed Private Investigator's Association, although they were limited to a P.O. box and a cell phone number. Griffin entered the number on his phone before immediately deleting it: he didn't want Jabal or Lucius to pick up his phone and find the detective's details on it. Instead he tore a scrap of paper from a take-out menu and wrote the number on that before folding it and placing it at the bottom of the watch pocket of his jeans, buried beneath his loose change. He wasn't going to call the detective yet, not until he was sure he had no other option. He'd go out and talk to some people about him first.

Griffin finished his beer, took a leak, and cleaned himself up. He still had a buzz on from drinking steadily all day. He reached for his car keys, briefly debated whether he was too drunk to drive, decided that if he was capable of assessing the scale of his inebriation he probably wasn't, and headed into Portland.

# XXXVIII

S hakey watched Harpur Griffin go, then called Parker to tell him that he was on the move again. Despite Parker's injunction to the contrary, Shakey had gone to Griffin's place on his own initiative, mostly because he was kind of enjoying having a purpose. Parker told him once again to go home, after first burning his ear for potentially putting himself at risk.

"I can stay," said Shakey. "It's not cold."

Actually, it was cold, but not by the standards Shakey applied to the weather. He was, after all, a man who had slept rough on Portland's streets in winter. It had almost killed him, and he wasn't anxious to repeat the experience, but it had given him a certain sense of perspective.

Parker was briefly tempted to take Shakey up on his offer, then decided against it. The two men who had been with Griffin at the Porterhouse had seen Shakey and were now aware of him. They might not yet have been suspicious of him, but if they glimpsed him again in their vicinity, or that of Griffin, they might hurt him.

So Shakey returned to his apartment. Thanks to the intercession of Parker and his friends in the city, he now lived in subsidized housing off Congress Street, not very far from the block that had briefly housed Jerome Burnel. Shakey's building had an on-site laundry, a library with computers, even blood pressure screening, and there was a bus stop

right out front, which made life easier. His ruined foot was already telling him that winter was on its way, and the hours spent trailing Harpur
Griffin had caused it to ache. Shakey pulled a piece of candy from his
pocket and chewed it all the way to the nearest bus stop, where he took
a seat and waited for the bus to take him back to Portland.

And all the time, Lucius and Jabal regarded him from the front seats
of their car, while a third figure sat in the back and mulled over everything he had already learned about the private detective named Charlie Parker.

Chapter

# XXXIX

Parker left Angel and Louis and returned to Scarborough. Like Shakey, he was feeling the approach of winter. His scalp itched where the shotgun pellets had cut through, a sure sign that a headache was on its way, for he had learned to spot the advance signals sent by his damaged body.

He took a couple of painkillers, then made a cup of coffee and sat out on his porch to drink it, even if the evening was a little more chilly than he might have preferred, and that damned left hand was letting him know it. Nevertheless, in Maine you learned to take your pleasures where you could. The marshes had no shortage of bugs in summer, and if he was fool enough to sit out on his porch once the snow came they'd have to chip the ice from him and break his bones in order to fit him in the casket. He liked October and November. They were his months.

He called Moxie Castin on his cell phone and told him about his encounter with the three men at the Porterhouse, although he withheld some details of their exchanges on the grounds that it was inadvisable to tell anyone everything, especially a lawyer, and he didn't know Castin as well as Aimee Price, who looked after his own legal affairs.

"And you believe that these men might have something to do with Burnel's disappearance?" asked Castin.

"They were from out of town, and didn't look like they were planning a sunset tour of the harbor followed by dinner at DiMillo's. If this was the Wild West, they'd have been up on a bluff watching for signs of pursuit from a posse."

"I never ate at DiMillo's," said Castin.

DiMillo's was Portland's floating seafood restaurant, situated in a former car ferry moored at Long Wharf. Whatever its qualities, Parker's natural aversion to eating anything with more than four legs, or no legs at all, had forced him to give it a miss.

"Me neither," said Parker, while not expressing surprise at Castin being distracted by talk of food. He knew the man's reputation as a gourmand.

"You think it's worth setting the police on them?" said Castin, once his train of thought found the right rails again.

"It's your call, Moxie, but I don't have anything more than Harpur Griffin's connection to Burnel, and by now those guys are nowhere near the Porterhouse."

"Then we wait."

"That was my feeling."

"Is Griffin at risk from them?"

"Maybe."

Parker let the lawyer consider the possible consequences.

"We still wait," said Castin.

"If it goes south—"

"I'll deal with it," said Castin.

"Okay."

There was a pause.

"How far south could it go?"

Parker recalled the faces of the two men.

"Antarctica," he said.

Castin thanked Parker, although even he didn't seem sure why, and hung up.

Next, Parker called Shakey to make sure he'd gotten home safely. The little man was sitting in his armchair, eating a sandwich and watching a VHS tape of *The Goonies*. Shakey didn't own a computer, and didn't have a credit card, so downloading movies was out, even though Parker had offered to share his Netflix password and buy him a Netflix-compatible Blu-ray player. But Shakey had a huge affection for VHS and old vinyl, both of which could be bought cheaply. His little apartment was now a repository of books, records, and VHS movies. It had taken Parker only a little while to realize Shakey was a man who had lived for years on the street, his only possessions those he could wheel in a cart or carry, and he was now enjoying owning things, and being surrounded by them without having to worry about mobility or potential theft.

Parker remembered a conversation with the teenage daughter of one of Rachel's friends, who couldn't understand why people still bought music, or spent money on DVDs, CDs, books, magazines, and a whole host of other items on which Parker was quite happy to drop the occasional dollar. "Our generation doesn't want to own things," she'd explained to Parker, in the manner of a teacher explaining to a slow pupil why it was important not to lick his fingers and stick them in an electrical outlet. Parker had nodded along politely while thinking that it was easy to decry ownership when almost everything you could want was at your fingertips, most of it for free, legally or otherwise. But ownership and possessions mattered when, like Shakey, you could remember not having very much at all. In the end, you had to be reasonably wealthy and privileged to choose not to own stuff.

He told Shakey that he'd see him around, then hung up. He was glad that Shakey was doing okay. At least some good had come out of that murderous business in Prosperous, a consequence of his investigation into the death of Shakey's friend Jude. He'd read about the town in the newspaper earlier that week. Apparently its supply of drinking water had become polluted, and the county was providing tanker trucks to supply the town's needs. The report included a picture of some of Prosperous's previously privileged inhabitants standing in line with containers like refugees in a war-torn city. First fire, the paper noted, now water. Pretty soon, Prosperous would be plagued by locusts and boils, or so Parker certainly hoped.

Thinking about Shakey brought him back to Harpur Griffin. Angel and Louis had gently suggested that some form of surveillance more professional than a crippled homeless man might have been appropriate, but it wasn't as if Parker had a huge pool of resources on which to draw. Griffin and his buddies had already seen Angel and Louis, and the Fulcis couldn't have been more conspicuous if they'd dressed up as brightly colored dinosaurs.

Also, Griffin didn't strike Parker as particularly bright, but the same couldn't be said of the men who'd been with him at the bar. They'd have been watching for a tail. Already they knew that they had strayed onto Parker's radar, and he onto theirs. It was a pity he hadn't anticipated that Griffin might have been enjoying such interesting company: he could have had Angel tag their car so it might be tracked by GPS.

But Griffin was the weak link, and it was in his own power to save himself, if he chose. To do so, he simply had to share what he knew about Jerome Burnel; about the men who Parker was now certain had played some part in Burnel's disappearance . . .

And about the Dead King.

There was no moon tonight, but he could still make out the gleam of the water on the marshes. He felt the urge to call Rachel. Sam might be up late, and he could talk with her before she went to bed. He missed her always, even though he could not think of her without being troubled.

He had visited her in Vermont at the end of the previous month. She had chatted unself-consciously with him over ice cream, and they'd gone to see a movie, Rachel joining them, so that they were almost a family once again. At no point did Sam give any indication that she was other than what she appeared to be: a slightly precocious little girl, happy in her own skin.

Yet Parker could not help but look at her and recall seeing another Sam, one who had stood in judgment over a dying man, and might even have willed his death; one who had whispered urgently to her father, warning him not to question her or speak of what he thought he might have seen, for fear of what he might bring down upon both of them. That Sam spoke with the voice of a child, but she was something stranger, something older . . .

He pushed these concerns away. They would do him no good. He understood now that his purpose on this earth, just like the purpose of any father, was to protect his child.

But this child was special. This child, he believed, could change worlds.

Chapter

# XL

I t was a miracle that Harpur Griffin even managed to find his car at the end of the night. If he hadn't been intoxicated when he left his apartment, he certainly was by the time 1:00 a.m. came. He'd drifted around some of Portland's less salubrious drinking establishments until he found a man named Benny Tosca smearing his face with chicken wing sauce at a bar out by Deering Junction.

Tosca had been bounced from one of the state's more rural police departments for something to do with hookers, parking violations, a rat-infested condo that he owned, and an attempt to drown a candidate for mayor, the details of which remained unclear since the mayoral candidate chose not to press any charges, and the chief of police had given Tosca the option of going quietly and saving the department some embarrassment, or going noisily and almost assuredly ending up in jail, with Benny sensibly taking the former course. He had ended up working as a PI until that career path also terminated in the weeds of illegality, and now he mostly chased down bad debts for a payday loan company that operated out of a former Armenian restaurant off Forest Avenue, and on weekends he occasionally manned the door at strip joints. Benny Tosca disliked everyone, but he reserved a particular hatred for those who had succeeded where he had not, which meant cops and PIs, along with fathers, husbands, dog owners, slum landlords, pimps, and regular human beings.

Not that he had any fondness for ex-cons either, but Griffin smoothed over Tosca's residual objections to convicted wrongdoers by offering to pay for a couple of rounds, and pretty soon Tosca was giving him a whole lot of information on Charlie Parker, some of which might actually have been true. Even allowing for exaggeration and bile, Tosca's description of Parker confirmed what Griffin had already suspected: he was principled, dangerous, and more than capable of taking on the Cut.

Tosca left the bar to return to his task of watching out for undesirables at the entrance to whatever show club was paying him that evening, while Griffin wandered off to retrieve his car, once he remembered where he'd left it. He'd parked behind an old brownstone that had been converted to commercial use, and was now probably locked up for the weekend. He struggled to open the driver's door, and then found himself unable to fit the key in the ignition. Griffin took this as a sign that it might be inadvisable to drive in his present condition. He was unlikely to attract the attention of any passing cops where he was parked, so he put the seat back to grab a nap in order to straighten himself out, and was unconscious within seconds.

———

GRIFFIN WOKE WHEN THE tape was placed over his mouth. More of it was wound around his head, securing him to the headrest. He tried to struggle, but two nylon straps had been passed over the seat and around his body, both of which were now instantly tightened. The first loop encircled his chest, efficiently restricting the movement of his arms. The second was around his throat.

Jabal appeared before him, staring at him through the windshield. Griffin heard the back door open and close, and then Lucius joined Jabal. Lucius had something in his hand, but in the darkness Griffin couldn't make out what it was.

Finally, the front passenger door opened, and a third man took the seat beside Griffin, who could just about turn his head to look at him.

Griffin recognized the new arrival immediately from the last time he'd seen him, which was when he was lying on the floor of Oakey's men's room with a fractured skull.

"Remember me?" asked Marius, and Griffin nodded. Even though his nostrils were not constricted, he was struggling to breathe. He needed to take a leak so badly. He knew that, right now, he had bigger troubles, but it was the immediacy of his aching bladder that most concerned him. Had he been a more philosophical man, and a less inebriated one, Griffin might have recognized it as the same impulse that causes a man on the gallows to fixate on a splinter, a hat, a face, anything but the enormity of his own imminent extinction.

"You owe a debt to me," said Marius. Against the gag, Griffin tried to tell him that he'd done all he had been asked to do, that he was sorry, that he'd been dumb and drunk back at Oakey's, just as he was dumb and drunk now.

"Hush," said Marius. "It'll all be over soon."

Griffin needed to pee: he needed to pee so badly that he started to cry. He thought of his mother. He tried to keep the image of her in his head. He hadn't spoken to her in a long time. He wasn't even sure that she knew he was out of jail.

Marius slipped something over the knuckles of his right hand, then showed it to Griffin, turning his fist in front of his face: it was a knuckle-duster, an old wooden one. Then Marius drew his hand back, striking Griffin just below the ear, and Griffin felt his jaw dislocate. He screamed against the gag as Marius climbed from the car, leaving Lucius to open the driver's door and begin dousing Griffin in gasoline.

Griffin closed his eyes and imagined his mother's hand stroking his hair as the gasoline poured down his face. The stink of the fumes burned his nostrils and stung his eyes, but he kept them shut even as he heard the striking of a match, followed by a surprised, angry hiss as the rest of the book burst into flame.

Then Harpur Griffin ignited too, burning a path into the next life.

# XLI

C omes the child through the marshes.
    Comes the child, comes the child . . .

———

JENNIFER PARKER HAD A memory of the moment of her dying. She experienced it as an instant of incandescence, of pain turned to light and heat, and so profound was it that it seemed the agony must last for eternity. She was trapped in it, and had always been and would always be, for she could no longer remember how it had begun.

And then—

Nothing.

———

SHE THOUGHT THAT SHE might have slept, except how could one sleep and wake into a dream? The world was changed, and she was changed. She was at one and the same time the "was," the "is," and the "might-have-been" of herself. She looked like a child, and spoke and thought like a child, but behind it all hovered another consciousness experiencing the world in ways she could not express. She was alone, but she was not afraid. She sat on a rock by the shore of a lake and watched the dead stream by to be absorbed into the bloody redness of the sky and the deep, dark blue of the sea. Sometimes they stopped and asked her to join them. Mothers reached out a hand to her, for she reminded them of their own lost children. Fathers sought to protect her, no longer having children of their own to shield. But she did not respond, and eventually they continued on their way, and were at last lost to sight. Only to the children did she consent to speak, because they were often frightened and confused, and so she would talk with them, and reassure them that all would be well, even though she did not know if this was true, and in time they, too, rejoined the great mass and vanished into the distant sea.

She did not count the days, because they were all the same. She had no concept of the passage of time, because the flow of people remained constant, only the faces changing, and soon she stopped noticing even these differences, and they became as one to her.

———

SHE THOUGHT OF HER father and mother, and felt herself as the last point of connection between them, as though they stood at opposite sides of a deep yet narrow chasm, with a stone stack between them, and on that stack she sat, one arm extended toward her father, the other toward her mother. She sensed her father as a cloud of red, and black, and fiery orange, but she could not touch him. Her mother she felt simultaneously as both an absence and a presence: near her father lurked something that had the form of her mother, but was not her mother entire. It was sad and angry, and so much of that sorrow and rage was directed at her father. But the best of her mother, the part that loved and was loved in turn, was elsewhere.

Then—and it might have been after an hour, or a month, or a year—that better part of her mother approached along the shore of the lake. The child watched her come, dressed in her favorite summer dress, but she did not rush to meet her. She remained seated on her rock, her knees drawn up beneath her chin, and felt the warmth of the passing dead.

And after a day, or an hour, or a moment, her mother was beside her, but she, too, was a being transformed. The child felt her mother's distraction, an irritation at being called from a higher realm to deal with this girl she had once known, seated on a rock by the paths of the dead.

"Hello, daughter."

"Hello, mother."

Her mother—no, her Almost-Mother—stood behind her, watching the dead.

"They are so many," said the Almost-Mother.

"I used to try to count them, but then I gave up. Now I just see lights."

The Almost-Mother sat down beside her.

"How long have you been here?" she asked.

"I don't know."

"How long will you stay?"

"I haven't decided."

"You can come with me, if you choose. You don't have to remain all alone."

And the child inhaled her father's pain, carried on a wind between worlds. It smelled of copper and dead flowers.

"And if I do, what will become of him?"

"I don't know."

"Don't you care?"

The landscape flickered, and the Almost-Mother and the Mother of Sorrow and Rage briefly became one, and somewhere in their conjoined hearts was a kind of love.

"I can't help him."

"Can I?"

"Perhaps."

"I want to go back."

"Then go."

And she did.

———

TIME PASSED. SHE WALKED in shadows. Once, maybe twice, the Almost-Mother joined her in the world of her father, and brought a child from the confusion of death to follow the water, but mostly she was alone, or drifted with the Mother of Sorrow and Rage, and watched her father from afar. She willed him to see her, and sometimes he almost did. She glimpsed as he came close to falling, felt him nearly touch damnation before drawing back. She—

———

SHE WAS ON THE rock again, and the dead flowed around her, and the Almost-Mother was seated beside her. But the air was different, and the sky had changed, and when Jennifer raised her hand blue light arced across her fingers.

"Listen to me," said the Almost-Mother. The child heard the fear and awe in her voice, and she listened. "That which once slept is awaking."

Jennifer felt it—a consciousness returning, exploring—and the ranks of the dead shivered. A few paused in uncertainty, and a man and woman drifted away hand-in-hand to wander among low hills, and the child could not tell what might befall them now that they turned their backs on the distant sea.

"What must I do?"

"Hold close. Listen. Listen hard."

She heard it—the crying of an infant: a girl, a new daughter. For the first time since the Traveling Man had come and cut her from her old life, she wept.

"He will forget me," she said. "I want to leave. I want to go with you. He doesn't need me anymore."

"No," said the Almost-Mother. "He will need you now more than ever."

And in the darkness of the depths between worlds, something stirred.

Chapter

# XLII

P arker's phone rang shortly after 7:00 a.m. No good could ever
come of a phone call at such a time on a Sunday.

It was Moxie Castin.

"Turn on Channel Six," he said. "It looks like someone burned
Harpur Griffin alive . . ."

———

PARKER WATCHED THE NEWS while he dressed, then drove over to Forest
Avenue, parked a couple of blocks from the scene, and walked as far
as the police cordon. Behind it was a mass of cars, both marked and
unmarked, and a crime-scene van. Over to the right, he saw the medical
examiner's vehicle, and a pair of figures dressed in overalls. Screens had
been placed around Griffin's car to protect it from curious onlookers, of
which there were already a few. A breeze blew the stink of the burned-out
car at them. Up close, the police would be able to smell Griffin as well.

His cell phone rang: Castin again.

"I've been asking around," he said. "There's no positive ID, not yet,
but it's definitely Griffin's car, and they found nylon and buckles fused
to the victim's chest and neck. Looks like he was strapped to his seat
and left to burn. Do you want me to arrange the sit-down with Portland
PD? The sooner we tell them some of what we know, the better."

"No, I'll make the call. If you do it, we'll look adversarial from the start."

"You have friends in the department?"

Parker watched as a detective appeared from behind the screen. Her face was concealed by a mask, and she was wearing blue plastic gloves. She tore off the gloves and dropped them in a waste bag before removing the mask, but Parker had recognized her the moment he saw her.

Sharon Macy. They'd dated, and it didn't take, but at least he hadn't left scorched earth in his wake.

"Kind of," he said.

"Since it's you, 'kind of' is the best that can be expected under the circumstances. Let me know the time, and I'll join you."

"Sure," said Parker.

"You told me it might go south," said Castin. "At least you didn't lie."

Parker hung up as Angel and Louis appeared. He'd called them from the house.

Louis stared at the screens and sniffed the air.

"Well," he said, "that didn't work out so good."

———

ANGEL AND LOUIS HEADED over to the Big Sky Bread Company to get coffee and breakfast, leaving Parker to attract Macy's attention. He skirted the cordon until he came into her line of sight. He didn't need to wave, or even whistle; she noticed him quickly enough. Anyway, if he'd tried whistling at Sharon Macy he might have ended up eating through a straw. He saw her say something to the other detective from the Criminal Investigation Division who was with her—Parker thought his name might be Farrow or Farnham, something like that, and he was enrolled in the Criminal Justice program at one of the local colleges, taking advantage of the department's 50 percent discount on tuition fees. That meant he was ambitious, and was probably secretly pleased that someone had set Harpur Griffin alight. Homicides were good for those hoping to gain a foothold on the career ladder. Farlow or Frobisher seemed inclined to follow Macy, but she waved a hand at him and he hung back, watching her depart with an abandoned expression, like a dog left behind when its owner has gone into a store.

Macy looked good, but then she always looked good. She was small, dark, and pretty. Parker had missed his chance with her, but he had no regrets. Well, few regrets. Local gossip claimed that she was seeing Cliff Sanders, one of the city's new tribe of restaurateurs. Sanders had already opened two Portland restaurants in which the size of the portions was inversely proportional to the price, and was planning to add two more to his roster before the next tourist season kicked in. It confirmed Parker's suspicion that pretty soon anyone on the state's average wage would be able to dine out in the greater Portland area only if they stuck to happy hours and buffets.

"Rubbernecking?" asked Macy, when she reached where Parker was waiting. "It's not really your style."

Parker indicated Griffin's car.

"You think it might be suicide, or a dropped cigarette?"

"We haven't made any official announcement yet. Maybe if you watch the news later, you'll learn something."

"Like that he was strapped to his seat before he was killed?"

Macy hadn't stopped smiling, but the smile seemed to be struggling to climb as far as her eyes, and was currently marooned somewhere around her cheekbones.

"You're well informed."

"Even without the TV news. I think we need to arrange a sit-down."

"You know who's in that car?"

"Harpur Griffin. If it's not him, I'll pay you a dollar."

"Friend?"

"Hardly."

"Client?"

"I'm not that desperate—yet. I've been doing some work for Moxie Castin, and Griffin wandered into range."

"In what way?"

"Well, that's why I thought we should meet: you, me, Moxie, and whoever. Look, this isn't about pulling privilege: I just thought it would be better if I made the first approach. I've got nothing to hide, but Moxie's client already has enough troubles, and this is Moxie's case, not mine."

"This client wouldn't be Jerome Burnel, would it?" asked Macy.

Damn, but the woman was smart.

"Impressive," said Parker.

"I read the bulletins. You tell Moxie to be at Middle Street in one hour. If he's not there on time, I'll personally come around to his office and see how many cans of that soda of his I can shove up his ass. And before you make the call"—she raised an index finger; the smile was entirely gone now—"do I need to start thinking about an arrest warrant for Burnel?"

Parker looked past her. From this angle, he could see the car in a gap through the screens. What was left of Harpur Griffin was covered by white plastic, but the blackness of him was visible beneath it. Macy's question was the reason Parker had wanted to hold off on saying anything about Burnel until Moxie Castin was present. He couldn't see Burnel tying someone to a car seat and setting him on fire, but then Burnel probably hadn't seemed like someone capable of shooting two men at a gas station until he'd pulled a gun and killed them, and if anyone had a reason for murdering Harpur Griffin, it was Jerome Burnel. Now that Griffin had been immolated, the possibility existed that Burnel hadn't been abducted at all, and had instead dropped out of sight in order to target his tormentor.

Except Parker couldn't really see it happening that way. Had Griffin been found stabbed or beaten in an act of panic or rage, then Parker might have been inclined to add Burnel's name to the list of suspects, but equally he would have expected Burnel to have been found beside the body. He wouldn't have run, but would instead have waited for the cops to come and get him. No, Griffin's murder suggested a degree of sadism and premeditation, and Parker believed it would probably have taken more than one man to carry it out. He couldn't picture Burnel with an accomplice. He didn't have many friends left.

Macy was waiting for his answer.

"No," he said. "Burnel didn't do this."

"You sound very sure of that."

"I've met him."

"And you don't think he's the type."

"Not to set a man alight, but that's only part of it."

"What's the rest?"

"I believe Burnel is dead. And if he's not, he may be wishing he was."

Macy thought about what he'd said, then turned slightly so that she, too, could see the ruin of the car, and the shape of the body inside.

"So you think that whoever did Griffin—"

"Did Burnel, too?" he finished for her. "Possibly. No, probably."

"Call Moxie," she said. "Now."

# XLIII

Shortly after eight that same morning, Sheriff Edward Henkel turned his cruiser into the parking lot of Shelby's Diner and killed the ignition. Since his divorce, and the decision not to haul the kids over to stay with him more than once every month, it had been his habit to take the early shift on weekends, if only because it gave him something to do. He had never been one for letting his deputies do all the hard work. Anyway, Plassey's size and population meant that its sheriff's department was small by the standards of the state, so everyone helped to carry the burden, Henkel included, which he was more than happy to do.

There wasn't much to Plassey County, but it was his. He knew every corner of its speed-trap towns, every trailer park, every creaking shack. He saw the beauty of it, even in its decline. The small mine at Berber Hill was long closed, but Plassey still bore the marks of a coal county in the disused railway lines, the locked-up storage yards by the Colney River, and the roadside advertisements for lawyers specializing in cancers and other ailments caused by years spent amid darkness and dust.

Even when he wasn't rostered, Henkel would sometimes put on his uniform and take a run along the county roads. Occasionally he'd pull someone over for speeding, or roust some kids who were indulging in a little illicit drinking, but mostly he'd just stop by homes and businesses, making sure that folks were happy, and if they weren't, finding a way to do something about it. He had an election coming up next year, and was conscious of Channer breathing down his neck. Rob was probably still too young and unseasoned to be considering a run for sheriff, but it remained good politics to make sure people understood that new blood wasn't always better than old.

Sheriffs in West Virginia were limited to two consecutive four-year terms, but Henkel was already grooming Ned Ralston, his chief deputy, to succeed him, assuming Henkel won the next election, which he fully intended to do. Ralston wasn't even very keen on being sheriff, but Henkel had assured Ralston that he'd back him all the way, and stay on as his chief deputy in turn. Then, four years later, if Ned decided that he'd had enough, well, Henkel would be happy to run again. Henkel liked to think of himself as a modest student of politics, which is why he made sure to read something more than the comics in the papers every day. You could say what you liked about that Putin fella in Russia, Henkel believed, but he certainly knew how to hold on to power, even if it meant becoming prime minister instead of president for a while in order to get around those term limits in Russia. He probably hadn't even moved out of his old office, but just found someone to switch the nameplates on the doors.

Part of Henkel's weekend routine was to pick up the thick Sunday copies of the *Washington Post* and the *Charleston Gazette-Mail* in order to continue his education on world affairs, and head to Shelby's not too long after Miss Queenie, Shelby's widow—Shelby having departed for the great diner in the sky some years earlier—opened the doors. Sundays tended to be pretty quiet, which was why Queenie opened at the later hour of 7:00 a.m., and stayed behind the register until 9:30, when it was time for her to go to church. Usually, if Henkel got in early enough, he would find himself alone in the diner for a while, during which time Miss Queenie made sure that he was adequately fed and watered, but otherwise left him to his reading. He was running a little late this morning, but the diner remained almost empty as far as he could see. Business would pick up after the church services finished, and the various congregations came to Shelby's for brunch and conversation.

There was a time when the background music in Shelby's on Sundays was WVGV 89.7 FM, West Virginia's Gospel Station, in honor of the Sabbath, but it meant that the accompaniment to Henkel's reading was *Preaching Time* with Dr. Larry Brown, and *Word of Life* with Michael Bailey, neither of which, for all their undoubted merits, Henkel found conducive to his enjoyment of the papers. After some consultation with her pastor, Miss Queenie agreed to replace WVGV with classical music, at least while Henkel was on the premises.

Miss Queenie had initially expressed some surprise that Pastor Dave should have been so amenable to the change, and Henkel had seen no reason to enlighten her to the fact that he and Pastor Dave liked to share a quiet restorative whiskey-scotch at weekends, and Henkel therefore had the ear of God. Pastor Dave was less fire-and-brimstone than steady-as-she-goes, which suited most of his congregation pretty well. A lot of people in Plassey County still recalled the unfortunate business of Pastor Ricky sucking off teenage boys in Charleston restrooms, which had resulted in a certain suspicion of men of the cloth who appeared to protest too much. Pastor Dave might have been a little too forgiving of the faults of others—and maybe his own as well—for the county hard core who felt Satan's immanence, but he had a good-looking wife, five children, and no apparent fondness for men's rooms beyond that commensurate to the call of nature.

Henkel saw Miss Queenie come to the door, as though concerned at his apparent reluctance to enter her premises, but he didn't move from his car. He had the newspapers on the seat beside him, the *Gazette-Mail* on top. According to the paper, a county circuit court judge in the Panhandle had issued a dress code for his courtroom, having grown tired of the sartorial sins of the people of Ohio County. The code forbade the wearing of pajamas, slippers, flip-flops, sunglasses, exposed underclothing, and shirts with obscene language or graphics. Henkel, who was not unfamiliar with the kind of people who passed through the state's courts, had to admire the judge's stance, although anyone who turned up to court wearing house slippers and a T-shirt reading, DON'T LIKE ME? TAKE A SEAT WITH THE REST OF THE BITCHES WAITING FOR ME TO GIVE A FUCK, as a woman in Plassey County did recently, shouldn't have been surprised if the judge sent her ass to jail until she did decide to give a fuck.

The dress code story might have given Henkel more pleasure had it not stood alongside the first section of a longer feature, continued inside, detailing the discovery of the bodies of Robbie Killian and Dustin Huff. The headline read, "KILLERS IN THE COUNTY: PLASSEY'S ROUGH 'JUSTICE,'" and the story itself detailed Killian and Huff's efforts to expand their narcotics operation, before they ran afoul of what the newspaper described as "rival forces." Henkel knew the story was coming because he'd been asked to contribute a quote. He'd given the reporter the standard boilerplate—inquiries continuing, number of leads, no suspects as yet—and referred her to the state police, who were handling the main investigation, for further comment.

The rest of the piece was essentially a history of Plassey County, and included a litany of killings and disappearances over the best part of a century and a half. True, there hadn't been quite as many over the past decade or so, but pulled all together in one place like that they certainly made an impression. The article didn't mention the Cut by name, but it wasn't hard to read between the lines. Regardless, it wasn't what Henkel wanted to read over his breakfast—like the Cut, he preferred not to make the papers—even if it did serve his purposes by putting pressure on the Cut and, more particularly, by perhaps making the state police look more closely at its activities.

He could smell frying bacon through the open window of the car. That was another thing: he'd received a call from the heart specialist on Friday afternoon. She was proposing a coronary angioplasty to relieve

Henkel's clogged artery, which would involve inserting and inflating a tiny balloon to widen the path. She also felt that it would be useful to put in a stent to help keep the artery open and prevent it from narrowing again. She suggested that this procedure should be carried out as soon as possible. In the meantime, she'd warned Henkel to avoid stress, and watch his diet. His diet he could do something about, but right now the only way he could avoid stress would be by retiring, and he wasn't ready to do that yet.

Miss Queenie was now standing outside the diner, her hands on her hips and her head tilted like an old bird's.

"Morning, Miss Queenie," said Henkel.

Everyone called her Miss Queenie. Even her husband had called her Miss Queenie, and he was married to her for forty-five years.

"You doing okay?" she asked. "I got bacon, hash browns, and a sausage omelet that aren't going to eat themselves."

And Henkel wondered why he had clogged arteries. *Ah*, he thought, *to hell with it.*

"Be right there, ma'am," he said.

# XLIV

Inside, Henkel did his rounds of the tables, greeting those already seated, and waving to Teona Watson in the kitchen. He asked how her boy, Odell, was doing, because he sometimes saw him on the road near his home, and received a smile in return.

"He's doing fine, Sheriff," said Teona. "Real good."

The lie tasted like sour milk in her mouth. Teona liked the sheriff, but she preferred to keep her distance. She knew that he had his informants in the county, including any number who lived within sight of the Cut, but she wasn't among them. She and her family were too close to it, and therefore too vulnerable. They all knew it, even Odell.

Henkel picked a table by a window, ordered breakfast, and drank coffee while he waited for his food to come. He was immersed in the *Post* when someone entered the diner and he sensed a change in the mood of those around him. Conversation briefly ceased, then resumed at a lower volume. He looked up to see Oberon standing before him. Outside in the parking lot sat Oberon's truck. One of the younger Cut boys, Benedict, was at the wheel. Benedict had been away for at least a week, or so those who knew of such matters had told Henkel. It was a shame, in Henkel's view, that Benedict had come back at all. The boy was wrong. Anyone who kept company with Lucius Hobb had to be.

Henkel made little effort to disguise his dislike of the Cut. He was no Russ Dugar. Henkel kept an eye on the Cut folk when they came into town, and his network kept him apprised of their movements, at least outside their own territory. But his dealings with Oberon were infrequent, each man circling the other warily. Henkel's last encounter with Oberon had come two months earlier, when Lucius Hobb had been involved in an altercation with some tourists at a gas station, during which the father of the family had been assaulted, and the woman threatened with having her breasts cut off. Cassander had apologized for any misunderstanding that might have occurred while simultaneously refusing to surrender his son to Henkel for questioning, and Oberon had been civility and reason itself, even while making it clear that Henkel would not be allowed to proceed into the Cut without a warrant, just as Cassander's son would not be produced without a warrant for his arrest. Henkel had stomped off in a fury, determined to get the authority he needed, but by the time he'd filled in the necessary paperwork, and was on his way to Judge Cryer to have the warrant issued, the complaint against Lucius had been withdrawn. The Cut had worked fast on that occasion, even by its own efficient standards.

When Henkel went to find the family at Dryden's Inn, on the outskirts of Turley, they had already checked out. Dryden's was just a motel, but it was the only such place in the county where anyone in his right mind would want to stay, if not for very long. The desk clerk, a cousin of Morton Dryden, the motel's owner, told Henkel that the family had headed west, and he caught up with them about three miles down the road. The father simply refused to talk to him, and two of his three kids started crying when Henkel appeared. The mother, meanwhile, just stared ahead, her face ashen. Henkel let them go. After all, what else could he do? He did return to the motel, though, and the clerk confirmed that the family had been visited by two men, but he claimed not to have seen them or their vehicle clearly, despite the fact that their room had been directly across from the motel office, and it was a bright, sunny day. Later, Henkel paid a visit to Morton Dryden, and suggested that he ought to look again at the caliber of his employees, and maybe consider having their eyesight checked, too.

The business with Lucius had been only the most recent in a series of confrontations with the Cut over the course of Henkel's career, but he knew that his were token gestures, and nothing more. Had he been serious about taking on the Cut, he'd have sat down with the FBI, or maybe the ATF, and told them—

But that was it: told them what? That a community of families, living in isolation on privately owned land, and leading an existence that appeared to be in no way luxurious or excessive, might, just might, be engaged in some form of criminal behavior, and could perhaps have been responsible for killings stretching back generations, although there was nothing to link them to such crimes other than local gossip and Henkel's own suspicions? Both the feds and the ATF had plenty to be getting along with, what with drug cartels, terrorists—domestic and otherwise— criminal gangs, and whatever other threats to society might be competing for their attention at any given time, without listening to the woes of some pissant sheriff in the smallest pissant county of a state that, last time Henkel bothered to check, was at the bottom of the national well-being list for the sixth year running, which meant that when it came to basic needs, sensible lifestyle choices, work environment, health, and optimism, residents in West Virginia were just shit out of luck.

So if the people of the Cut took it upon themselves to give Plassey County an edge by warning off anyone who viewed it as an easy conquest for drugs, prostitution, racketeering, or excessive corruption— because a little corruption always needed to be factored into things, as it was the oil that kept the machinery of commerce rolling—then good for them, or so common, unspoken wisdom might have put it. And if certain nefarious individuals, who meant no good for beast or man, chose to ignore those warnings, and maybe the beatings that followed, or the torching of their homes, business premises, or meeting spaces, and ended up inspecting tree roots from below, then so be it. They had been given the opportunity to repent of their sins, or seek alternative locations in which to indulge them, and were no loss to society anyhow.

This had been Russ Dugar's view, and that of most of his predecessors, until Henkel arrived and began, if not to rock the boat, then to make its passage less smooth than before. Perhaps he was fortunate that the Cut had become less active—or as Henkel suspected, less obvious and open in its activities, in part as a reaction to his presence—and that he himself maintained a certain level of support in the county. The result was an uneasy status quo between Henkel and the Cut.

But with the election on the horizon, Henkel had begun to worry that the Cut might be considering an intervention to tilt the balance back in its favor. It wouldn't take much—a quiet word with some influential figures, a veiled threat or two where necessary—to sow doubts in the minds of voters about the wisdom of reelecting Henkel as sheriff, with Ned Ralston hovering behind, ready to become a puppet sheriff another term down the line.

Now here was Oberon, his hair hanging down his back in a carefully worked ponytail, his red checked shirt neatly pressed, his jeans worn but clean, his work boots old but freshly treated with dubbin in anticipation of the coming winter. His beard was thick but not unruly, the ends of his mustache hanging almost to his chin, giving him the aspect of a Viking, as though by his very presence he offered proof to those who believed that Norsemen had done more than establish short-term settlements in these lands.

"Mind if I join you?" asked Oberon.

Henkel saw that Miss Queenie was watching them from her post by the register. Some of the younger men and women of the Cut occasionally came into her place of business, always maintaining a low-key presence and paying in cash, but she could not recall ever seeing Oberon darken her door. Her hand hovered over the push-button phone on the wall, Miss Queenie having no truck with cell phones, but Henkel caught her eye and gave the slightest shake of his head.

Oberon didn't turn his back, but he must have guessed what was happening.

"I just want to talk," he said.

Henkel indicated the seat opposite, and Oberon sat. Connie, the waitress, came over and asked if he'd like to order anything. She regarded Oberon curiously, and not without a certain interest, for he was an imposing man, and Connie and he were of a similar age.

"Some mint tea, if you have it," said Oberon, and Connie told him she'd be right back with it. He and Henkel didn't speak until the tea arrived, and Connie gave them some space. The booths and tables nearest to them were all empty, so there was no chance that they might be overheard.

"I saw the Charleston paper on the front seat of your car," said Oberon. "You had a chance to read it yet?"

"I skimmed through it," said Henkel.

"You see the story about those two young men, the ones that the Lutter boy stumbled on over by Mortonsville?"

"I did."

"I hear you were there when they were found."

"I came later, but not by much."

Oberon nodded. "After Clyde Bentley, right?"

"That's correct."

"The newspaper story claimed those boys—Killian and Huff, if I have their names right—might have been engaged in the distribution of narcotics."

"That's what I read."

"It's a dangerous business to be in."

"It was for them."

Oberon nodded again and tugged gently at his beard, as though contemplating the profundity of Henkel's observation.

"Do you have any information you'd like to share about the circumstances of their deaths?" asked Henkel.

Oberon's expression didn't change, but his body seemed to relax into position, like a fencer's after an opponent's first thrust has confirmed that the match is on.

"No, I don't think that I do," said Oberon.

"Well, if that situation changes, you ought to contact the Bureau of Criminal Investigation. They have the lead, on account of their resources."

Oberon looked out the window to where Benedict was seated in the truck with the windows down, his left hand tapping a cadence on the door.

"Sheriff Henkel," said Oberon, "I sometimes think we got off on the wrong foot from the start."

"Why is that?"

"Well, in the event of something like this happening in the past, your predecessor, Sheriff Dugar, would have taken the time to inform me and my people of it, just as a matter of courtesy. The Cut occupies a significant area of Plassey County. What affects the county affects the Cut."

"Sheriff Dugar did a lot of things differently, and not all of them in ways of which I approve."

"I understand that. I don't have any illusions but that you're your own man. But two bodies being discovered so close to the Cut is obviously a matter of concern to us. Those boys were found early in the morning, yet it was almost noon when we heard about it, and then only because one of my people was driving out that way and saw the commotion."

"Well, I'm real sorry I couldn't spare a deputy to bring you the news in person," said Henkel. "As you can imagine, moving two bodies from a shallow grave eats up a lot of time and resources. It's smelly work, too, and dirty. Makes you feel bad for the men and women who have to do it, bad for the victims, too, and inculcates a certain negative disposition toward whomever might have put them in the ground to begin with."

"I'm sure," said Oberon. He was listening intently to Henkel, both to what was being said and what lay behind it.

"I have been considering how they came to be found so easily, though," Henkel continued. "Seems to me that it was a botched job, burying them so shallow like that. Makes me wonder if the people responsible might have been interrupted, or believed they were at risk of discovery. It could be that somebody saw them or their vehicle, and maybe doesn't realize the significance of it as of yet. But, like I said, that's mostly a matter for the state police, although we'll provide any assistance we can."

Henkel leaned forward and clasped his hands before him.

"What I'm saying is, somebody fucked up. They killed those boys, rushed their burial, and managed to put them in the ground on the wrong side of the county line. Worse, what I hear is that Killian and Huff weren't just on the radar of the state police here and in Ohio, but the DEA had started to take an interest in them as well. So who knows what kind of shit is going to start spilling into Plassey County on account of all this? And, as you just told me, what flows into this county flows into the Cut."

Oberon took a sip of his mint tea, the first time he'd touched it since it arrived at the table. He didn't seem to find it to his liking, and pushed it away.

"Sheriff, you sound almost pleased about all this attention," he said.

"I enjoy seeing the law in operation," said Henkel. "It gives me faith in the future of our society."

Oberon stood.

"Thank you for your time," he said. "My apologies for interrupting your reading."

"No apologies necessary," Henkel replied. "Oh, and you might want to tell the boy with you that the wearing of seat belts is mandatory in the state of West Virginia, and violators can be fined up to twenty-five dollars. I wouldn't want to have to pull him over and ruin his day. Come to think of it, I haven't seen him around much until this morning. He been away?"

"He had some business to conduct," said Oberon.

"And where would that have been?"

"Elsewhere."

"Elsewhere, right," said Henkel. "I just hope it turned out satisfactorily, because what's good for the Cut is good for the county, right? And the mint tea is on me. Anytime you need to talk again, you know where to find me."

"I do," said Oberon. "Here, obviously. At your office. And—"

Henkel wagged a finger, but he did not smile.

"And that's it. I like to think of my home as inviolate. You could almost say I'm excessively protective of it."

"I'll remember that."

"Make sure that you do," said Henkel. "Because I'll kill anyone who walks through my door uninvited."

"Likewise," said Oberon.

Henkel stared after him as he left, and continued watching him as he climbed back into his truck and said something to Benedict. The boy reached into his pocket, pulled out three bills, and sent them fluttering to the ground, grinning all the time at Henkel as the wind carried the $25 away. The truck pulled out and turned right, bound for the Cut.

Henkel sat back in his chair. There was sweat on his palms, and his chest hurt. He reached under the table and touched the grip of his gun. It was time, he thought.

Time to bring the Cut to an end.

P arker called Castin and told him about the imminent meeting with the Portland PD, although he decided to leave out the part about Macy shoving cans of soda up his ass, as he didn't want to prejudice proceedings before they'd even begun. He joined Angel and Louis for a quick coffee at Big Sky, and asked them to swing by Harpur Griffin's place and then cruise the streets. Griffin's building would already be swarming with police, but at least Angel and Louis would be able to identify the vehicle driven by the two men who'd been with Griffin at the Porterhouse, and it was just possible that they were still in the vicinity: possible, but unlikely.

Parker headed down to Portland PD headquarters on Middle Street, and parked by the Portland Regency Hotel. Castin was waiting for him at the corner, with a soda in one hand and a cigarette in the other. Despite this, he looked surprisingly relaxed, but Parker guessed that he had probably been smoking, as well as drinking sugary carbonated drinks, for so long that he was largely immune from the effects of both, and only withdrawal was likely to cause him complications.

They consulted for a minute or two before heading into the lobby to wait for Macy to escort them to the meeting room. Fortnum or Franks was already present, along with a lieutenant from CID named Dundonald, who Parker vaguely knew by sight, and—hey!—Gordon Walsh.

Once the introductions were complete, and coffee was offered and declined, Castin explained how Parker had been engaged to search for the recently released Jerome Burnel, for whose safety Castin was now concerned. Parker, in turn, explained how he had come to track Harpur Griffin to the Porterhouse, which was when the ears of the detectives in the room pricked up. Parker knew that they'd like the sound of Burnel bearing a grudge against Griffin for his treatment of him in Warren, but there was nothing he could do about it. He still didn't believe Burnel had anything to do with Griffin's death, but if he had, there was no point in trying to protect him by concealing the truth from detectives like Macy and Walsh, who were smart enough to figure it out for themselves. He gave them detailed descriptions of the two men who had been with Griffin at the bar, along with the make and license number of the vehicle they'd been driving. It was at this point that Macy's face clouded.

"What is it?" asked Parker.

"That car was found burned out early this morning," said Macy, "in a disused lot off Route One in Saco. We only received the notification from Saco PD an hour ago, after they heard about our own burned-out vehicle and wondered if there could be a connection between the two incidents."

"Might have helped us if you'd come forward earlier to tell us about the men at the Porterhouse," said Furnish, now that the earlier introductions had clarified just what his name was.

"Why would I have done that?" asked Parker. He wasn't about to let Furnish score points off him. "I had no knowledge of the commission of a crime."

"You were looking for a man in violation of his probation."

"I was searching for Mr. Castin's client. I wasn't aware that the law had changed to oblige me to keep you notified of my movements."

"Boys, boys," said Macy. Walsh just grunted. Dundonald made a note of something, then crossed it out. Furnish folded his arms and tried not to look like he was sulking.

"And you have no knowledge of Mr. Burnel's current whereabouts?" Macy asked Castin.

"No."

"He hasn't been in contact since he asked you to pay Mr. Parker for his services?"

"No."

"Has any further attempt been made to withdraw money from his account?"

"He doesn't have a bank card. Any withdrawal would have to be made through me, or in person at the counter, and neither of those instances has occurred. Naturally, I'll keep an eye open for any withdrawals once the bank opens tomorrow. I may even have the account frozen."

"I have to advise you," said Macy, "that your client is a suspect in what we now believe to be the murder of Harpur Griffin—at least, we're assuming that it's Griffin in the car, pending the arrival of dental records from Warren."

"Understood," said Castin.

"Is there anything else Mr. Parker would like to share with us?" asked Dundonald.

"No, I think that's everything," said Parker. Walsh grunted again. Parker gave him the hard eye, and he looked away, but Macy had picked up on Walsh's skepticism. She waited until everyone else had left, and Castin was on his way out, before grabbing Parker's arm and yanking him toward a window.

"If you're withholding information that may be of use in this investigation," she said quietly, "and I find out, I'll have you charged with obstruction of justice."

"You've been spending too long with Furnish," said Parker. "I'm not psychic so I can't tell what seemingly irrelevant detail might prove pertinent at some point in the future. I have no interest in protecting Burnel if he's a killer, but I've told you already that I don't believe he is. The ones you should be looking for are the two men who were with Griffin at the

Porterhouse, but I don't have any more idea of who they might be, or where they've gone, than you do. Right now, we're on the same page."

"I don't believe that for a moment. You remember what I said: I'll come after you."

Parker shrugged, and said, "I hear you're dating that restaurant guy, Sanders."

Macy looked slightly stunned at the sudden change in direction that the conversation had taken.

"What the hell has that got to do with anything?"

"Nothing. Just what I heard."

"Is this where I tell you that you had your chance?"

"If you like. Why are you dating Sanders anyway? I've seen him. He looks like he eats all his meals at Denny's."

"You're a piece of work, you know that?"

"I think you're dating him because it's the only way you can afford to eat in his restaurants."

"Fuck you."

But she was grinning.

"You're right," said Parker. "I had my chance."

"Yeah, you did. Are you going to keep looking for Burnel?"

"I'll talk to Moxie, see what he says."

"And if he says no?"

"I think I'll keep looking anyway."

"You find out anything, you call me."

"I have your number," he said.

"No, you never had my number," she replied, and she left him to find his own way out of the building.

———

CASTIN WAS WAITING FOR Parker outside. He was smoking another cigarette and drinking from a new can of soda, which Parker could only assume he had been keeping in his briefcase for emergency use.

"I always felt sorry for Jerome Burnel," said Castin, between puffs and slurps.

"You may have more cause to feel sorry for him now than before."

"I think you're right, although I hope you're not. So what do you need?"

"You want to keep paying me to look for him?"

"You know, I figure I could set you to search for him for free, because I can see in your eyes that you're not going to let this thing go. I don't work that way, though. Bill me for your hours, and try not to kill anybody. If you do, call Aimee Price up in South Freeport. She must be used to you by now."

"Well, since I'm on your dime I'll draw on your resources. Can you have someone dig out everything to be found on Harpur Griffin, including the name of his lawyer in Maine. I'd be surprised if it wasn't a court-appointed attorney, in which case he, or she, might be more amenable to talking about him than someone in private practice. Once you get me the details, I'll cross-check them with what I have on Burnel."

"I'll call my secretary and have her come in. She could use the overtime." Castin looked at the glowing tip of his cigarette. "Hell of a way to go, being burned alive."

"Yeah."

"Someone must really not have cared much for Harpur Griffin."

"I met him. He was hard to warm to."

"Easier after they burned him," said Castin, smiling at his own joke.

But Castin was right, thought Parker. If the object of the exercise had been to silence Griffin, there were simpler and more efficient ways of going about it. Burning a man alive in his car was a severe punishment. Had Griffin earned it in the eyes of his killers by being foolish enough to talk about the Dead King while in Warren? It still seemed excessive to Parker, unless a message was being sent to someone else, a warning to remain silent. But if that was the case, then at whom was it directed?

Moxie finished his cigarette and soda, and trashed the can and the butt.

"I'll be on my way, then," he said.

"Sure. And Moxie?"

"What?"

"Does anyone ever call you Oleg?"

Castin thought for a moment.

"Who's Oleg?"

# XLVI

P arker took another run past the scene of Griffin's murder. The
cordon was still in place, and a fingertip search of the scene had
commenced, but the body was gone and the car had been placed
on the back of a flatbed truck for transportation to the lab.

Parker called Angel and arranged to meet him and Louis for brunch at
the Bayside American Cafe, which used to be called Bintliff's, although
thankfully only the name had changed and not the quality of the food.
Angel and Louis both ordered the lobster eggs Benedict, as was their
admittedly expensive habit, while Parker stuck with bacon and eggs. As
anticipated, Griffin's apartment had been sealed by the police, and Angel
and Louis found no trace of the men who had been with him at the Porterhouse. Parker, in turn, went over all that had transpired in the course
of the meeting at Middle Street, and watched a light begin to glow in
Louis's eyes at the news that Castin was paying Parker to find out what
might have befallen Jerome Burnel. The two men at the bar had raised
Louis's hackles, and he was now almost certainly guaranteed another
encounter with them, one that might result in violence and death.

If he was lucky.

They talked as they ate. Louis agreed with Parker that Griffin's
murder had not simply been a matter of expediency, but a form of
extreme retribution.

"It could also be a warning," said Angel, following the second train of thought.

"Yes, but to whom?" said Parker.

"Us, maybe."

Parker hadn't considered that possibility.

"If it was," said Louis, "then they don't know us very well."

"No," admitted Angel, "they don't. After all, when have we ever paid attention to warnings?"

"I prefer to think of them as invitations," said Louis.

The check arrived. Parker picked it up.

"You gonna pay that?" asked Angel.

"I'll bill Moxie for it. This was a business meeting."

"You think he'd spring for champagne later?"

"Maybe if we find Burnel alive."

"So no champagne, then."

"Probably not."

———

BACK IN SCARBOROUGH, PARKER began examining Jerome Burnel's case files for a third time. He was almost finished when a driver arrived with a stack of paperwork relating to Harpur Griffin, including his personal details and a list of previous convictions, for some of which he'd served time in Ohio and West Virginia. Parker flicked through the documents, establishing their order and relevance, before returning to the beginning. He made one quick run-through, then called the lawyer who had defended Griffin during his most recent trial. Her name was Beth Shears and, according to an Internet search, she had since moved on to work in the state's Department of Professional and Financial Regulation. Parker wasn't surprised. Maine didn't have a public defender's office, and instead the state hired private attorneys to take on court-appointed work. The rates were far lower than those in private practice, and the state's budget for court-appointed and indigent defense wasn't enough to meet demand. Lawyers either supplemented state work as best they could or, like Shears, went in search of positions with more money and security.

He found Shears's number in the phone book, and was lucky enough to get her at home. She'd seen the TV reports on Griffin, and so wasn't surprised to be receiving a call about him, although she'd expected the first one to come from the police. She couldn't tell Parker a lot about her former client. He'd pleaded not guilty, despite fingerprint and DNA evidence to the contrary. Oh, and he'd also been apprehended at the scene, which hadn't helped his cause. He was only lucky that the old woman hit hardest didn't die in the immediate aftermath of the attack, or else he'd still be in Warren now.

"He came on to me," said Shears.

"Really?"

"Yeah, three times. I should have thrown him to the wolves, but I needed the money."

"What, so you let him?"

It took Shears a moment to figure out that Parker was joking.

"No, smart-ass, I held my temper and told him that I'd walk away if he even looked at me strangely again. I did my best for him, but, between us, I just wanted the judge to lock him up."

"Did he ever mention a king to you?"

He was being careful here. He knew the police would talk to Shears eventually.

"As in royalty?"

"Anything like that."

"No, I don't believe so."

Parker thanked her, looked at his notes, and decided that he hadn't learned much of use. He returned to the files, but only got as far as the second page when he paused, flicked back, found the reference that had caught his attention, then put the Griffin material aside and reached for Burnel's file. It took him a while to find the papers he wanted: the background information on Burnel's ex-wife, Norah Meddows, born June 19, 1971, in Deep Dell, West Virginia. He held her details in his left hand, and Harpur Griffin's in his right. Harpur Griffin: born November 20, 1979, in Turley, West Virginia.

Parker pulled up a map of West Virginia on his computer, and saw that Deep Dell and Turley were both in Plassey County, the smallest county in the state.

Curious.

He spent another hour working Norah Meddows alone, using the social security number contained in the file given to him by Castin. By the time he was done, he had her current address, place of employment, and the make of car she drove. She was living in Columbus, Ohio, about a four-hour ride from Plassey County. She hadn't quite returned home, but it was close enough.

What was it one of the men had said to Burnel? *I like your jacket.* That was it. He could have meant nothing by it, or else something very significant indeed: not just that he liked the jacket, but the gemstones he knew it contained.

How badly could a wife hate her husband? Parker supposed there were no limits, not really. Badly enough to arrange for him to be robbed and murdered, only to have it all fall apart when Burnel pulled a gun and started shooting? Maybe. But badly enough to set him up for a prison fall? Badly enough to have him brutalized while inside?

Unless Norah Meddows was a complete sadist, why go to the trouble of ruining her husband's life in the aftermath of a failed robbery? They weren't getting along, and divorces weren't so hard to come by. She'd have been entitled to alimony. Maybe she was just greedy and wanted everything.

No, he was missing something. He knew it. A point of contact between Griffin and Norah Meddows was absent. True, they came from the same county, but Griffin had entered the picture only after Burnel was incarcerated, and Griffin, high on Adderall, hadn't let slip that

Burnel had enraged Norah Meddows. No, he claimed that Burnel had somehow crossed the Dead King, and it was the mention of the Dead King at the Porterhouse that had brought a reaction from the two men with Griffin, and almost certainly contributed to his death.

It was a pity Parker didn't know anyone in West Virginia. He performed one more Internet search, and was grateful that he did. Sometimes, life dealt you a halfway decent hand.

As it turned out, he did know someone in West Virginia. Parker was about to renew an old acquaintanceship. He just didn't think that the other half of this relationship would be very pleased to hear from him again.

He continued working late in the evening and into the night. He sat on the couch in his office, his legs stretched before him, his back supported by cushions. All he needed was a rug and a bath chair and he'd officially be an old geezer. Only at 2:00 a.m. did he cease taking notes, because he'd found at last what he had been looking for from the start: a Dead King.

And then he saw the name attached to the academic reference, and a prickle of disquiet crept across him like the touch of a spider in the dark.

# XLVII

O nly about eighteen hundred students were enrolled at Bowdoin College, but given that its hometown of Brunswick had a population just north of 20,000, their presence exerted a significant influence on the community. The vibe in summer was laid-back. Now that the students had returned, the vibe in fall was also laid-back—as befitted a small, private liberal arts college—but with slightly more noise.

Parker liked Brunswick. It had a Bull Moose store that crammed a lot of books and music into its small space, which Parker regarded as an indication that all might not yet be lost for humanity, and the town itself was pretty, once you got past the logjam on Route 1 and progressed to the appropriately named Pleasant Street. He passed the First Parish Church, where, in pew 23, Harriet Beecher Stowe first conceived of *Uncle Tom's Cabin*, and continued along Maine Street until he came to Ashby House, home of the college's faculty of religion.

———

PROFESSOR IAN WILLIAMSON WAS sitting at his office window in Ashby House, amusing himself by counting the remaining leaves on the nearest tree while half-listening to one of his students complain of how GWS 1017, the Christian Sexual Ethics offering, was making her feel uneasy due to its use of explicit language. Williamson wasn't actually sure that there *was* any explicit language in the Christian Sexual Ethics option, or none that he would have regarded as such, but then he had to admit that students these days appeared more ready to take umbrage than those of previous generations. He had a vague longing for the student radicalism of the sixties and seventies, mainly because he had been too young to experience it himself. It seemed to him that the youth of that era had been looking for reasons to be angry, which was perfectly understandable because the young were supposed to be angry. Now the young were just looking for reasons to feel offended, and that wasn't the same thing at all. The four ages of man, as far as Williamson was concerned, were confusion, anger, complacency, and grumpiness, but it was important to embrace them in the right order.

The Christian Sexual Ethics course wasn't even one of his own, but because he was English and the girl was an international student from his homeland, albeit one with a remarkably sheltered upbringing, she had turned to him in her moment of need. He was about to suggest that she switch to Rel 216, The New Testament in Its World, which would provide less scope for unhappiness, provided she called in sick should it appear to be about to touch on matters circumcisional in its rituals section, when he saw the distinctive Mustang pull up outside Ashby House and Parker emerge from it.

"Penny," he said, interrupting her in mid-flow about what she believed to be soft-pedaling on matters of sexual orientation, "I'm afraid I have another meeting that's about to begin. Leave me to think about this for the rest of the day, and I'll have an answer for you in the morning."

He smiled his best smile, the one that had brought a thousand American women—well, a few: three, actually, depending on how one chose to define a sexual encounter—to his bed when he was still a single man. Not that he had any intention of trying to lure Penny to his bed, nor would he have done so even had he been a young and single doctorate student. Frankly, after hearing her views on GWS 1017, there wouldn't have been much point.

He heard the door close behind her, but by then he was standing at his window, watching Parker's progress, and had anyone been present to witness it, the expression on Williamson's face might have led them to believe that the impending visit was not entirely a welcome one.

It had been many months since Williamson and Parker had last met, when the detective had come to discuss the qualifications, real or fraudulently claimed, of a preacher named Michael Warraner, who had ministered to the town of Prosperous. Warraner had come to regret Parker's interest in his affairs, but from what Williamson knew of Parker, regret, injury, and sudden mortality were associated risks when dealing with him, which might have explained some of his nervousness at the detective's return to Bowdoin. But Williamson greeted him warmly, asked after his health, and offered coffee or tea, both of which were declined. He thought that Parker looked thinner, which was to be expected after what he had endured, but the effect was not to diminish him but rather to concentrate, and perhaps even enhance, his sense of energy and mission.

As for Williamson himself, he remained unchanged as far as Parker was concerned: the same disheveled hair and the same worn Converse sneakers, although combined now with clothing of browns and reds, perhaps as a gesture to the season, or so that he could, if necessary, hide himself from his students in a pile of leaves. It looked like he'd added some more religious artifacts to the collection in his office, and several extra piles of books, although that hardly seemed possible given how crammed the shelves and floor space had been when Parker last visited.

"I noticed in the college guide that the faculty has a new option in Paganism, Christianity, and the Occult," said Parker. "That wouldn't be one of yours, by any chance?"

"Am I that obvious?" said Williamson. "It's turned out to be one of the most popular courses we've ever offered. Booked out. Standing room only. Although I'm not sure that we'll have enough cauldrons for everybody. That's a joke, by the way."

"I got it. I even understand irony. I've seen *Frasier*."

"Well, then I may try some irony later, just to test you."

Williamson invited Parker to take a seat while he assumed the chair opposite, a low coffee table between them. Parker reached into his satchel and produced two books: the studies of the Green Man, the pagan figure represented on some old European churches, that Williamson had loaned him many months before, when Parker was investigating the town of Prosperous. Williamson thanked him, and gave the covers of the volumes a little pat, like a man greeting his returning dogs.

"I visited Prosperous," said Williamson.

"Really?"

"Yes, out of curiosity as much as anything else. It's changed considerably."

"For the better, I hope."

"I suppose that depends on whether you have to live there or not. They still seem to be rebuilding parts of it, but it appears to have survived—as, more to the point, and more to be welcomed, have you. There are lots of rumors about what happened to you, and how it might have been linked to the fate of Prosperous."

"I've heard most of them."

"Are they true?"

"I think they're called rumors for a reason."

"That's not quite an answer."

Parker relented, but only slightly.

"I'm not sure I'm ready to give any answers yet, or at least not ones that might incriminate me or anyone else."

"We have an archive—well, more correctly, I have an archive, which the college kindly keeps under lock and key. If you did feel the urge, I'd like to hear more about the fall of Prosperous, and have it on record. It could be arranged that the papers would remain sealed until after your death."

"I'll bear it in mind, but I can't say that it appeals."

"If that sounds too formal, or too risky, I'd be happy to listen to a tale told over a drink. A story, after all, is just a story."

"That might work."

"Right, then. Now, I sense that you didn't just come here to return my books. Is there something I can help you with?"

"Perhaps," said Parker. "I'd like you to tell me about dead kings."

Chapter

# XLVIII

Leaves falling; the coming and going of students. Across Maine Street, Bowdoin College Museum of Art was hosting an exhibition entitled *Night Vision: Nocturnes in American Art, 1860–1960*. Parker thought that he might take a look at it later, if there was time.

Williamson fiddled with his Nespresso machine. The act of making a cup of coffee appeared to help him arrange his thoughts, the physical routines echoing his mental processes. Parker had told him something of how he had come to be asking about dead kings, and Williamson had blanched as he made the connection to the man who had been found burned alive in his car over the previous weekend.

"That—and I'm sure you'll forgive me if I sound impressed—is a very obscure piece of folklore," said Williamson, as the coffee began to pour. "What makes you think that this man Griffin wasn't simply referring to an individual, someone with an ear for striking nomenclature?"

"As far as I can tell, there isn't even a rapper called Dead King, and those guys pick up on all the good names," said Parker. "But I admit I believed I'd exhausted every avenue of inquiry, and was thinking along those same lines—that Griffin was using someone's nickname—until I found one reference to a 'dead king' in a book called *Violence and Devotion in Medieval Society*, published back in 1945."

"Which brought you to me."

"That's why I get to put the word 'investigator' on my business cards, helped by the fact that the book was written by an English academic named Norman Williamson, which led me to wonder if you might not have entered the family business."

"My grandfather," said Williamson. He searched his shelves, found his copy of the book, and handed it to Parker. "I wasn't even aware that the book could be found on the Internet."

"Someone scanned and posted it. I'd say that you were being hurt for royalties, except I suspect it's out of copyright by now."

"Not quite," said Williamson. "Nevertheless, I don't believe that I'd have been buying a yacht with the proceeds in any case."

The book was in plain brown boards, with the gold lettering of the author's name and the title almost entirely rubbed away. Parker flicked to the title page and saw that it had been inscribed "with paternal affection and admiration" to someone named Alice.

"Your mother?" asked Parker.

"My aunt. I'm sure my mother must have had a copy too, at one point, but it went missing somewhere along the way. My mother preferred romantic fiction, which is no judgment upon the woman herself, of whom I remain very fond."

He added milk to his coffee, and resumed his seat. Parker, meanwhile, found the page that he had printed from the Internet and brought with him, just in case Williamson, Ian, wasn't related to Williamson, Norman, or didn't possess a copy of the book in question.

"The study makes only a passing reference to a dead king in the section on totems," said Parker. "Would you have anything more detailed, or more recent?"

"I don't think very much has been done on it," said Williamson. "Entire dictionaries and encyclopedias have been devoted to superstitions and folklore; even the best can barely find space for all of them, and that's before you get down to the micro level. Blakeborough's *Wit, Character, Folklore and Customs of the North Riding of Yorkshire*, published in

1898, runs to five hundred pages and includes more than four thousand idioms, and that's just one third of the county. Or take a look at this."

He opened a door under the shelves, and Parker saw layers of bound documents. Williamson ran a finger along the spines until he came to the one that he wanted, and gave it to Parker, who glanced at the title page.

"*Examples of Printed Folk-Lore Concerning the East Riding of Yorkshire, Collected and Edited by Mrs. Gutch*," Parker read aloud. "Who's Mrs. Gutch?"

"Eliza Gutch. It was she who suggested the foundation of the Folklore Society in England in the nineteenth century. Take a look at the contents page."

Parker did. It covered Natural and Inorganic Objects; Respect Paid to Trees and Plants in Alphabetical Order; and Beasts, Birds, Insects. But all of this represented only Mrs. Gutch's efforts to soften the reader up for the good stuff, including Goblindom; Leechcraft; Witchcraft; Wife-Selling; Death Portent; Dog-Whipping Day; Finding of Drowned Body; and Creaking Boots.

"It looks like Mrs. Gutch embraced a wide range of interests," he said.

"Disturbingly so," said Williamson. "Useful woman, though. Without her efforts, a great deal of valuable material might have been lost. That study of the East Riding is especially meticulous, which makes what it leaves out even more fascinating."

"Dead kings?"

"Very good."

"Maybe she just hadn't heard of them."

"If she hadn't heard of something, then it didn't exist. That's just it, though: she *had* heard of dead kings, but she chose not to include them in her collection."

"How do you know?"

"Because my grandfather interviewed her for his book, and she confirmed it in private to him."

"So why exclude them?"

"Because someone told her to."

"She said that?"

"More or less. My grandfather's notes indicate that it was the only time he detected signs of evasiveness in Mrs. Gutch. This was a woman perfectly at home with mythology and folklore. I can't say how much of it she believed was real, but she clearly wasn't easily disturbed."

"Did your grandfather draw any conclusions from this?"

"He suspected, but could never prove, that somewhere in the East Riding of Yorkshire was a dead king."

"Which brings us to the core question," said Parker. "Namely, what exactly is a dead king?"

———

OUTSIDE ASHBY HOUSE, a group of students tossed a miniature football around the parking lot. Across the street, a small line had formed to enter the art museum. Most of the buildings along Maine Street were owned by, or connected to, Bowdoin, even if Massachusetts Hall, the oldest college building in the state, was some distance away, on the north side of the original quadrangle. It gave the individual departments the feeling of outposts, of being their own self-contained universes, and Williamson's office, with its crosses and mandalas, its shofars, its *murtis* of the Hindu deities, seemed particularly like a world of its own, especially when the pagan artifacts were included: images of fertility goddesses or massively phallic males, and half-glimpsed demons carved in stone so worn by time that, from a certain angle, they might be viewed as retreating into the material as belief in them faded or, alternatively, emerging slowly from the rocks in which they had hidden themselves, believing that their time had come again.

"What do you know of hands of glory?" asked Williamson.

"Nothing that wouldn't be considered rude."

Williamson raised his eyes to whatever god he happened to be researching at that particular time. "I already have hundreds of teen-agers to try my patience," he said, "but you just had to add yourself to their number."

"Sorry."

"Never mind, I'm used to it. A hand of glory is the dried, preserved hand of a hanged man: it's usually the left although, in the case of a murderer, a preference might be expressed for the hand that commit-ted the crime. Numerous preparations were suggested for its preser-vation, including soaking it in varieties of urine, but the ultimate end was to ensure that what remained was a talisman that could be used to cure illness or, if fitted with a candle, to take away the power of motion and speech. It wasn't just hands, either. People fought under the scaf-fold for teeth, ears, bits of hair, anything that might retain the essence of the dead.

"Even severed heads."

Here he gave a tug at his chin, as though to ensure that his own head remained intact and in place.

"Heads, heads, heads . . ."

Williamson went to a shelf and found a small silver coin, which he handed to Parker. The coin had a hole cut close to the edge, perhaps through which to pass a chain.

"What is it?" asked Parker.

"An Aethelred penny, minted in Cambridge, England. It's over a mil-lennium old. What you're holding may once have been in contact with a dead king."

Parker stopped gently rubbing the coin and put it on the table between them. He still wasn't sure what a dead king was, and until he was, he wanted to limit his exposure.

"Dead kings could have originated in England—certainly, the oldest of them was found there—but it's possible the tradition may have been influenced by Viking mercenaries. In 2009, a burial pit was revealed at Ridgeway Hill, Dorset, in the southwest of England, which is where that coin was discovered. The pit contained the remains of more than fifty young Viking men—fifty-four, to be exact, for reasons that will become clear in a moment—all of whom had been murdered and then decapitated. While it's not entirely certain who they were, a Cambridge researcher named Dr. Britt Baillie has concluded that they were Jomsvikings: elite killers, mercenaries who operated from a base in Jomsborg on the Baltic coast. The order to kill them may have come from the Anglo-Saxon ruler Aethelred II, known as Aethelred the Unready because of his reluctance to listen to counsel, who decided to have all the Vikings in England slaughtered on St. Brice's Day, November 13, 1002. Aethelred employed bands of Viking mercenaries to do his dirty work, but he was growing tired of Viking raids on his coast, and feared for his life, so he seems to have decided to get rid of the lot of them, and have done with it. At Ridgeway Hill, the Jomsvikings, if that is indeed who they were, were systematically executed from the front. In other words, they were looking their executioners in the eye when they were beheaded, which bespeaks no small amount of bravery.

"So fifty-four bodies were found in the grave, which would lead one to suspect that there should also be fifty-four skulls, as the heads were all piled together at the far side of the pit. Yet there were not fifty-four heads at Ridgeway, but fifty-five."

"A lost body?" Parker suggested. "Someone executed elsewhere, with only the head transported because it was too much trouble to haul along the corpse?"

"It would make sense if the fifty-fifth head was also that of a Norseman, but it wasn't. Isotope testing on the teeth revealed that the head originated in southern Europe, probably from what was then the Caliphate of Córdoba. It was also at least a century and a half older than the other remains, and holes in the skull suggested that it had once been adorned in some way, probably with gold or precious stones, or coins"—he gestured at the silver penny on the table—"all of which had been removed by the killers of the Vikings."

"What's the explanation?"

"The skull was a totem, a talisman. One of the first—maybe even *the* first—of the dead kings. The Vikings roamed as far east as the Khazar Khanate, between the Black and Caspian Seas. Córdoba was on that route, and had been raided as early as the ninth century.

"My grandfather, it's safe to say, would have been fascinated by the Ridgeway find. In his absence, I took the time to visit the site when I was home for a few weeks. It seemed the least I could do to honor the first Professor Williamson. A dead king, then, is a kind of effigy, typically centered on the skull of a victim, but very rare, even in its most basic form, and the creation of one, as far as we can tell, is entirely the preserve of the most extreme of criminal groups or gangs. By its nature, it requires a certain specialization in killing, because the potency, and therefore the efficacy, of the totem is enhanced by the addition of further body parts from new victims. It doesn't really matter how big or small the remains are; what's important is that they represent something of the life force of the dead.

"Think of it like the natives of certain tribes who consumed the flesh of those whom they had killed in battle. The braver the dead warrior, the more potent the meat. Potency is linked to belief. In a way, you have one of the greatest dead kings of them all visible in almost every Christian church: the crucified Christ. He may not be constructed from actual body parts, but the Christian church makes up for it by having enough relics of saints to fill a good-sized cemetery. And in the Catholic faith transubstantiation turns the bread and wine in the sacrament of the Eucharist into not merely the figurative or symbolic, but the actual body and blood of Christ—if that's what you're prepared to believe.

"Anyway, when those natives eat their enemies, the vitality of the fallen warrior passes to them. A dead king is trickier: it's not just a symbol, and it's not lightly named. You *serve* a dead king. You're its subject. As it is added to, and its potency grows, so too does its hold on those who created it increase."

Parker watched Williamson as he spoke, his hands moving rapidly to emphasize his pronouncements. Beside the silver coin on the table lay the copy of his grandfather's work. All this, Parker thought, from a single reference in an old work, happened across after hours of searching on the Internet. He should have thought it odd that a link to what he might be seeking had come in the form of a man who lived only thirty minutes up the highway from Portland, an academic from whom he had sought help in the past, and whose grandfather happened to have been the one to make a passing reference to dead kings in his work.

But he did not find it strange at all.

There was a time when the detective had almost lost his faith, in the weeks and months after the loss of his wife and first daughter. He wondered what kind of god would allow that level of suffering and violence to be inflicted on two innocents, and had been tempted to conclude that the only answer was no god at all. But he had seen too much since then to believe that what lay beyond death was nothingness, for Jennifer had returned, and others, too, and he himself had sat by the shores of a still lake, waiting for a car to take him on the last journey, the Long Ride.

Whatever entity ruled in the next world—benevolent, uncaring, or simply wanton in its cruelty—had not burned every clue. It had left traces of itself, and if one glanced over them, not heeding, not noticing, they could be passed off as coincidence, or luck. And sometimes that was all it was, but the trick was to be able to discern the difference between accident and intent.

If what Williamson was telling him was correct, then the men who had been with Harpur Griffin at the Porterhouse were involved in the creation of a dead king. Jerome Burnel, it seemed, had come to their attention when he killed two of their number at Dunstan's Gas Station, and that had doomed him.

But what of Burnel's wife? She and Griffin came from the same county in West Virginia. If she had somehow sold out her husband to the servants of a dead king, a plan undone by her husband's secret acquisition of a weapon, and had then set out to ruin him, did she do so on her own initiative or at the instigation of others? If it was the latter, then it could only be that those same individuals had also urged Griffin to make Burnel's time in prison as miserable and painful as possible. What linked Griffin to Burnel's wife, Burnel himself apart, was where they had come from.

Somewhere in Plassey County, West Virginia, was a dead king.

"There is one more thing you should consider," said Williamson. He looked serious, and almost sad.

"What would that be?"

"This man Griffin didn't say 'a' dead king, he specified 'the' dead king. It may just have been a turn of phrase, and could mean nothing."

"Or?"

"What Mrs. Gutch told my grandfather was this: if you create a dry, safe place in your garden, then a creature will make its home there. You'll find a spider or an earwig, or even a larger animal, like a bat or a bird. A dead king is similar: if it becomes strong enough, potent enough, it can act as a magnet. It'll attract something to itself, something that will be happy to make its nest amid old bones. It may not have a name, or a form, not until a composite of the dead supplies it, but once it gets in there, it won't leave. Suddenly, those who wanted a talisman to protect them, who paid a kind of lip service to it in return, and called it a dead king, will find that their ruler isn't quite as lifeless as they once thought. They may even discover that they prefer it this way.

"So if that nest of bones is old and powerful enough, it will draw to it a malignancy of similar age and power, and then what you have isn't just *a* dead king anymore. You've given physicality and purpose to something very unpleasant indeed. If Harpur Griffin didn't misspeak, then he wasn't just referring to a talismanic object.

"He was speaking of an entity."

Chapter

# XLIX

As he had watched Parker arrive, so too did Williamson watch him leave. The academic stood at his office window, keeping the private detective in sight as he crossed Maine Street and headed in the direction of the museum and its *Nocturnes* exhibition. It was appropriate, thought Williamson: Parker was a creature of the dark.

Almost absentmindedly, Williamson reached for a round glass display case on a nearby shelf. Contained within it was a fragment of the ruined church at Prosperous. He lifted the glass and rolled the piece of stone between his fingers. He thought he felt the slightest of vibrations from it, the vestigial remains of the power that it had once contained.

Williamson had traveled a long way to get close to Parker. He had turned down better-paying jobs in favor of the post at Bowdoin, and had exhausted every testimonial and promise of support in order to obtain it.

Now Parker had come to him.

# L

O beron was working on the engine of his truck, winterizing it for the months ahead. It was a little early to be starting on it, but it paid to be careful with the weather being as unpredictable as it was. Regardless, the routine allowed him a degree of solitude and space to think, his hands and eyes taking care of the actions while his mind worked on the problems to hand.

Around him the branches of the ash trees were bare, retaining only the dark seed bunches. The leaves of the beeches had turned a deep yellow, the Virginia creeper the red of wine. The scent of apples was in the air as a team of women and small children manipulated the cast-iron presses behind the Square, filling bottles with juice and setting the mush aside to feed to the pigs.

Oberon worked up a 50/50 mix of antifreeze and water that would protect the truck against temperatures as low as twenty degrees below zero. The Cut was unusual meteorologically as well as geographically: its temperature was always a couple of degrees lower than the rest of the county, which was welcome in summer but less so in winter.

*Henkel. Henkel was a threat.*

Oberon added distilled water to the battery to cover the lead plates, checked the cables and terminals, then set the battery to recharge because the water would have diluted the electrolyte solution.

*Killian and Huff. Those damned bodies . . .*

He then went through the truck's 4WD system, ensuring that the transfer lever, locking hubs, and push-button engagement were all moving well. He didn't bother to install new wipers, as the ones in place were only a couple of months old, and he'd performed an oil check a week or two before. Finally, he gave the truck a good coat of wax to protect the finish from ice and salt, took a soda from the little refrigerator in his garage, and walked into the woods. He'd placed a carved wooden bench in a glade well out of sight of the house, and his family tried not to disturb him when he went there. Oberon brushed some leaves from the seat, then sat and watched a pair of deer move through a big stand of conifers that his father had planted to provide the animals with winter cover from wind and snow. The deer, Oberon knew, would already have begun to decrease their food consumption in preparation for the coming cold, during which they'd rely on their fat reserves and their ability to conserve energy to survive, as deer could live for up to a month without eating. People who didn't know any better sometimes put out food for them in winter, but deer were sensitive creatures, and could take weeks to adjust to a new food source. Corn was the worst: it caused acute acidosis, which could kill a deer agonizingly within days.

Nobody hunted in the Cut except the people of the Cut themselves, and they were careful to take no more than they needed. Oberon didn't hunt at all because he no longer ate meat; he'd stopped a decade before because it made him feel sluggish, and now he consumed mostly vegetables and fruit, with some fish for protein.

Life in the Cut, although hard, was also somewhat idyllic, but an idyll had to be protected and supported, which required funds. Some of that came from the ranges, the name the Cut gave to their systemized robberies and burglaries, but less so than in the past ever since the deaths of his sons. Oberon thought of them often. Years had gone by before he risked the trip to Maine to visit their pauper's graves, and even then he had not lingered.

Up there, where the law had failed to trace their origins, they were Henry Forde and Tobin Simus. To Oberon, they were Balder and Gideon—Balder the prince, the heir—born to different mothers but of the same father. Oberon knew that Russ Dugar might have been aware of who they were, even though they had left the Cut years earlier to roam as part of Balder's apprenticeship, returning only rarely and discreetly to their home. The old sheriff had handed Oberon a copy of photographs from the men's licenses, which had been circulated to law enforcement agencies around the country following their deaths in Maine. Dugar had torn the document into four neat pieces before placing them in an envelope and giving them to Oberon. Neither had said a single word about it again, not even after Oberon left a package containing $10,000 on Dugar's porch mat.

Gideon, the younger of his sons, had been dangerously depraved, and Oberon recognized that he might have been forced to kill him himself if his behavior continued to deteriorate, had Jerome Burnel not done it for him, but Balder was to have been his successor, the leader of the Cut. Now Oberon had no male heirs, and Cassander might soon make a move against him.

It was Oberon who had determined that the Cut would no longer engage in the same degree of criminality that had sustained it until the second half of the last century. Larceny, burglary, kidnapping, bank robbery, and the targeting of rival organizations and the sequestration of their assets, usually at gunpoint and occasionally with associated fatalities, had been the Cut's methods for most of its existence. But the world had changed, and such activities were no longer worth the risk, although the recent killings of Killian and Huff had netted $48,000, after Lucius and Benedict, Zachary Bowman's fool son, had convinced them that they could buy their lives if they handed over all the money they had and promised never to set foot in West Virginia again. Once the cash was theirs, Lucius and Benedict had shot the two men, and then mishandled the disposal of the bodies.

Lucius, aided by his younger brother, Marius, and their comrade Jabal, had also later mishandled the killing of Harpur Griffin. Oberon had not sanctioned Griffin's death, but he should not have been surprised that Marius chose to revenge himself upon Griffin after all these years. Only the public nature of Griffin's murder angered him. It was unnecessary, and risked drawing attention.

Cassander's sons had returned from Maine earlier that day. Marius and Jabal instantly vanished, leaving Lucius to relay the details of what had happened in Maine, and then explain why he and Benedict had not buried Killian and Huff deeper, and farther from the Cut. Oberon blamed Lucius for the mess, because Lucius was the elder of the two. But then Lucius had always been unreliable; it came with his propensity for violence, which was useful on some occasions. Not everyone in the Cut had the stomach for what sometimes needed to be done.

But what Lucius told him had simply added to Oberon's worries. Lucius said that they'd had to rush the job of burial because he'd seen Charlie Lutter's boy—Perry, the idiot—walking through the woods, and if Perry came across them with the bodies they'd have a bigger problem, because something would have to be done about him.

"You should have come clean with me when it happened," said Oberon, as Cassander watched and listened, one hand on his son's left shoulder in a gesture of protection and support. *My blood, right or wrong*, thought Oberon.

"We didn't want to get Perry in trouble," said Lucius, but that wasn't the reason, and Oberon knew it. He had just decided to keep quiet about the possibility of a witness until the discovery of the grave had forced him to be honest.

It was then that Benedict, who was standing by Lucius, spoke up.

"The grave wasn't so shallow," he said.

"What?" said Oberon.

"I helped dig it, and we put those bodies nearly three feet down. I even had time to put stones on them before we covered them up with dirt."

"Yeah," said Lucius, and his sullen expression changed as Benedict threw him a line that might enable him to escape Oberon's anger. "Hey, I remember that!"

"It didn't stop an animal digging it up," said Oberon.

"What animal?" asked Lucius.

Oberon thought. His informant had been detailed, and quite specific, in his description of the scene.

"Fox tracks."

"No fox could have uncovered those bodies," said Benedict.

Cassander spoke.

"If not an animal, then who was it?"

But Oberon already had an answer, and it made him feel tired and old.

Perry Lutter.

———

THE DEER MOVED OFF, ears and tails flicking. Oberon was still angry with Lucius and Benedict. They hadn't handled the situation well, even if, as they claimed, they'd been forced to shoot Killian and Huff earlier than anticipated after Killian made a grab for Benedict's gun. That left them with two bodies to bury, and they didn't want to risk being pulled over for any reason with corpses in the bed of their truck, so they'd made a judgment call and buried them at dusk close to Charlie Lutter's land. They believed themselves to be in the next county, but they were mistaken.

The question was: had Perry Lutter simply stumbled upon the disturbed ground, and out of curiosity begun to dig, or had he witnessed the burial? Perry might not have been about to join Mensa anytime soon, but Oberon had enough experience of his ways to recognize that he possessed an innate cunning. He liked the woods, and was known to wander many miles from home while always finding his way back again, unless he was given a ride by someone from the county, because everyone knew Perry.

He saw a lot, but he gabbed a lot too.

Officially, the police had not confirmed the identity of the person who found the burial site, but even without his sources it wouldn't have been hard for Oberon to guess that it might have been Perry Lutter, and Henkel hadn't denied it when Oberon mentioned Perry's name at the diner. Except now it appeared that Perry might not simply have stumbled across the grave accidentally. Oberon would have to talk with him, and away from his father and mother, who were as protective of their son as bears with a cub.

Then there was the private investigator, the one who had confronted Lucius and Jabal in Portland, necessitating the killing of Griffin in order to ensure that he didn't talk, as well as satisfying Marius's blood urges. With luck, Griffin's death would mark an end to his inquiries, but Oberon decided that he would look into this man Parker, just in case. The Cut did not have Internet access, just as it did not have cable TV, or use any but a handful of the most basic burner phones that were replaced every two weeks. Oberon would have to visit an Internet café outside the county to research Parker.

Which left the matter of Sheriff Edward Henkel. Oberon wanted him gone, but had resigned himself to waiting until the election. Henkel was a respected figure in the county, and had easily won his first term. It had rapidly become clear, though, that he was no friend of the Cut. Still, serious confrontations had largely been avoided in the early days, but recently Henkel was becoming markedly more hostile, and Oberon had decided that he didn't want him working against them for another four years. He had already put together a list of influential individuals who were to be targeted with polite requests, bribes, and what could be viewed—depending on how one took them—as threats in order to ensure that a less proactive sheriff was installed in Plassey County.

But the discovery of the bodies of Killian and Huff was the most immediate threat to the Cut. Following his meeting with Henkel in the diner, Oberon was convinced that the sheriff would exploit any opportunity offered by the investigation to direct its resources toward the secretive community at the heart of the county. He might already be doing so, for who knew to whom he might be speaking, or what kind of friends he had at the state or federal level? It wasn't hard to kill a sheriff—Russ Dugar had learned that, in his last moments—but it was a whole lot harder to deal with the consequences.

Oberon didn't believe that the sheriff's department, or anyone else, had enough evidence to secure a warrant to search the Cut, not yet, but he had made a couple of calls in an effort to muddy the waters. It would buy them some time, at least, and divert resources. If county, state, or federal forces were about to make a move on the Cut, he would almost certainly be given some warning. He would set out a plan of action, and share it with Cassander and the other elders. Each would be assigned a task to carry out in the event of an impending raid. In the meantime, he would find Perry Lutter, and try to establish what he had or had not seen on the night that Killian and Huff were killed.

But there was one loose end that he could take care of right away.

———

OBERON RETURNED TO HIS home. The whole house smelled of vinegar as Sherah, his wife, and their daughter, Tamara, were preserving tomatoes, cucumbers, and capers for the winter. Sherah was his second wife. He had married her a decade to the day after his first wife, Jael, died of pneumonia. Sherah was Jael's younger sister, and both were daughters of Zachary. In a close-knit community like the Cut, such second unions were not unusual. Gideon had been born to another woman between his marriages, and it was this woman whom Oberon blamed for his son's deficiencies. She, like their troubled offspring, was now dead.

He picked up Tamara and raised her high above his head. She was four years old, and one of the youngest children in the Cut. He had hoped for a boy, but had grown to dote on Tamara. He continued to be surprised by just how much love he felt for her. He thought he might even love her more than he had Jael, and certainly more than he loved Sherah. He still wanted another son, but so far Sherah had not conceived again.

"Have you finished your work for the day?" Sherah asked him.

"No, I have one more task to complete."

"Will it take long?"

"It shouldn't, but I'll have to wash when I'm done."

He did not take his eyes from his daughter's face during the entire conversation. Sherah did not mind. She was used to her husband's ways. She knew that she was little more than a replacement for her sister, and new breeding stock for her husband. She wanted to give him the son he desired. She enjoyed the process of trying, and she thought Oberon did too, but she did not know whose body was failing them.

Oberon put his daughter down and went to his private office. When he returned to the kitchen, Sherah saw that he had added to his belt a long knife in a scabbard. She did not comment on it, nor did she do more than pause for a moment in the pouring of vinegar when she saw him take a spade from the shed, and a sealed green bucket, the one in which he stored the quicklime.

"Where is Daddy going?" asked Tamara from her perch on the chair by her mother.

"He has something he needs to finish."

"Can I help him?"

Sherah pulled her daughter to her and kissed her on the crown of her head.

"Maybe when you're older."

# LI

C assander was crossing the Square to his house, one of his dogs trotting alongside him, when he saw Oberon approaching, the spade in his left hand, the knife hanging against his right leg. Cassander knew that knife. Oberon used it only on meat.

Cassander opened his mouth to speak, but Oberon threw the spade in his direction before he could say anything. Cassander caught it, and registered the expression on Oberon's face. It boded well for no one.

"Tell Lucius to dig the hole," said Oberon, without pausing in his stride. "And make sure that it's deep this time."

———

HENKEL RECEIVED THE CALL shortly after 4:00 p.m., from a buddy in the Bureau of Criminal Investigation, an investigator named Scott Stokes. According to Stokes, the investigation into the deaths of Killian and Huff had taken a new turn, based on intelligence received from a CI, a confidential informant. It now looked likely that they'd crossed one of the four cartels—most likely Sinaloa, which controlled 80 percent of the meth trade in the United States, largely through its aggressive policy of combining high purity with lower prices.

"That's bullshit," said Henkel. "Sinaloa doesn't have a cell in West Virginia."

"They're in Ohio, and that's close enough, in case you haven't looked at a map since high school. And Killian and Huff were out of Columbus, which DEA says is simmering nicely for Sinaloa."

"No, you have to listen to me here, Scotty: this is local business. It's tied to the Cut."

"DEA says otherwise, and they're all over this one. They were convinced Huff in particular would lead them to Sinaloa's door. They figured he was ripe for the turning."

"Aw, damn it . . ."

"Look, if you find anything solid that says otherwise, then let me know and I'll run it up the chain. I don't understand why you're getting all hot and bothered about this anyway. Nobody here is complaining about the DEA taking two corpses off our hands."

"Yeah, well, that's where we're different, I guess."

"Come on, don't get all sanctimonious on me."

"I think you've been in Charleston too long, Scotty. You're becoming citified."

"And you've been out there with the hillbillies for too long. You need to try living somewhere with a hard road. If the mood takes you, come on down here for an evening and I'll feed you something better than hoecake."

Henkel told Stokes that he'd think about it, and hung up. He was furious, but there was no point in taking it out on Stokes, and Henkel wanted to remain on good terms with him. He sat back in his chair and dug a pencil into the wood of his desk until the point snapped. A CI? Maybe he'd been mistaken about the Cut's involvement, but he didn't think so. Someone was baiting a hook, knowing that the DEA would bite.

Oberon. It had to be.

———

JEROME BURNEL WAS BLINDED shortly after he was brought to the Cut. It had been a simple thing to do—two flicks of a blade—but it made the

Dead King's influence more profound. Still, before Oberon had taken away his eyes he'd permitted him to catch a glimpse of the king, just so Burnel would understand the nature of the entity with which he had been imprisoned.

By now, Burnel was as good as insane.

He was chained to a stake that was anchored in the concrete floor of the blockhouse. He slept on dirt, and was fed only water and grits. He stank of his own filth, and no longer tried to speak, reason, or bargain with his captors. Instead he lay flat on the ground, and emitted a low keening. His head barely turned at the sound of Oberon entering the blockhouse.

Oberon knew how the voice of the Dead King sounded. It was unsettling to hear, like small bones rattling in a sack. It spoke in no intelligible tongue, and yet those familiar with its timbre held no illusions about its needs and desires. They were unceasing, and foul. Even after all these years, Oberon tried to limit his exposure to the Dead King.

Burnel had been alone with it for days.

The original dead king was almost as old as the Cut, a relic from another age and culture brought to the New World by the earliest Nordic settlers. But the Dead King, the force that now inhabited it, was older than worlds.

Oberon lit a lamp that hung from one of the lower tree branches that ran through the interior. The lamp cast its illumination over Burnel and the Dead King. Its chatter came clearly to Oberon, rendered only slightly more bearable by the fact that it was directed at Burnel.

Oberon knelt beside the blinded man and drew the knife. In all the time that he had been here, no one had confirmed to Burnel the one thing he surely wanted to know above any other:

Why?

Oberon could have told him, and now, at the last, he decided to do so, although he was not certain that Burnel, in his madness, would understand. He grabbed Burnel by the hair and raised his head. Burnel's ruined eyes stared up, unseeing. His mouth hung open, and Oberon saw that part of his tongue was missing. He had chewed it off. Oberon wondered if the Dead King had told him to do it. Probably, just as it had encouraged him to draw out his fingernails with his teeth and pile them in a cairn by his water bowl, and pluck the hairs from his head, one by one, leaving him with scattered bald patches like a mangy hound.

"They were my sons," Oberon whispered. "All of this is because you killed them, and it will still never be enough. But it's over now. Your time of torment is done."

He had intended simply to cut Burnel's throat, but at the final moment he turned the knife and stabbed him in the chest, and once the first wound was inflicted he found that he could not stop, and so Oberon struck at the dying man over and over—jabbing, slicing, tearing—until he knelt in a pool of blood and flesh, his head filled with the chittering of the Dead King.

———

OBERON REGAINED CONSCIOUSNESS BY the mutilated body of Jerome Burnel. He did not know how much time had passed, only that the light was different and the lamp had gone out. The Dead King was now talking to itself.

Oberon left the blockhouse. He walked down to the river, laid his bloodstained clothes by the bank, and immersed himself in its depths, the blood indistinguishable from the darkness of the water as it flowed around him. When eventually he emerged, he was shivering with cold and shock. He put on only his trousers, and used the end of his shirt to clean most of the blood from his knife. He returned to the Square to discover Cassander seated on the grass by his house, smoking a cigarette, the spade at his feet. The porch light caught him, revealing the dirt on his hands and clothes. He rose as he saw Oberon, took the fleece from his upper body, and placed it on the shoulders of the older man. He didn't need to ask if it was done.

Oberon glanced at the spade, and the mud on Cassander's skin.

"I told you to get Lucius to dig that hole."

"I couldn't find him, so I dug it myself."

"Where is he?"

"I don't know."

It was a lie, but Oberon did not call him on it. The two brothers, Lucius and Marius, were plotting somewhere, now that they had returned to the Cut. Maybe even Cassander did not realize how dangerous they really were.

Oberon glanced back over his shoulder. The blockhouse was not visible from where he stood.

"You'll need a sheet of plastic to carry him in. It'll have to be burned after. The quicklime is still up there somewhere."

"I'll take care of it."

"There's a lot of blood. If they come—"

"I told you: I'll take care of it."

He walked Oberon to the door of his home, where Sherah was waiting for him, but Oberon did not eat, and later he did not sleep, for he had spent too long in the blockhouse, and the voice of the Dead King was in his head. Instead he watched the darkening of the Cut, and felt the cold air from the north creeping into his bones.

# LII

Jennifer drifted through her father's house, aware of him as he slept upstairs, but not daring to approach his room, much as she loved to be close to him. He was acutely sensitive to her now; sometimes, even when she watched him from a distance, or silently from the shadows, she would find him turning as if to catch a glimpse of her, the expression on his face that of one who simultaneously wishes to see yet is fearful of seeing.

While she had no sense of time passing when she sat by the lake, here she was aware of the ticking of the clock in the hall, the buzzing of the refrigerator in the kitchen, the flickering of the lamp that her father always kept lit in his office. She thought it might be for her, so that she could find him in the night, although she would never have any difficulty making her way through the marshes to the house on the hill. She enjoyed once again being part of this world that she had left—the transience of it, the slow decay measured in minutes and hours. The lake was always still, set in an airless landscape. Only her father's brief presence there, lingering between realms of existence, had altered it for a time: the shell of a building had appeared, and an old car, driven by entities that had taken the form of grandparents she had never known. He had caused them to manifest themselves, and they had vanished as soon as he turned away from them, electing not to take the Long Ride.

Jennifer wondered what lay at the end of the paths of the dead, beyond the crashing of the waves, where the Long Ride ceased. She recalled the Almost-Mother, and thought that what waited for all was both being and nonbeing—a loss of self, and its absorption into the whole. But Jennifer did not want to lose herself. She desired to hold on to the complexity of her emotions, to fascination and confusion and love and hate and joy and sadness and envy and rage and—

All of it: she wanted to retain all of it, and by returning to the world from which she had been so violently torn she was reminded of why. Perhaps if her father came with her, it might be different. He had changed the other world once: was it not possible that he could do so again? Or maybe they could stay together by the lake, watching the dead go by, like sentinels at a gateway.

Yet in the end, was it not just that her father remained here while she and her mother were elsewhere, and when he died so also would her connection to this mortal world cease? Then, together, they would join the ranks of the dead, walking hand-in-hand into an existence where old names had no meaning, where something so small and fleeting, yet so deep and enduring, as human love would be lost forever, like a tear shed into the sea.

She walked to his desk. A book lay open, and beside it an array of papers: notes in his handwriting, photocopies, maps, flight reservations for the morning to Columbus, Ohio, and a rental car confirmation. She leafed through them, and had someone been passing in the hall, someone who was not her father, they might have thought that the wind had found its way beneath the window frame to sow disorder while it could.

She read the name on the papers.

Dead King.

The rustling stopped.

She was gone.

S am stirred in her sleep and opened her eyes. Jennifer stood at the end of her bed. She had not been there for long, Sam thought. The crackle of static electricity that she usually brought with her was absent. Sam could neither feel it nor smell it in the air.

Sam raised herself on one elbow.

"What is it?" she asked. She was tired, and had a spelling bee the next morning. She resented being disturbed.

"Our father is hunting the Dead King," said Jennifer. She sounded concerned, even frightened.

Sam thought for a moment or two.

"Good," she said, and returned to sleep.

# LIV

**N** orah Meddows took delivery of eight bags of clothing and two boxes of shoes from the Salvadoran immigrant named Hector, whom she employed to pick up consignments from homes in an increasingly wide radius of Columbus. This represented the cream of the week's donations as determined by Hector's wife, who had a good eye for fashion and was, Meddows believed, reasonably honest, at least to the extent of not stealing too obviously from her employer. Actually, Meddows had no evidence to suggest that Elisa Rios Silva had ever stolen anything in her life, from Meddows or anyone else, but since she was herself dishonest she naturally ascribed a similar or greater degree of dishonesty to everyone she encountered.

Meddows was breaking the law, of course, but not in any way that harmed folk, although she wasn't sure that the Attorney General's Office, which regulated charities, would see matters the same way. Meddows used Hector and his family to distribute flyers seeking donations of good used clothing which would either be sold to aid poor families in Latin America or, in the case of items not suitable for sale to the discerning U.S. consumer, sent directly to those most in need. People with clothes to donate were invited to leave them on their doorsteps on a given day, when they would be collected without fuss and put to good use.

Meddows made sure to target only relatively well-to-do neighborhoods: she didn't want any old JC Penney shit, even if she inevitably got more than her fair share of the kind of attire that, curiously enough, many poor citizens would have been grateful to receive, and not only south of the border but closer to home. No, Meddows was seeking designer items—or clothing that could be passed off as designer in the absence of the real thing—aided by the labels of real but obscure European fashion houses that Hector's wife produced using a series of templates supplied by her employer. The rest Meddows sold by the pound to people even less scrupulous than herself, and did pretty well off it, all things considered, to the extent that she had been forced to rent a unit off Route 23 in which to store and sort the donations, a task with which Hector's family was happy to assist for a few bucks an hour and their pick of the cheap stuff. Really, Meddows would have been lost without Hector. She couldn't understand why so many of her neighbors complained about immigrants. Without Hector and his kin, she'd have been forced to do all these shit jobs herself.

Now she began sorting through the bags in the back room of Old and New by Sue, her "vintage clothing boutique" off Neil Avenue near Ohio State. She was proud of the store's name, having come up with it herself. Sue, she told customers who asked, was her middle name, even though it was really Alison. But by this point, Norah Meddows was so mired in fraud and deceit that even she could no longer conclusively tell the difference between what was true and what was false, and wasn't particularly troubled by the distinction anyhow.

She placed the clothing on the tailoring table in the back room. The donations had already been washed and folded by Elisa's sister, Elisa having first applied some eye-catching designer labels where required. The third bag contained a nice little windfall, though: a Sasha Kanevski shirt that looked like it had never been worn, and a guipure lace print stretch cotton dress by Oscar de la Renta that had probably retailed for close to a thousand dollars when new. Meddows cast an expert eye over it, and only on the third examination did she discern the repair job carried out by Elisa on a nasty triangular tear under the left arm. She made a mental note to slip Elisa an extra twenty bucks at the end of the week—such good service should not go unrewarded—while simultaneously giving thanks for the excesses of consumer culture. Better still, according to Elisa's note on the bag, the dress was part of a consignment from Hector's run to Cincinnati the previous month, so there was little danger of its original owner stumbling across it in the boutique. Even were such an unlikely circumstance to arise, Meddows had a get-out clause. On the wall against which the front door of the store opened, and therefore almost invisible to any but the most eagle-eyed of customers, was a small sign advising that a percentage of the store's profits went to support charitable causes in Latin America, that percentage varying between negligible and zero depending on Meddows's income and mood.

A buzzer sounded, indicating that someone had entered the store. Meddows had installed cameras in two corners, but they were just dummies designed to discourage the cruder breed of shoplifter. Hers was largely a one-woman operation, so there was nobody to check monitors in any case, and Meddows was more than capable of keeping an eye on her own stock. She had designed the layout of the store herself so that it had almost no blind spots, and every item was secured to its hanger by a plastic tie. It meant that Meddows had to cut the ties in order for women to try on clothes, but it represented only a little trouble and less expense, and enabled her to keep count of the items in a customer's possession at any one time. She had been in the business long enough not to be surprised at the willingness and ability of even the most prosperous-looking of women to steal if given the opportunity. Forget all that bullshit about such acts of theft being a cry for help: the poor sometimes stole because they had to, but the wealthy stole because they could.

Meddows stepped into the store and was only slightly surprised to find a man standing before the counter. Men occasionally came in looking for designer bags for their wives, or unusual scarves. Some were hoping to pick up something that looked impressive for a fraction of its retail price. One or two were simply seeking directions to some-place else. This man, though, had the demeanor of one who didn't enter through a door until he knew that there was at least one other way out. His eyes were gray-blue, or greenish blue, depending on the light, with a kind of wintry warmth to them. He was wearing a nicely cut black jacket over jeans, and a small-collared white shirt open at the neck. He wasn't tall—not more than five-ten at most—and not handsome exactly, but you'd notice him if he entered a room.

"Can I help you?" she asked.

"You can if you're Ms. Meddows," he replied, and she instantly grew wary. He didn't look like a cop, but he had something of the cop about him. She thought again of the attorney general: if required, she had enough doctored records to give even the best of accountants a head-ache. The flyers distributed by Hector gave no clue as to the ultimate destination of the donations, and the small print at the bottom made reference to codes and licenses, with some random figures thrown in to fool the unwary.

Hector, in turn, was under strict instructions to plead ignorance and lack of English if questioned by anyone who might appear to know what he or she was talking about, before running for the hills. In the event of the police becoming involved, he was to keep his mouth shut except to call the law firm of Painter-Maynes, which also acted for the Croatians who bought Meddows's cast-off clothing, and was connected to the offices of one Daniel Starcher in Lewisburg, West Virginia. They would have Hector back on the street in time to enjoy that evening's meal of beans and rice, or whatever the hell else he and his family chose to eat in the confines of the apartment rented to them by Meddows, which was another reason for Hector to embrace silence and discretion if the law became involved.

Thankfully, that situation had yet to arise, Hector having an innate ability to sense the proximity of the forces of the state, a consequence of several branches of his extended family having been wiped out by the Salvadoran Guardia Nacional during his country's protracted civil war. That same National Guard—including, according to Hector, some of the same individuals, but now in higher positions—had raped and murdered three American nuns and a Catholic laywoman back in 1982, an outrage that caused the U.S. government to discontinue military aid to the Salvadoran regime for a whole six weeks. Hearing about this had made Norah Meddows even happier about screwing over the IRS. After all, she didn't want her tax dollars put to that kind of use.

And now here was a man with a certain authority, asking after her by name. She smiled brightly, giving him the full two rows, newly whitened, and confirmed that she was indeed Norah Meddows.

He took his wallet from his jacket and produced a business card.

"My name's Charlie Parker," he said. "I'm a private investigator."

He passed the card to her, and she read its contents carefully, right down to the cell phone number at the bottom, while giving herself some time to think.

"Maine," she said.

"That's right."

"I used to live in Maine." If he was standing in her store then he already knew this, but she thought it made her appear more open.

"I'm aware of that."

"I suppose that's why you're here. If you've come from Maine, then it must be about my ex-husband. I can think of no other reason why you'd have made a trip all the way to Ohio."

"Did you know that he'd been released from prison?"

"No. I figured he must be due for release sometime soon, but I didn't know when, exactly."

"He got out last week."

"Oh."

Just oh.

P arker took in the woman before him. She was good-looking without being attractive, her features lacking the animation and character required to earn more than a passing glance. Only her eyes had any real life to them, but it was the gleam of avarice. She looked like a hungry doll.

"Has your ex-husband been in contact with you since his release?" he asked.

"No. Why would he be?"

"Because you were once married to him. Because someone who has been in prison for five years won't have many friends on the outside, and will usually turn to old ones instead."

"My ex-husband and I aren't friends. He's a deviant. I want nothing to do with him. That's why I divorced him. Look, what is this about? Did he hire you?"

"Yes."

"Why?"

"He claimed to be innocent of the crimes for which he served time. He was convinced he'd been set up."

She laughed, and shook her head in pity at the man before her, as though anyone could be so dumb.

"You can't be much of a detective," she said, "if you believe every hard-luck story that a convict puts before you."

Parker smiled back.

"I don't believe every hard-luck story," he said, "just the ones that ring true."

"My god, you're serious! Look, he had child pornography on his computer. He had photographs that he kept hidden in a box in the basement. I saw some of them. The police showed them to me. They were appalling, just the worst things I've ever had to view. I'd lived with this man; I'd taken his name. He pretended to be a loving husband, but in reality he was someone who got off on looking at pictures of naked children—and worse: kids being sexually assaulted in every possible way you can imagine. He should have died in jail."

"He didn't die, at least not in jail, but he suffered a lot."

"Good."

It didn't appear to be a reflex response, or a glib effort to shield herself from any residual affection she might have felt for her ex-husband. Parker doubted that she had any affection at all, residual or otherwise, for Jerome Burnel. He wondered if she ever did. She must have had some reason for marrying him, but who could say what it might have been? Boredom, perhaps, or a lust that burned itself out in the years after the vows were exchanged. It might even simply have been a matter of money and security. That would not have surprised Parker in the least: with her shiny magpie eyes, her pinched cheeks, and slightly pursed lips, Norah Meddows was almost vampiric in aspect.

"Before these images were found, had he ever given any indication that he might have an interest in pornography of that nature?"

"No," she replied. "Do you think I'd have stayed with him if I suspected?"

"People sometimes do."

"Not people like me."

*No*, thought Parker, *definitely not people like you.*

Meddows was self-aware enough to recognize that the man before her was immune from whatever allure she might have believed herself to have possessed, and sufficiently clever to realize that his arrival at the store presaged no good for her.

"If you'll forgive me," she said, "I'm very busy. I have a lot to do."

She indicated the door behind him and waited for him to leave. She didn't want to turn her back. She wanted to be sure that he was gone, and then she would lock the door and close up for the rest of the day. She could slip out through the office, and return for her car later. He probably knew where she lived, though: if he'd tracked her to the store, he could just as easily find his way to her home. She might go to a movie for the afternoon, or even check into a motel for the night, in the hope that he grew tired of hanging around.

But it was as if she had not spoken, and he appeared heedless of her obvious unhappiness at his continued presence. She, in turn, decided to dispense with any attempt at civility.

"Look, why are you here?" she asked.

"Your ex-husband is missing," said Parker.

"He just got out of jail. How can he be missing?"

"He didn't appear for a scheduled meeting with his probation officer. His clothing, and whatever possessions he took out of storage, are still at his apartment."

"Maybe he skipped. Isn't that what they call it, 'skipping'? I think I heard it mentioned on TV once."

"It's hard to skip without money. Your husband left what little he had in the bank, and he doesn't have a debit or credit card."

She folded her arms. Her very white teeth nibbled at her lower lip as though, in the absence of anything else to consume, she might feed upon herself. Jerome Burnel's disappearance seemed to have come as news to her, but her attitude wasn't entirely one of surprise. She didn't know about it, Parker guessed, but it still wasn't unexpected.

"And what has any of this to do with me?"

"You were born in Plassey County, West Virginia."

There it was: a kind of shiver.

"So?"

"Did you know a man named Harpur Griffin?"

A breath. He heard it being released.

"No."

And a lie.

All that stuff about people looking to the right when constructing untruths—or it might have been the left; Parker could never remember, not that it mattered anyway—was so much mumbo jumbo: smoke from the pseudoscience of neurolinguistic programming. It was the pauses, or absence of them, that gave a liar away: either taking too much time to think, or not enough time at all. He could see Norah Meddows weighing her options, and deciding that deception represented her best hope.

"You're sure?" he prompted her.

"Don't be rude, Mr. Parker. It's a sign of poor breeding."

"Deceit, on the other hand, is universal."

"Get out of my store, or I'll call the police."

"Oh, I don't much care if you call the police or not," said Parker. "I'll be talking to them myself pretty soon anyway. I just thought I'd give you the chance to tell the truth before all this got out of hand. Harpur Griffin did time with your ex-husband. Griffin was burned alive in his car in Portland a couple of days ago. It made the papers—some of them, anyway. He also came from Plassey County. That makes two people from one small region in West Virginia with ties to Jerome Burnel. I find that odd."

"Just leave. Please."

"I think I will." He sniffed the air. "You know, the smell of old clothes always reminds me of mortality."

She couldn't help but bridle at the implied insult to her business, even at the risk of further time in his company.

"This isn't a thrift store."

"Right, it's 'vintage.' I forgot, like most antiques are just junk until somebody wants them badly enough. You have my card, in case you need to call me and prepare."

"Prepare for what?"

"The questions that the police will ask you, eventually: Did you set up your ex-husband to be robbed back in Maine? Did you know that he carried a gun? How did you recruit the men who ended up dying at your husband's hand? Did you help to plant the child pornography that convicted him? Why did you have Harpur Griffin killed?"

"I didn't have—"

The words tumbled out before she could stop herself. Parker turned toward the door.

"It sounds like you do need to practice your answers," he said.

"Go fuck yourself."

He raised the index finger of his right hand.

"Remember: it's a sign of poor breeding."

And he closed the door gently behind him.

# LVI

**N**orah Meddows waited until Parker had driven off in his car—a rental, she thought, noting the make, color, and license number—then locked the door and turned the sign to CLOSED. She killed the lights in the store and returned to the back room, where she dashed the new stock from the table and scattered it on the floor. She looked at the phone. She'd have to call them. They might—no, they would—hurt her if they found out that the detective had been here and she'd kept it from them. He'd made the connection with Plassey County, although that was their fault, not hers. They were the ones who'd recruited Harpur Griffin to do their dirty work.

She couldn't understand why they hadn't just killed her husband, either before he went to prison or while he was behind bars. Instead, they'd opted to inflict years of misery upon him, and even she hadn't hated him that much. She'd just found him dull and weak, although she had been surprised by his actions at the gas station—but again, why the hell couldn't they have taken her husband on a quiet stretch of road instead? But whatever his previously unsuspected depths, it still turned out that not everyone in the jewelry trade made enough money to shower a good wife in wealth and diamonds. Who knew?

They'd kill the detective, of course. If they were smart, they'd just make him disappear. But she was seriously starting to wonder how clever they really were, after botching a simple robbery that she'd gifted to them, and then burning a man alive and allowing his remains to be found—because they must have been the ones who murdered Griffin, although she had no idea why.

And then there were the two bodies discovered in the county, the ones that had been all over the papers at the weekend. If the Cut had also put them in the ground, they were definitely losing their touch. Maybe she should just keep her mouth shut after all. It wasn't like Parker was going to advertise that he'd spoken with her, or was it? Damn. No, she'd have to tell them. They were her occasional suppliers as well, after all. Their "ranges" often produced some nice items of clothing for her store. More to the point, they were her silent partners, and their monthly share wasn't linked to gross or net: it was a set fee, and it hurt every time.

She had watched enough crime shows to know that she shouldn't use any of her own phones to make the call. She picked up the clothes from the floor, and spent an hour sorting and pricing most of them before driving all the way to the Mall at Tuttle Crossing, keeping an eye in the rearview mirror for the detective's car, but finding no sign of it. She watched out for him inside, too, even taking a detour to Panera Bread just to grab a coffee and sit by the window, all the time trying to catch sight of him or his vehicle. When she was as certain as she could be that he had not followed her, she went to Sears, got a cart, bought some towels, stockings, and a handful of other stuff that she barely needed, before adding a cheap cell phone to the pile. She then headed to an Internet cafe and activated the phone on one of its computers.

When all that was done, she made the call.

# LVII

Perry Lutter liked walking. He liked being outdoors. When he was in his little bedroom in his parents' house—the same bedroom that he'd occupied for as long as he could remember, complete with some of the childish things that he'd never put away, and the adult things that were now also part of his twin lives, for he was both young and old—he would feel the walls closing in around him, and hear voices speaking to him in the night. The voices, the Bad Speakers, used dirty words, sometimes about women and girls, and Perry didn't think he liked to hear those words, although among his adult things were some magazines that he had found on his travels, and hidden as best he could behind the dusty childhood books on his shelves.

But when he was outside, the voices usually went away, or were lost in the sounds of birds and animals, wind and water. In the summer, Perry would often sleep outdoors, either on the porch or, if the air didn't smell like rain, in his sleeping bag in the woods behind his father's toolshed. His parents didn't try to stop him, just as long as he stayed within sight of the house at night.

There were times, though, when the voices persisted, the babble of them so loud that they made Perry wail. When that happened, Perry would pray, and if he prayed hard enough the other voices would come, the soft ones, and they would shoo the Bad Speakers away, and eventually Perry would fall asleep to the whispering of them, which was like the hushing of the sea.

Perry stayed away from the Cut. He kept to roads and forests that did not abut it, maintaining a buffer between himself and whatever dwelt in that place. He would hear it if he accidentally drew too close, as he sometimes did if he grew disoriented and confused, but that happened only when he was tired or hungry, so he'd learned always to keep some candy and fruit in his pack when he went wandering.

The thing in the Cut sounded like the rattle he'd had as a child, and which his mother still kept in a drawer in the living room, along with one of Perry's earliest pairs of shoes, a picture of her that he'd drawn on his first day at the special school, and old photographs of him as a baby and a little boy. Perry loved it when she took them from the drawer and told him the stories connected with each item, even though he'd heard them hundreds of times before. The sound of his mother speaking was one of the few voices that could drown out the Bad Speakers.

Another was the voice of the thing in the Cut, because even the Bad Speakers were afraid of it.

*Rattle-rattle, chatter-chatter, hiss-hiss*: not separately but all at once, a communication in a language that could only be heard and never understood, yet the baseness of it was clear to any who were exposed to it, and to Perry Lutter in particular because he had no filters to protect himself from it. So he avoided the Cut, and also the people who lived there, because they brought with them the taint of the thing that dwelt among them, and behind every word they spoke was its echo.

Perry was almost six feet tall, but had never shed the baby fat of childhood. Regardless of the weather, he always wore a long-sleeved shirt buttoned to the neck, either brown or blue chinos, depending on the day of the week, and a windbreaker. His hair was black, and he wore it brushed straight back from his forehead and held in place by a generous dab from his supply of Reuzel's water-based pomade. His father used Murray's pomade, which was cheaper, but Murray's was oil-based and gave Perry acne along his hairline, so his mother insisted that he use Reuzel's instead, although his father bitched about the extra cost every time he saw Perry with the tin in his hand. Perry's eyes were slightly too small for his face, but he had a kind smile, and neither meant nor did any harm. He worked three afternoons each week, and all day Saturday, washing dishes for Miss Queenie at the diner, for which she paid him three dollars an hour, which he stored in a vintage Nabisco cookie tin and counted every Sunday afternoon, carefully writing the new total on a sheet of paper that he kept with the money.

Perry's mind was mostly a happy blank when he rambled through the woods and fields, because he was at peace with himself when he wandered. Lately, though, that peace had been taken from him, ever since he had witnessed the two men from the Cut digging the hole. He'd tried to pretend that he hadn't seen what they were doing, but he wasn't sure he'd fooled them. Then he'd made the mistake of going back early the next morning to see what they'd put in the hole, digging with a little shovel that he'd borrowed from his father's toolshed. He thought that the men might have buried treasure in the hole.

But it wasn't treasure.

He'd thrown up all over his shirt and pants when he saw what lay under the dirt. He didn't know what else to do, so he covered the bodies as best he could before returning home to clean himself up and put on a new shirt and pants. That was how his mother had found him, crying in his underwear and pulling on a pair of chinos backward, crying because his clothes had gotten dirty, and the chinos were the wrong color for the day, and his hands smelled of dead boys.

Perry Lutter was incapable of lying; such a level of outright deception was beyond him. The closest he could come to it was in a withholding of the truth, or a refusal to speak at all. It took his mother half an hour to calm him to the point where he would even begin to talk to her about what had happened, and another half hour later the police were at the scene. Afterward, Sheriff Henkel came to speak to Perry, with his father and mother present, but Henkel could get little out of him because Perry had a profound fear of men and women in uniform, a consequence of an incident in his twenties when one of Russ Dugar's idiot deputies had come across Perry just off Mortonsville's main street, tearing apart the contents of a garbage can. The deputy, who was new on the job and unfamiliar with Perry, although he could clearly see that he was mentally challenged in some way, ordered him to stop, but Perry persisted in redistributing the trash, whereupon the deputy pushed him to the ground, cuffed him, and drove him to the sheriff's department, where he was put in a cell to cool off.

It was a perfect storm of misfortune, because the incident occurred on a Sunday afternoon, when the only other deputy in the department was just as wet behind the ears as his comrade, if marginally more sensitive to Perry's condition. When Perry wouldn't stop crying, and began banging his head against the bars, the deputy took it upon himself to call Russ Dugar at home for advice.

Dugar, despite all his flaws, was not an unkind man, and knew the Lutters well. He drove to the sheriff's department, still dressed in his Sunday shirt and tie, stopping off only to pick up Perry's mother along the way. Together they managed to calm her son down, and discovered that Perry, who had been buying candy, had accidentally dropped his mom's change in the garbage can, and was afraid of getting in trouble for not being able to produce it when he returned home. A doctor had to be called to put some stitches in Perry's forehead, and he had remained understandably fearful of uniforms, and particularly the attire and patrol vehicles of the Plassey County Sheriff's Department, ever since. As for the unfortunate deputy who had arrested Perry in the first place, Dugar ground his face so hard against the bloodied cell bars that he bore the mark of them on his skin for days.

It wouldn't have done Henkel any good even if he'd arrived out of uniform, because Perry knew that he was the sheriff, which brought with it the same set of traumatic associations. The best Henkel could get out of Perry was that he had been curious about the disturbed earth and started digging. And if Perry knew more than he was saying, as Henkel quietly suspected, in part because of the way Perry's mother had tightened her grip on her boy's hand when the questions got too near the truth, then he wasn't going to share it with Henkel anyway. Later, on his porch, Charlie Lutter again asked if the police could gloss over the fact that Perry had found the bodies, and Henkel had consented, seeing no benefit to anyone involved in publicizing Perry's involvement, especially not if this was Cut work. They'd find out in the end, though, no matter what Henkel did or did not say. Charlie Lutter knew it, too. He was just doing his best to shield his son.

"Is there any chance Perry saw more than he's saying?" Henkel asked Lutter.

"He's a good boy," said Lutter.

"That wasn't the question, Charlie."

"He only told me what he told you."

Which could have been true, but it wasn't answering the question either. Perry was his mother's boy. She might well have shared things with her husband that Perry told her, but likewise she might not. Either way, Charlie Lutter knew less about his boy than his wife did, and that was God's truth.

Henkel had put his hat on, and told Lutter to make sure Perry knew the importance of staying quiet about those bodies, and Lutter said that he would, and thanked him, and Henkel had looked away so Lutter could dry the tears of gratitude and relief that were welling up in his eyes.

But Perry Lutter knew none of this. He only understood that he mustn't talk, not ever, about those bodies in the woods. His father had told him not to, and Perry always obeyed his father. He loved his mother, and dreaded her moments of anger less than the potential withdrawal of affection that might accompany them, but his fear of his father was not as complicated by love, and consequently Perry followed his instructions to the letter.

Now here was Perry, a strange, distracted smile on his face, wearing his favorite green windbreaker to ward off the gathering cold, tramping through his beloved woods, keeping count of squirrels, and the flight of birds disturbed by his presence. The thing in the Cut was far away, the Bad Speakers reduced to a sullen background murmur, and Perry was counting, counting, counting because when he looked at the ground he sometimes saw mounds of dirt, and they brought to mind the bodies in the hole, and by a process of association both illogical yet profound, it seemed to Perry that each mound might house its own bodies, all crying out for him to start digging so that their resting places might be discovered and their moms and dads could come and take them home.

*Eight, nine.*

*Thirty-one, thirty-two.*

"Perry! Hey, Perry! Hold up there."

To Perry's right, where the woods ended and the road began, stood a figure with red hair, and sharp nails and teeth. Perry knew his name. It was Lucius, and he came from the Cut. Perry had seen him around town, at the diner, driving by in his big truck.

Digging a hole in the woods in which to bury two dead boys.

*Seventeen, eighteen.*

*Thirty-three. Jesus's age. Amen.*

Lucius started walking toward Perry. Another man appeared behind him, and Perry recognized him, too: Benedict.

*Christ, Lucius, this one already smells bad. I think he shat himself.*

*He's gonna start smelling worse if we don't get him in the ground.*

Perry wanted to run, but he couldn't.

*Thirty-four. Thirty—*

"Don't be afraid," said Lucius. "We just want to talk to you."

"I gots to go home," said Perry.

Lucius drew nearer. He was almost within touching distance of Perry. Behind him, Benedict had not moved.

"We'll give you a ride. It's going to rain."

Perry glanced at the sky. There were clouds, but they were white and wispy. He had not smelled rain. He would not have come out if he had.

"No, it's not," said Perry. "No rain."

Benedict started walking. He did so slowly, reluctantly, coming down to join Lucius, coming to damn himself. Perry started to cry.

"Perry," said Lucius, "just get in the fucking truck."

———

WHEN IT WAS DONE, and the sun had set, Lucius took Benedict's chin in his right hand, still smeared with blood and dirt, and said, "We tell no one about this, you understand?"

And Benedict understood.

# LVIII

Sherah was asleep. She had tried to make love to Oberon, not knowing what else to do to draw him out of himself. He had been gentle in his refusal, and she had not been offended, for she understood him better than he realized, although she was younger than him by nearly three decades. She stroked his head before she went to bed, as he sat by the window staring out upon the Cut, and noticed a patch of dried blood behind his left ear. She wet a handkerchief with her spit and cleaned it away.

"What is it?" he asked.

"Nothing," she said. "A stain, no more."

She tried to slip the handkerchief into her sleeve, but he caught her hand and opened her bunched fist. The redness was visible against the white of the material. It might almost have been mistaken for a smear of lipstick, had both of them not known better. Oberon looked up at his wife from where he sat, and she stared back at him without blinking.

"I'm sure it was necessary," she said, for want of something else to say. She did not know if it was true or not, and it didn't matter anyway.

"It was not," he replied. "I did it because I wanted to. I did it because I hoped that it would give me some peace."

"And it didn't?"

"No."

"He killed your sons."

"He did what he thought was right. And he paid for it."

One of my boys was sick, he wanted to tell her, although she would not have needed his testimony to confirm the depravity of Gideon's nature. It had been familiar to all of them. Gideon was a mad animal, just like Lucius—maybe even worse than him, because Lucius had some semblance of reason, but Gideon had none. His brother, Balder, who died alongside him, had enjoyed hurting women: that was his weakness. Oberon also sometimes hurt them, but it gave him little pleasure, and the end for them, when it came, was always quick.

If his sons had been so damaged, then what did it say about himself? Could he really only blame the mother for Gideon's profound physical, psychological, and moral decay? The blood of the Cut was tainted: how could it not be, after all this time, and generations of intermarriage? Even the occasional introduction of new stock could only dilute the contamination, not eradicate it entirely. The flaw was in Sherah, too, he thought, or how else could she wipe another man's blood from her husband's skin without a blink of her eyes?

Oberon shivered, despite the glowing embers of the fire, and the heat that remained in the room.

"It's airish," he said. "Don't you feel it?"

"What?"

"That chill. It's coming from the north, but the trees are still, and there is no sign of wind. What carries it here?"

"I feel nothing, and it's been mild these last days."

She put the back of her hand to his forehead, but it was no warmer than it should have been. She did not like seeing her husband this way. It wasn't usual for him to be so odd-turned. He was their rock, but perhaps Cassander was right, and that rock was now weakening and fracturing.

It was then that she moved her hand from his head to his chest, and down over his belly to the bulge of his crotch.

"Come to bed," she said, "and I'll warm you up."

He had lifted her hand from him, held it to his lips, and kissed it once.

"You go," he said. "I need to sit up awhile."

That had been two hours earlier. The lights of the nearest houses were extinguished, all but one: a lamp still burned on Cassander's porch. In time there came the sound of a truck approaching, and from the shadows of his post by the window Oberon saw Lucius emerge and walk toward his father's house. The door opened and Cassander appeared. He said something to his son, and both looked over in Oberon's direction. Then Lucius entered, the door closed upon them, and the porch light went out.

Oberon remained in his chair, his fingernails scratching at his thighs like a man who feels the dirt conspiring against him as he tries to halt his final, fatal fall.

————

OBERON WAS NOT THE only one sitting awake by a window. At the edge of the Cut, where the back road from Turley sliced a ragged, uneven route through the trees, Odell Watson gazed into the darkness. Odell had been woken by the sound of a truck: Lucius and Benedict returning to the Cut.

Odell had overheard his mother and grandmother talking. Oberon, the one who led the Cut, had come to the diner and spoken with the sheriff. His mother had watched them unnoticed from her place at the serving hatch, and caught a little of what was said; not all, but enough to know that the sheriff and the Cut were not far from each other's throats.

"Sheriff don't have the strength to face down the Cut," his grandmother had said.

"I think the sheriff is a good man," his mother replied. She would not tell him what she knew of the Cut, but she still wished him to prevail against it. He would just have to do so without her help.

"They're the worst kind."

"Oh, you don't know what you're saying."

"I do, and you better listen to it, girl. Good won't avail against the Cut, or not good alone. They're like a pack of wolves. And the sheriff, he's no better than a rabbit. They'll tear him apart."

"Then what will avail, huh?"

And Odell's grandmother had taken a moment before replying.

"Hunters," she said.

Now Odell sat by his window and thought of men like wolves, but the only images that came to mind were ones from old movies, or the werewolves from *Twilight* that didn't look right when they talked. He thought also of Lucius. His grandmother was wrong about him: Lucius wasn't a wolf but a fox, like old Brer Fox in the tales, except Brer Fox wasn't smart and always lost, while Lucius and his kind didn't ever seem to lose. Lucius even looked like a fox, all red and sharp.

Odell was growing sleepy. He turned from the window, and a bird shrieked from somewhere in the dark. He paused and the sound came again, except now it was more like the noise foxes made when they were mating: it had a human quality to it, like a child weeping. Odell listened until it faded away, then climbed between his sheets. Only on the verge of sleep did it strike him that the cries from the woods were deeper than those of any fox he had heard, and might almost have been calling "Momma" over and over again.

# LIX

The day dawned bright and clear: blue skies, the barest fragments of cloud, and a sense of the world transforming itself once again, the beauty of fall still lingering but the trees barer than before, and arrowheads of geese drifting high above, less like birds than the impression of them, as of a child's hurried marks on a blue page.

Miss Queenie opened the doors of Shelby's Diner, Teona Watson setting the first pots of coffee to brew before returning to the kitchen to start on the bacon. Brewing the coffee was usually one of the waitresses' tasks, but they'd both arrived late that morning, drawing glares from Miss Queenie that could freeze piss on an icicle, as Connie, the older of the two, put it, as they were putting on their faces in the restroom. Miss Queenie thought that Teona appeared tired, and had asked her if everything was okay at home. Teona told Miss Queenie that she'd been kept awake by an animal crying in the woods. She had wondered if it might be the copulation of foxes, but it was too early for mating season—the peak would come in January.

By 8:00 a.m. nearly every table in Shelby's was full, and men and women stood talking by the stools at the counter, because the community always drifted to Shelby's when there was news to discuss or be disseminated. Perry Lutter had not returned home the night before, and a search by his parents at first light had not discovered him in his usual haunts. A call had been made to the sheriff's department, and the patrol cars were out searching for him. In the meantime, Sheriff Henkel had asked those with time on their hands to check their lands, just in case Perry had met with some accident and was lying incapacitated, and anyone with business on the roads was keeping one eye peeled for him.

"He'll turn up," said Miss Queenie, with the assurance of a woman who had lived in this community for more than seventy years, and knew the rhythms of its inhabitants—Perry Lutter's more than most. But she had heard the whispers: that it was Perry who had found the bodies of those two boys, and might have seen the ones who put them in the ground. The talk was of Mexicans out of Ohio, and those people didn't fuck around, although this last observation was couched in more delicate terms for Miss Queenie's ears.

And so distracted were Miss Queenie and her staff that they paid less attention than usual to the two strangers sitting at the back of the restaurant, for unfamiliar faces in such environs usually attracted some small interest. The taller of the two, a black man in a dark sports jacket, was reading the *New York Times*, which was available only at one gas station in the county, a fact of which the man in question was now acutely aware, given that he and his colleague might have been eating an hour earlier had they not had to learn this the hard way. The other— smaller, and significantly less dapper than his companion—had a magazine open on the table, and was turning the pages with conspicuous regularity while taking in little that he was reading, and everything he was hearing and seeing around him.

A patrol car pulled into the parking lot and a deputy got out. He wandered into Shelby's, ordered a coffee, and quickly found himself surrounded by a small group of people, Miss Queenie among them, with others hovering at the periphery, or keeping an ear cocked from their chairs, but there was no news, and no sign of Perry Lutter. Folk were being asked to convene at the sheriff's department at 11:00 a.m., where they'd be organized into teams and given areas to cover. Ordinarily, forty-eight hours would have to elapse before someone could formally be declared missing, but this was Perry Lutter, and no such declaration was necessary.

And the two men sat in their corner, drinking their coffee and listening to all that was said.

―――――

THERE WERE OTHER STRANGERS circling the Cut too: a pair of Japanese tourists had to be sent on their way by Jason Hayward after they drove as far as the barrier that blocked the road onto his property, then started smiling and babbling at him when he pointed out that they must have ignored half a dozen PRIVATE PROPERTY signs on their way in. He'd had to help them perform close to a ten-point turn to get them facing in the right direction again, and then one of them had tried to thank Hayward by pressing some kind of Hello fucking Kitty candy on him. Later, Brion Moline told Hayward that he'd encountered the same two men on the southern road into the Cut, hunched over Stan Tekiela's *Birds of West Virginia* field guide, but by then the Cut had bigger worries than errant Japanese tourists.

Sheriff Henkel had come down the same road shortly before noon, and when Hayward asked him his business, Henkel advised him in no uncertain terms not to fuck with him, and informed Hayward that if he didn't lift the barrier within ten seconds Henkel would cuff him to a tree and deal with the legal consequences later. He wanted to see Oberon, he said, and Hayward, catching the look in the sheriff's eye, decided that the best thing to do was raise the barrier and lead him in, keeping the pace slow in order to contact Oberon from his truck and give him any time he might need to prepare.

Oberon was waiting for them at the southern edge of the Square, and Hayward noticed that the barrier had been lowered behind him, sealing off the heart of the community: the sheriff wasn't advancing any deeper into the Cut than this. Henkel got out of his car and straight into Oberon's face.

"Perry Lutter's missing," he said.

"How can you be sure?" asked Oberon. "Perry Lutter takes walks right across this county."

"Does he walk in the Cut?"

"I don't believe so."

"Well, we need to know for sure. I want your permission to search it."

"This is private land, Sheriff."

"That's why I'm asking."

"I can't let you do it. We value our solitude."

"Bullshit."

Oberon remained silent. He wasn't used to being spoken to in this way.

"I don't like your tone, Sheriff Henkel, or your language."

"I don't much care. Perry's not in the habit of staying out overnight, not without telling his mom and pop where he's going to be, and even then he always remains within sight of his home. We're concerned for his safety. This is the largest section of privately owned land in the county. It's possible that he might have wandered into it."

"If he'd wandered into the Cut, we'd know," said Oberon.

"Is that a fact?"

"It is."

Hayward watched it all, waiting for the inevitable eruption. He wouldn't have been surprised if one of the two men had suddenly leaped at the other, precipitating a confrontation that would bring the Cut into outright conflict with the county. Instead, it was Oberon who relented.

"I'll organize a search of the Cut," he said.

"Not good enough."

"What more do you want?"

"I want my people to join the search."

"This is our land."

"And this is a man's life."

And, again, Oberon retreated.

"All right, but I get to approve the outsiders. There are people from the county who will only come onto this land over my dead body."

Even Henkel appeared surprised at the compromise being offered. It was, Hayward guessed, more than he had expected.

"Agreed."

"And they stay out of our houses and outbuildings."

Henkel's mouth twisted.

"Agreed," he said again, but more reluctantly than before.

"Give me an hour," said Oberon. "I'll arrange for men to wait at each of the main entry routes. Who will you be sending?"

Henkel considered the question, then gave a list of names, two of which were immediately discounted by Oberon without explanation. Henkel substituted two replacements, and Oberon gave his approval.

"If Perry isn't found soon," said Henkel, "I'm going to start talking to people about their movements over the last twenty-four hours. That'll include your folk, understood? You'll make them available to me if required."

"I have no difficulty with that. Let's just hope Perry turns up safe, so it won't be necessary."

Henkel glanced over Oberon's shoulder to where three men had appeared from a house on the right of the Square. Even from a distance, he recognized the bulk of Cassander, and beside him his two sons. They were watching from a distance, but did not approach. Marius was putting on his coat, and the engine of his truck was running.

"Yeah," said Henkel. "Let's hope."

Chapter

# LX

Oberon had less than an hour to prepare for the arrival of the searchers, and ensure that certain areas remained out of bounds. He certainly didn't want the blockhouse or anywhere in its vicinity to be inspected, which meant that those who entered the Cut from the north needed to be steered either east or west as they approached the Square. It was all a game anyway: even if Henkel suspected the Cut's involvement in Perry Lutter's disappearance, he must know that they wouldn't be dumb enough to dispose of him on their own land.

Oberon's next move was a distraction from the main business, but a necessary one, if only for the sake of his own authority, and as an outlet for his rage. He headed to Cassander's house. Marius had already left to source parts for a generator, or so Oberon was told by Cassander. Lucius was in the backyard, checking on the cold frames that would be used to grow vegetables over the winter. His father was at the other end of the garden, spreading a mulch of peat moss, bark, and shredded newspaper to insulate the plants and prevent erosion. All this, instead of coming to find out the reason for Henkel's appearance in the Cut. They were deliberately distancing themselves from Oberon.

Lucius turned at the sound of Oberon's approach, and was just in time to take a blow to his chin from the heel of Oberon's hand. It sent him sprawling to the ground, and he tasted blood, although he managed to avoid biting his tongue.

"What did you do?" shouted Oberon.

Lucius tried to rise, but Oberon pursued him, kicking at his thighs, his ass, his back, until Lucius gave up the attempt to flee and simply curled in upon himself in an effort to protect his face and his groin from damage. By then Cassander was coming at a run, and he tackled Oberon, hurling himself with full force at the older man so that both of them ended up in the dirt beside Lucius.

Oberon was first to his feet, but he quickly found himself facing both Cassander and his son. He noted with satisfaction the blood running from Lucius's mouth, and the swelling by his right eye where one of Oberon's kicks had connected.

"What did you do to Perry Lutter?" asked Oberon.

Lucius wiped some of the blood away. Despite his injunction to Benedict to remain silent, he heard himself start talking before he could think straight. He hated Oberon, because Oberon frightened him.

"He saw us," said Lucius.

"When?"

"When we were burying Killian and Huff."

"How do you know?"

"I caught him watching us from the woods. It was only for a couple of seconds, and then he was gone, but it was him. I'm sure of it. I should have told you before, but—"

"Go on."

"I was scared." The humiliation of the admission made Lucius want to throw up.

"And?"

Lucius glanced at his father, who nodded once.

"We took care of him."

"You 'took care' of him?"

"It was quick. He didn't suffer. I didn't want him to. I always liked Perry."

Oberon turned to Cassander.

"You knew about this? You knew, and said nothing?"

Cassander didn't look away, and Oberon thought: *They're openly challenging me. This is how it starts.*

"We were going to tell you," he said. "*I* was going to tell you."

"When?"

Cassander shrugged. Today, tomorrow, next week—it didn't matter. It was done.

"Henkel is coming," said Oberon. "He's bringing search parties into the Cut."

Cassander appeared shocked. Even Lucius stopped dabbing at his bleeding mouth.

"We have to stop him," said Cassander.

"You don't appear to understand," said Oberon. "Your son, by his actions, has brought them down on us. I'm not going to prevent Henkel from entering. I gave him my permission to come."

"You're *allowing* him into the Cut?"

"If I don't, he'll go looking for a warrant—and he'll get it. It'll draw more trouble to us, and we're already engaged in damage control over Killian and Huff. Half the county is probably looking for Perry Lutter. If we stand in their way, they'll turn against us. We have no reason not to allow a search, unless we have something to hide."

Reluctantly, Oberon turned his attention to Lucius.

"Where did you put him?"

"Over the county line. We buried him deep, and put bricks on top. He won't be found."

"We?"

"Benedict and me."

Oberon clenched his fists. He wanted to pummel Lucius some more, and his father along with him. Instead he said, "When this is done, you'll answer for Perry Lutter's death. Until then, get to the western road, and wait for the searchers to come. Make sure nobody wanders off the path, and delay them all for as long as you can. Cassander, organize guides to join the teams at the other approaches, then take four men and monitor the area around the blockhouse. If anyone comes near, head him off. I don't want any outsiders to get close enough even to see it, am I clear?"

"Yes. And what about you?"

"I'll join Henkel once I'm done."

"You won't—"

"What?"

"You won't kill them?" said Cassander.

They all knew to whom he was referring. There was no need to speak it aloud.

"They're worth too much to us to kill," said Oberon. "My wife will keep them quiet. But your son has just cost your family fifty percent of your share. You'd better hope those plants make it through the winter, or you'll be begging others for food."

Cassander didn't try to argue. He and his son watched Oberon walk away. His time was drawing to a close, and Cassander's was about to begin.

"Fifty percent!" said Lucius. "We can't let him do that to us. We earned our full share. I earned it for us in Maine."

"I know," said Cassander. "Don't worry. It won't come to pass."

"He thinks that it was my decision alone to kill Perry."

"For now. You said nothing to Benedict to make him suspect otherwise?"

"Not a word. You still believe it was the right thing to do?"

"Yes."

Oberon was almost at his house. His back was still impossibly broad, but he walked with a slight stoop. He was aging.

"If you want me to do it, I'll kill him," said Lucius.

Cassander gripped his son by the back of the neck.

"We'll see. Now get ready to meet the outsiders."

———

WORD WAS ALREADY SPREADING that the Cut was about to be violated, but it was made clear to all what was expected of them. Men, women, and children old enough to understand the importance of what was happening slipped into the woods to shadow the search parties as they moved deeper into the realm.

Oberon went to Sherah. He needed her for what was to come: she was a calming influence. She sent Tamara to summon Hannah, Bram's wife, to assist her. When Hannah arrived, the two women walked quickly to the whelping shed where the bitches were kept. Sherah opened the outer door, revealing the second, inner door with its heavy window of reinforced plastic.

And from behind the window, two pregnant women stared back at her with mute hostility.

# LXI

Paige Dunstan had been a prisoner of the Cut for three years. In that time, she had given birth to two children, both girls, by Cassander and Oberon respectively. She was now six months pregnant with a third child, this time again by Oberon. Each pregnancy was the result of rape, although after the early assaults she had given up trying to fight and had learned to hold the best part of herself apart from what was occurring, so that her body and her consciousness became separate entities. It was an imperfect arrangement, but it was the best she could come up with under the circumstances.

Paige had been abducted from her home near Ashland, Oregon, by Cassander Hobb. She could remember little about it: a dark night, a van, a sudden sharp pain in the side of her neck, and when she woke she was trapped behind a false panel in the back of the vehicle. She ate there, slept there, pissed and crapped there, and was not permitted to leave the van until it reached its destination, by which point her legs were so weak and cramped that she collapsed to the ground as soon as she got outside, and had to be carried to the building that had been her prison ever since.

The prison house had armchairs; two bedrooms; a supply of books and magazines that were regularly refreshed; a laptop without Internet access but on which DVDs could be watched; and a cupboard filled with food. It did not have a stove or a microwave, so the foodstuffs consisted of candy, cereals, fruit, potato chips, processed meats—anything that could be eaten cold or uncooked. Once a day, she was brought a hot meal. Her utensils were all plastic, and none of her food was stored in cans or metal containers that could be used as a weapon to harm herself or others. The Cut, it seemed, had learned that particular lesson at a price: after two years as a prisoner, Paige was informed by Sherah, who was marginally more forthcoming than some of the other women who tended to her, that her predecessor had slit her wrists with the lid of a baked bean can. Paige had only been told the woman's first name: Sally. She was buried in the Cut's cemetery, in a grave marked by another's name.

It had been a better end than Corrie's. Paige still thought of her. She had spent a year with Corrie, who was already pregnant when Paige arrived, and who gave birth to a boy shortly after. Paige had not been able to run when Corrie tried to make her escape. By then Paige had been eight months pregnant with her first child and couldn't fit through the window from which Corrie had painstakingly removed the mortar, replacing it with chewing gum and wet newspaper where the loosened original material was too damaged to sit unnoticed in the frame. They'd sent the dogs after her, but one of them had nicked an artery in her neck when it brought her down, and she'd bled out among the trees. They'd buried her with Sally, and the bigger windows were subsequently bricked up to become slits.

Paige had miscarried once, and received no pre- or postnatal care beyond what was offered by the women of the Cut, but they had been giving birth in its environs for centuries and their midwifery skills, while primitive, were accomplished. The sex was entirely functional on the part of the men involved, although with some degree of care and solicitude from Cassander and Oberon. The rapes largely continued only until she became pregnant, at which point they would almost immediately cease, although some men had been permitted to use her once the pregnancy had been confirmed, just as long as they did not damage her or the fetus.

She did not know what had happened to the children. Hannah and Sherah would say only that they were no longer in the Cut. Paige had given the girls names: Dorothy, after her mother, and Meredith, after her sister. Although they were the offspring of sexual assault, she continued to feel the pain of their loss. She tried to hide it from herself, but the trauma of her separation from them, even given the circumstances of their conception, was like an open wound in her flesh. Hardly a day went by that she did not weep for them.

She wondered if her mother was still alive. She wondered if her family was still searching for her, holding out hope that she might yet be returned to them, living or dead. She wondered if she ever would be, or if she, too, would eventually be laid to rest beneath a liar's cross. She wasn't sure that she could endure another assault, and this latest pregnancy was telling on her. Her body was worn out. When she looked in the plastic mirror that hung in the bathroom, she saw a woman she could barely recognize: older than her years, harder.

Sometimes—most of the time—Paige wanted to die, but if she died no one would ever discover what had befallen her, and this horror would go on: there would be more girls, more rapes, more pregnancies, more vanished children. So Paige endured, and waited patiently for her chance, because she knew that a chance must surely come. She refused to despair, because if she despaired she would go mad: mad, like Gayle.

Gayle had been plucked by the Cut from the streets of Washington, D.C., another kid fleeing a bad home life for a chance in the big city, although what she imagined she'd find once she got there, apart from an even harder life in a bigger place, Paige wasn't sure. Gayle had begun crying and screaming from the moment she regained consciousness. Paige had tried her best to quiet Gayle down, but it wasn't as though she could offer her any great consolation. Paige even held back from Gayle, for a while, the length of time she herself had been kept prisoner in the hut. Eventually, though, she couldn't keep the truth from the girl. She told her what would happen to her, and how best to cope with it, but Gayle had broken before the first assault even began. Perhaps she'd been broken before she ever got to D.C. Paige suspected as much. She bore the mark of a girl who believed that she had already seen the worst of men, but the ones in the Cut proved her wrong.

Sometimes Paige was able to have a coherent conversation with Gayle, but those times were growing less frequent since she had conceived. Mostly, Gayle just crooned, although Paige didn't think she was singing to the child. During one of their rare substantial discussions, Gayle had asked Paige how she might go about aborting the baby. Paige dissuaded her from that line of thought, mainly because she'd initially contemplated the same action herself. Two things had caused her to reconsider. The first was that, even if she found some means of inducing an abortion, she might well damage herself fatally along with the fetus. The second was something Sherah told her after she conceived for the first time.

"If you hurt the baby," Sherah said, "they'll kill you. They'll bury you in the woods along with the others. But if you carry it to term, they'll look after you, and you won't be harmed."

Paige had stared at Sherah in disbelief when she'd said that. She'd been abducted, imprisoned, and raped until she conceived: if that wasn't being "harmed," then Paige didn't know what was.

Sherah guessed the direction of her thoughts.

"You'll go hard," said Sherah. "Don't think it'll just be a bullet or a blade. They'll burn you."

Paige thought she'd misheard.

"Burn?"

"You wouldn't be the first."

Paige struggled to find the words to express what she was feeling. Imprisonment, rape, forced childbirth, and now burning? It was like she'd tumbled back into the Middle Ages.

"Why are you letting them do this to me?" she asked.

And Sherah had shrugged.

"I don't want you to suffer," she said, "and I'll do my best to keep you safe and healthy: all of the women here will. But you're not of the Cut, and the Cut looks after its own."

———

IN THE BEGINNING, PAIGE had screamed for help, just like, later, Gayle did, but no one outside the Cut heard her. Hannah had arrived to warn her to be quiet, but Paige had told her to go fuck herself.

After that, Oberon came, and Paige didn't scream anymore.

Paige had tried to escape once, shortly after the first birth, when Martha, an older woman who had since died, came to bring Paige her daily hot meal. Paige had knocked her down and started running, but they caught her within minutes. Lucius had reached her first, and he'd struck her so hard on the side of the head that she was still partially deaf in her right ear. As punishment, she was placed in the unfinished basement under the floor of the hut. She hadn't even known that there was a basement, so well had they hidden the entrance beneath a section of board. They left her down there in the blackness for two days with just bread and water, and a bucket to use for her ablutions. That was as close to madness as she had come.

For so long she had waited for someone to arrive in the Cut, some-one from outside, but nobody ever came. Still, she had not entirely lost hope, or not until she overheard Cassander talking with Hannah after her latest pregnancy was confirmed. Paige had experienced trouble conceiving again, and the earlier miscarriage had been a source of con-cern. If she couldn't give birth again, then what good would be she be to them? Hannah and Cassander had believed her to be sleeping, but Paige woke up to pee, and heard them speaking not far from one of the vents in the wall.

"It's about time," said Cassander. "I thought we'd bled her dry."

"Perhaps you should think about looking for another. Three births would be as many as we've ever had from one woman. They get damaged. It's not the same as it is between husband and wife."

"I know the difference."

"Good. Sherah would be unhappy otherwise."

Cassander had laughed, and Paige had returned to bed, storing away this little piece of information even as she feared for her own life. Sherah was Oberon's wife. Could Cassander possibly be sleeping with her behind his back?

But she had other, more immediate concerns. After this one, they would kill her. Paige knew it. She would have to try to run again, but they let her out for only an hour a day to exercise in the fenced-in yard behind the hut, and she was always being watched. The Cut women were careful to keep their distance, and they were sometimes armed. Even when they came to check on her and Gayle, they would do so by first separating them, and at least two women would always be present. Paige would be locked in her room while Gayle was being examined, and vice versa. No matter how often she considered the problem, and from how many angles, Paige could find no way to make her escape. She would die in the Cut, and soon.

The biggest of the slit windows was no more than a foot wide and three feet long, and fitted with Plexiglas that had grown worn over the years so that it gave a misty perspective to everything. Still, Paige liked to stand on a chair and gaze out on the world beyond the walls. When she lost the will and energy even to do that, then she'd probably welcome the final visit, and the walk into the woods to the waiting grave.

Now, at the window, she saw movement: Sherah and Hannah, coming up fast. They looked worried.

"Something's happening," she said.

Gayle stopped crooning and looked up at the older woman.

"Maybe they're going to let us leave," said Gayle. She began to giggle, then stopped.

"I think I'm going to hurt one of them," she said. She spoke as though she were considering trying on a different dress: the white one, or maybe the blue, but it was a tone that Paige had never heard her use before.

"Which one?" asked Paige, curious about this pronouncement.

"Hannah. No, Sherah. She pretends that she cares, but she doesn't care. At least Hannah doesn't try to pretend."

"And when will you do this?"

Gayle mused on the question.

"Today?"

Paige heard the question in it. *Maybe all is not lost for this girl*, she thought.

The Cut women were drawing nearer. Paige moved away from the window and knelt carefully before Gayle, aware of the weight of the child she was carrying. "I'll help you to hurt one of them, okay, but not today. Soon, though. You'll just have to wait for my signal. Will you do that?"

"Yes."

"Good."

"And then I want to hurt Cassander, and Oberon, and Marius, and Lucius . . ."

*First things first*, thought Paige.

"Yes, we'll find a way to hurt them, too."

Chapter

# LXII

Henkel was part of the team that moved into the Cut from the south: they were ten in total, including their Cut minders, and they spread out in a line that permitted each man or woman to see the others to the right and left. They called out Perry Lutter's name as they went, waited for a response, then moved on. They only had enough dogs to place one with each team, but so far none of them had picked up Perry's scent. Although Henkel would never have said as much aloud, he didn't hold out much hope of finding Perry in the Cut. If anyone from the Cut was responsible for Perry's disappearance—or, God forbid, his murder—then a lesson would have been learned from the discovery of Killian and Huff, and he would have been buried far from this place.

Henkel also knew that his animosity toward Oberon and his kind was prejudicing the conduct of the search. It was entirely possible that the Cut had nothing to do with whatever had befallen Perry—and, most assuredly, something had—which meant that Henkel was wasting valuable time and resources on this incursion.

But while he had no direct evidence to link Perry to the Cut, he had nearly two decades of experience in law enforcement on which to draw. The Cut's history of violence, and the rumors of possible criminality on its part, were an open secret in Plassey County. The only current point of contention was whether or not the Cut was winding down, and turning its back on its past in favor of a more conventional lifestyle, or as conventional as could be expected from a reclusive community that had sequestered itself away on private land and appeared never to have heard of an ordinary name like Dave or Steve. There might have been some element of truth to the belief that the Cut's more dubious activities were in abeyance, but this did not mean they had ceased entirely. There was badness yet in the Cut.

The search was Henkel's way of maintaining pressure on Oberon and his people. For now, with the focus of the investigation into Killian and Huff directed elsewhere, it was the best he could do. And if Perry Lutter didn't show up soon, Henkel would be shouting his name on every TV channel and radio station that would broadcast it, and talking to every journalist who would listen, and would sow further seeds of doubt about the Cut's nature. Pressure, pressure, pressure; soon, cracks would appear. Henkel was certain of it.

The line moved on. The dog sniffed and whined. When Henkel paused for a leak, taking some small pleasure in pissing on the Cut, he thought that he caught sight of at least two children following the searchers. A man named Bryan Kibble, who had once owned a hardware store in Turley that somehow managed to stay in business for thirty years, despite the presence of the big Sears just over the county line, waited for Henkel to rejoin the search, briefly shifting position to the right so that he and the sheriff were within earshot of each other.

"You see them?" said Kibble.

"Yeah."

"Spooky little shits, and rough as pig iron. This whole place gives me the dismals."

"It's just wood and dirt, like any other place."

"No it ain't, and you know it."

A figure moved across the back of the line, checking to see what was delaying the progress of the two men: Lucius, Cassander's son. Henkel had noticed the bruising on his face as soon as he arrived, but it had swollen badly in the hour that had gone by since, and Lucius's right eye was now half-closed.

"Everything all right here?" Lucius asked.

"Catching a breath," said Henkel. "You ought to put something on that eye of yours."

"Truck door hit me," said Lucius.

"Yeah," said Kibble drily. "They'll do that if you sneak up on 'em unexpected."

Henkel, meanwhile, thought he could make out a tread mark on Lucius's face, even amid the swelling. He might have been mistaken, but he was pretty certain Lucius had taken a boot to the face. It wasn't from Perry Lutter, though: Perry always wore sneakers, rain or shine.

"We ought to keep moving," said Lucius. "Don't want to break the line."

Henkel nodded and took a final glance over his shoulder. A girl stood watching him from amid knee-high weeds, half-hidden by the trunk of a tree. She was wearing clothing of green and brown, so that she seemed almost an extension of the natural world, a sprite taking form from leaf and bark.

Henkel shivered, and gave his back to her as he and Kibble returned to the search.

# LXIII

The lawyer named Daniel Starcher operated out of a small suite of offices in the pretty historic town of Lewisburg. He blended in perfectly amid its galleries and wine shops, its antiques stores and Realtors, striding the old and new worlds like a genial legal colossus, Southern manners allied to modern nous. From his office window he could see the monuments of the Old Presbyterian Church Cemetery, and the BMW that was currently his vehicle of choice. His walls displayed a carefully curated mix of art, most of it by young Southern artists. His practice specialized in civil cases, with only a little criminal work on the side. It was said locally that Daniel Starcher didn't like to get his hands dirty, and preferred any clients who broke the law to have the decency to wear a white collar when they did it.

Starcher was the Cut's lawyer, chosen as much for the unlikeliness of the juxtaposition between advocate and client as for his ability and discretion. On those rare occasions when denizens of the Cut found themselves in legal difficulties of a criminal or civil nature, Starcher would farm the work out to one of a handful of tame litigators in nearby towns or cities, all of whom had trained under Starcher's aegis and thus exposed themselves to his gentle but potent corruption. Starcher was a moral abyss, entirely sociopathic. In Lewisburg it was generally assumed he was gay, but Starcher was in fact virtually without a sexual drive. He did, though, very much like money. As far as he was concerned, those who claimed that wealth never made anyone happy simply hadn't attained the correct level of financial security.

Starcher arranged the private adoptions on behalf of the Cut. He was very good at it. When required, he could even provide a "straw" mother to attest that the child was hers, and perform the requisite pantomime of regret at handing over her baby, and relief that it would now receive a better life than she could have offered. Such acts had rarely proved necessary over the course of his long relationship with the Cut, the adoptive parents mostly being relieved simply to receive a healthy Caucasian child, and with as few legal complications as possible. Most, Starcher knew, understood that it was better if the adoption was not subjected to undue scrutiny. They were buying a baby, and paying a premium for it, which also covered the fast tracking of any paperwork. Once the child was delivered, Starcher never expected to hear from them again, and he had yet to be disappointed in this regard.

He had lined up three prospective sets of parents for the two children promised by the Cut, and after a short bidding war the list had been narrowed by a third. Fortunately—or unfortunately, depending on one's perspective as a potential parent—a new buyer had emerged in recent days, or rather a consortium of buyers. They had presented themselves in the form of a standard, middle-aged couple seeking to adopt the child that they themselves could no longer create, but Starcher was no fool, and always performed his own background checks. He couldn't quite nail down their references, and a perusal of their bank records revealed a series of large payments lodged to a new account during the previous month.

Deeper background searches had turned up a connection to a man named Paulo Torak, a pornographer with a lucrative sideline in child pornography of the most vicious kind. Starcher knew of Torak because it was through one of his associates that Starcher had acquired the

material used to incriminate, and imprison, Jerome Burnel. Starcher
sent some of his less scrupulous associates to question Torak, and
although he declined to name names, he admitted that a group of men
of very particular tastes were prepared to spend a significant sum of
money to acquire a child—preferably male, although female would also
be acceptable—for their own enjoyment. When he informed Starcher
of the upper limit to the money on offer, and promised him a further
10 percent for his cooperation, Starcher immediately culled his previous list of two sets of parents by a further 50 percent, and consented to
sell a child to the consortium.

He knew that he would have to keep the nature of the sale from
Oberon, who was very uncompromising in such matters. This would
require a little lying, at which Starcher was adept. But Starcher also
knew that Oberon's time was drawing to a close, and he had encouraged Cassander Hobb in his ambitions to lead the Cut. Cassander was
less rigid than Oberon, but also more dangerous. Starcher decided not
to lie to him about the sale, and offered him a quarter of his own bonus
to sweeten the deal.

Cassander had accepted, although once again Starcher would have
been surprised had he raised any objections. Starcher was a fine judge
of character, having none of his own worth mentioning, which left him
free to make accurate assessments of the character of others.

The call from Cassander came as Starcher was opening a very good
bottle of Cabernet Sauvignon to celebrate the successful conclusion of
a piece of civil litigation. He had also shed his shoes, and was about to
immerse himself in a Wilbur Smith novel. Cassander's interruption
would have been unwelcome at any time, but especially this one. He
was calling from somewhere outdoors, and kept his voice low so that he
would not be overheard.

Oberon had permitted a search of the Cut. This was bad enough, but
Cassander had also learned—and Starcher did not want to know how,

though he had his suspicions—that Oberon might be about to renege on the sale of at least one child, if it was a boy, and keep it for himself.

"It's time for new leadership," said Cassander.

Starcher, reflecting on his promised bonus, replied: "I think that might be for the best."

And so it was decided.

Chapter

# LXIV

Major Alvin Martin of the West Virginia State Police had come a long way from Haven County, Virginia: not physically, because a swift car ride would take him back there soon enough, if he chose—which he most certainly did not—but in terms of rank, income, and further career opportunities. He did not miss being the sheriff of Haven County. He had one son about to graduate high school, another in middle school, and a daughter who was studying to be a lawyer. He had a wife who was aging better than he was—and didn't rub it in, which was damn Christian of her—and a dog named Rocco, who was just about the dumbest animal in canine history but didn't have a single bad bone in his admittedly mangy body.

Sometimes, whole days could go by without Martin thinking about the dead children, and the man in Haven County who had been complicit in their murders more than a decade before. Martin had spent a long time wondering if there was anything he could have done to stop the killings earlier, and bring those involved to justice. After much searching of his soul, and long talks with his pastor and his wife, he had decided that there wasn't, but it didn't give him much consolation.

Two bodies still hadn't been identified. Martin didn't know how that could be. Somewhere, a mother or father—natural, adoptive, or foster—was aware of a missing child, but either didn't know or didn't care enough to make the pilgrimage to New York to investigate further. Those two anonymous children had been buried in a pauper's grave, with tissue samples retained in case someone did eventually come forward to claim them. Until then, they rested beneath the shadows of a pair of small white crosses, largely unmourned except by Martin and his wife—who visited the grave once a year to lay flowers and pray for the souls of the children sleeping under the earth—and one other person.

The groundskeeper at the cemetery had mentioned it to Martin a couple of years before, when he noticed him tending to the grave. He told Martin that a man came to the same resting place quite regularly, although he never left flowers. Martin asked for a description, and within moments he knew who the visitor was: the private detective Charlie Parker.

The groundskeeper recalled him clearly, he said, because of an incident that still troubled him. It was a clear spring afternoon, and he saw the man enter the cemetery, and then later caught sight of him sitting on a bench just as the sun was setting, with two children standing behind him. Although the man did not appear to register their presence, or turn to speak with them, the groundskeeper was certain that he was aware the children were there.

"Why didn't he try to find out who they were?" Martin asked.

"I think he knew exactly who they were," the groundskeeper replied. "That's why he didn't turn around."

That conversation still gave Martin a chill. He had never felt at ease in the cemetery since.

His thoughts did not often turn to Parker, largely by force of will—which meant, Martin supposed, that he kind of *was* thinking about the detective, mainly by trying not to. The detective was a presence in his subconscious, like a stain that would not be erased and simply must be ignored as best one could. True, Parker had uncovered a great evil, and brought it to an end, but he had also left wreckage in his wake, and Martin's own career was almost part of it. Martin had put Haven behind him, and had risen to his current position despite, and not because of, Parker.

Or that was what he told himself. As a black man who had worked his way up through a number of largely white law enforcement agencies, he had grown adept at learning to ignore what was uncomfortable or demeaning, and to believe his own lies when required. He could not have survived otherwise.

He was so lost in his thoughts that he barely noticed Estelle, one of the desk staff, standing at his door.

"I'm sorry to disturb you, sir," she said, "but there's a man downstairs who says he's come to see you."

"Did he give you a name?"

"No, just this."

She handed him a matchbook from the Haven View Motel in Haven County. The motel had closed many years before, a fact not unconnected to its briefly accepting Parker as a guest. Martin flicked the matchbook open. Written inside were the words "I bet you still keep your cells nice and clean."

Martin had the strangest sensation.

*I thought about him*, he said to himself. *I brought him to mind, and in doing so I summoned him up, like a ghost.*

*Or a demon.*

"What should I tell him?" asked Estelle.

"That I'll be down in a few minutes."

Estelle turned to go, but Martin summoned her back.

"Actually," he said, getting to his feet and finding his hat and coat, "I think I'll just deal with this right now."

# LXV

Martin led Parker to Capitol Roasters at the Capitol Market on Smith Street, which was far enough away from the state police barracks on the other side of Charleston's Kanawha River to make it unlikely that they'd be spotted by anyone who might take an interest in the company Martin was keeping, although even drinking coffee with this man in one of the contiguous states would still have been too close to 725 Jefferson for Martin's liking. The two men took seats outside, overlooking the produce sellers. Martin still did not know what Parker might want. He'd just told Martin that he wanted to talk with him, and Martin had considered it wise to do so somewhere with far fewer uniforms around.

They'd both changed. They were older, grayer, possibly a little wiser—and Parker had more blood on his hands. Like most of those who had crossed his path, Martin had some awareness of the cases in which the detective had involved himself. He should have been dead ten times over, yet here he was, drinking expensive coffee on Martin's dime, since Parker had insisted on making Martin pay for the best cup of coffee that Capitol could offer, if only to be annoying. Parker's continued survival was enough to make one believe in the existence of God, if one were so inclined, or to dispute it, according to one's view of his endurance. They made no small talk, just sipped their beverages until Parker was ready to begin.

"A man named Harpur Griffin got himself burned alive in his car in Portland last weekend," said Parker.

"I saw that."

"You know him?"

"He had a record, but nothing significant."

"Did Portland PD get in touch with you?"

"Not with me personally, but they made contact. Wanted to know who in West Virginia might be inclined to do such a thing, like burning folk was something we liked to get up to on a regular basis, maybe when there wasn't a Mountaineers game on."

It was clear from Martin's tone that whoever got in touch with the West Virginia State Police on behalf of the Portland PD had not done much for relations between North and South.

"Any idea who made the call?"

"Function, Farnold, something like that."

"Furnish."

"Yeah, that was him. Friend of yours?"

"This is me looking offended at the suggestion."

Parker took a long draft of coffee. *Damn*, thought Martin, *that was one* muy caro *cup of beans and water. The least the son of a bitch could do is sip it and make it last.*

"And what was Griffin to you?" he asked.

"I think he may have been involved in the disappearance of a client."

"Who?"

"Jerome Burnel."

"Faraday—"

"Furnish."

"Yeah, him, he mentioned that name, but it didn't set off any alarms down here."

"I think there's a connection through Plassey County."

Parker caught just the slightest hesitation as Martin raised his cup to his mouth. *Many a slip*, he thought.

"Yeah?" said Martin.

"That's in West Virginia."

"I know where it is."

"So what's the problem with Plassey County?"

"Did I say there was a problem?"

"You'd be a good poker player, but not a great one."

Martin leaned back against the wall. He wished he'd called in sick that morning. Too late now.

"Plassey County is home to fewer than five thousand people," said Martin. "It's small, quiet, pretty, dirt-poor, and has virtually no crime worth mentioning. It's a little bit of not much at all."

"It sounds great," said Parker, "apart from that bit about being poor. But poverty breeds crime, and crime breeds violence, so how come Plassey is such a haven?"

"Officially, it's because it's got an older population, and the county offices function efficiently. In a jurisdiction that small, the law usually gets to know the people who might be of a mind to cause trouble, and works with them to ensure that they exercise an element of self-restraint."

"Is that what the law does in Plassey County?"

"No," said Martin. "Someone else does it for them."

Martin removed a stray piece of dirt from his uniform trousers. They were otherwise spotless. Martin was a straight arrow. What had annoyed him about Parker's matchbook message was that his cells were, in fact, still clean. He was doing his best to ensure that the state police maintained a similar standard of purity, but West Virginia was peculiar. Violence had been endemic to it since its foundation, and its mountainous terrain had long inhibited effective law enforcement, along with the personal nature of feuds in small isolated rural communities, which placed a premium on settling disputes with force and without recourse to the police. When coal mining began, the nature of the violence in the state became linked to industrial development, so along with prostitution, gambling, and narcotics came confrontations between the mine bosses and the unions. Add in the effects of Prohibition, and West Virginia was stewing nicely during the first half of the last century, and that kind of history was akin to poisonous chemicals that leached into the soil. What grew out of it—if anything did—would bear the mark of those contaminants.

And worst of all was the coal industry. Sure, it provided jobs—in grim, dangerous conditions that wouldn't have been entirely foreign to miners from centuries earlier, so that those familiar with the pits described descending into them as similar to drowning—but at the price of the state's blind loyalty to its needs, and the slow destruction of the land itself.

Now those jobs were disappearing, and Walmart had become West Virginia's largest employer, yet the aftereffects of generations of underachievement could not easily be erased, which meant obesity, drug abuse, kidney disease, emphysema, and the least college-educated population in the country. West Virginia was trapped in a spiral of decline.

But Martin, like Edward Henkel, loved the state: the glory of its landscape, despite the efforts of the mining and chemical companies; the decency of its people, even in the face of the corruption of those who were supposed to represent their best interests; and the stubbornness of that same population, which saw generations of men and women work themselves to death for an industry that could, as late as 1972, watch one of its coal slurry dams burst, flooding sixteen towns along Buffalo Creek Hollow and killing 125 people, and declare it an "act of God."

All this Martin told Parker while the sun shone on the market and, to the east, Henkel and his people moved ineffectually through the Cut.

"The Cut runs Plassey County," said Martin. "And the reason it has been allowed to do so for centuries is that it's better at it than the institutions of the state. If you screw with the water supply in Plassey, or pollute a river or stream, you answer to the Cut. If you try to set up a meth lab, the Cut will destroy it and give you twenty-four hours to leave, and you'd better not ever return. If you engage in any kind of criminal activity—hell, if you raise your hand to your wife—the Cut will come calling, and it'll be the last time you do it."

Parker thought about this.

"And all in the interests of order and good governance?"

"All in the interests of being left in peace."

"To do what?"

"The official line? To live, to work, to mind their own business."

"And the unofficial line?"

"Well, you could ask what that business might be."

"Would I get an answer?"

"Not from me, but I'm not the right person to ask."

"And who is?"

"The sheriff of Plassey County, Ed Henkel. He has no love for the Cut, to the extent that there are people in Charleston who regard him as a pain in the ass. He cries wolf on the Cut. If the weather changes, he blames them. If he could, he'd burn the entire Cut down to the ground and sow salt in the ashes."

"So how did he get elected?"

"Because maybe there are enough people in Plassey who believe that the rule of law shouldn't be beholden to the Cut, or should have the power to hold it in check."

"Will Henkel talk to me?"

"You can ask him."

"Will you tell him I'm coming?"

"Bet your life on it."

"I'd prefer if you didn't."

"With respect, your preferences don't come into it. My turn: how much trouble are you going to cause in Plassey County?"

"I haven't decided yet."

Martin imagined a sliding scale, with a desired level of trouble right down at the bottom, and Parker hovering near the top, just prior to blowing off the scale entirely.

"I'd prefer if you kept it to a minimum."

"With respect, your preferences—"

"All right, I get it."

Parker stood. He put out his hand. Martin shook it.

"You know, I like my job," said Martin.

"It certainly comes with a very nice uniform."

"If anyone asks me, I'll say that I told you to get the hell out of West Virginia."

"I understand."

"So get the hell out of West Virginia, and stay away from the Cut."

"Was that Henkel with one 'l' or two?"

"One."

"Thanks."

"Don't mention it. Seriously: don't mention it."

Martin didn't turn to watch him go. He needed to head back to Jefferson Road to pick up some paperwork. If he waited long enough, then Estelle might have gone home, and he knew that she was heading off the next day for a vacation in Aruba. By the time he saw her again she would, with luck, have forgotten entirely about Parker. Perhaps Martin could start trying to forget about him again too, or just exile him back to the dark places in his mind, where buried children waited for someone to call their names.

Martin glanced to his left.

"He didn't even finish his damn coffee," he said aloud. He turned in his chair and caught a passing barista.

"Hey," he said, "can you heat this coffee up, please? And maybe find me a newspaper . . ."

# LXVI

The searchers continued moving through the Cut, the four teams gradually approaching the Square. Oberon remained discreetly in touch with each group, mainly by using the shortwave radios that the Cut preferred to cell phones within their own borders, but also through updates delivered by a series of children, so that by the time Henkel's group reached the Square they were no longer being followed, and the children had vanished back into the woods.

The searchers were met with hot soup, chunks of freshly baked bread, and pots of coffee, served by both women and men. Henkel knew most of the faces and names, although some of the older inhabitants were such infrequent venturers from the Cut that Henkel at first struggled to recall them. They watched the strangers with a kind of muted hostility tempered by curiosity: this was probably the first time in years, certainly since before the reign of Sheriff Dugar, that outsiders had been allowed so deep into the Cut.

Henkel sipped his coffee and strolled with exaggerated casualness around the Square, taking in all that he was seeing, marking the position of houses, outbuildings, and paths, and calculating the distances between each. When he returned home, he would create a map of the Cut, initially from his own observations and later by adding what others had seen as they progressed through it. Google Maps wasn't much use where the Cut was concerned: apart from the Square itself, much of the land was covered with evergreen forest and perennials, and even the main roads were narrow enough to be overhung by branches.

Oberon stood by the steps of the largest house on the Square, monitoring Henkel's movements. It had been a calculated gamble on his part to allow Henkel to search the Cut, and they both knew that it was all for show. Perry Lutter had not wandered into the Cut, and even if he had, and was lying somewhere within it, unconscious or dead, the searchers would have discovered him only if they had physically stumbled across him. The search for Perry was little more than a cursory effort. Oberon understood that its true purpose was to plant a flag in the Cut, to show them all that the sheriff was no longer prepared to stand by and allow it to remain a private fiefdom. The search represented a significant escalation of hostilities between Henkel and the Cut, but it remained to be seen if Henkel would be able to accumulate enough evidence to mount a bigger challenge, or if Oberon and the others could wait him out until his term began to draw to a close, and then ensure that his replacement was someone more willing to leave them unmolested.

Henkel had not seen Cassander. Oberon's second-in-command usually made his presence felt. He was, in his way, even more protective of the Cut than Oberon. On this occasion, though, he seemed to have appointed the more disturbed of his two sons to be his eyes and ears while he was engaged elsewhere. Lucius was sitting at a table constructed from a single massive slab of wood, clearly sawn from close to the base of an ancient tree, and set to rest on four smaller trunks to which sections of bark still clung. Lucius was using a long knife to hack at the edge of the table. His attention was fixed on the knife and the wood, the only distraction from his mutilation of the furniture being a single glance in Oberon's direction that Henkel caught, the naked hostility of it as bright and clean as the blade in Lucius's hand.

*What might you have done*, Henkel wondered of Lucius, *to earn Oberon's boot in your face?* Had he and Oberon been other than antagonists, Henkel might well have advised him to watch his back around Lucius, especially when the boy had a knife in his hand. But Henkel figured that Oberon wouldn't have needed his advice anyway. If he hadn't realized the threat posed by Lucius, whatever the cause, then he had no business running the Cut, and someone else might take his place before long: possibly Cassander, but not Lucius himself. Nobody in the Cut was crazy enough to follow him. Marius, his brother, was hardly a genius, or overburdened with charisma, but he had the benefit of not being actively insane. He was no leader, though. If something happened to Oberon, it would fall to Cassander to take his place. Henkel wasn't sure how he felt about that. Oberon was bad enough, but not beyond comprehension, while Cassander remained largely a mystery.

Henkel was now at the northern edge of the Square. Through the trees, he glimpsed a long, shedlike structure with a tin roof and windows that were barely more than slits. He had not noticed it before, and since his team had entered the Square from the south he'd had no cause to pass that way. He looked around. Rob Channer was speaking with some of his cronies, his back to Henkel. Channer had taken it upon himself to reorganize the groups that had entered the Cut from the north, west, and east, which Henkel had discovered only when the four teams met in the Square. He'd have a word with Channer about that later, because the Cut wasn't the place in which to discuss it, but that northern team, with Channer leading it, should have taken a look at the building.

Off to Channer's right, and out of earshot, sat Kyle Fogle, who had been part of the Channer group. Kyle was an okay kid, but easily led. He wanted to be a sheriff's deputy, but had already failed the written test once. This, Henkel felt, was probably for the best.

Now Henkel sidled up to Fogle, asked him how the search had gone, and then, as an afterthought, inquired if his team had taken a look at the structure behind him. Fogle told him that they hadn't, and it turned out that Channer's team hadn't taken a direct route from north to south but had drifted slightly southwest as it drew nearer to the Square, so that it met up with the party heading from the west about a quarter of a mile out, and entered more from that direction than the north.

*Huh*, thought Henkel. Maybe he'd underestimated Kyle Fogle after all. He might have another chat with him about that written test at a later date. Henkel thanked Fogle, dumped the last of his coffee on the ground, and headed for the building.

Cassander sat within touching distance of the blockhouse, and listened to the voice of the Dead King as it conjured up images in his head, like a mood evoked by a song in a foreign tongue. He saw the Cut in bloom, a blaze of green foliage and flowering plants in the heat of summer. He saw children. He saw his wife's grave slowly disappear, covered over by creeping vines, and another woman drifting through his home, adding her own music to rooms that had not heard a female voice in three years. Her face remained hidden from Cassander, but her body was young.

He saw a primitive wooden coffin being lowered into the dirt. The female figure in his house grew clearer. He descried its features: the shape of its breasts, the swell of its hips, the welcoming darkness between its thighs. A light caught the woman in her nakedness, and Sherah turned to welcome him, her widow's weeds put away.

And Cassander took her, and made her his own.

# LXVIII

I t had been clear from the moment they arrived in the prison house that Sherah and Hannah were not screwing around. Paige and Gayle were told to sit facing the wall, with their hands clasped before them. Sherah had a gun, but Paige didn't think that she was likely to use it. It was mostly for show. Hannah, though, held a cattle prod, and Paige knew from experience that it was most certainly not just for show: Hannah had turned it on her after the first escape attempt, and it wasn't an encounter Paige was eager to repeat, so she did as she was told, and Gayle followed her lead.

Three men and two more women entered the prison house, all of whom Paige knew by sight but not by name. They moved quickly to strip the accommodation of any signs of recent habitation. Cereals and foodstuffs were taken from the closets and put in boxes and plastic bags, and the pictures that she and Gayle had pulled from magazines to brighten the walls were torn down.

Plastic ties were placed around their wrists and pulled tight, followed by a ball gag to the mouth against which Gayle tried to struggle. The panel on the floor was lifted, exposing the entrance to the basement. Now it was Paige's turn to start panicking. She didn't want to go back down there. It would break her.

"Hush," said Sherah. "I'll be with you, and we'll have a lamp. It won't be for long, I promise."

And then Paige knew: someone was coming, someone from outside.

# Chapter

# LXIX

Henkel heard a voice shouting his name as he left the Square, following a trail worn by footsteps to the door of the building, but he didn't look back. He rose on his toes to try to peer in the windows, but they were too high. He could just tell that it was dark inside, while the surrounding trees obscured even the dying of the day's light. He tried the steel door, but it appeared to be locked.

"Can I help you, Sheriff Henkel?"

He turned. Oberon was standing halfway up the trail. He wasn't smiling, but he didn't appear troubled either.

"What is this place?" Henkel asked, indicating behind him with his thumb.

"We use it for storage. It also has beds, and it's plumbed for a toilet and shower."

"Why?"

"Sometimes there are arguments," said Oberon. "A wife fights with a husband, or a son with a father. This is an enclosed, tight-knit community, and that's good for the most part, but if you're not getting along with someone in your family, then it's hard to find space to cool off. This is somewhere that people can come if they need to."

"It looks like a jailhouse."

"It's been used for that in its time as well. Men have too much to drink, they get angry, and this becomes a drunk tank."

Henkel took in the well-worn trail.

"Looks like they come here pretty regularly."

"I told you: it's used for storage as well."

"Open it, please."

"Perry Lutter isn't in there, and I shouldn't need to remind you that you don't have a warrant."

Oberon didn't move. Farther back, Henkel glimpsed a handful of the Cut watching from the base of the trail. Lucius was one of them.

"I did say 'please,'" Henkel reminded him.

Oberon unclipped a key from his belt, concealing its bone fob in the palm of his hand, and joined Henkel at the door. It opened easily, revealing an unlocked second door with a plastic window, beyond which was a large room piled up with a random assortment of boxes, some old chairs, a couple of couches, and a table. At one end was a pair of bedrooms, each containing a single bed and a locker, and between them a small bathroom barely big enough to accommodate the shower stall, toilet, and sink that it contained. It smelled of a scented soap or gel. Henkel saw hairs around the drain of the shower. They looked damp to him. The shower, at least, had been used recently.

Only bare mattresses remained on the beds. The lockers were open and empty. There were marks on the wall where pictures of some kind had been stuck up. Traces of adhesive material still clung to the paintwork.

The walls of the building were thick. They'd keep the rooms cool in summer, thought Henkel, and warm in winter. The roof might have been tin, but it had been well insulated. The floor was wood laminate, and free of dust. It felt solid enough under Henkel's feet. A couple of rugs had been rolled up and stood in a corner of the main room.

"What's in the boxes?" Henkel asked Oberon.

"I don't know. I haven't been in here for a while. If you want to search them, feel free."

Henkel didn't bother. If Oberon was happy to let him poke around in the boxes, then they contained nothing worth seeing. He stood in the center of the room, his hands in his pockets. Something about the building wasn't right, but he couldn't put his finger on what it might be.

"If you're done?" said Oberon.

*What am I missing?* Henkel wondered. *What am I not seeing here?*

"Yes," he said. "I'm done."

# LXX

aige could just about make out the sound of two voices—one of them Oberon's—from down in the basement, but not what they were saying. She was seated on the dirt floor against a wall. A pair of battery-powered lamps provided the sole illumination. There was one beside her and another by Gayle, who sat directly across from her. The younger woman was watching Paige carefully, fully engaged with her environment for the first time in months. If they were down here, it was because the man speaking with Oberon represented a threat. This wasn't just some casual visitor: a threat meant more than an outsider. A threat meant the law.

But Paige didn't dare move or make a sound because Hannah was beside her, whispering in her ear. Her every word made it clear that if Paige so much as breathed too loudly then what would follow would make her previous punishments seem like blessings by comparison. She held the cattle prod in front of Paige's face.

"I'll touch this to places it was never meant to touch," said Hannah. "Do you understand?"

Just in case Paige didn't, Hannah placed the tip against Paige's right nipple.

"Zzzzt," said Hannah. "Zzzzt. Zzzzt."

She moved the prod down, over Paige's belly, her groin, before letting it rest between her legs.

*"Zzzzzzzzzt!"*

The voices ceased. Footsteps resounded dully from above. A little dust fell from the ceiling. Paige heard the sound of the door closing.

No. No, no, no, no . . .

But Sherah and Hannah did not move, and the four women remained in the basement for what felt like an hour to Paige, but was almost certainly less, until the door above their heads was opened again, footsteps came across the floor, and the section of laminate hiding the basement entrance was removed. Oberon appeared in the gap that was revealed.

"Bring them up," he said. "It's safe now."

The ball gags were removed, and Sherah cut the plastic restraints with a small knife. Paige shot Hannah a look of pure vitriol as she helped Gayle up the rough wooden steps to the main room, but said nothing. She thought that Hannah was disappointed not to have been able to hurt her with the prod.

Their few possessions were returned, although nobody offered to help them restore the food to the cupboards, or put the pictures back on the walls. Some of the latter were crumpled and torn, including a poster of some boy band of which Gayle was inexplicably fond, as though Paige needed reminding of just how young she really was. A couple of hours later, Sherah and another woman, Agathe, brought the evening meal. It was better and bigger than usual—roast turkey, mashed potatoes, gravy, carrots, and peas, all freshly made—and included cupcakes for Paige and Gayle: their reward for being well behaved in the basement. Paige could still taste the rubber of the ball gag in her mouth, and not even the sweetness of the cupcake could overcome it, but she ate everything. Gayle did the same. She had not spoken a word since they had been released from the basement. She had not even recommenced her crooning, and ignored Paige when she asked her if she wanted to wash or dry the dishes and utensils tonight, so Paige did both. Whatever was up with Gayle would reveal itself in time.

Lights-out was usually at 9:00 p.m., but both women had small battery-powered book lamps to use for reading, and a pair of flashlights that weren't much more powerful than the lamps. The computer was charged for them twice daily since the hut had no outlets that the women could access. It was currently fully juiced, so Paige watched a couple of episodes of *That '70s Show* from a box set that someone from the Cut had bought well used. Gayle didn't join her, and Paige didn't laugh at the sitcom. It was just an escape—meaningless sound and light in which she could lose herself for a while, because she didn't think she could focus on a book, or even a magazine article. For the first time since she had been abducted, someone from outside the Cut had come to the house, and it was probably a lawman. What had brought him? Was there progress at last into the investigation, something to link her or Gayle to the Cut? No, it couldn't be that: a solid lead would have resulted in more than a cursory examination of their prison. Nevertheless, an outsider had been here, in this room. He would have heard her if she'd been able to cry out.

So close, so close.

And what then? The Cut would have killed him, lawman or not. Kidnapping was good for ten years in West Virginia—Paige had read about it in a newspaper article—and a single rape conviction could put someone away for up to thirty-five years, never mind multiple charges linked to any number of women. Nobody that Paige had encountered so far in this place—not Cassander or Oberon, and certainly not fucking Hannah—was going down without a fight.

Sherah came to check on them shortly after nine, and then the main lights were extinguished. Paige had gone to the bathroom while there was still power, but Gayle had not, and Paige heard her fumbling around by the flashlight's illumination while she undressed in her room. Paige ran her hands over the swelling at her belly. She felt heavy and tender. She also thought that she might have to pee again. She wished Gayle would hurry up. She pulled her nightgown over her head and sat on the edge of her bed. A few minutes later she heard the toilet flush, and then Gayle appeared at her door.

"I have a present for you," she said. As she came closer, Paige could see that she was smiling.

Paige wasn't sure that she liked the sound of this. She knew all of Gayle's possessions by heart. There was nothing that the girl could give her, or nothing that she might want.

"What is it?" she asked.

Gayle held out her hands, palms down, clenched into fists. She had big hands for a small girl, with long, muscular fingers. She'd told Paige that she used to play the piano, before—well, before whatever it was that had made her run away, which she still hadn't shared with Paige, but about which the older woman had her suspicions. It was in the way Gayle said the words "my mom's boyfriend," and the expression on her face that came with them, like she'd just swallowed something bad.

"Pick one."

"I need to pee."

"Please, just pick."

"The left."

Gayle opened her fist. Lying in the palm was a section of red brick: a good heavy one, too, by the looks of it. Paige took it from her and weighed it in her own hand.

"Where did you get it?" she asked.

"The same place I got this," said Gayle, opening her right fist to reveal a long, narrow stone, with a kind of dull point at the end, like some ancient tool discovered in the course of an archaeological dig. "In the basement. I dug them up with my fingers while we were stuck down there."

Paige stared at Gayle with new eyes. While she'd been listening to voices and footsteps that might represent the possibility of rescue, and thinking about how much she hated Hannah, Gayle had been proactive.

These weren't just stones. These were weapons.

"So when can we use them?" asked Gayle.

Paige tightened her grip on the piece of brick, lifted her hand, and brought it down in a single swift movement. *Yes*, she thought, *I can do this.* She pictured Sherah's nose breaking and Hannah bleeding from the ears.

"Soon," said Paige.

Real soon.

# 4

And ye shall overthrow their altars, and break their
pillars, and burn their groves with fire; and ye shall
hew down the graven images of their gods, and
destroy the names of them out of that place.

—Deuteronomy 12:3

Chapter

# LXXI

P arker headed east not long after his talk with Alvin Martin, just
as the light was starting to fail. The clouds hung low over ver-
dant hills, white wisps trailing from the woods like the smoke
from unseen fires. He passed houses with too much junk in their yards,
and too little money to maintain them. He saw cheap signs for clothing
alterations, barbers, and hair salons, the kinds of businesses that could
easily be opened with only a little investment, and just as easily closed
again. Mailboxes gaped emptily for houses hidden among the trees, and
he lost count of the number of PRIVATE ROAD signs. Baptists, Method-
ists, and Presbyterians fought for believers alongside roadside churches
that gave no hint of the substance of their beliefs beyond plain crosses
and plainer exteriors, most of them indistinguishable from the beaten-
down stores and battered homes that surrounded them. If there were
any Catholics down here, Parker thought, they were staying low, and
out of range.

He had learned little from Norah Meddows, but had anticipated as
much. It was enough that he had rattled her, and through Alvin Martin
he now believed that he had a name and location for those involved in
the torment of Jerome Burnel: the Cut.

If, as he thought, Meddows was involved in all that had befallen her
husband, she would call her accomplices in the Cut, and the decision

would be theirs to make: whether to continue to ignore Parker's interest in their affairs—which seemed unlikely, even unwise—or take action against him. They might delay for a time, but eventually, if only by his presence, he would force them to move against him. He would draw them down upon himself, and in doing so, they would reveal themselves. After that, he could start picking them off.

He did not think it strange that the investigation into Jerome Burnel's disappearance had brought him into contact once again with Alvin Martin, just as he had not considered it particularly odd that Ian Williamson's grandfather should have provided him with a link to the Dead King. Parker was a weapon in the hands of an unseen god. He walked tangled paths, and the surprise was not that they sometimes crossed, but that they did not do so more often.

But seeing Alvin Martin had reminded Parker of another time, when he was less than he was now, a creature composed of rage and pain, risking his own destruction by seeking out the man who had butchered his family in order to avenge himself upon him. Speaking with Martin brought Parker back to the Traveling Man, and a house in Brooklyn that had once promised so much, and a vision of himself bathed by police lights with the blood of his wife and child on his hands. Some of that anger still remained within him, but now he could feed on it without allowing himself to be consumed in turn.

Or so he assured himself.

He drove in silence toward Plassey County until the rain came and the road grew slick beneath his wheels. A tiredness came over him, and his side and back began to ache. He saw a red-and-yellow light manifest itself among the trees and pulled into a parking lot sprinkled with wood chips, behind which stood a low building with a log facade, and windows of stained glass. It appeared more church than diner, but the sign—Rickett's Country Provisions—promised coffee and baked goods, along with "hand-crafted religious iconography." Ordinarily, the promise of the latter might have caused Parker to seek more conventional surroundings in which to rest, but the pain was insistent, and he needed to get out of the car and stretch his legs.

Inside, Rickett's smelled of coffee beans and freshly shaved wood. A counter to the left held mugs and paper cups, and a glass display case with muffins, cinnamon rolls, and slices of pound cake. A series of windows ran along the wall behind it, while in front were three tables with mismatched chairs. Choral music was playing in the background, although Parker could not identify it. It didn't matter. His attention was on the rest of the interior.

Every available space—walls, floors, even the beams under the roof—was covered with carvings. Some were merely heads or busts, others entire bodies. All were images of saints and angels, although Parker recognized only a handful, a holdover from a childhood that had included time spent as an altar boy. Icons of the four evangelists were in a cluster to his left, each depicted in various forms, so that Matthew was a winged man with a lance in one version, and in another he held a purse; John bore a chalice with a snake emerging from it, but beside it, in the guise of a smaller carving, he carried an eagle on his arm. Elsewhere, Francis of Assisi was surrounded by a phantasmagoria of birds, fish, and wolf heads, while behind him an armored Gabriel blew a trumpet blast to herald the resurrection of the dead and the coming of the Lord, although Parker recalled Father Flannan telling him that the Bible did not identify the herald by name, and such iconography was a product of Byzantine art, of which Parker knew little then and less now.

Parker moved deeper inside, through carven stillness and sightless eyes, until he was brought up short by a form that sent him tumbling back through the years, just as his meeting with Alvin Martin had hours earlier, except this time with a force that was visceral and smelled of blood. It was a statue of St. Bartholomew, life-sized and anatomically correct, his skin flayed from his body and draped like a stole over his shoulders and around his waist, covering his groin as it flowed to the right, and hanging almost to his feet at the left. He held a blade in one hand, and a Bible in the other.

And in the saint's agony, Parker was reminded of the final sufferings of his wife and daughter, and in turn his own. He wanted to look away, but could not bring himself to do so, for the statue was at once both terrible and beautiful. He did not even notice the man who joined him until he heard an exhalation from behind, and discovered beside him a figure who might almost have been the image of a saint himself, some martyr from the ancient world, his beard white against his olive skin even in the dimness of the workshop, his head entirely bald and unnaturally smooth, with only the spectacles that magnified his light brown eyes to hint at his modernity.

"You know who it is?" he asked. His voice was soft and high.

"Saint Bartholomew," said Parker.

"Very good." He nodded his approval. "Some sources claim that he was put in a sack and thrown into the sea, but that's not an image to inspire great art. The Christian tradition states that he was flayed alive in Armenia, and then beheaded. They called it the 'Syrian Martyrdom.' The beheading part tends to be left out of depictions, though. It's hard to make beauty from a headless martyr."

"Did you carve this?"

"Well, this version is my work, but I can't claim credit for any more than that. I copied it. The original was created by Marco d'Agrate in 1562, and stands in the transept of Milan Cathedral. I'd always hoped to visit it someday, but I don't see it happening now. I worked from pictures. Funny—or maybe it isn't, come to think of it—but nobody has ever asked to buy it. Not sure I'd sell it, though, even if someone did want it. Mind you, that would depend on what was being offered. Feel free to name a price, if the mood strikes you."

"It doesn't," said Parker, "but thank you anyway." He tore his gaze from the carving. "Who *does* buy your work?" he asked.

"Oh, churches mostly," came the reply, "though not so many of the

storefront kind around here; they don't hold with idolatry. Some col-
lectors. I've even sold to bars and restaurants, because it's not like these
statues have been blessed or anything. But they have a power, you
know, doesn't matter if they've been sprinkled with holy water or not. I
make more of them than I'll ever sell. They watch over me. When one
departs, I carve another, but I always try to keep a few in reserve."

He put out his hand.

"I'm Thomas Rickett."

"Charlie Parker."

They shook.

"You know you share a name—?"

"I know."

"Guess you've heard that before."

"Some."

"It's no bad thing. I almost share a name with an ailment, but my
father always claimed we were related to General James Brewerton Rick-
etts, who fought for the Union Army during the Civil War. He tried to
keep that claim to family circles, being aware of which side of the Mason-
Dixon Line he happened to reside on. You want a coffee or something?"

"A coffee would be good."

"Take-out, or a civilized man's mug?"

"The mug, if it's no trouble."

"None at all. My wife usually takes care of that side of the business,
but she's out shooting the breeze with her sister."

Rickett went behind the counter and poured the coffee.

"Pastry?"

Parker ordered a slice of pound cake, although he wasn't hungry. It
just seemed proper to give Rickett the business.

"It's an unusual combination," said Parker. "A coffee shop and a religious workshop."

"The coffee brings folks in, and sometimes they buy a souvenir." He
gestured to a set of shelves by the door, laden down with small cruci-

fixes, nativity scenes, and statues of the Virgin Mary with rubber suckers on the bottom to fix them to a car dashboard. "It might seem odd, but it works."

Rickett poured the coffee, and served Parker his cake on an old china plate.

"Where are you from?"

"Portland, Maine."

"What brings you down here?"

"Business."

"Uh-huh?" Rickett nodded politely, waiting for Parker to continue, if he chose.

"In Plassey County," Parker added. He figured that it couldn't hurt. He still knew very little about Plassey, beyond what he'd learned from Alvin Martin.

"You're right on the border, then," said Rickett. "Another mile, and you'll be in Plassey. Only trees between here and there."

"You haven't asked what business I'm in."

"That's because if it's to do with Plassey, could be I'd be better off not knowing."

"I might be a salesman."

"You don't look like a salesman. You look like the law."

"Private."

"Like on TV."

"Just like it," said Parker.

He drank his coffee and took a bite of pound cake for appearance's sake. It was good, so he ate some more.

"You go into Plassey County much?" he asked Rickett.

"No, I do not."

"That sounds pretty definite."

"It is."

Rickett's expression never altered. It was benign, smiling, and very, very careful about what it kept concealed.

"I see you wear a cross," he said.

Parker's shirt was open at the neck, revealing a small pilgrim's cross.

"I do."

"Looks old."

"Byzantine."

"Well, that is old. Does it have any meaning for you?"

"In what sense?"

"Are you a Christian man, or is it just something beautiful to wear?"

"Both, I think."

"Good," said Rickett. "No harm in beauty if it's used right, but it's the belief that imbues a thing with power. I believe that the spirit of God inhabits every one of these saints and angels. That's why I really don't worry too much about them going to fancy restaurants, or dark bars that are looking to buy some atmosphere. Can't do the people in those places any harm to have a saint keeping watch over them."

And in his comment on power and belief, Parker heard something similar coming from the mouth of Ian Williamson, and wondered again at the nature of the Dead King in the Cut.

"You be sure to keep wearing that cross, where you're going," Rickett continued.

"In Plassey County?"

"Yes, in Plassey County. If you're going there, and you're the law— private or not—you're going to run into the Cut."

"You know about them?"

"Most people in the county, and at its borders, know about the Cut."

"Are they criminals?"

"They're criminals, and more than that."

"How much more?"

"I only know what the saints tell me," said Rickett.

"And what do they tell you?"

"That I'm not the only one around here who believes in the power of a graven image."

Parker opened his mouth to speak again, but Rickett held up his right hand in warning.

"No, I know what's on your lips, but you don't go saying that name aloud. Folks come in here—tourists, travelers—and they think they see a workshop, a store, a collection. But that's not what this is. You want to take a guess at what I have here, Mr. Parker?"

"Protection?"

"An army of it," Rickett confirmed. "All to keep at bay whatever lies in the Cut."

He reached for Parker's cup.

"You want more coffee?"

"No, thank you," said Parker. "That was enough. I'm done with the cake, too," he added, although it was mostly crumbs by now.

Rickett took the cup and plate and placed them in a dishwasher under the counter. He looked at his watch.

"I don't imagine there'll be any more business coming my way this evening," he said. "It's time to turn off the lights."

Parker took it as his cue to leave. He had more questions he wanted to ask, but it was clear that he wasn't going to get much more from Rickett. He began walking to the door, and Rickett followed him.

"I'm sorry about the statue," said Rickett, as Parker opened the door.

"Why?"

"The flayed man. I saw in your eyes how the sight of it affected you. It took me a little while to make the connection. Your name was familiar, but not because of music."

"Did the saints tell you that, too?"

"You know, I reckon they probably did. I wouldn't have spoken so openly otherwise."

They both looked to the darkness in the east, where the Cut waited.

"I used to think this was all about good and evil," said Rickett, "but it's not."

"No?"

"There's a kind of evil that isn't even in opposition to good, because good is an irrelevance to it. It's a foulness that's right at the heart of existence, born with the stuff of the universe. It's in the decay to which all things tend. It is, and it always will be, but in dying we leave it behind."

"And while we're alive?"

"We set our souls against it, and our saints and angels, too." He patted Parker on the shoulder. "Especially the destroying ones."

Parker walked to his car, got in, and started the engine. *The past is more real than the present,* he thought, *and we carry our histories with us.* He pulled out of the lot and turned right. Only when he was safely on the road was Rickett's sign extinguished, leaving him with just his own lights to guide him. Parker was already half a mile away when he realized that every face in Rickett's workshop had been facing east.

Toward the Cut.

Toward the Dead King.

# LXXII

Henkel had been brooding over the Cut ever since the end of the search. Whatever he'd hoped to find there—and it wasn't primarily Perry Lutter—had proved elusive. If he had been forced to put a name on it, he'd have called it "proof": proof that his instincts about the Cut were right.

The hunt for Perry had gone statewide, and the newspapers and TV had picked up on it, because Henkel had made damn sure that they did. The staties also shook off some of their slack because Perry was the one who had discovered Killian and Huff, and Henkel had suggested to them that he might have seen whoever was responsible for disposing of them. Once again, though, he had no proof, and Perry's parents were sticking to their story that Perry had told them nothing to indicate he was a witness to a crime. Henkel didn't want to turn the screws on them, not yet. They were in a state of desperate equilibrium, afraid of the Cut on one hand, and of losing their son entirely on the other.

Henkel had heard through the local chain of whispers that Charlie Lutter had sent an intermediary, Morton Dryden, to the Cut after the search of its territory had concluded. That was a delicate, dangerous thing to do without effectively accusing them of committing a crime, but the message was couched carefully, or so Henkel's informant told him. Dryden had apparently told Oberon that Charlie wished his son

had never found those bodies, and neither Perry nor anyone else in his
family knew how they had come to be there. Maybe they were hoping
that, if Oberon was holding Perry, or had knowledge of his whereabouts, then he might release him, just in case Perry was being used as
some kind of leverage until the investigation petered out.

But the investigation had already turned toward the cartels, so any
move by the Cut on Perry would just have brought attention back on
Plassey County again. There was no percentage in holding Perry in
order to encourage his folks to remain silent, and if the Cut had taken
him, they'd have been sure to let the Lutters know that Perry was with
them. There was no point in keeping a hostage if nobody knew about it.

So if the Cut wasn't holding Perry, what were the other options?
Henkel was still hoping Perry might be found alive, maybe at the
bottom of a hollow or down by a streambed, with a busted leg that had
prevented him from walking, but searchers had scoured Plassey pretty
thoroughly and found no trace of him. Then again, Plassey might have
been a small county, but there was still a lot of territory to cover, and an
injured man might easily be missed, especially if he was unconscious,
or too weak to cry out for help.

Sitting in the darkness of his kitchen, Henkel knew that hope didn't
count for much. He felt in his heart that Perry Lutter was dead, and if his
death wasn't accidental, then the Cut had to be responsible, because all
that stuff about Mexicans was so much bullshit. But once again, like that
image of the snake chewing its own tail, Henkel came back in a circle to
the question of why the Cut would risk more trouble by killing Perry if
the law was already looking elsewhere for the murderers of Killian and
Huff. Oberon and his people would have to be desperate or foolish to
do that, which meant that a) Perry Lutter definitely saw the man or men
responsible for burying Killian and Huff; b) he could identify them,
which indicated they were locals; and c) those involved were intimate
enough with Perry to know that he liked to talk, and would inevitably
reveal what he knew. Warnings wouldn't be enough to dissuade him.

Henkel heard sounds from the bedroom, and Irene appeared in the doorway. He had left her in a postcoital doze. She was wearing one of his T-shirts, which showed off her legs to good effect. She was a fine-looking woman: long dark hair, in her forties, looks that were maturing with age. Henkel had no idea what she was doing with him, and didn't even know much about where she'd come from. She'd said something about an ex-husband, but it was long ago and he was yesterday's news. She and Henkel hadn't discussed where the relationship might be going—it was all too recent for that—but for now he was glad of the company.

"What are you doing?" she asked him.

"Thinking."

"About what?"

"Perry Lutter."

"I was hoping that you might be thinking about me."

"I'm thinking about you now," he said. "Hard not to with pins like those."

"Come back to bed, then."

"I'll be there in a minute. Just let me finish my milk."

She didn't move.

"You still think the Cut killed him, don't you?"

"I've ruled out ghost Mexicans."

"Why do you hate the Cut so much?"

"I don't hate them."

"You do. You may not know it, but I can see it in you."

Henkel tried to find the right words, but couldn't, so he settled for: "They're just wrong."

"But you've got no proof."

"They have a history of violence and criminality."

"So the stories go, but even if they were like that in the past, it doesn't mean they're the same now."

"You sound like you're on their side."

"I'm not on anyone's side!"

"Not even mine?"

She shook her head.

"I don't want to see you hurt."

"You think the Cut will try to hurt me?"

"If you keep pushing them."

"Seems to go against what you were saying just a few seconds ago."

"They don't have to hurt you physically. They can exert pressure on people, make sure that you lose the election. Once they have someone in place who they can manipulate, you'll be forced out of the department, even the county, too, assuming you don't resign immediately after the votes are counted."

"There are enough people in Plassey who don't believe the Cut should be the law here. That's how I got voted in to start with."

"And the Cut have seen what you can do, and know for sure that you're set against them. They don't like it."

"That's the voice of the well-informed."

"Anyone with two ears can hear what's being said."

Henkel drained the last of his milk, went to the sink, and ran some water into the glass.

"Why are you with me?" he asked.

"What?"

"Why are you here, with me, in this house, in this . . ."

"Relationship?"

"Yes."

"Because I like you."

"Do you respect me?"

"Of course. I wouldn't be with you otherwise. It would mean that I didn't respect myself."

"Then you must understand why I can't let the Cut be. And it's not just about Perry, or what's happened in the past."

"Then what is it?"

He hadn't told anyone else. He wasn't sure it would make any sense. But he liked her, and she was a woman, so it might be that she'd understand.

"They have a building in the woods, up back of the Cut's heart. I looked in it. They told me it was used for storage, or a place for folks to sleep if they weren't getting along with their families. It seemed like it had been occupied recently. I caught a smell of soap in the air, the kind a woman would use, and there were hairs in the shower drain that looked damp."

"So? They have women in the Cut, and I know I'd want to get away from some of their menfolk once in a while if I was married to any of them. One of those women could have been using the hut."

"The hut has a lock on the outside, but not on the inside. There isn't even a bolt."

"What does that mean?"

"That it can only be closed from the outside. If I was staying in a hut to be safe, I'd want to be able to lock it myself. Admittedly, there's an inner door that could be locked, but it still doesn't sit right with me."

She thought about it.

"That is odd."

"I also couldn't see any switches inside, or even electrical outlets. It's wired for light and heat, but the lights are covered in steel grids so no one can get at them."

Irene joined him at the kitchen table. She sat across from him, and held his hands in hers, but said nothing.

"That's not a place for people to live," he said. "It's a place for people to be kept. It's a cell."

"But who would they keep in there?" she asked. "Perry?"

"No, not Perry."

"Then who?"

"I don't know," he said.

And they stayed like that for a time, joined by touch, unspeaking in the listening dark.

# LXXIII

To the west, in her comfortable German Village home, Norah Meddows ran a bath and poured herself a glass of wine to drink while she lay soaking. Her mother had been born in Columbus, but had married a man from Plassey County. It hadn't lasted, so maybe it was in the family genes, but Meddows had retained an affection for the city of her mother's birth. She'd always loved German Village in particular, with its cobbled streets and gaslights, and it had taken a lot of saving and going without to build up enough money for a deposit on a house there, even if it was one of the smallest on the street. If she looked out her bedroom window, she could just see the lights of the Old Mohawk restaurant, a former general store that had operated as a brothel and speakeasy during Prohibition before opening as a tavern in the thirties, serving a famous soup made from turtles raised in the mud pit in the basement. It had brick walls, a pressed tin ceiling, and a $10.99 sirloin steak special on Sundays. It was her escape and refuge. She'd gone there earlier—not to eat, just to drink. The familiar environment helped to calm her nerves. With one call, she'd condemned the private detective to death, but the likelihood of his murder wasn't what had driven her to the Old Mohawk's bar. Instead, she just hoped that none of it rebounded on her.

Sometimes, Columbus seemed too close to West Virginia and the

Cut for comfort, but after the shooting at the gas station, they wanted her near, just in case anyone came calling. It had taken years, but eventually someone did.

The lawyer Starcher had always been her point of contact with the Cut. She'd known about him since her time in Plassey County, when her father had gotten into some trouble with the Cut over a land deal and Starcher helped straighten it out. It was to Starcher that she turned when she came up with the plan to rob her husband of his gems and split the proceeds with the Cut. He'd also acted as the attorney for her divorce under a *pro hac vice* admission. It had been made clear to her that she didn't have much choice in the matter, and the Cut had levied a fine on her settlement, just as it continued to do on her business each month. She could have complained, since it was their fault a simple robbery had deteriorated into a gunfight that left two of them dead, but the consequences would have been an increase in the levy at best, and at worst a shallow grave somewhere, with any number of unpleasant gradations between those two extremes. The Cut blamed her for what had happened in Maine, and she was unlikely to be forgiven for it in this world.

The bath was slowly filling. She lit a cigarette. She never smoked in the store because she didn't want to make the clothes smell, but she liked having a cigarette with a glass of wine. She looked at the burning tip and thought of Harpur Griffin. She still couldn't figure out why they'd killed him.

The doorbell rang. She walked to the intercom in the hall and pushed the button.

"Yes, who is it?"

"Is Hector, Miss Meddow."

He always called her Miss Meddow. He just couldn't get his tongue around that final "s."

"Is it urgent? I'm about to take a bath."

"We have fire at storage. Is big mess."

"Shit."

She dropped the cigarette in the bathroom sink. She no longer wanted it. Cinching her robe tighter her around her, she turned off the faucet in the bathroom and headed for the door in her bare feet. She noticed that a thread had come away from the robe, and the phrase "loose end" came to mind. Was that why they'd killed Harpur Griffin? God, had Parker come calling on him as well, and did he tell the Cut about it?

And a fire. A fucking fire. That was all she needed.

She opened the door. Hector was standing on the step, but behind him were two other men. Both wore black ski masks, and both held pistols. The pistols were .22 Rugers, and barely used, each fitted with a suppressor. The bullet from the first hit Hector in the base of his skull, severing his spinal cord and causing instant paralysis from the neck down. As he collapsed, the shooter stepped forward and dragged the dying Hector into the house while the other man kept his gun on Meddows.

The door closed behind them. Hector, Meddows noticed, wasn't bleeding much. She thought that was odd. She would have expected more blood. Only then did she start to tremble.

One of the men lifted his mask, revealing the face of Marius, the younger son of Cassander Hobb.

"I didn't tell him anything," said Meddows. "I wouldn't."

"It doesn't matter," said Marius.

He struck her once with the gun. Meddows went down.

She did not even hear the shot that killed her.

# LXXIV

Early the next morning, after stopping at Shelby's to pick up coffee and a doughnut, Henkel made a circuit of the Cut, but no vehicles emerged from it and he saw none of its people. The evergreens formed a barrier around it, a physical manifestation of its essential impenetrability. He had led searchers into the Cut, yet was no closer to discovering its secrets.

Henkel ate only half the doughnut. He'd ordered it without thinking, but now when he snacked on something that he shouldn't be eating, he felt his heart hurt. He had to confirm a date for his procedure soon. Once he did, his health problems would all come out. There would be no way to keep something like that a secret, not even if he recovered rapidly. The Cut would exploit it. A sheriff with a heart condition? Folks, they'd whisper, would need to be careful about voting for a man with such a weakness.

The Cut was winning. He realized that now. It always won. You didn't survive for centuries without learning the skills to cope with those who might mean you harm. The Cut had escaped being connected to the murders of Killian and Huff, and had so far avoided being implicated in the disappearance of Perry Lutter. Perhaps Irene was right: he had allowed all of this to become personal, and it might be that it was blinding him to the truth. And in the end, what did it matter? Most of the people in Plassey County didn't want the Cut to cease to exist. They had grown accustomed to its evil, to the point where they no longer even recognized it as such. Its malevolence had become diffused over the years. It was in everything and of everything, and so its presence hardly registered any longer. Even the disappearance of Perry Lutter was already being explained away.

*Perry fell. He had a fit. You know what his kind are like. They're special, but they don't live as long as normal folk. The Cut? Nah, the Cut wouldn't harm Perry Lutter. Nobody would, not in this county.*

The law, for what it was, existed only to provide a counterweight. Henkel wasn't excessively loved by the county. No man whose job description included the words "tax collector" would ever inspire any deep affection in the general populace.

As he circled the Cut, Henkel determined to let the dice fall as they may. He would book his appointment at the hospital; he would let the relevant people know why he was taking some time off, and they would whisper it to the rest of the county; he would run for reelection the following year, and if he didn't get the job, well, he might just head west to be closer to his kids.

He drove to the sheriff's department, where a message was waiting for him, asking him to call Major Alvin Martin of the West Virginia State Police.

———

HENKEL VAGUELY KNEW MARTIN from conferences, and the occasional telephone conversation when county and state business intersected. Martin's position was essentially administrative. He no longer took an active role in investigations, which probably explained how he managed to stay so neat and clean. For some reason, Martin always reminded Henkel of a new car before it was driven off the lot.

Henkel closed his office door, sat at his desk, and dialed Martin's number. It was a direct line, and Martin picked up on the second ring.

They exchanged pleasantries, asked after each other's family, and then Martin started talking about some interagency initiative designed to combat sexism in recruitment procedures, at which point Henkel's ass began slowly unscrewing with boredom. He couldn't understand what was so urgent about this shit. Martin could have sent it in an e-mail, which would have made it easier for Henkel to ignore. He wasn't sexist. One of his best deputies was a woman, and he'd hired her. She was one of only two hires he'd been permitted in three years due to budget constraints and an absence of retirements and resignations among existing deputies. If this was what Martin was being paid to do, then Henkel wanted some of the good money that the state was clearly throwing around freely in the vicinity of Jefferson Road.

Henkel tuned out, so it took him a moment to realize that Martin had ceased talking.

"When did you stop listening?" Martin asked.

"A while back," said Henkel. "Nothing personal."

"Well, if anyone asks, you can tell them the official reason for my call."

"Is there an unofficial reason?"

"You have a man coming to your county. His name is Charlie Parker. He's a private investigator out of Portland, Maine."

"If he's here to sightsee, we don't have much."

"I think he's going after the Cut."

There was a long silence.

"Why would you say that?" asked Henkel.

"You read about that guy got himself set on fire in his car up in Portland?"

"Harpur Griffin."

"One of yours, right?"

"From a ways back. He hasn't troubled us with his presence for a long time, helped by a judge putting him behind bars."

Henkel sat up straighter behind his desk. He hadn't immediately connected Griffin's immolation to the Cut. There had been no cause. But this was interesting.

"Well, he's unlikely to be troubling you again," said Martin. "Burning: story was that in the dim, dark days, it was the way the Cut dealt with folk who crossed them."

"So they say. Was Griffin a friend of this investigator?"

"I don't imagine so. One of Parker's clients has gone missing, and there's a link to Griffin. I'll let him tell you the rest."

"He ask you to call me?"

"No, he asked me *not* to call you."

Henkel had picked up a pen and doodled a hanged man.

"What do you want me to do here, Major?"

"That's up to you. In my experience—my bitter experience—you have two choices: you can cooperate with him, or not cooperate with him, but whichever you decide, it won't make much difference. He'll stay with it until the job is done."

"I think the Cut murdered our missing boy, Perry Lutter," said Henkel, "and I'm pretty sure they killed Killian and Huff. I also believe they may be holding a woman in their compound against her will."

"A woman? Do you have proof?"

"No, not yet."

"Then let Parker look for it, but don't get your hands dirty. If you find a reason to go in there, with or without a warrant, either through Parker or by your own initiative, and need support, then you call me, day or night."

He gave Henkel his cell phone and home numbers, and the sheriff wrote them down on a pad of Post-it notes from Kibble's old hardware store.

"They'll kill him if he gets in their face," said Henkel, once he'd finished writing.

"They'll try. Others have."

"He's just one man."

"I don't think he'll come alone. From what I hear, he travels with an armed entourage."

"Jesus."

"I don't think Jesus is part of it, but I'm open to correction. If you're looking to tear down the Cut, then this is the guy. Basically, my advice is just to light the blue fuse and step away."

Henkel glanced out his office window, as though he could already see smoke rising over the Cut.

"And remember," added Martin. "Sexism Is the Enemy of Good Policing. I'll be sending you a poster with that on it. Be sure to put it up somewhere it can be seen."

———

ONCE HE'D HUNG UP on Henkel, Martin made a second call. In the aftermath of the hunt for the Traveling Man, the FBI had visited Haven County, specifically in the form of an agent named Ross. He told Martin that if Charlie Parker ever contacted him again, the FBI was to be informed. Ross had made it very clear that this wasn't a request, and had no expiration date.

Martin made the call.

# LXXV

When Parker did appear, he wasn't what Henkel had been anticipating. Martin's call had caused him to expect something approaching a one-man army, bristling with attitude and weaponry; a heavyweight. Instead he was confronted with an individual a couple of inches shorter than he was, with an air of what Henkel could only think of as haunted amusement, like someone trying to recall the substance of a joke that still made him smile. He didn't look ill exactly, but he had wrinkles on his face that weren't a product of age, and a scattering of white slashes and spots in his hair that reminded Henkel of the markings of a jungle animal.

He was shown into Henkel's office by one of the secretaries that the sheriff's department shared with the other county offices, including the circuit clerk, the surveyor of lands, and the prosecuting attorney, Adel Wickins. Although it appeared superficially hearty and civil, Wickins and Henkel had a poor relationship. Being the prosecuting attorney of Plassey County was an easy way to bank $60,000 a year, especially when, like Wickins, you chose to pretend that the Cut didn't exist. Wickins wasn't completely useless—he came down hard on child abuse and neglect, and had filed a number of civil suits for county agencies on environmental issues—but he preferred to let his assistant do most of the drudge work, including making the majority of court appearances, and the consultancy business Wickins ran on the side regularly threw up conflicts of interest that might have troubled someone with a more sensitive or developed conscience.

The unspoken agreement between Henkel and Wickins was that the latter would leave the sheriff to go about his business as long as it didn't involve the Cut, which was why Wickins had done his best to tear Henkel a new one after he learned of his actions during the search for Perry Lutter. Henkel had been forced to point out that Wickins was participating in a golf tournament at Pikewood National while the search was being conducted, and therefore wasn't really available to be consulted. It seemed likely that Wickins wouldn't be voting for Henkel come election day, and he'd be doing his damnedest to make sure nobody else did either. But few people really listened to Adel Wickins anyhow—even most judges regarded him as inconsequential—so Henkel wasn't overly concerned.

Nevertheless, he was glad that Wickins was in Charleston on business that day, and so was not present to witness the arrival of Charlie Parker. Rob Channer was, though, and the deputy gave the private investigator a curious look as he passed, causing Henkel to wonder if Channer somehow recognized Parker's face.

Henkel and Parker shook hands.

"I know who you are," said Henkel, as he closed his office door behind Parker, "and I know why you're here."

"Alvin Martin?"

"Helped by the Google machine."

"Don't believe everything you read."

The sheriff's cell phone rang. He looked at the caller ID, saw that it was Irene, and answered.

"Can I call you back?" he said. "That visitor I mentioned to you has just arrived."

She'd come by earlier to say hi, and he'd told her about the call from Martin, and the man who was coming, perhaps to face down the Cut.

It was the first time since she'd known him that Irene had seen hope in her lover's face.

Henkel put away his phone and reached for his hat.

"Why don't you and I take a ride, Mr. Parker?"

———

FOR THE SECOND TIME that day, Henkel drove around the perimeter of the Cut, but now with Parker in the passenger seat. He explained its history to the investigator, for he had delved long and hard into its origins, until he arrived at more recent times. He made a clear distinction between what he knew for sure, what he strongly suspected, and what was simply conjecture on his part. He told Parker of Killian and Huff, and Perry Lutter, and the building at the heart of the Cut that smelled faintly of a woman's presence. It took an hour, and by the end of it Parker had heard a litany of threats, intimidation, disappearances, and killings spanning centuries.

"How have they survived for so long?" he asked.

"They're part of the fabric of the county," said Henkel, "and the county is part of the fabric of the state. And they don't leave tracks, not usually. That's the important thing about them. They're careful, or they have been until recently."

"What's caused the change?"

"Young blood. It runs hotter than the old. Also, I think there's some competition for the position of alpha male. Oberon, their leader, has no male heirs. He had at least one son, although I've heard tell that there might have been another born out of wedlock. This is all rumor, but they left the Cut a long time ago, and the best guess is that they're both dead now."

"Oberon?" said Parker. "For real?"

"The Cut give weird names to their children. Always have. They take them from the Bible, history, mythology. It's their way. Anyway, Cassander, Oberon's lieutenant, has two sons, and Cassander himself is about ten years younger than Oberon. Again, it's just gossip, but Cassander thinks it's time that Oberon stepped aside in favor of his line."

"And Oberon isn't moving."

"Not yet."

They drove on to Shelby's Diner, where Henkel took his usual seat.

"I'd suggest keeping a low profile," said Henkel, "but my guess is, if you'd wanted to do that, you wouldn't have wandered into my office and shown yourself like you did."

"They'll find out I'm here soon enough. I noticed that you haven't asked me the specifics."

"I figured you'd share those with me in your own time."

They ordered coffee and two slices of pie, and Parker told Henkel everything.

———

OBERON RECEIVED THE CALL as he was driving toward Turley. He pulled over to the side of the road, listened, and then killed the connection without saying anything at all. When the phone rang again, he ignored it. He climbed out of his truck, walked into the woods, and stared up at the sky. The trees were almost bare, making their branches appear as cracks in the cosmos. Oberon picked at a piece of bark and rolled it between his fingers. He felt like a condemned man who has just heard confirmation of the date and time of his execution, so that the world around him becomes more beautiful because of it, with every sight, sound, and smell seeming new to him. The chill from the north that had been cutting him to the bone had arrived at last, not in the form of winter but in the shape of a man. The Cut had been threatened before, but never like this. They had brought the investigator down upon them by their own actions, by the carelessness and savagery of young men.

He had thought the worst was past. They had overcome the discovery of two bodies, and the murder of a mentally challenged man who had never hurt a soul in his life. An incursion into the Cut by outsiders had been authorized, and the risk had paid off. Even Henkel could be contained, given time.

But this man, this Parker, was a born hunter, and more, much more. In his head, Oberon heard the Dead King howl a warning.

Now, alone among the trees, Oberon wondered if the time had not come for him to leave the Cut. He could take Sherah and Tamara with him. They would start again somewhere else, far from Plassey County. He had some money hidden away, enough to buy them new identities and the foundations of a modest life. He was skilled with his hands. He could find work as a mechanic, even set up his own business. It wouldn't be hard.

But he wanted a son to replace those he had lost, and so far Sherah had not provided. The woman Paige seemed likely to give birth to a boy, and by Oberon's seed. Hannah could tell these things; she had never yet failed to correctly predict the sex of a child. That boy, Oberon had decided, would not be sold. It didn't matter that Cassander and many others wanted the infant to be exchanged for cash as planned. The Cut needed new blood more than money. Oberon's intention was to raise the boy as his own, and eventually make a good match for him from within the Cut, assuring the continuation of his line. He had been forced to confirm this intention just that morning with Cassander and the lawyer Starcher, in order to ensure that no further money changed hands in anticipation of an adoption. It was another nail in the coffin of his deteriorating relationship with Cassander, whom he had once regarded as his closest friend and confidant.

In response, Cassander warned Oberon that he was not alone among the Cut in believing that the child should be sold as planned. They had buyers waiting for the baby, and a sum of money agreed. Oberon did not have enough funds of his own to compensate them for the loss. But Oberon had reminded Cassander that he was under no obligation to compensate anyone. When the Cut needed to keep a child, it had always done so. Cassander, though, would not agree, and they had parted on bad terms. It was this final argument, more than any other, that had convinced Oberon he would have to kill Cassander, and probably his sons, too.

Yet all that was before the coming of the hunter from the north.

So what now? The Cut was not as strong as it once was: the fear and respect that it evoked in the people of Plassey County were products of an accumulated store of dread, and powered by past actions. The Cut as it now existed was a shadow of what it once had been, and not even the Dead King could arrest its decline.

He and his family could leave the Cut behind, Oberon theorized, and bring Paige with them. It would be dangerous, but she only had a few months left. Sherah could take care of her, and when the baby was born, Oberon would deal with Paige. Her kidnapping had been a consequence of his fury at the loss of his sons, just like the tracking and snatching of Corrie Wyatt. He would have killed the old man, too, the gas station owner, had nature not taken care of him first. Oberon had been blinded by grief, but the decision was a good one, in the end, because Paige had served them well. Corrie Wyatt had given them just one child before she died, but she and Paige between them had still provided the Cut with a significant amount of money.

He would like to have been able to let Paige go. He respected her more than the younger woman. She had real strength. If he could have trusted her to remain silent, then he would have released her, but he knew she would go to the police at the first opportunity. Her rage had kept her sane, and the fire of it would not be extinguished simply by offering the promise of freedom to her. Cassander wanted to kill her after the third child was born. In this, at least, Cassander was probably correct.

A soft rain began to fall. Oberon closed his eyes and allowed it to settle on his face. He felt it gather in the hollows of his eyes and roll down his cheeks. It soaked his hair, and penetrated his skin, and slowly washed away all his dreams and fantasies. He sighed, and let them go.

No, there would be no flight from this land. He was of the Cut, and the Cut was in him. It was their place, and if they had to make a stand, then so be it. It had served as a fortress once, and would do so again. They had watched generations of adversaries turn to dust and ash, and they had endured. Henkel would be dealt with, and Parker, too. In the face of their enemies, they would hold the Cut.

And still the Dead King howled.

---

"I'VE NEVER HEARD THAT name," said Henkel.

"You're sure?" asked Parker.

"It's not something I'd forget easily. If they have a king, it's Oberon. He may be many things, but dead isn't one of them."

"And yet Harpur Griffin claimed he was acting in the name of the Dead King."

He watched Henkel molding his thoughts, choosing his next words carefully.

"I was familiar with Griffin by reputation," he said. "He was real popular: good-looking, and kind of charming if you were easily sold. He wasn't completely dumb, but he was conceited, which meant he didn't use the intelligence that he had, and eventually it just withered away. But there was a time when he would have been considered a catch by a lot of the girls in this county—and not just the ones beyond the Cut."

"He had a girlfriend from the Cut?"

"I never had it confirmed for me."

"It doesn't matter."

"If the story's true, the girl's name was Sherah. She was sister-in-law to Oberon, and now she's his wife. It didn't last long—the Cut doesn't marry outside its borders, and definitely doesn't approve of its women consorting with the likes of Harpur Griffin—but I think that when Griffin put his life on the line by assaulting Cassander's son at Oakey's, it might have been Sherah who interceded on his behalf."

"She wasn't prepared to intervene a second time, judging by what happened to him in Portland."

"Could be that she didn't know what was planned for him. But Sherah's with Oberon now, and whatever she had with Griffin was a long time ago. She's a cold one. I doubt she shed many tears for Harpur Griffin when he died."

"What about Norah Meddows, Burnel's ex-wife?"

"I know the name. The Cut's women weren't alone in occasionally venturing beyond dirt roads for their pleasures. They say she was with Cassander for a time."

"You have a complicated county here, Sheriff Henkel."

"It does keep me entertained. Obviously, I'm obliged to warn you that if you're considering starting trouble with the Cut, I'll have you arrested and charged in the event of any injury—or, God forbid, fatalities."

"What about self-defense?"

"As long as you can prove it with independent witnesses."

"I'll bear it in mind."

"You do that. May I ask what it is that you're planning on doing next?"

"I'm going to talk to Oberon, and ask him to deliver up the two men who were last seen with Harpur Griffin before he died." Parker had described them in detail to Henkel, and the sheriff had been pretty certain that the individuals in question were Lucius, the older son of Cassander, and another man named Jabal. "Unless the Portland PD's budget extends to sending detectives down here to question them, they'll accompany me back north of their own volition, where they'll be handed over for questioning about Griffin's death and the disappearance of my client, Jerome Burnel."

"I can tell you now that Oberon's not going to let that happen."

"I'm obliged to ask. It's only polite."

"And after he refuses?"

"Then I'll have to go in and get them myself."

"With company, I hope?"

"With company."

"The Cut may decide to come at you first."

"Good."

Henkel stared at him. *By Christ*, he thought, *this guy means it.*

"You've been shot before, if what I read about you is true."

"Yes."

"For a man who's been shot a lot, you sure seem anxious to get shot again."

"I'd like to think I've learned some avoidance tactics since the last time."

"I certainly hope so."

Henkel raised his hand for the check and simultaneously slid a piece of folded paper across the table to Parker. When Henkel looked back, the paper was already gone.

"What is it?" asked Parker.

"A map of the Cut. The distances are approximate, and it's only partial. There are parts of it I didn't see, and about which I couldn't approach anyone else for information. Before you go wandering in there, you should know that they've secured it over the years. Shortly before I became sheriff, a couple of good old boys headed in after a twenty-point buck, figuring it was worth the risk."

"And?"

"One of them lost a foot to a bear trap, and I don't believe they get too many bears through the Cut. In other words, I wouldn't venture into it without a guide, but the only guides who know the Cut are its own people, and they're not likely to be offering their help to you."

The check came. Henkel paid it, and carefully placed his copy in his wallet.

"What about you?" asked Parker. "If they know I'm here, then they'll also know that we've been talking."

"Let them."

"You don't think they'll come after you, too?"

"They haven't yet, and killing a sheriff might be a step too far, even for them. Or that's what I'm banking on."

But he sounded uncertain as he spoke, and his smile was strained.

"Come on," he said. "I'll give you a ride back to your car."

Parker followed him, and did not even glance at the table beside the register, where Angel and Louis, each with a gun close at hand, were seated by a window, watching the vehicles come and go, waiting patiently for violence to erupt.

# LXXVI

Ross knocked on the door of Conrad Holt's office. His superior was working through a mound of paperwork, a task that appeared to be giving him little joy, so he looked almost relieved when Ross appeared, at least until he saw the look on Ross's face.

"What is it?" Holt asked.

"You asked me to keep you apprised of Parker's movements."

"And?"

"He's in West Virginia."

"Why?"

"He's investigating something called the Cut—a community of recluses, possibly with criminal connections."

"Anything we should be concerned about?"

"Probably no more than usual."

Holt scowled.

"That bad, huh?" he said.

"It remains to be seen. And there's this."

Ross produced a wrinkled map of the United States from a file beneath his arm. He spread it on Holt's desk, allowing him to see the markings that had been added. They were GPS coordinates, written in red ink. Holt instantly felt a chill. He'd seen such maps before.

"Body dumps?" he asked.

"I wish," said Ross. He handed over a small index card to Holt. On it, in the same hand as the GPS coordinates, were written the words "FBI Restrooms" followed by a question mark.

Ross pointed a finger at a set of coordinates in the Midwest.

"This," he said, "is the location of the National Mustard Museum in Middleton, Wisconsin. Close to it, in Neillsville, and also marked, is the location of Chatty Belle, the World's Largest Talking Cow." His finger moved south. "Here is the Chasing Rainbows Museum at the Dollywood theme park in Pigeon Forge, Tennessee. That, in San Antonio, is Barney Smith's Toilet Seat Art Museum. We've also got the Idaho Potato Museum, the International Banana Museum in Mecca, California, and the World's Largest Chest of Drawers in High Point, North Carolina."

"And that?" asked Holt, gesturing resignedly at a set of coordinates in the Mojave Desert.

"Area Fifty-one," said Ross. "I don't think we need to run a fingerprint analysis to figure out who sent it."

"That fucking Angel," said Holt. "I hate these guys."

# LXXVII

Cassander lay on the bed, and considered when might be best to deal with Oberon, who seemed determined to retain control of the Cut even as his hold on it continued to weaken.

That morning, Oberon had informed the elders of the Cut of his intention to take Paige's next—and final—child, and raise it in his house. Few voices had been raised in open dissent, but Cassander's was among them, restating publicly what he had told Oberon in private. He pointed out that it had been agreed the next two children would be sold, and the proceeds divided equally. These last years had been difficult for them all. In his desire to prolong his line, said Cassander, Oberon was forcing hardship upon everyone in the Cut.

But Oberon was their leader, and the decision was ultimately his to make. Afterward, Cassander heard a few mutters of discontent from those who had kept their peace during the meeting, but he ignored them all. They were no use to him after the fact. There would be no open rebellion by the Cut against Oberon's leadership, but that in itself was not entirely bad news. It meant that Cassander and his sons could take control without fear of competition.

Although Lucius was the elder of Cassander's boys, he was not a leader by temperament, only by inclination. Marius was more balanced—even if it had been his decision to burn Harpur Griffin—and it was he to whom Cassander was intent upon entrusting the future of the Cut. Of course, Marius was not yet ready: he was too green, too weak. If Oberon were no more, Cassander would have to take on the leadership of the Cut, with Marius shadowing him until the father adjudged the son ready to succeed him. It was a responsibility Cassander was prepared to assume. He had spoken to the Dead King about it, and received its blessing.

And Cassander had already begun taking on the mantle of leader. It was he who had received the call from Starcher informing him of Parker's visit to Norah Meddows, and he who had sent Marius and Jabal to make her disappear. When the detective came to Plassey—as he most assuredly would—then Cassander would deal with him if Oberon was too cautious to act.

A hand splayed itself over Cassander's chest, the fingers like pale snakes writhing through the graying hairs. Sherah was naked beside him. Her child was playing in the house of Hannah, far to the south.

"Again," she said. "Do it again."

Oberon was probably on his way, but still Cassander took Sherah for a second time, heedless of the risk of discovery, even desirous of it, so that the hostility between the two men might come to a head and be decided at last.

But Oberon did not arrive, for he was engaged in a confrontation of his own.

# LXXVIII

O beron had stopped to pick up a few essentials at Sampson's, Turley's largest general store. The Cut was almost entirely self-sufficient, but some items still needed to be brought in, coffee, sugar, and salt among them. After a moment's thought, Oberon had also purchased a box of 9mm ammunition, two boxes of buckshot for his 12-gauge, and three boxes of 7.62x39mm rounds for the AR-15.

Cassander was the Cut's armorer, but Oberon no longer trusted him. It wasn't just about Cassander's apparent unwillingness—or inability—to control Lucius, or his objections to Oberon's plans for Paige's infant, or even Oberon's belief that Cassander wished to rule the Cut. No, Oberon had seen the way Cassander looked at his wife. He still trusted Sherah, or thought he did.

In truth, he was no longer sure.

He hefted one of the boxes of bullets in his hand. In terms of accuracy, the AR-15 ammunition wouldn't be much good beyond 200 yards, but it wasn't meant to be. If trouble came to the Cut, the fighting would be at close quarters. He savored the weight of the box for a few seconds more, and was just stowing it in the cab of his truck when he had the sense that he was being watched. He looked up to see a man leaning against a nondescript sedan, the car too clean and too new for these parts to be anything other than a rental.

The investigator: Parker.

Oberon closed the truck door, checked the lot for oncoming traffic, and walked over to stand before the hunter.

"I know you," said Oberon.

"Then you know my purpose."

"No, that you'll have to tell me."

"I want you to hand over the two men, Lucius and Jabal, who were recently in Portland, Maine."

"To what end?"

"So that they can be interviewed here or back in the Northeast about the death of Harpur Griffin and the disappearance of Jerome Burnel."

"I don't know either of those names."

"I didn't ask if you knew them. I asked for Lucius and Jabal."

"You're a private investigator. You have no authority here, and neither Lucius nor Jabal has been charged with any crime. You need to go back to Maine, before this gets ugly for you."

"I can't do that."

"Then it will play out as it must."

Oberon began to move away, then paused.

"Why can't you just leave us in peace?" he asked.

"I don't believe you're a peaceful man, or that the Cut is a peaceful place," said Parker, "so the question has no meaning."

"I'm warning you," said Oberon. "You should stay away from us."

"Lucius," said Parker. "And Jabal."

Oberon said nothing more, but climbed in his truck and drove away. When he glanced in his rearview mirror, Parker was already gone.

————

IT DIDN'T TAKE OBERON long to establish where Parker was staying, because there weren't many places to stay in Plassey County, or none in which a man would want to linger. Parker had a room at Dryden's Inn, and Morton Dryden knew better than to cross the Cut.

Oberon headed back to his home. The bedroom windows were open, the mattress was bare, and the damp sheets were hanging on a line to blow in the breeze. They had been on the bed for less than a week. Oberon did not comment on it, but kissed Sherah and asked her how Paige and Gayle were faring. She told him that she had not yet visited that day, but would check on them after the evening meal. She would bring Hannah with her. The women had not been examined since the previous week, and Hannah was the expert in these matters.

Oberon left his wife and walked across the Square to Cassander's house. Cassander appeared on his porch before Oberon reached the steps. He did not seem surprised to see Oberon, who noted that Cassander's hands had bunched instinctively into fists at his approach. He was also wearing a jacket indoors, which could only mean that he had a gun under it.

Oberon was too old, and too wise, to pretend that there was nothing wrong.

"We have matters to discuss, you and I," he said, "but now is not the time for them. There is a bigger problem."

Cassander relaxed slightly and waited to be told.

"Parker has come."

# LXXIX

Paige had spent so long in the Cut that despite being trapped in the hut, and able to observe the community only from a distance, she had become attuned to its rhythms. Just by taking in the comings and goings from her window, she could tell when there was trouble, or a cause for celebration. She had also become quietly adept at manipulating Sherah, Hannah, and the other women for hints of useful information, and had even managed to glean a little about the organization of the Cut during the sexual assaults that had culminated in her three pregnancies, every grain of insight purchased with a violation. Now she could feel it in the air: something was wrong. It was in the way that Oberon and Cassander had emerged from the latter's house and begun gathering men to themselves, and she was not particularly surprised when the guns appeared. Her only concern was what it might mean for her and Gayle. She was not going back into that basement. She'd die first.

*Actually*, she realized, *I might die anyway.*

She and Gayle had hidden the stone and the brick in the toilet cistern. Gayle's eyes had retained a disconcerting animation ever since she'd acquired the weapons. It wasn't quite the light of sanity, but at least it was some form of engagement with the world around her. It had been all the older woman could do to prevent Gayle from sulking, and thereby drawing attention to the captives, when her prizes were not put to immediate use.

Later, Paige slept, but while it was still dark she woke to the sound of vehicles. Two trucks and a car pulled up in the Square, lit by flashlights, and she saw a group of armed men join the drivers before the vehicles headed away again. Oberon and Cassander were not among them, but it didn't matter. What was important was that the Cut's numbers had just been depleted considerably, and within hours Sherah and Hannah would be coming with breakfast, because they typically fed the women between 6:00 and 7:00 a.m.

Paige turned to see Gayle, who had come into the room and was sitting on the floor in her nightdress, her arms folded on her knees, her chin resting on her arms, her eyes fixed on the woman at the window.

"Why don't you go get our new toys?" said Paige.

# LXXX

enkel had gone to bed aching. Earlier in the day he had removed the back door from its frame because the hinges were busted, and next thing he'd started sanding it where it was sticking, and pretty soon he was all sawdust and sweat, but at least it was a distraction from the business of the Cut, and the arrival of Parker. He was sure that his physician would have advised against wrestling with a door until she'd done something about his heart, but if he started thinking like that then he'd never leave the house at all.

He was so deep in sleep when his cell phone rang that he incorporated it into his dream, and a shadow version of himself reached for it only to hear the sound of Perry Lutter's voice emerge. Perry was crying for his mother. He asked Henkel if he could go get her for him, because his tummy hurt.

*"I's got blood on my shirt,"* said Perry. *"I's got blood everywhere."*

Then Henkel woke, but the phone was still ringing. It was Irene.

"I know it's still dark," she said, "but can you come over here?"

Henkel sat up.

"What's wrong?"

"I think there are men in the woods, watching the house. I could be mistaken, which is why I called you, and not 911. I didn't want to look stupid if it was just shadows caused by the breeze."

"Lock the doors," said Henkel. "I'll be there in ten."

————

DEPUTY ROB CHANNER HAD just gone to check on Della Watkins in the drunk tank when Henkel got in touch with the dispatcher. Della wasn't a regular visitor to the cells, but when she did tie one on—which was about three times a year—she was prone to kicking up a fuss, and trying to break objects that weren't hers to break, like doors, windows, and other people's heads. This time she'd limited herself to one of the old mirrors in Burry's Bar, but it was unlikely that Burry would press charges. He would just want the repairs to the mirror covered, and Della would be all contrite once she'd sobered up, so the bill would be paid within a day.

"Problem, Lucy?" Channer asked the dispatcher, as she logged the call.

"Sheriff is heading over to Irene Colter's place. She thought she might have seen some men moving around."

"He sound worried?"

"Does he ever sound any other way lately?"

Channer looked at the coffeepot. He'd just started a fresh brew, in case Della began coming around sooner than expected.

Damn.

————

ODELL WATSON WAS SITTING at his bedroom window, trying to finish his geography homework, which involved mapping all the great rivers of the United States. Odell had no idea why this might be useful to him in later life, unless he planned on becoming the captain of a ship, which he did not. Being able to name them was one thing, but drawing them, tributaries included, was a bitch. He should have been asleep, but sleep seemed intent on evading him that night. He had woken shortly before 3:00 a.m., and read for a while using his night-light before he realized that he'd forgotten all about the great rivers. He figured that was why he had been unable to sleep, and marveled for a time at the ways of the brain before retrieving his schoolbooks from his bag and settling down to work. He had just finished connecting the Pecos with the Rio Grande when Perry Lutter appeared at the garden gate.

Odell knew all about the search for Perry, and he'd heard some of the rumors about his disappearance, too, because his mother and grand-mother had been whispering about it. Perry was still the main sub-ject of conversation at the diner, where his continued absence had cast a pall over the staff, and Miss Queenie in particular, who had become more fractious than ever. But now here was Perry: sneakers, pants, buttoned-up shirt, windbreaker.

Yet this wasn't Perry Lutter, not really. Odell had known Perry all his life, ever since his mother used to take him to the diner when he was an infant, just so she could fit in a couple of extra hours. Miss Queenie hadn't minded much, as long as Odell was quiet, which he usually was, Odell being one of those children who never cried much when he was young, remaining largely content to observe the world when he was awake, and dream about it when he was not, with the rest of the time occupied by food and play.

So Perry's face was one of the first with which Odell had become familiar at the diner. It was ingrained in his memory, and while the figure at the gate bore a certain resemblance to Perry, it was similar to that between the airbrushed photographs of models in some of his mother's magazines and the reality of them in the tawdrier journals that she secretly preferred, the ones in which women's bellies sagged over their bathing suits, and circles were drawn around the fat on their thighs. It was as though someone had subtly rearranged Perry's fea-tures, making his eyes—always too small for his face—more in propor-tion with the rest of him, and cleared up the spots that plagued his skin.

He was almost handsome now, Odell thought. He was looking at the Perry who might have existed if the doctors hadn't messed up during his difficult birth, clamping down on his skull just a fraction too hard with the forceps. This was Perry as he should have been, the man whom Perry Lutter saw in the mirror when he looked at himself.

Perhaps Odell should have been frightened, but he was not. He knew for certain that Perry was dead, because otherwise this entity in the shape of Perry wouldn't be standing at the end of the front yard, but Odell detected no threat. The man still had Perry's eyes, and they were as soft and friendly as ever, but an intelligence inhabited them that had not been present before, and it lit him up from within, like someone had put a lightbulb in Perry's head and flipped the switch.

Odell's mother and grandmother were sleeping. He didn't call them, but instead opened his bedroom window and jumped down. He walked toward the figure at the gate—Perry, or this version of him—and stood within touching distance. A light breeze blew, and it carried the new scent of Perry to Odell: smoke, burnt timber, and mud, as though someone had set a fire in a swamp.

There was blood on Perry Lutter's left sneaker, and not just drops of it: it was the kind of stain that came from a wound that didn't stop bleeding until there was no more blood left to give.

"Did it hurt?" asked Odell.

Perry didn't answer. He just smiled.

"I'm sorry," said Odell, although he could not have said for what, exactly. He hadn't done anything wrong, and he didn't think he could have prevented whatever had happened to Perry. He was just sorry for all of it, he supposed.

Perry nodded. He turned his back on Odell, crossed the road, and waited for Odell to join him. Odell looked left and right, then followed. He knew that Perry wouldn't hurt him, and wherever they were going was where they were meant to be.

Odell didn't even hesitate as they headed into the Cut.

# LXXXI

The best thing about Dryden's Inn, in Louis's opinion, was that it was probably destined to fall down before too long, and then nobody else would ever have to stay there again. Maybe sometime in the past, long before people knew about fripperies like proper plumbing, A/C that didn't sound like a failing jet engine, and towels with a consistency softer than sandpaper, Dryden's might have served as an acceptable rest stop for those with suitably low expectations, but it now belonged to another, distant century, just like smallpox and tuberculosis, although Louis wouldn't have been surprised if a sample of some of the gunk behind the sink in his bathroom had revealed traces of both.

Dryden's consisted of twenty-four rooms organized in what Louis was convinced was a swastika pattern, with a small office at its heart. The walls of his room were lime green, which contrasted sharply, even painfully, with the brown carpet and harvest gold drapes. The chairs matched the walls, the lamps matched the carpet, and the bedspreads matched nothing at all. His room had two beds and two chairs, none of which was actually comfortable, although each was uncomfortable in a subtly different way, making Louis feel like Goldilocks wandering through the Three Bears' house after Baby Bear had left for college and Momma and Poppa Bear had put all his stuff in storage.

He and Angel had opted for separate but adjoining rooms, mainly in order to draw as little attention to themselves as possible. When Morton Dryden, the motel's proprietor, had asked them their business in Plassey County, in the manner of a man who already believed that they had no business being there at all, Louis told him they were researching a book on famous folk and country musicians from West Virginia, which softened the old man up somewhat, especially once Louis revealed that he knew the difference between Mollie O'Brien and Molly O'Day, and knew that Milt Haley, father of the blind fiddle player Ed Haley, had been murdered by a lynch mob in 1889 during the Lincoln County Feud.

If Dryden was tempted to ask what a black man was doing listening to music performed primarily by white musicians, and traditionally associated with Caucasian audiences, he resisted the urge. Instead, he supplied the names of a handful of local good old boys who could play a mean tune, and even burned a few CDs for Louis from his own collection. Louis had to admit that some of it was pretty good, although it all fell on deaf ears where Angel was concerned, for whom any music that involved fiddles, banjos, or tunes that Casey Kasem wouldn't have played on *American Top 40* was safely to be dismissed as "hillbilly shit." To maintain the cover story, Louis had acquired a small library on the area's music, including Ivan Tribe's *Mountaineer Jamboree* and John Lilly's *Mountains of Music*, to leave in his room, and had spent two very contented evenings at the Hope Tavern in Mortonsville listening to the pick-up bands that performed there most nights.

Now, though, other matters were about to come to a head. Parker had returned, and Oberon had been baited. The Cut could either wait to see what Parker did next, or it could strike. Louis was hoping for the latter: it was a while since he had killed anyone.

It was after 4 a.m., and Louis could not rest. Angel was fast asleep in his room, as was Parker in his, which was three doors down from Louis's own. So far, they had not interacted publicly. Better that the Cut believed Parker to be alone. Dryden's appeared to have a handful of other occupants that night, all of whom were in other wings of the motel. The building was quiet, and only the occasional car passing on the road broke the silence.

Louis usually slept well, but he had been on edge ever since his arrival in Plassey County. He was a man born of the South, but he no longer felt at home there, if he ever really had. He was also anticipating the violence to come. Louis, through his own observations and the probings of those who had come south with him—including a pair of departed Japanese visitors—had developed a sense of the Cut's people. They were simmering, and soon they would boil over.

But for now, Louis was on a mission of his own. Not only was his latest change of towels more threadbare than usual, they were also pitted with cigarette burns, some of them fresh. Every man has his limits, and Louis had just reached his. So it was that he marched toward the motel office, the towels under his left arm, and a final glass of Vergelegen Reserve Cabernet Sauvignon in his right hand. Improbably, Turley boasted a gourmet store off its main street, with a small but perfectly formed selection of imported wines from which Louis had selected the Vergelegen. He had also bought a box of four Riedel glasses from which to drink it, because he didn't want to sip good Cab Sauv from motel tooth glasses wrapped in paper that boasted of their hygiene and cleanliness while containing what looked like spider eggs.

He reached the motel office. The door was closed, and a sign announced that the proprietor would be back shortly. Louis turned the handle. The door opened. A TV was playing softly, but there was no sign of Dryden or any of the kids who looked after the desk in his absence. A cigarette lay in an ashtray, smokeless but still warm.

Louis put down the towels. Behind the main desk were two rooms, one of which was a sleeping area for staff to use in the small hours. The bed bore the impression of a body, and the sheets were disturbed. A connecting door stood open, revealing an empty bathroom. Next to the bedroom was a small office that, upon closer investigation, proved to contain filing cabinets, boxes of soap and tissues, and two cartons of frozen doughnuts thawing on a table prior to being presented the next morning as part of the motel's breakfast of coffee and pastries. After some exploration, Louis discovered a couple of packs of thick, fresh towels wrapped in plastic, and apparently never used. He exchanged his own for three of them, stepped into the main office, and departed, closing the door behind him.

He looked at the lot behind the office, where two spaces were reserved for staff. No car sat in either of them. Wherever Dryden or the night manager had gone, he'd taken his wheels with him.

It was a cool night. Louis took a deep breath and inhaled smoke, and the earthy aroma of dead leaves. Now that he had satisfied himself by solving the towel problem, he thought that he might sleep for a few hours.

To his right, a truck pulled up at the edge of the main lot, and three men got out. He heard a second vehicle draw to a halt to his left, although he couldn't see it, blocked as it was by that wing of the motel. Seconds later, another smell joined the evening's scents: that of strong, cheap aftershave. The men from the truck were now moving quickly but quietly across the lot. Two were carrying rifles, while the other had what looked like a bottle in each hand.

Louis heard footsteps approaching from his left. He drained the last of the wine from his glass, placed one towel on the ground, laid the glass on its side on top of it, then covered it with a second towel. He put his heel on the bowl of the glass, broke it, and gently scattered the fragments on the ground between the office and the wall of the main building. When that was done, he retrieved the stem and moved into the shadows.

The man was careless: careless about where he placed his feet, careless in his approach, careless in not holding the pistol, bulbous with its added suppressor, closer to his body. He barely had time to react to the crunching of the shards beneath his boot before Louis stepped into his right side, his left hand grabbing the pistol while his right, the base of the wine glass flat against the palm, sent the sharp stem into the man's throat, then twisted it to do maximum damage. It broke off in the wound, sending a gush of red against the night sky, and the motel wall blushed crimson. The man staggered backward and went down, his hand to his throat in an effort to stop the flow of blood, a wet noise heaving from him like a child gathering the strength to cry. Louis recognized him from the Porterhouse. Parker had told him the names of the two men who had sat alongside Harpur Griffin. This was not Lucius, the red-haired one, but the other: Jabal.

Louis didn't have time to watch him die. A second gunman appeared, armed with a shotgun, and almost stumbled over Jabal's body. Louis shot him through the heart with Jabal's gun, the noise loud in the night even with the suppressor. Another truck pulled into the lot at speed, but Louis was already moving to his right, where he risked a glance at the three men who had been advancing across the lot. One was heading Louis's way, alerted by the gunshot, using the parked cars for cover. The others, farther behind, were trying to get a lighter to strike. Louis could see it sparking, and glimpsed the bottle held close, a second one standing between the feet of the two men. As Louis watched, a flame appeared, and a rag ignited.

And Louis understood. They were going to burn Parker in his room. If he came out, or tried to make a run for it, the men in the lot would shoot him, presumably aided by the two who were now lying dead on the ground, had they survived. The second vehicle, and whoever might be left in it, would cover the back, in case Parker tried to escape through a bathroom window.

The man with the Molotov cocktail drew his arm back to throw, and Louis shot him. The bottle dropped and exploded into flame on the ground, the fire engulfing the legs of his companion as the wounded man dropped to his knees before collapsing face-first into the blaze. There was a rattle of semiautomatic fire, and the motel wall to Louis's left spat fragments of masonry into the air. He pulled back to the office, which had a brick surround beneath its large windows, and tried to draw a bead on the gunman by the cars. Now he heard more shots coming from near Parker's room—an exchange of fire, which meant Parker and Angel were alert to the danger. Glass broke seconds later, followed by the boom of another Molotov igniting, and the eruption was reflected in the windshields of the cars. Someone cried out in pain, and another of the attackers in the lot wandered aimlessly into Louis's sights, the legs of his trousers still smoldering. Before Louis could shoot, the figure tripped over his own feet and lay unmoving on the ground. Behind him, a pyre burned in the shape of a man.

Semiautomatic fire came Louis's way, this time cutting a swath through the glass of the office, forcing him to lie flat on the ground. He prayed that they had no more Molotovs. If one were lobbed into the office, he wouldn't stand a chance.

The onslaught on the office ceased, then recommenced piecemeal. Covering fire, thought Louis. He got to his knees and moved around the wall toward the door, just in time to see a pair of feet disappear around the corner, leaving a smear of blood behind them. They were removing their dead and wounded. He made an attempt to go after them, but the semiautomatic opened up on him for a final time, keeping him pinned down. Somewhere a woman was screaming, and then the sound was lost in the roar of a departing truck. One more pistol sounded, and all went quiet.

"Louis?"

It was Angel.

"Here," he called. "In the office."

"They're gone," said Angel. "But we got one of them alive."

———

THE EAST ARM OF the motel was entirely engulfed in flames. The sound of sirens came from the north. Three women and a man were standing in the lot, having emerged from their rooms in the other parts of the motel. One of the women was staring in horror at the shattered windows and bullet-pocked body of her car.

But Parker, Angel, and Louis were already leaving the motel behind them. Parker drove, Louis in the passenger seat, his gun fixed on the man who sat beside Angel in the back. Benedict's right elbow was shattered, and he was in considerable pain, but he'd live. He'd been initially reluctant to tell his captors anything, not even his name, but Angel had tapped him on his damaged elbow with the barrel of a Glock, and that seemed to do the trick.

They could have waited for the police to arrive, but Parker knew that their enemies would be shocked and panicked after the failure of the assault on the motel. It was the time to counterattack, and Benedict would provide them with a way in.

The hours of the Cut were numbered.

# LXXXII

Henkel arrived at Irene Colter's property to find the house lit up, but no signs of movement inside or out. He took in the woods as his headlights moved across them. He stopped the car, and heard no sound beyond the faint clicking of the turret lights above his head. He'd come in with the roof blazing, because if it was the Cut then he wanted them to know he was on his way, although he couldn't imagine what business they might have had with Irene, beyond trying to get at him through her.

He climbed from his vehicle. His M&P9 was sitting in a holster on his belt, and in his arms he carried one of the department's Remington 870 shotguns. He called Irene's name, but received no reply, so he backed up to her porch steps, keeping his eyes on the woods, and knocked. Still nothing. He tried the door, but it was locked, so he moved around the house until he came to the back entrance. This too was locked.

He thought for a moment. If she'd done as he asked, then she was still inside. He could see no indications of a break-in, but it was always possible that intruders could have gained access to the house before she'd had a chance to secure it, and locked the doors behind them. He had no choice: he'd have to break the glass to get inside.

He twisted the shotgun so the stock was against the glass, and was about to shatter the pane when he caught a flash of reflected movement. He went right and brought the gun up, his finger already on the trigger. He eased the pressure when he saw Irene standing before him.

"God," he said, "don't sneak up on me like that. Why aren't you inside like I told you?"

"It's complicated," she said.

He moved to join her, his attention focused solely on her face, and a man stepped from the shadows to his right and held a pistol about a foot from his head.

Henkel froze.

*Maybe this is just a warning*, he thought. *Maybe they'll let me live.*

The figure to his right shifted position. It was Nestor, one of Brion Moline's sons from the Cut, and he wasn't wearing a mask, which meant this wasn't going to be simply a warning. Henkel had never figured Nestor for a killer, but it seemed that he'd been wrong. It looked like he wasn't going to live after all, not if Nestor was prepared to show his face like this, but maybe he could still save Irene.

Then she spoke to him.

"I'm sorry," she said. "I did kind of like you."

"No," said Henkel, and in that one syllable he heard all the tiredness and disappointment of a life that had never worked out as he might have hoped, and now seemed destined to end in a manner befitting all that had gone before.

Irene turned to Nestor.

"Just do it," she said, like Henkel was some old dog that needed to be put down swiftly and painlessly.

Henkel heard the shot. He shouldn't have, not if it was meant for him, not at that range. Nestor fell to the ground. The bullet had taken him under his raised right arm and passed straight through his torso. He made a low wheezing sound, and a blood bubble sprang from his lips before bursting with his last breath.

Irene stood openmouthed, staring at the body between them. Henkel didn't know if she'd ever watched a man die before. Right now, he didn't much care. He saw Rob Channer advancing across the lawn, and for a moment thought that someone else must have killed Nestor, and now Channer was going to finish the job for the Cut, but he couldn't make the logic of it work.

Channer kicked the gun away from beside Nestor's hand, all the time keeping his own weapon fixed on Irene.

"On your knees!" he told her.

Irene looked beseechingly at Henkel.

"They made me do it," she said. "They threatened me."

*Just do it.*

"You heard the man," said Henkel. "On your knees."

She knelt. Channer pushed her down flat on her stomach and searched her before holstering his weapon and cuffing her. When Channer was done, Henkel said to him, "I didn't expect it to be her, and I didn't expect it to be you."

"I wanted your job," said Channer, "but not like this."

The radio in Henkel's car squawked to life from the front of the house. He stepped over his ex-girlfriend—because that was what she most assuredly was, and he didn't believe he needed to confirm for her that they were no longer an item—and went to pick up the handset.

"Henkel."

Lucy's voice was both urgent and excited.

"We have reports of shots fired at Dryden's Inn," she said. "And it's burning."

# LXXXIII

Hannah and Sherah entered the prison house earlier than usual, Hannah leading, Sherah with two meals on a tray: bread, cereal, fruit, and some lukewarm coffee in plastic cups, to avoid any chance of the captives using them as scalding weapons.

The routine was well established. Paige and Gayle were required to be seated at the table when the women entered, so that the inner door could be locked before the meal was served. One woman would place the food before them while the other maintained her distance, just in case an attempt was made to get at the keys. In reality, though, the procedures had become more relaxed as the years had gone by, with either Hannah or Sherah—because they were the ones who most frequently tended to the breeders—taking care of the food while the other checked the rooms, or replenished the supplies, or just looked bored. On this occasion, though, there was clearly some urgency involved, and Hannah was standing close by Sherah as she served, keys jangling in her left hand.

This was all good.

Paige gave the slightest of nods to Gayle, who toppled her cereal bowl to the floor and began to wail. Hannah turned away to grab a cloth while Sherah squatted to rescue the food, which was when Paige brought the piece of brick in her right hand down hard on Sherah's left temple. Paige thought she felt something crack, but Sherah didn't fall. She just rocked on her feet, and made a sound like an old crow on a branch, so Paige hit her again, and Sherah dropped.

Gayle moved as soon as Paige struck the first blow. She pushed Hannah so hard from behind that the older woman tumbled face-first to the floor, but Hannah managed to get on her back and started struggling against Gayle, who was sitting on her stomach and working her way up Hannah's body in order to pin her arms.

Beside Paige, Sherah was trying to rise. She pushed herself up on her hands and knees, and shook her head. There was a swelling on her temple where the brick had connected, with a slight cut to the skin that wasn't bleeding much. Most of the blood was coming from her right ear, a steady *drip-drip-drip* that pooled on the floorboards, and her right eye now had a downward cast to it. Sherah's lips moved, and an assemblage of noises emerged, but they made no sense to Paige. She raised the brick again, Sherah's remaining good eye trying to follow its progress as Paige put all her upper-body power behind the blow. This time, Paige both felt and heard the crack, and Sherah's eyes rolled up in her skull as she slipped sideways and lay twitching on the floor.

Now that Sherah was taken care of, Paige could help Gayle, but Gayle needed no assistance. She was standing beside Hannah, who was convulsing on her back by the kitchen closets, her hands clawing at her mouth and neck. Hannah appeared to be having some sort of seizure. Her face had turned purple, and a series of clicking noises were emerging from her throat. Paige didn't make any move to help her, or to reach for the discarded keys. She was fascinated by Hannah's suffering, but she also noticed that Gayle's left cheek was bleeding.

"What happened to your face?" Paige asked.

"She cut me with a key."

"Ah."

They returned to watching Hannah, whose struggles were clearly nearing their climax.

"And what did you do to her?" asked Paige.

"I made her eat the stone," said Gayle.

"Ah," said Paige, again.

The top of Hannah's head banged hard against one of the closet doors. Her eyes grew very large, her throat clicked one last time, and her struggles ceased. Paige stepped around her and picked up the keys from the floor. She went to the window and saw that the Square was clear, with nobody in sight of the prison house. She removed Hannah's shoes, while Gayle took off Sherah's. They were about the right size for Gayle's feet, but Hannah's were too big for Paige, so she stuffed some newspaper into the toes, which helped.

Paige had no idea of their location. She knew only that the window onto the Square faced south, but as for where the nearest road or even town might be, she could not say. Ultimately, it didn't matter. They couldn't stay here, not now. They could only flee, and hope.

The door was to the far side of the house, which meant that the safest exit would be to turn left out of it, skirt the eastern wall, and then allow the building and the early morning gloom to shield them while they made their way into the woods at the rear. She explained this to Gayle, who took her hand as they walked to the door. Paige thought that she looked sad.

"What's wrong?" Paige asked.

"It's silly," said Gayle.

Paige released her hand, put the key in the first lock, and turned it. The outer door was slightly ajar. She peered through the gap, but there was still no one in sight.

"Tell me."

"I wanted to kill more of them," said Gayle.

"Honey," said Paige, as they prepared to run, "I know just how you feel."

———

ODELL FOLLOWED PERRY LUTTER deeper into the Cut. He'd heard stories about the dangers of this place, and his momma had warned him against venturing into it. Some kids in school said that the Cut's territory was guarded by metal traps, and pits with spikes, and explosives that would blow your dick and balls off so you'd have to pee out of a hole below your belly. Odell didn't know how much of that was true, but he understood that the people of the Cut were dangerous. He had the evidence of his own eyes. He sometimes wondered what had happened to the prisoner he had witnessed being bundled out of the van and into the trees. Nothing good, Odell thought. Now he himself was following a similar path, walking as if in a dream, descending into the Cut with a presence that was as much of another world as this one.

Gosh, but his mom would be mad.

And still he was not afraid, because Perry was with him, and he had something that he wanted Odell to see.

Odell stayed very close to Perry, walking in his footsteps, because Perry left marks on the ground, which made Odell question whether he was really a ghost at all. He could see the patterns indented in the dirt and grass by the soles of Perry's sneakers, and the bushes and branches moved as Perry pushed his way through them. If he was a ghost, then he wasn't like the ones in movies. You couldn't look through him. He had substance.

But Perry was dead. Odell would have been certain of that even if he hadn't glimpsed the hole in the crown of Perry's head, the hair around it scorched away, the entry wound rimmed with red and pink, and a whiteness glistening inside the skull. The bullet hole was just confirmation, although it didn't explain where the blood on Perry's sneaker had come from.

Perry stopped and stared back at him. He wasn't smiling anymore. He looked sad and angry.

*He knows what I'm thinking*, thought Odell. *He knows I've been staring at the hole in his head.*

Perry untucked the front of his shirt from his pants and lifted it up with both hands. There were stab wounds in his belly, some of them so close to each other that they'd combined to form a single, larger lesion. Perry turned, hoisting the shirt at the back, and Odell saw more gashes revealed. He had a vision of Perry crawling through mud and dirt, crying for his momma, before a shadow fell across him, and a gun uttered his name.

Perry tucked his shirt back in. Odell couldn't figure out how his clothes were so clean, with only a single sneaker bearing the trace of what had happened to him, but then Perry had always liked being neatly turned out. It didn't seem like death had changed that situation much at all.

Perry pointed into the undergrowth to Odell's left, where a trail of sorts ran between the trees. Metal gleamed in the dawning light, and sharp teeth were revealed. It was an animal trap, laid just where a stranger might have walked had they chosen to take the easy way into the Cut, which explained why Perry was leading Odell along a rougher path.

They resumed their advance, Odell keeping an even closer eye now on where Perry put his feet. He didn't want to die out here. He didn't want to be like Perry.

And he didn't want to look any longer at the hole in Perry's head.

# LXXXIV

One truck returned to the Cut bearing the dead and wounded in the back, the two remaining vehicles having been abandoned at the inn. Cassander, Lucius, and Marius watched them come. Oberon joined them, tucking a pistol into the band of his trousers. They'd been warned in advance that all had not gone well at Dryden's. It had been a mistake to entrust the attack to Jabal and Benedict, and now it seemed that Parker had the latter. None of the survivors knew whether he was dead or alive. They'd fled to save themselves.

The police would come. That was inevitable. There had been witnesses.

A wailing arose from the women as the bodies were passed down. One of them was wrapped in an old blanket, and a strong smell of burned flesh came from it. A scorched arm slipped from the blanket, and the wailing increased in pitch.

Oberon looked around for Sherah and Hannah, but could not find them. They'd be needed, Hannah especially, because she was the most skilled physician among them. When last he'd seen them, they'd been preparing food for the bitches in the hut.

Cassander approached him.

"What should we do?" he asked.

"We blame the dead," said Oberon. "Some of our young men argued with Parker and tried to kill him. We knew nothing about it until the truck appeared, but the driver was the only survivor, and he died of his injuries. Have the wounded tended to, then get them away from here."

*It might work*, thought Oberon.

*It won't work. It will just buy time.*

Cassander couldn't believe what he was hearing.

"We're going to brazen this out?"

"What choice do we have?"

Lucius, who had been listening in, interjected.

"We can fight."

"This isn't just going to be a local dispute with Henkel. This will be the state police, maybe even the FBI and the ATF. We can't stand against them all."

*And maybe it's best that we don't. I should have left while I had the chance. I could have taken Tamara, and Sherah—if she'd been willing to come.*

He stared at Cassander, and felt a rage sweep over him at the betrayal that he suspected, before his gaze passed on to the prison house. Sherah and Hannah had still not appeared. Something was wrong. Maybe one of the bitches was ill.

"We don't have to worry about Henkel," said Cassander.

"Why not?"

"He's dead."

"What?"

"I sent Nestor after him."

"I didn't authorize any move on Henkel."

"I know," said Cassander. "I did."

Which was when Lucius moved behind Oberon, placed the gun close to the back of his head, and pulled the trigger.

# LXXXV

Cassander walked to the prison house, Lucius ahead of him. The women would have to be moved out. They were worth too much to kill, but if they were discovered by the police then all would be lost. Blame the dead, Oberon had advised. Well, that was just what Cassander planned to do. Oberon had ordered the attack on Dryden's Inn, and on Henkel. He had then tried to kill Cassander, and Lucius had been forced to intervene. They had witnesses who would swear that this was the case. The Cut might yet survive. But the women had to be hidden away.

The women, and the Dead King.

Lucius tried the door. It was unlocked, as was the inner door, and it was never supposed to be open, not even when meals were being served. He stepped inside and saw Sherah lying on her side on the floor, and Hannah on her back by the kitchen closets. Cassander was right behind him, and pushed him aside to get to Sherah. He found a pulse, but it was faint. His fingers hovered over her damaged skull.

"Hannah's dead," said Lucius.

*Sherah is not*, thought Cassander, but he could see the severity of her injuries. Nobody in the Cut was skilled enough to deal with this kind of damage. Sherah would have to be taken to a hospital. More questions would be asked.

The piece of brick that had been used on Sherah lay beside her body. Cassander saw traces of blood and hair on it. He took a handkerchief from his pocket, used it to pick up the stone, and said to the unconscious Sherah, "I'm sorry."

He hit her twice, but she made no sound. When he was finished, the pulse had been stilled.

Cassander cast the brick aside.

"Find the women," he told Lucius, "and bring them back here. *Alive.*"

Chapter

# LXXXVI

Paige had tried to keep herself in shape as best she could, but walking around a fenced yard for an hour a day at best, in between sexual assaults, pregnancies, and the aftermath of difficult births, wasn't conducive to flight.

*Jesus, I'm joking about it*, she realized. *I'm running—no, stumbling— for my life. I've been raped, abused, and I'll soon give birth to a third child, but I'm joking.*

*And I thought Gayle was insane.*

Her legs were weak, she was struggling to catch her breath, and the weight of the child in her belly kept threatening to drag her to her knees. The paper in her shoes was coming away from the toes, and her feet were moving around freely inside them. She'd already fallen twice, and was bleeding badly from her right knee and shin. Gayle had helped her up each time. She was having less trouble than Paige, but then she wasn't as far along in her pregnancy and she'd spent months instead of years cooped up in the prison house like a battery hen. But Paige also noticed that something of the girl that Gayle once was had reared its head, as though it had been lying dormant beneath a veneer of craziness in order to protect itself. Now it was Gayle who was supporting Paige, encouraging her to keep going and not look back. But, Christ, she was tired, and her damn feet hurt so much.

"Wait," said Paige.

She paused, slipped Hannah's shoes off, and cast them into the woods. She'd take her chances without them. It would be less painful, or so she believed until she started walking again and the first of the twigs and stones bit into her soles and heels.

"Shit!" she said, as a particularly sharp pebble lanced her right foot and lodged itself in her flesh. She stopped again, dug it out, and ran straight into Gayle's back.

"What's wrong?" she asked.

And then they were both staring at the small black boy who stood amid the trees, watching them with surprise.

———

PERRY LUTTER HAD DISAPPEARED. One moment he was walking in front of Odell, the next he was gone, and in his place were two white women, both of them with swollen bellies, although the older one's was bigger than the younger's. Odell knew what a pregnant woman looked like, and he was pretty certain that he was looking at two right now. Were they from the Cut? If so, why were they out here, and one of them barefoot? Odell didn't want to get into trouble with the Cut. He wasn't supposed to be on their land. He'd been following Perry, but now Perry had vanished, and it wasn't like he'd left Odell with detailed instructions about what he was supposed to do in the event of meeting two women with babies in their bellies.

Then the younger one said, "Help us. Please!"

And Odell Watson knew why Perry Lutter had lured him into the Cut.

———

LUCIUS AND MARIUS WERE tracking the women. It wasn't difficult. They'd left a trail through the woods that a child could follow.

Cassander's instructions had been clear: the women weren't to

be killed, not even after what they'd done to Hannah and Sherah—
although Sherah's death couldn't entirely be blamed on them, not that
Lucius would ever let anyone know what his father had done to her in
the prison house. Lucius had never liked Sherah anyway. He knew that
his father had started sleeping with her, and a woman who'd cheat on
her husband wasn't to be trusted.

And a man who slept with the wife of another—was he to be trusted?
Lucius wasn't sure. His feelings about his father were complex. He
loved him, but at the same time he understood that Cassander favored
Marius, and had always viewed him as a potential leader of the Cut.
But by the laws of primogeniture, Lucius was the one who should have
been groomed to assume authority after Cassander, now that Oberon
was dead. That would have to be discussed once their current problems were dealt with. Marius might have been smart, but it was Lucius
who was always left to do the dirty work, such as killing and burying
Killian and Huff, or putting a bullet in Perry Lutter's head after Benedict had fucked up the knife work. Marius wouldn't have been capable of performing any of those tasks, even if Cassander hadn't done his
utmost to ensure that his younger son maintained a distance from the
Cut's bloodier tasks. True, Marius had set Harpur Griffin alight, but
only when Griffin was too drunk to struggle much against his bonds.
Marius wasn't a leader. He had no guts. But still Cassander preferred
him to Lucius.

In his darker moments, Lucius sometimes wondered if he was being
set up by his own family. If someone had to take the fall, then let it be
the troubled elder son, it seemed, and not the cautious—no, call it what
it was: *cowardly*—younger one.

Lucius stopped to let Marius catch up with him. This was all his
brother was good for: hunting women and killing drunks. And when
they apprehended Paige and Gayle, would Marius join his brother in
inflicting some punishment on them, because bringing them back alive
wasn't the same as bringing them back unharmed? Lucius had always

wondered what it might be like to take Gayle by force. There was something vulnerable about her that appealed to the baseness in him. As for Paige, he might take her, too, just to teach her a lesson, and, while he fucked her, he'd let her know that he'd be the one to kill her once her baby was born, and would make sure that she went slowly. There'd be no mercy for her. It was what Hannah and Sherah would have wanted.

"Look," said Marius. He pointed to the undergrowth, where two shoes lay discarded. One of the women was now barefoot. It wouldn't make any difference. They couldn't be moving fast, either with shoes or without. The two men must be almost on top of them.

"We're coming!" shouted Lucius. "You hear me? We're coming!"

And he raised his face to the sky and howled.

———

ODELL WAS LEADING THE women back to the road. The older one—who said her name was Paige; the younger one was Gayle—told him that the Cut had been holding them prisoner, but they'd escaped, and Odell had no reason to doubt the truth of this. He'd take them back to his home, and then his momma and grandma would know what to do. For now, Odell's attention was fixed on finding his way to the road. It was still murky, although there was light to the east, but Odell had good eyes, and because Perry had made him follow a rough, less-trodden path, he could pick out the places through which they'd passed by the broken bushes and flattened undergrowth. He also kept the trail to his right, because it had been mostly to his left when they'd entered the Cut. He tried to explain to the women how important it was that they follow his footsteps as closely as possible, because traps had been laid by the Cut, but he wasn't sure that they understood. They kept forcing the pace, and once he caught them walking almost alongside him, and had to warn them to stay behind. It was hard for them, though. Paige's feet were all cut up, and Odell couldn't be certain, and was too embarrassed to point it out, but he thought she might be bleeding from under her dress.

A man's voice came from very close behind them, followed by a howl.

"We have to go faster!" said Paige, and Odell saw a peculiar expression sweep across Gayle's face, like the tide rolling in over a beach and erasing any sign that people might have passed that way—writing, footprints, sandcastles—leaving only blankness behind. She released her hold on Paige and stepped to her right, but the bank wasn't level and she slid down a couple of feet on wet leaves and dirt. Gayle was trying to drag herself back up again, and Odell was reaching over to help her, when he heard a snapping sound and Gayle screamed in pain and lost her footing entirely. Odell glimpsed a thin line of silver wrapped around her left leg, just above the ankle. Gayle tried to get up, and the wire of the snare rose out of the leaves, stretching taut from the tree trunk to which it was anchored.

Odell turned to Paige, but Paige was gone, and then a hand clasped itself over Odell's mouth as he was yanked from his feet and carried into the trees.

# Chapter

# LXXXVII

Lucius was the first to find her, Marius trailing behind. Gayle was sitting amid a pile of wet leaves, scratching with her nails at the snare around her leg. She stared up at Lucius even as her nails continued to work, digging through the skin and into the flesh. If she'd been left alone, Lucius thought she might even have tried to gnaw her leg off, like a trapped wolf.

Lucius drew his knife and let her see the blade.

"Go after the other one," he told Marius.

"What about her?"

"I'll take care of her."

"You can't hurt her," said Marius. "Father warned us."

*Father warned us. Fuck that.*

"He told us not to kill her," Lucius corrected him. "He never said anything about not hurting her. You just worry about the other bitch. Go on, now. I don't want no audience for what I'm about to do."

———

ODELL HAD STOPPED STRUGGLING. The hand over his mouth was black, just like the face beside his, and the voice in his ear that told him to be quiet, that they were on his side, except Odell didn't have a side, or not one he knew about. And who were "they" anyway? He saw two other men, both armed, hiding behind trees, and a third who was lying flat on the ground, his hands tied behind his back, a gag over his mouth and a length of barbed wire around his neck. The rest of the barbed wire was connected to what looked like a broom handle, creating an instrument of control, the way someone cruel might force a bear to perform tricks. Odell couldn't see the man's face properly, but he thought he recognized him as Benedict.

A shape appeared on a small rise, and Odell identified another of the Cut. He had a gun in his right hand. He progressed warily along the trail, watching his feet, the woods, even the branches above his head, as though what he sought might be lurking up there like a bat or a bird.

"Come on out, now," said Marius. "It'll just go worse for you the longer this goes on."

He stopped, his attention caught by a mark on the ground before him. He knelt, and put his fingers to fresh blood. He raised it before his face and smeared it with his thumb. It was still warm.

When he looked up again, a man stood on the path before him. He was small and unshaven, and wore a knit cap against the cold. Like Marius, he also held a gun in his hand.

"Keep quiet," he said, "and let the gun drop."

A more experienced thug than Marius might have done as he was ordered, recognizing the futility of trying to bring up a weapon to counter another who already had a gun leveled at him. He might even have decided that it was better not to move at all.

But Marius panicked. He tried to stand. He wasn't even sure that he intended to use the gun. He'd never shot anyone before, and now he never would, for Angel killed him as soon as his knees left the ground.

———

LUCIUS WAS STANDING OVER Gayle, his belt already unbuckled, when the shot came.

"What the fuck?"

He refastened his belt and backed away from Gayle. He called his brother's name, but received no reply. Maybe Paige had tried to jump him, and he'd fired off a shot to scare her. He'd better not have injured her enough to harm the baby. That child she was carrying was pure gold to them.

Lucius was halfway up the bank, his gun in his hand, when he saw a pair of sneakers before him, one of them bloody. His gaze moved up from the sneakers to the neatly pressed pants, past the clean shirt, and finally to the placid, smiling face of Perry Lutter.

"I told you I'd see you again," said Perry, except it wasn't Perry's voice that came out of his mouth, but a deeper male voice, a black voice. Then Perry wasn't there anymore, and in his place stood a man with a shaved head and a circle of silvered beard, the mocking, dangerous presence from the bar in Portland, the one, according to the survivors, who'd started all the shooting back at Dryden's Inn.

Lucius let the gun drop and raised his hands.

"I give up," he said.

"I don't care," said Louis, and he sent Lucius to join his brother in the fires of the next world.

———

HENKEL, MEANWHILE, WAS ENGAGED with the fires of this world, in his case the remnants of one wing of Dryden's Inn that was crumbling to charred wood and ash as two fire trucks struggled to ensure that the blaze didn't spread to the rest of the building. They were aided in this by an easterly breeze that was blowing the sparks and flames away from the motel complex and toward a disused lot that had once housed a bar named Whitney's, which everyone in Plassey County knew as Whitey's due to its famed lack of tolerance for non-Caucasian customers. Whitney's particular brand of Jim Crow nostalgia had come to an end in 1997, when members of an African American gang named the L8 took a detour while transporting two thousand stamp bags of heroin from

Pittsburgh to Weirton in a pair of jitneys, and reduced Whitney's to broken glass and splinters using an IED made from ammonium nitrate.

Morton Dryden claimed not to have known what had happened in the course of a night that apparently encompassed a full-on battle at his inn, and the subsequent incineration of a quarter of his rooms, he and his desk clerk having conveniently been elsewhere at the time. Henkel didn't much care what Dryden knew or didn't know, and was only sorry that the wind seemed intent on not burning down the rest of his shithole establishment. What Henkel knew was that Charlie Parker had been staying at Dryden's, and witnesses confirmed he had left the scene, with two or three other men, in pursuit of one of the vehicles involved in the attack. Two more remained in the parking lot, but had deliberately been set on fire in an effort to hamper identification.

But Henkel didn't need papers or plates to know it was the Cut that had come after Parker, and messed up the job, just as they had sent Nestor to kill him, and screwed that one up, too. Irene Colter was in a cell back at the sheriff's building, guarded by two armed deputies. Since her arrest, she had only spoken to ask for her phone call, which she'd used to contact a lawyer named Daniel Starcher in Lewisburg, a man with links to the Cut.

The state police, summoned by Henkel, were on their way, accompanied by at least one armored Humvee and the McDowell County MRAP, the Mine Resistant Ambush Protected vehicle acquired under the Department of Defense's 1033 Program, which was basically a way for the government to sell off some of its heavy armor now that Afghanistan and Iraq had been saved by regime change and democratization. At the time, Henkel thought the purchase of the MRAP was just about the dumbest thing he'd ever heard, given that the chances of anyone in McDowell County utilizing mines in a dispute were slim to none. Now, though, he wasn't about to ride into the Cut without as much armor and firepower as he could find, and the MRAP was starting to look like a pretty good purchase, all things considered.

His cell phone rang. He looked at the number, but didn't recognize it. "Henkel," he said.

"It's Parker."

Henkel took the phone from his ear and held it toward the fire, just in time for it to catch the crash of three rooms collapsing in on themselves.

"You hear that?" he said. "That's the sound of a building burning down. Where the hell are you? Wherever you are, you're under arrest."

"I'm at the home of a woman named Teona Watson," Parker replied. "She says you know where she lives. I have two pregnant women here who've been held prisoner and repeatedly raped by the Cut."

# LXXXVIII

C assander had heard the gunshots. They were faint, but boded ill. He'd warned his sons not to harm the women. If they were shoot- ing, then it wasn't at the escapees. He sent two men to investigate. They came back as soon as they found the bodies. Cassander shed no tears. There was no time. He would weep later, if he lived.

On Cassander's orders, the Cut was preparing to fight. Men and women were equipping themselves with shotguns and semiautomatic weapons. Vehicles were being moved onto the roads, each of them loaded with sacks of cement, bags of fertilizer, anything to add weight before the tires were punctured and the engines crippled. Once the roads were blocked, Cassander's instructions were for the majority of the inhabitants to retreat to the Square, where the Cut would make its stand.

But they would not be many: just over thirty adults at most. The Cut had been surviving on its reputation, coasting on fumes. Perhaps Oberon was right after all, and its time was coming to an end. If so, it would not be a slow decay, but a final great conflagration, and the Dead King would be part of it.

The Cut had been forced to hide the Dead King only twice in its his- tory, when it had believed itself to be under imminent threat. A bunker in the woods had been constructed especially for that purpose, but

Cassander no longer intended to utilize it. He had spread gasoline in and around the blockhouse, and would position himself there. If the end came, he would lock himself inside, set the fire, and die with the Dead King.

Nikolas, one of Micah Morcamb's sons, came to Cassander as he was tossing the last of the gasoline cans into the woods. Nikolas looked frightened. He had good cause to be. Most of them would not survive what was coming.

"What is it?" asked Cassander.

"The Holberts have fled," said Nikolas. "The Lunns, too."

"What do you mean?"

"Their trucks are gone. They've left us."

The Holberts had three sons, the youngest seventeen. The Lunns had two, both in their twenties. It meant Cassander's force had been cut by almost a third in a single stroke.

"Who knows?"

"Just me and Damon, so far." Damon was Nikolas's younger brother.

Cassander grabbed Nikolas by the right shoulder.

"You keep this to yourself, you hear?"

"Yes."

Nikolas had an AR-15 on his shoulder. He was small for his age, and the gun looked far too big for him.

"You know how to use that weapon?" asked Cassander.

"My daddy taught me," said Nikolas.

"Good. When they come, they won't care who they hurt. You saw what they did in Waco. Women, children—everybody died. It was all the same to the government. We have to hold them off for as long as we can, make them negotiate with us. We can't just let them roll in here, understand?"

"Yes."

"You're a good boy. Now go join your father and brother."

Nikolas left him and walked out of the woods, the rifle bouncing against his back, and a voice spoke Cassander's name. He turned to find the source, but no one was near. He listened and heard his name being called again.

This time he knew.

He returned to the blockhouse and stood before the Dead King.

———

AT THE WATSON HOME, Henkel, with Rob Channer beside him, listened to Paige Dunstan recount the essential details of the women's story. He didn't have time to hear it all, and he didn't need to. He already wanted to kill someone.

Parker leaned against the wall of the living room. Across from him sat two other men, whom Parker had introduced to Henkel as Angel and Louis. The one named Angel made Henkel want to hide his wallet. Louis stone cold scared the shit out of him. They'd been forced to kill two of the Cut in self-defense getting the women out, Parker said, and Paige had confirmed his story, identifying the dead men as Lucius and Marius, Cassander's sons. The tale might even have been true. Henkel added it to the list of things that he didn't care much about either way. It was growing at a frightening speed.

Benedict, Zachary Bowman's son, was bound with barbed wire to the Watsons' gate, a piece of broom handle still attached to the back of his neck. Parker had used him to enter the Cut, relying on Benedict's instinct for self-preservation to avoid any traps. Benedict didn't say a whole lot when Henkel removed the gag from his mouth, beyond babbling about kidnapping and murder, so Henkel had simply gagged him again.

"So what now?" asked Parker.

Henkel told him about the arrival of additional firepower in the form of state troopers and armored vehicles. He'd have called in the National Guard, too, if he thought it might have helped. Henkel was royally pissed off, and his blood was up: the town's only inn was on fire, most of the men in the room with him had recently been involved in a gunfight on his territory, the Cut had been raping women and doing God alone knew what with the resultant babies, and his girlfriend had just tried to have him killed. It was hard to see how the day could get much worse, but Parker found a way.

"What will the Cut do when all those guns start appearing on their land?" he asked.

"They'll fight," said Henkel.

"There are women and children in there."

"Some of them will fight, too."

"Then you'll have a bloodbath on your hands."

That wasn't what Henkel wanted to hear, but he knew it might be true. He'd been so concerned about dealing with the Cut once and for all that he hadn't fully considered the consequences.

"What's the alternative?" he asked.

"You hold off on the state troopers, and the armored vehicles, and we go back in. Maybe Oberon can be reasoned with. He won't want to see his people killed."

"He and his 'people' are looking at federal charges on the kidnappings," said Henkel, "or worse if we find evidence of capital crimes."

"Not in this state," said Channer.

West Virginia had abolished the death penalty back in 1965, and the last federal capital trials in 2007 had resulted in the overturning of the death penalties in favor of sentences of life without parole and thirty-five years respectively. With good lawyers, anyone in the Cut accused of capital crimes would be almost guaranteed to avoid the federal needle. It was a bargaining tool.

"You may have a point," Henkel conceded. "There's just one problem: who's to say that Oberon is still in charge in there? He may be a son of a bitch, but he cares about those families. Even if he was responsible for the attacks on both of us, he'd know by now that his best option was negotiation. He'd have called and tried to open a channel of communi-cation. It's his way."

"If Oberon isn't holding the reins," said Parker, "then who is?"

Henkel sighed.

"Cassander Hobb," he replied. "And you and your friends just killed his boys."

# LXXXIX

Fallen trees, heavy furniture, and sandbags were being used to create fortified positions around the Square. Most of the women and older men, and all of the young children, had been moved to the prison house formerly occupied by Paige and Gayle. They had no weapons, and in the event of the Cut falling they were under instructions to surrender to the authorities. There was no sign of Cassander, but Cassia and Jana, two of the younger women with infant sons, had gone to the blockhouse to beg him to reconsider, and send someone to negotiate with law enforcement before they entered the Cut. They were kept back by Koli and Logmar, two Cassander loyalists, who told them that Cassander was seeking guidance.

And so they waited, but Cassander did not emerge.

———

HENKEL MADE SOME CALLS. The first of the state troopers had arrived at the sheriff's office, and more were on their way. According to Lucy, the FBI had also made contact, and two of its agents were eager to speak with the sheriff. They seemed very concerned about Parker, which didn't surprise Henkel, even if he wasn't sure how they'd found out that he was in Plassey County. Pretty soon, Henkel knew, the whole business would be out of his hands. The FBI, if—or when—it became formally involved, would have professional negotiators, but Henkel thought that local knowledge of the Cut might best avail. He didn't want a slaughter: he wanted surrender. He just hoped that it might still be Oberon from whom he would be trying to secure it.

"We'll make an effort to negotiate," he told Parker. "But it might be better if you and your friends stayed back here."

"I came to find Jerome Burnel," said Parker. Paige Dunstan had told him of seeing a hooded man being brought into the Cut some nights earlier, and forced into the woods, and Teona Watson's son had confirmed a similar sighting. It was possible that Burnel might still be alive somewhere in there.

Henkel looked to Channer for an opinion. If this all went badly, Channer might be sitting in the sheriff's chair a lot sooner than he'd anticipated.

"I'd prefer to go in with five guns instead of two," said Channer. "And maybe the fewer uniforms the Cut sees, the better."

That settled it, then, Henkel supposed.

"I have a heart condition," said Henkel.

"I know."

"This can't be good for it."

"I guess not."

Henkel got to his feet. He wasn't feeling great. What he had to do next wasn't about to make him feel any better.

"All right, then," he told Parker. "Raise your right hand. I'm deputizing you and your friends here. You're operating under the authority of the Plassey County sheriff from this point on, with all the power and protections of that office, but if you fire another shot without just cause, I'll kill you myself. Any questions?" said Henkel.

Only Angel raised a hand.

"Does the position come with a restroom key?"

———

THEY ENTERED THE CUT in two vehicles, Henkel and Parker in the sheriff's truck, with Benedict acting as a reluctant guide, and Channer, with Angel and Louis in back, following behind in his car. They encountered the first roadblock half a mile in. It was simple, but efficient. An ancient Buick with flat tires, presumably used for the scavenging of parts, lay on its collapsed roof in the middle of the road, a thick line of trees at either side.

"We can push it out of the way," said Parker. "Use the truck to spin it, then work around it."

Henkel took in the woods. Through them he could see a house, but it appeared quiet.

"That's the Tinsley place, right?" he asked Benedict.

"Yeah."

Achim Tinsley had two children, a boy and a girl. The boy was about twenty, the girl a year younger. Achim was all right, as far as the Cut went, but his wife, Priska, was a piece of work.

Henkel activated the speaker on the truck, then instructed Benedict to call Achim's name, and told him what to say. He placed the handset close to Benedict's mouth, and nodded.

"Achim! It's Benedict. The sheriff just wants to talk to Oberon. He says we can find a peaceful way out of this."

They heard no response for about ten seconds before a male voice answered from among the trees. It sounded young.

"Oberon's dead."

"That's not any of the Tinsleys," said Benedict.

"Then who is—" Henkel started to ask, just before the truck was raked by bullets from the house and the trees. The windshield exploded as Henkel and Parker ducked low. They heard more shooting from behind as Channer and the others returned fire. Benedict didn't move. One bullet had hit him in the chest, and another in the chin. He slumped sideways as Parker and Henkel opened the doors and hit the dirt, using the Buick for cover. Channer's shotgun boomed twice, and someone cried out from the bushes to the left. The shooting stopped.

Carefully, Channer and Henkel moved into the undergrowth. Lying on a patch of bare ground with a hole in the center of his torso and a pistol by his side was a boy of no more than sixteen or seventeen. He was blinking repeatedly, trying to focus on the sky above his head. Henkel thought that Parker had been right: if they went into the Cut in force, then they risked having the blood of children on their hands, even if they were children with guns. It should never have come to this.

"Ah, hell," said Channer. "It's one of the Parsons' boys—the youngest, Nicon."

The Parsons had been so close to the Hobbs for generations that they were virtually the same family.

"Parsons has one more son and—" Henkel began to say, just as two things happened. The Parsons boy stopped blinking as the life left him; and a flap of scalp rose from Rob Channer's skull, followed by a cloud of blood and bone, and the crack of the rifle shot that had just killed him. Channer toppled on his side, and Henkel dropped with him, Channer's corpse absorbing the second bullet and saving Henkel's life. This time, the fusillade that followed in reply from Parker, Angel, and Louis was aimed at one window of the Tinsley house, and when it was over all was quiet again.

Henkel got out from behind Channer's corpse and crawled into the trees.

"Please," said a woman's voice from inside the house. "No more shooting."

Henkel recognized the speaker as Priska Tinsley. He looked at his dead deputy, and tried to keep his voice level.

"Priska, this is Ed Henkel. We got an awful mess out here, and I don't want it to get any worse."

"Achim's hurt," said Priska. "He was hit in the gunfire. I can't move him."

"Just the two of you in there?"

"Jason Parsons is here too, but he's dead. The rest are up in the Square. Only Achim and me are left."

"Then you come out with your hands up, and we'll see to Achim."

The front door of the house opened, and a slim woman in her fifties emerged. Her yellow blouse and blue jeans were heavily stained with blood. Parker and the others kept her under their guns while Henkel approached, his weapon raised.

"Lie down on the ground, Priska," he said.

The woman descended unsteadily to her knees, and used her hands to brace herself before lying flat in the dirt. Henkel searched her, but found nothing. Parker joined him, and together they advanced on the house. Parker risked a glance inside. A man with long white hair, who looked decades older than the woman outside, was slumped against a pockmarked wall in a widening pool of blood. His eyes were open, but whatever they were seeing wasn't in this world. A hunting rifle lay beside him.

Parker went in first, and together he and Henkel cleared the single-story house. They found one other body, and immediately saw its resemblance to the boy who had died outside. He'd been hit twice in the upper body. He was a year or two older than his brother. He, too, had a rifle. Either he or Tinsley could have killed Channer.

"So much for negotiation," said Henkel.

"Let's talk to the woman."

They went back outside. Priska Tinsley was still lying on the ground, Angel and Louis keeping watch on her.

"We need to get help for Achim," she was telling them, over and over.

Henkel knelt beside her, this woman whom he believed to have conspired in the killing of his deputy, and spoke as tenderly as he could with Channer's remains lying in sight.

"He's beyond caring now, Priska," he said. "But maybe you can help us to save the others."

# XC

H enkel was reluctant to advance any farther into the Cut without support. Channer's death had tipped the balance against its
inhabitants, and it was all that Henkel could do to restrain himself from wiping his hands of them and letting events take their course.
But at the same time, he didn't want his name to be associated with
another Waco. The radio in his truck was busted, so he used his cell
phone to contact his department.

Unfortunately, any remaining doubts about how to deal with the
Cut had been dispelled by the testimony of Paige and Gayle to the
state police, and the two FBI agents who had just joined them. In addition, the Holbert and Lunn families had voluntarily surrendered to
the authorities, claiming sanctuary from Cassander Hobb and those
who stood alongside him, and state troopers were apparently already
advancing into the Cut from the north, east, and west.

Parker heard a rumble to the south as Henkel tried to take in what
he was being told, and moments later the MRAP appeared, followed by
a state police SUV and a cruiser, only to find their progress blocked by
two disabled vehicles—the first a wreck on its roof, the second Henkel's
truck, with its engine pumping steam from bullet holes—and one reasonably intact sheriff's department cruiser.

"Well," said Louis, taking in the bulk of the MRAP and thinking that a bad situation was about to get a whole lot worse, "at least now we can get rid of the Buick."

———

HENKEL DECIDED THAT THE MRAP, complete with SWAT team, should lead the way, on the grounds that opposition might crumble at the first sight of the combat wagon. What mattered now was reaching the Square before any of the other advancing forces, because that was most assuredly where Cassander and his loyalists would be waiting. If Henkel could get to Cassander and reason with him, he might be able to prevent further bloodshed, but already reports were coming through of troopers exchanging fire with members of the Cut—they could faintly hear some of the shots from where they stood—and there was also the problem of Cassander himself.

Priska Tinsley confirmed the truth of what the voice had called out from the house: Oberon was dead, killed by Cassander's son Lucius, but almost certainly on the orders of his father. Priska couldn't say if Cassander had also ordered Henkel's murder, but it now seemed highly likely. In addition, word had spread through the Cut via burner phones and shortwave radios that Cassander's sons were dead. Being reasonable, Henkel guessed, was unlikely to be foremost in Cassander's mind.

Troopers pushed the crippled Plassey County sheriff's vehicle off the road, Henkel being understandably reluctant to incur further damage by letting the MRAP take care of his truck, a decision for which he was doubly thankful after he saw what it did to the Buick, which the MRAP crushed as much as moved. Priska Tinsley was put in the back of the state police car, just in case she might be able to talk sense into any Cut skirmishers, but they encountered only one further roadblock along the way, this one constructed from logs and sandbags, and after some cursory shots at the MRAP, and a warning to lay down their arms, the defenders surrendered. Two of them were teenagers, the other a girl in her twenties, and all seemed grateful to be under arrest. They hadn't been in a hurry to die. None of them could offer any clue as to what might be waiting in the Square, beyond giving a rough estimate of the size of the force holed up there: no more than twenty men and women, all told, with the elderly and very young kept back in the prison hut for safety. Using the map he had given Parker, Henkel indicated the position of the building in which the old and the children were gathered, and gave two troopers orders to get to it and keep those inside calm. This would also ensure that it was less likely to be fired upon accidentally by any members of law enforcement entering the Cut from other directions. Although there was a state police lieutenant with the SWAT team from the MRAP, he was smart enough to defer to Henkel. Like the sheriff, he wasn't eager to have the blood of women and children on his hands.

They were within sight of the Square when the first shots came, both from the buildings before them and from hidden positions to the right and left of the road. Parker saw a trooper go down, hit in the leg, and then they were all in it: blood, smoke, noise.

Dying.

———

LATER IT WOULD COME back to Parker as fragments, pieces of a vast diorama that had somehow shattered and then scattered itself through his memory: the MRAP opening to disgorge the SWAT team, and the ragged shooting of the Cut being answered with heavy, disciplined fire; glass shattering, and someone shouting for help; a middle-aged man in camouflage gear rising from the undergrowth with a shotgun at his shoulder only to be almost torn in half by a stream of automatic fire from close to the MRAP; the turret gunner opening fire on one of the houses in the Square with a .50-caliber sniper rifle, its suppository-shaped bullets ripping through the walls and anyone inside unfortunate enough to get in their way; the MRAP crawling forward, and then the ground collapsing to its right, for the road had been built with deliberate weaknesses at its edges precisely to thwart an advance by heavy vehicles. The MRAP tumbled to its side, ejecting the sniper from the turret, his momentum sending him smashing into a tree before he fell at its base and did not move.

By then, Parker was close to the Square, Angel and Louis at his heels, troopers shooting at the houses until Henkel's voice sounded over a loudspeaker, calling for everyone to cease fire. The last thing he wanted was to engage in a house-to-house clearance of the Square. So far, he had two injured troopers, and Channer was dead. The Cut's casualties were higher, but only one of the defenders on the outskirts of the Square had been added to the list of the dead. Three more were wounded, and some of the rest were already laying down their weapons and raising their hands. Like a street fight, the conflict in the Cut seemed set to burn briefly; there was not enough determination, or desperation, among its inhabitants for a sustained battle. Most of these people were not killers. They probably didn't even consider themselves criminals.

Parker, flanked by Angel and Louis, continued around the east of the Square, keeping to the trees, not drawing fire. Priska Tinsley had shared one crucial detail with them before the assault began: the blockhouse was where Cassander would be. It was their shrine, the heart of the Cut, although she claimed never to have been inside it, and when Parker mentioned the Dead King she looked away and went silent. Whatever lay at the heart of the Cut's existence, whatever the Dead King might be, it was in that sanctuary.

They cleared the Square and moved north into the woods, until the blockhouse was revealed to them, and they paused to take it in. It resembled a construct from a child's fairy tale, a castle for an ogre; squat and dark, with branches thrusting themselves through its walls, and a thinning crown towering above its roof, so that the whole resembled a head, torso, and arms, as though the blockhouse might in an instant uproot itself and disappear into the forest. The material of the structure and the wood of the tree had weathered together over the years, making it difficult to say precisely where one ended and the other began.

A door stood open at the foot of the blockhouse, but before they could get any nearer to it a shotgun blast tore the branches and leaves from the evergreen above Louis's head, and a second later a burst of fire raked the ground beside Angel.

"I have one of them," said Louis.

He drew a bead on a figure in brown moving through the trees to the west of the blockhouse, and fired three times. The man fell. Louis waited to be sure that he was down before he began to move toward him, keeping low. The shotgun fired again, but the blast was wild, the action of someone who could no longer lift his weapon from the ground. Louis circled, and came in behind, but by then the man was already dead.

Angel and Parker concentrated their attention on the second shooter. He was staying under cover, using the undergrowth to change position without being seen before opening fire again. With his target neutralized, Louis continued on behind the blockhouse, while Angel kept shooting to the right and left of the gunman's last position, keeping him down so that Parker could make a run for the building.

The rattle of sustained fire came from beyond the Square, followed by an explosion that might have been a grenade. Parker heard a woman screaming, and men shouting, and Henkel's amplified tones once again urged calm and ordered the defenders of the Square to lay down their weapons and come out, assuring them they would not be hurt. Parker saw Angel dart behind a tree, advancing cautiously as he and Louis closed in on the remaining gunman.

"Cassander Hobb?" Parker called. "It's over."

He stayed away from the door, although he wasn't sure how much protection the old wood of the blockhouse would provide if someone inside decided to shoot. Then again, it had survived for this long, and the logs at his back felt as cold and hard as stone. Was Hobb even in there?

There was no reply. Parker risked pushing the door further ajar, and waited for the gunfire to come, but all remained dark and silent.

He stepped inside and found himself in the court of the Dead King.

# XCI

The interior of the blockhouse was lit only by the spears of morning sunlight that pierced its windows. The walls were hung with old standards and flags, some of them little more than rags, with only the barest trace of color remaining on them. Parker picked out a royal standard that might have been Spanish, judging by the preponderance of reds and golds; a colonial flag with the British colors in one corner alongside a series of faded stripes; and the distinctive red-and-white guidon of the 9th Cavalry Regiment, the black fighters nicknamed "Buffalo Soldiers" by the natives. Alongside them were nineteenth-century U.S. flags, one with as few as twenty stars upon it, and a number of Confederate Stars and Bars, mostly tattered and stained. Despite the strangeness of the blockhouse's appearance, and its obvious antiquity, the air inside was peculiarly dry, which might have explained how the delicate banners had not just rotted away. They were less decorations than trophies of war, relics of those who had crossed the Cut during its history and not lived long enough to regret the encounter.

Parker smelled gasoline. He touched the walls, and his fingers came away damp. They must have been preparing to burn the blockhouse when the assault on the Cut began. Why it had not been accomplished, he could not say. Perhaps they had been holding off in the hope that the spiritual home of the Cut might yet be saved.

The floor was made of wood and stone, and strewn with fresh straw, but Parker barely glanced at it, his attention drawn instead to two phantasmagorical sights. The first was the great tree that seemed to have birthed the dwelling, its trunk rising like a supporting column from the ground, its branches the beams upon which the roof appeared to rest. It was an awesome natural entity, which accentuated the contrast with the unnatural thing that sat at its base.

The Dead King rested on a throne carved from a single massive block of black wood. The throne stood at the top of a short flight of wooden steps, so that the figure dominated the room. A cloak of dark furs covered its shoulders and upper arms, and gold rings glittered on its fingers. It sat entirely upright, skeletal hands clasped on the arms of the throne, its feet flat on a small stool. Its ribs were unbroken beneath the cloak, its lumbar vertebrae straight and undamaged, the hollows of the ilium free of dirt and insects.

But it was the skull that haunted. It was the color of amber, although the lower jaw was slightly lighter in color, and better preserved than the rest. All of the teeth were still intact, but the nasal bone had been broken at some point, enlarging the fissure at the center of the skull. Parker looked into the hollows of its eyes, and the Dead King stared back, a messenger from a world into which all others must inevitably pass. A band of beaten gold lay upon its brow, decorated with finger bones that pointed to the heavens.

But as Parker stepped closer, he saw, despite the dim light, that the bones of the Dead King did not quite match: some were smaller and yellower than others; the right tibia was significantly shorter than the left; and the teeth were jagged and uneven, incisors and molars alternating with canines. Parker discerned the wires that held the bones in place, the careful acts of restoration and attachment, and he understood.

The Dead King was not one but many, a being fashioned from the victims of the Cut, each contributing bones to its creation, each death enhancing its potency. Parker wondered if something of Jerome Burnel was among them, and felt certain that there was. Only the neurocranium and facial skeleton came from a single source, the mandible excepted, and it struck Parker as older than the rest. This was the point of origin, the first victim. If the Dead King had any identity beyond that of the wretches who comprised it, then it lay there, but whatever name it might once have borne was now long forgotten.

A metal spike was set in the ground close to the throne, and from it hung two sets of manacles. Parker tested their mechanisms, and found that they moved easily. He thought again of Burnel, and the other unfortunates who might have spent their final days and hours in the company of the Dead King.

The blockhouse felt empty. Parker had been anticipating a sense of malevolence, of palpable evil, but he felt nothing beyond the deluded human baseness that had led the Cut to create a god of bone from the remains of its victims. The Dead King existed because the Cut wanted it to exist, but Parker did not have to believe in it. He turned away from the abomination. He did not want to look upon it any longer.

Angel and Louis were standing at the door, gazing at the hollow god on his throne. Henkel appeared behind them, and all three stood in silence for a time, taking in its decayed majesty.

"What is it?" asked Henkel at last.

"Evidence," said Parker.

"Of what?"

"Generations of murders. Have you found Hobb?"

"Not yet."

"When you do, that thing will damn him."

"This place stinks of gasoline. Nobody better strike a match."

Louis had moved to the right, the better to examine the Dead King, when he paused.

"Shit," he said.

Parker followed his gaze. A discarded cigarette pack, seemingly still full, lay open by Louis's feet. It rested on a mound of earth.

"Out," said Parker. "Now!"

Nobody needed to be told twice, not with the smell of gas in their nostrils. All firing in the Cut had ceased, and the muted sound of voices carried to them from the Square. Three state troopers were moving up the slope toward them as they emerged.

"Get back," said Henkel. "We have a potential problem here."

From inside the blockhouse came a hissing sound, followed by a low *whump*, like someone lighting a stove, and the problem moved from potential to actual. The blockhouse was illuminated from within as the incendiary device ignited the gasoline, and even from a distance Parker felt a blast of heat before the door slammed shut, as though the fire itself had decided that the Dead King's immolation should be hidden from sight. The walls began to smoke before the first fingers of flame reached through, and then the whole structure was ablaze, tree and building burning together. All who were able to do so gathered to watch as the fire grew higher, and the walls and roof collapsed. The oak began to burn like a great hand, and in the midst of the conflagration they glimpsed a figure on a black throne, grinning as it was consumed.

Chapter

# XCII

Cassander paused momentarily to watch the smoke rising above the Cut. Had there been anyone to witness it, his expression would have appeared entirely neutral: no rage, no regret, no sadness. The Cut, as he had known it all his life, was gone forever. He would never return there.

But Cassander was not alone.

For the Dead King was in him.

# XCIII

It took most of the rest of that day to round up the remnants of the Cut, and transport the injured to hospitals and the dead to the morgue. The process of questioning and interrogation would require days, even weeks. As a precaution, every adult member of the Cut was arrested and Mirandized, while arrangements were made to get them before a magistrate as soon as possible, when they would again be informed of their rights and, where appropriate, granted bail. In West Virginia, any person accused of a felony offense had the right to request a preliminary hearing, either within ten days if the defendant was being held in custody, or within twenty days if released on bail. Plassey County, and the state of West Virginia, were about to have a lot of legal work on their hands.

But it was being made clear to the Cut that those who cooperated with the investigation, and helped with the recovery and identification of the remains of victims, would receive an easier ride. Already, fingers were pointing at maps, and tales were being told of the last days of men and women. Most were buried in the Cut's cemetery, hidden beneath its own dead. Odell Watson, meanwhile, told for the first time of the woman he had seen brought down by dogs, and recounted again his tale of the hooded man being led into the Cut by night.

The next day, the digging would begin.

The West Virginia Department of Health and Human Resources stepped in to advise on how best to deal with the minors involved. After hurried discussions, it was decided that all the adults who had taken shelter in the prison hut during the fighting in the Cut should be charged initially as possible accessories to kidnapping, rape, sexual assault, and murder, with further charges potentially to follow, but the state would not object to bail, under strict conditions, among them that the Cut should remain sealed off from its former inhabitants pending forensic examination. The Plassey County Recreation Complex was designated as a temporary holding center, which enabled the state to kick a little farther down the road any decision on what to do about the children. The male prisoners were split between the Plassey County Jail and a handful of the state's correctional facilities.

But of Cassander Hobb there was no trace.

————

CASSANDER HADN'T INTENDED TO run. His two sons had been taken from him, and Cassander in turn had ordered the killing of the Cut's leader, the man who was once his closest friend, and finished off Sherah, the woman he and Oberon had shared. The attacks on Henkel and the private investigator had failed, and the captive women had managed to get away. The Cut was lost, but Cassander's intention had been to die defending it, until he heard the Dead King call his name.

In the darkness of its court, the Dead King entered him, and any thoughts of fighting for the Cut vanished from Cassander's mind. What was important now was that the Dead King should survive, and so Cassander would have to carry it inside him until a new nest of bones could be found. He felt the Dead King's presence as a weight upon his soul and a shadow across his vision. It whispered and chittered in his head, and its madness infected him.

Cassander emerged from the Cut to the northeast, close to the Barnett property. Millard Barnett was a bachelor who used to raise broiler chickens with his two older brothers until his siblings passed away within a month of each other, whereupon Barnett stopped caring about chickens, or anything else, and settled into solitary retirement. Cassander shot Barnett dead when he answered the knock on his front door, and dumped his body down a disused well. He then took Barnett's Saturn Ion and drove into Virginia. He made only one stop, and that was to call Daniel Starcher from a pay phone to alert him to all that had occurred, although Starcher didn't need Cassander to tell him since he could see it for himself on TV. Starcher had already set about erasing any incriminating traces of his ties to the Cut, including the unofficial adoption service. He'd leave it for as long as possible before breaking the news to the unhappy prospective purchasers that they wouldn't be receiving their little bundles of joy anytime soon. He'd also have to refund them their money, which included the large goodwill deposit put down by the consortium for one of the children.

*Shit.*

Cassander had cash, but he'd need more. Starcher asked Cassander what his plans were. Cassander said that he didn't know, but to begin with he would head for a safe house in Bedford, one of a number that the Cut maintained to serve as temporary refuges and storage facilities. Starcher told him that he'd arrange to have cash delivered to Cassander there, and hung up. Later that evening, having given Cassander time to get to the safe house and settle in, Starcher commissioned two freelance button men named Purvis and Stone to head to Bedford and kill him.

When they arrived, Purvis and Stone discovered the house empty. Cassander had been there—they found some fast-food boxes and empty beer bottles, along with the remains of a fire that had been set in a garbage can—but had clearly left again. They waited all that night and most of the next day, but Cassander did not return. Perhaps, they suggested to Starcher, he had been forewarned, but Starcher assured them that only three people knew of the planned hit, and Cassander was not one of them.

Starcher wanted Cassander dead. If the police captured him, and he tried to strike a deal, Starcher's position could be uncomfortably altered from defender to defendant. But Cassander had disappeared, and unbeknownst to Starcher, the police were already on their way to Lewisburg. Within hours, Starcher would be under arrest.

———

THE DEAD KING HAD warned Cassander that the killers were coming: not in words, or images, but feelings. Starcher could no longer be trusted, but Cassander would deal with him in time. He stayed at the safe house only long enough to eat, change his clothes, and add some fresh ones to a small case from the supply kept in the basement. He also shaved off his beard and most of his hair, and dyed what was left from a bottle kept in the bathroom for that very purpose, before burning the discarded hair in a garbage can and disposing of the bottle in the trash as he drove away.

The Dead King never stopped speaking, even if only to itself. It was almost enough to prevent Cassander from sleeping, and when he did manage to doze the Dead King took shape in his dreams, and Cassander would wake screaming. Cassander's sanity was eroding, but while it still remained to him he debated the existence of the Dead King, even as he heard it whispering in his head in an unknown tongue. Was it a symptom of their collective madness, an infection of the mind passed down through generations, a voice given to a form that they themselves had created? In that sense, were they not all the Dead King?

Only then did he notice the silence in his head. He waited, barely able to breathe. It was gone. Whatever it was, it—

And he heard the Dead King laughing.

———

PARKER, ANGEL, AND LOUIS could not avoid being questioned by the state police and the FBI. It was an especially uncomfortable experience for the latter pair, and only a request from Parker for Ross's intervention prevented it from becoming something worse than that. Ross made it clear to Parker that a favor had been called in, and he would be expected to return it, with interest.

"Whatever deal you struck with him," said Louis, as they prepared to leave Plassey County, "it was a bad one."

———

JEROME BURNEL'S WAS ONE of the first bodies uncovered, because it was the most recently interred. He had been buried in a pit used for the remains of the Cut's dogs.

———

THE DEAD KING WAS uncomfortable sharing Cassander's skin. It was not a thing of the living, but of the dead. It needed to hide among bare bones.

Cassander, in turn, wanted to punish someone for what had befallen the Cut, and he had two targets: Henkel and the private investigator named Charlie Parker. Henkel was out of reach for the moment—perhaps forever, given the near-impossibility of Cassander's return to Plassey County. That left Parker. Cassander knew a lot about the private detective. Oberon had spoken about him, and the Dead King had sensed his coming. Parker was dangerous, and Cassander wasn't certain he could go up against him and survive. As he drove, Cassander thought about Roger Ormsby, the abductor and killer of children whom Parker had tracked down. Ormsby hadn't just killed his victims: he'd made them vanish without trace, adding an exquisite layer of torment to the lives of those left behind.

Cassander knew all about the stripping of flesh from bones, of boiling and preservation. So he began to formulate a plan, one that would serve both his desire for revenge and the needs of the Dead King.

# 5

It should be noted that children at play are not merely playing; their games should be seen as their most serious actions.

—Michel de Montaigne (1533–1592), *Essays* I, 23

Sam sat on the ground at the edge of her grandparents' property, where a small copse of trees surrounded a pond. She wasn't supposed to go there alone. Her grandfather had warned her about the dangers of even shallow bodies of water, but then her grandfather warned her about lots of things: crossing the road, boys, eating undercooked chicken, strangers, her father, her father's friends . . .

In Sam's right hand lay the near-desiccated body of a dead bird: a little whip-poor-will that she'd found hidden amid bark and leaves by the entrance to its nest. She had no idea how it had died, but it appeared largely undamaged. Slowly, using a box cutter that she'd liberated from her grandfather's toolbox, she cut the bird open and discarded what was left of its internal organs, carefully reducing it to feather and bone.

Jennifer, Sam's half-sister, watched from over her shoulder.

The dead daughter and the living, together.

Jennifer spoke.

*it's coming*

"Yes."

*are you frightened?*

"No."

It wasn't quite a lie, but Jennifer sensed doubt.

*maybe—*

"Go away," said Sam. "You're distracting me."

Jennifer left her to her work. She returned to her own place to sit on her rock and watch the dead go by. She thought that Sam didn't love their father in the same way she did. How could she, when she was both human and something more, something beyond comprehension? Their father had once asked Jennifer if Sam frightened her, and she had not answered. She did not want to say it.

Sam did not frighten her.

Sam terrified her.

———

TWO DAYS LATER, CASSANDER Hobb snatched Samantha Wolfe, the daughter of Charlie Parker, while she was playing by that same pond. It was, Cassander thought, his good fortune that she should be alone, and out of sight of her house, when he came for her. He showed the child the gun, and warned her to be quiet, before cuffing her hands in front of her, binding and gagging her with tape, and forcing her into the trunk of the car. He warned her that he'd cut off one of her ears if she tried to escape. By the time she was missed, and the alarm raised, he was already halfway to New Hampshire.

He feared to use any of the safe houses, and had instead checked into a motel at the edge of the White Mountain National Forest that was content to take cash on the nail. He was given a quiet room at the end, but since only two other rooms were occupied, he had little fear of being seen or heard. He waited until the evening darkness descended before carrying the girl from the car into the room. He barely noticed how little she struggled, or the excited, insane chitters of the Dead King. He just wanted it all to be done with.

He placed her in the bathtub, lit himself a cigarette, and regarded her in silence while he smoked. She stared back at him, but did not move. Eventually, she tried to speak. He showed her the gun in one hand, and the knife in the other, before putting the gun away and cutting the tape from her mouth and body.

"I need to pee," she said.

"Pee in the tub."

"I'll get it on my clothes."

"I don't care."

She shook her head, but he noticed that she didn't pee. It was probably a trick, he thought. Still, she was a strange kid. She hadn't cried once. She just sat there, her eyes fixed on him, waiting for something to happen. It would, and soon. He was working up the strength to cut her throat. The Dead King wanted it.

Finally, she spoke again.

"Your nose is bleeding," she said.

A drop of red exploded on Cassander's jeans, closely followed by a second. He put the fingers of his left hand to his nose, and they came back stained. He reached for some toilet paper, wadded it into balls, and pressed it to his nostrils.

"Soon you'll start bleeding from other places, too," said Sam.

"What are you talking about?"

"Your ears, your eyes, the pores of your skin."

Cassander felt a sharp pain deep in his head. The Dead King asked a question only it could understand, and to which no living creature had an answer.

"What's inside you isn't supposed to be there," said Sam. "It can't survive for long in a body that's alive, so it kills it, in the end. It's not just the Dead King. It's the King of Dead Things."

Cassander coughed, and blood sprayed over the tiled floor and the edge of the tub. His vision was blurring. He rose unsteadily, and saw in the mirror that he was weeping tears of blood. Pinpricks of red appeared on the white of his shirt, growing in size. He felt dampness in his jeans as their fabric began to darken. He couldn't stay upright so he slumped down on the toilet and let his face rest against the cool of the tiles.

The child rose, and the Dead King started screaming. Sam was wearing a blue jacket. Awkwardly, her hands still cuffed, she unzipped one of its pockets and reached inside. When her hands opened again, they held the remains of the whip-poor-will, its chest opened and its wings cut to reveal the bones inside. It was wet against her fingers, and smelled faintly of lighter fluid.

Blood was now flowing from the sleeves of Cassander's shirt and the bottoms of his jeans. His face was entirely red, as were his eyes, the whiteness of them lost in the bursting of the capillaries. He was barely conscious, his brain already failing.

But Sam didn't want him to die, not yet.

She held up the body of the bird, and felt it stir against her fingers as the Dead King passed into it. She climbed from the tub and dropped the delicate remains in the sink. She took the toilet paper from its holder and wrapped the bird in layers of it. Finally, because it was easier than searching with her cuffed hands for the book of matches concealed in her windbreaker pocket, she removed Cassander's Zippo from his shirt, and used it to set the bird alight.

Behind her, Jennifer appeared, and together they watched as the Dead King, caught in its snare of bones, passed from this world in smoke and fire.

————

KIMBERLY BECKMAN, OWNER OF the Low Mountain Motel, looked up from her chair to see a little girl in a blue jacket standing in front of the reception desk. The TV behind her was carrying a news report about a missing child.

"Can I help you, honey?"

The girl held up her cuffed hands.

"My name is Samantha Wolfe," she said. "That's me on TV."

# XCV

Cassander Hobb was still alive when the police reached the motel. He was still alive when they got him to the hospital and put him on life support.

He's still alive now, if you can call it living.

Parker went to visit him once. Cassander's eyes were closed. He was being fed through a tube, and the medical staff assured Parker that he was brain-dead. In time, his body would follow.

Just as Parker was leaving, Cassander jerked on the bed.

"What was that?"

"Spinal cord neurons," said the nurse. "Reflexes. Have you ever heard of the Lazarus sign?"

"No."

"It's when brain-dead patients spontaneously raise their arms and drop them again. Scared the living Jesus out of me the first time I saw it happen."

"Does Hobb exhibit the Lazarus sign?"

"Not anymore. He just spasms now and again. There's nothing in there, Mr. Parker. He's gone."

———

CASSANDER'S MIND IS LIKE an empty house: no furnishings, no decoration, no life. Beyond its windows there is only darkness, broken by flashes of lightning as a stray neuron flares.

A presence moves through the house. It has no form, and no name. It chitters endlessly. It smells of smoke and burned feathers. It is waiting: waiting for Cassander to die, waiting for him to be reduced to bone in a pauper's grave.

Waiting, so that it may be reborn.

# Acknowledgments

I'm grateful to John Lorenzen, regional correctional manager in the Maine Department of Corrections, Division of Adult Services, for his patience in explaining to me the intricacies of the probation system in the state of Maine, but he remains one of the few human points of contact in the research for this odd book. The majority of the background work involved trawling through works of folklore and myth, most of which are namechecked in the novel itself, although *Severed: A History of Heads Lost and Heads Found*, by Frances Larson (Granta, 2004), provided a wonderful guide to concretizing some of the ideas and images that were roiling in my mind as the book progressed.

The band Espers very kindly allowed me to quote from their song "Dead King," which could almost serve as an accompaniment to sections of this book. They also declined to charge a fee, which says a great deal about them. Details of their work can be found at www.dragcity .com/artists/espers.

As always, I'm indebted to Emily Bestler, my editor at Atria Books, and all those who work alongside her, including Lara Jones, David Brown, and Albert Tang; to Sue Fletcher, my editor at Hodder & Stoughton, and to Carolyn Mays, Swati Gamble, Kerry Hood, Breda Purdue, Jim Binchy, Ruth Shern, Siobhan Tierney, and everyone at Hodder & Stoughton and Hachette Books Ireland. My agent, Darley Anderson, continues to show remarkable forbearance in the face of an author who is both awkward and a Liverpool fan. Thanks, too, to Clair Lamb, Madeira James, and Kate O'Hearn, writer and friend, for her hard work in securing clearances for quotes and CDs.

Finally, love to Jennie, Cameron, and Alistair.